Vienna Blood

Vienna Blood

LAURENCE PAYNE

PUBLISHED FOR THE CRIME CLUB BY

DOUBLEDAY & COMPANY

GARDEN CITY, NEW YORK

1986

All of the characters in this book
are fictitious, and any resemblance
to actual persons, living or dead,
is purely coincidental.

Library of Congress Cataloging in Publication Data
Payne, Laurence.
Vienna blood.
I. Title.
PR6066.A93V5   1986   823'.914   85-12909

For
Norman Bailey, CBE
Mastersinger

My grateful thanks to Herr Udo Proksch-Kirchhofer Director and General Manager of Demel K.u.K. Hofzuckerbäcker, Wien, for granting not only his permission to incorporate that establishment in the context of the following story but also the use of his own invaluable personality in the telling of it.

Thanks too to Herren Wolfgang Leschanz and Jürgen Meingast and to Demel's entire staff for their patience and courtesy.

L.P.

CHAPTER ONE

I should never have gone back to Vienna. I had been there only once before. As an actor, back in the seventies, hauling myself around the tiny stage of the English Theatre in Josefsgasse playing Konstantin in Chekhov's *Sea Gull*. I had hobnobbed with the upper classes, browsed among the Breughels, ridden the Ferris wheel and stood in awed solemnity before the grave of Beethoven. A city of trams and music and Lippizaner horses, Baroque churches, sombre palaces and a neo-Gothic city hall which looked like a cathedral, Vienna exuded the smiling and gently dimpled benignity I had been led to expect, and I had dutifully fallen in love with every stick and stone of her.

It was a mistake to return and spoil it all, but how could I have known that the dimples would turn to iron?

I had been idling through *The Times* in my eyrie of an office in London EC1 when a brief announcement at the bottom of page three caught my eye.

I said to the world at large, "My Auntie Alice has had a heart attack."

The world at large consisted only of Mitch, my assistant, creaking away in her chair in the outer office and immersed in something important like *The Gulag Archipelago*, Parts I and II—the sort of light relief she is apt to turn to when the hurly-burly of life in the office of a private investigator becomes too much for her.

"I didn't know you had an Auntie Alice," she said, getting up and coming to lean on the doorpost.

I handed her the paper. "Maybe I haven't any more."

She read aloud. " 'Alicia Sternberg. Heart Attack.' " She raised a questioning eyebrow at me. "*The* Alicia Sternberg?" I nodded. "She's your auntie?"

I nodded again, more smugly this time. "Great auntie, actually. She's my father's mother's sister."

She stared at me in silence for a second before carrying on with her reading. "The internationally famous dramatic soprano Alicia Sternberg has suffered a heart attack at her home in Vienna. Yorkshire-born Madame Sternberg, 84, one of the great operatic divas of the twentieth century, studied at the Royal College of Music in London and later in Berlin and Vienna. In 1928 she married diamond merchant Ernst Sternberg and thereafter settled in Vienna. She gave her farewell performance at Covent Garden in 1956 when she sang what was perhaps her most prestigious role, Puccini's *Turandot*. Madame Sternberg's condition is understood to be stable and satisfactory."

Mitch lowered the paper thoughtfully. "Well . . ." She blinked wide blue eyes. "Who's been keeping Great Aunt Alice under his hat then?"

I shrugged. "She never loomed all that large in my young life."

"Did you ever meet her?"

"My dad took me to that last *Turandot* of hers and we went backstage afterwards. I was all of nine years old at the time. She scared the living daylights out of me. It was like coming face to face with Dr. Fu Manchu, only not so cuddly—all teeth and fingernails. It was years before I realised she didn't actually walk the streets looking like that. The only other time we met was when I was out there myself doing the acting and she turned up after our last performance with the Spanish ambassador in tow and a couple of dozen unidentified odd-bods—all trying to squash into a dressing-room the size of a snooker table. Poor old duck. Maybe I ought to try to contact someone over there. I might easily be her last surviving relative. Not that she'll be alone—not with all her money."

Dollar signs pinged up in Mitch's pale eyeballs. I wagged an admonishing finger at her which she ignored; she was staring gloomily at the brown lino. "We could hire a carpet, perhaps," she said. "Or even," she added as the phone rang and she made her way to the instrument clamouring on her desk, "a telephone operator."

A second later, hand clamped over the mouthpiece, she was whispering hoarsely: "Talk of the devil . . . Auntie from Vienna."

She switched me through.

It wasn't Aunt Alice but someone calling herself Emily Hargreaves: ". . . friend and companion to Madame Sternberg," the voice explained in a resolutely British and businesslike manner. Madame was extremely unwell, and would it be possible for me to come to Vienna? If so, could I arrange it tonight?

I replied that I had only just learned of Madame's heart attack and how serious was it?

"A heart attack is always serious, Mr. Mark," said the voice in prim reproof. "This is her fourth in eighteen months." She made it sound as if it were some sort of record. I made a face at Mitch, who was lounging in the doorway and signed for her to come over and listen in.

"Are you still there?" asked Emily Hargreaves as Mitch leant over with an unladylike grunt. "Madame led me to understand that your visit, should it prove possible, would be on a strictly business basis—all expenses incurred to be paid by her."

I said grittily, "If you'll give me your number, I'll ring you back. It may not be possible to get a flight at this late stage."

"There's a departure from Heathrow at 5:45 this evening. I took the liberty of reserving you a place on it. Flight OS 458. You have only to confirm the booking with Austrian Airlines. Your ETA is 8:55. A car will pick you up at the airport and bring you here. And please not to bother about an hotel—you can stay here; there's plenty of room."

I crossed desperate eyes at Mitch. "Miss Hargreaves . . . just a minute . . . hold on a second . . . I'm not even sure if my passport is valid. Look," I galloped on as I heard her draw breath, "let your arrangements stand; if there's any hitch this end, I'll contact you. All right? And incidentally, if I do manage it, I'd prefer to stay in a hotel. I'm liable to keep funny hours. I'll fix that myself. So if you don't hear from me, I'll be on that flight. Give me those details again, will you?"

While I was taking them down, Mitch rummaged around in one of my side-drawers and unearthed my passport, which she placed open on the desk before me. I winced at the photograph which stared out of it and whilst grunting acknowledgment of Hargreaves' gratitude pencilled in a pair of horn-rimmed glasses and a long Chinese moustache which improved it no end. Mitch slapped the back of my hand and removed the pencil from my nerveless fingers. I bade Miss Hargreaves *"auf Wiedersehen"* and sat back in a dazed heap.

"How's your German?" asked Mitch drily.

"What?"

"German. You might need more than *'auf Wiedersehen.'* "

"German is the least of my problems," I wailed. "I can't go to bloody Vienna tonight."

"Why not?" She sounded sharp.

"And drop everything? Just like that?"

"You haven't got anything to drop." She was tetchily rubbing out the improvements on my photograph. "You're in the hiring business, aren't you? You've been hired. Aunt Alice has hired you. Not only do you get a free trip to Vienna, the city of song, but play your cards right and you might well retire on the proceeds. Why should the Bayrischer Rundfunk get all her money?"

"You're just a bloody mercenary, you know that, don't you?"

"Thank God one of us is."

* * *

When I eventually arrived—thirty-five minutes late—Vienna was dark and wet. A uniformed driver with rain-bespattered cap and shoulders stood stoically at the barrier staring without interest at the feet of the new arrivals; against his chest he held a card which had "Herr Savage" scrawled upon it in large black letters. I gave him a brisk "Bon soir," which surprised both of us, and then asked him if he spoke English. I was not yet ready to launch into pidgin German. He lifted wary wet shoulders as he took possession of my small and solitary bag. "Little," he admitted. "Little." Then gathering courage, he added with a shy smile, "Rain, *ja?*"

He led me to a smart black BMW and installed me in the back seat.

"Hotel Bristol," I told him.

"Nein." He gave an emphatic shake of his head. "Madame Sternberg."

"*Nein.*" I was equally emphatic. "First Hotel Bristol. *Mit* bag, right? You wait. *Warten Sie. Then* Madame Sternberg. *Comprenez?*"

He gave a heavy sigh and a non-committal shrug and we splashed off into the night, two abrupt and consecutive left turns having me almost on the floor.

The interior of the car was warm and smelled of expensive leather but did little to comfort me. Only the occasional flare of oncoming headlights relieved the blackness of the night outside. With the airport behind us there was not a lot to look at except the silhouette of the driver hunched against the glow of the dashboard and the streaming rectangle of windscreen. He had switched on his radio, but with the communicating panel now shut between us, I was only dimly aware of the dreary thud of pop, its persistent beat merging depressingly with the drumming of rain and the hiss of tyres.

I closed my eyes. I was uneasy and disconsolate. Quick decisions and unpremeditated journeys had never appealed to me. I hated being uprooted and sent forth into the unknown with nothing but a toothbrush and a passport.

Again I found myself pondering the affairs of my Great Aunt Alice; the entire journey had been occupied with little else.

Setting aside the remote possibility that I was about to feature as sole beneficiary of her last will and testament—a stimulating fantasy—I could only surmise that she was in trouble and needed help. A prospect which made my toes curl.

A private investigator at large in his own environment is something quite different from one on the prowl in a foreign country, and though a working knowledge of German was one of my few accomplishments in the world of foreign affairs, treachery could still lurk among the umlauts and colloquialisms. On my previous visit I'd had no trouble at all, my requirements being principally concerned with the intake of food and drink, where to post a letter and how to ride the trams without getting arrested for travelling without a ticket. On this occasion, however, assuming that Aunt Alice wished to hire me in a professional capacity, I would be living and breathing German, needing to ask pertinent questions and, having asked them, understand some of the answers.

A sudden burst of song from the front seat roused me from my brooding. Something on the radio tickled the driver's fancy, and he was booming away beyond the panel with the swashbuckling bravura of the Canadian Mounted Police in *Rose Marie*. It was neither a pleasant noise nor conducive to present safety, for, arriving at a climactic *rallentando*, he let go of the wheel and waved both hands above his head whilst the well-tempered BMW drove itself nonchalantly through a lengthy and excruciating B flat and into the city limits. I ducked my head to watch the lights reflected in the glistening tarmac. When I eventually recognised something, it turned out, not surprisingly, to be the Hilton Hotel. Later I caught sight of the illuminated dome and columns of the Karlskirche. Soon after, we glided to a halt.

The driver slid back his panel. "Hotel Bristol," he said in a calm voice. A man in a waterproof and a truncated brown top hat opened the door and bowed expectantly. The driver said as I clambered out, "You want wait?" I looked at him enquiringly. He pointed "Madame Sternberg . . . *zwei hundert Meter . . .*"

"Wait please," I told him. "I'll get drowned."

I checked in at the desk, asked them to have my bag taken up to the room and rejoined my driver, who, now silent and morose, shunted me a couple of hundred yards up the road, around a corner, and set me down almost opposite the Opera House. He waved aside my money and, when I refused to allow him to get out in the rain, pointed to a building with a light in the porch and took off before I could think of the German for "thank you."

My arrival had been anticipated. The door stood open, a shadowy figure awaiting me.

"Emily Hargreaves." A firm masculine hand seized mine, pumped at it vigorously and then drew me into the building. "So good of you to come. Madame will be delighted. Let me take your coat. If you wouldn't mind, we'll go up immediately. It's getting late. Just to set her mind at rest."

Allowing me no time to demur, she ushered me into a blaze of light, asked if I'd had a good flight and without pausing for a reply told me again how welcome I was, adding that though the others were there I was not to mind them. "It's you she'll be wanting to see. But don't expect too much. She won't want to talk tonight, I'm sure. But perhaps we might have a little chat later on, just you and I. I'm sure there are lots of things you'll want to know."

Resisting the temptation to say "Hello" and "Good evening" and "Yes, I had a good flight," I followed her up a noble staircase, wide and crimson-carpeted, through a glass-panelled door and into a spacious, softly lit corridor which reminded me of a theatre foyer. When she paused dramatically with her hand on a door handle, I had the fanciful notion that she was about to tear my ticket in half.

I stared for a moment into her dark eyes. "Thank you, Mr. Mark, for coming so readily," she whispered and pushed open the door.

The room was heavy with shadow. Candles guttered at my entrance. I peered blindly into the gloom. She was right: others were there before me, rustling and creaking like raptors folding their wings, bright-eyed and expectant. A throat was cleared, a shoe squeaked like a frightened mouse; someone was breathing heavily through an open mouth; someone else had recently doused himself with a particularly distinctive cologne.

It was a grossly unreal situation—as if I had stumbled upon the deathbed of a pope or a monarch.

Behind me the door closed stealthily. The candle flames steadied. Emily Hargreaves touched my arm, urging me forward. Spectral faces glowed momentarily in my path to fade into shadow at a muttered word from my guide. Now for the first time I could make out the bed, a four-poster, ornate and canopied like a funeral barge.

A dark-faced nun with flaring white head-dress, a rosary glimmering in her hand, made grudging way for me.

I stared down at the tiny, doll-like figure mummified in the white expanse of the bed. Lank grey hair trailed over the crumpled pillows.

Emily leaned in close, whispering gently. "Alicia . . . your nephew is here."

The murmuring grew more urgent as those not understanding English demanded translation. I turned my head. Silence fell.

The eyes were open now, colourless in dark sockets. The lips moved. "Lorenz?" The word was little more than a breath.

Emily Hargreaves drew me closer. "No, my dear. It's Mark, your great nephew, Mark . . ."

A frail blotched hand clutched at the coverlet, the eyes suddenly bright. I bent over the bed and took the hand in mine, a tiny birdlike claw, cold. The room had become deadly quiet, every eye and ear alert. Even the heavy breather had fallen silent.

"Lorenz?" The pale eyes searched mine. "Is it Lorenz?"

I shook my head, bending low over her. "It's Mark—from England. Your great nephew. Your nephew George's son . . ."

The bony hand tightened on mine. "Mark? You are Mark? Of course you are." Tears welled suddenly. Emily leaned in with a tiny lace-edged handkerchief. I took it from her and gently dried the eyes. The hand fluttered excitedly in mine. "Dear Mark . . . to have come all this way." Her eyes, furtive with sudden apprehension, flickered warily about the room. Her lips moved. I leant in closer. "Tomorrow, Mark dear . . ." The faintest whisper.

"Tomorrow," I nodded.

A tremulous finger touched my cheek. "Sleep now," she murmured. "Tomorrow we'll talk." A secret smile glimmered in the depths of her eyes, and I could have sworn that one heavy lid drooped in a sly wink. I drew the coverlet over her hand.

On the landing again, blinking in the dazzle from the outsize chandelier suspended above the stair-well, I waited for Emily Hargreaves to close the door quietly behind her.

"Who is Lorenz?" I asked abruptly.

I couldn't make out whether she hadn't heard the question or simply chose to ignore it. Whichever it was, she led the way in silence down the staircase to the hall below.

Unbridled Baroque extravagances roistered everywhere, chipped and chubby cherubs armed at all points with bows and arrows, garlands and plaster grapes, peeped coyly from every nook and cranny. In stern contrast the walls bore a formidable abundance of portraiture of Aunt Alice in a cross-section of her most famous roles.

I paused in front of one of them. The life-sized buxom beauty eyeing me from the confines of an ornate gilt frame seemed to shimmer with energy and wisdom. The flowing silks, the square-cut eighteenth-century *décolletage*, the lofty white powdered wig and the beribboned fan poised in an arched and elegant hand belied the dehydrated frailty enshrouded in that outrageous bed upstairs.

Emily stood beside me. *"Rosenkavalier,"* she said quietly. "Did you ever see her Marschallin?" I shook my head. "She came to it late, already in her fifties, long after the Bayreuth seasons. In my opinion it was the glory of her career."

She moved on, promenading from picture to picture like Her Majesty conducting a VIP through her gallery of ancestors. "Tosca . . . the first Bayreuth Brünnhilde . . . the Covent Garden Sieglinde . . . Lady Macbeth, Salome, Elektra . . . she really used to frighten me as Elektra . . ."

"She scared the life out of me as Turandot," I confessed.

"You saw her Turandot?"

"When I was nine. Her farewell at the Garden. I only remember her long fingernails."

By the time the tour was complete, we had become quite companionable, and I had become accustomed to her baggy maroon cardigan, tartan skirt and sensible shoes. We passed through a baize-covered door along a dimly lit passage and finally into a bright and well-appointed kitchen.

"This is the beginning of my own little domain," she informed me comfortably. "My apartments are just through here."

She showed me into a room which was an ugly corner of early twentieth-century English Vicarage, with frumpy furniture, crocheted antimacassars, lace curtains, a couple of wilting aspidistras and a bentwood rocking chair. The massive fireplace of sculpted white marble, redundant since the advent of central heating, served now as a proscenium arch to a television set which glowered from the recess where fire-basket and iron dogs should have been. Above a wide mantelshelf loaded with framed photographs, matching vases and a large black clock hung a depressing print of *The Light of the World.* The lampshades were of pale mauve silk and trailed three-inch fringes.

"You'll see that I have nothing to do with those dreadful excesses outside," Emily was saying with some pride. "I simply cannot abide fat little cherubs. There's one up there." She indicated a dusky corner where an overfed cupid blew on a gilded trumpet. "There's nothing at all I can do about him other than keep the light off him. Now sit down and make yourself at home. I'll get us some tea. And food; what about something to eat? You can't have eaten for ages."

I explained about the ham and potato salad they had supplied me with on the plane but said that a cup of tea would be appreciated.

She took my coat and disappeared into the kitchen, where I could hear her carrying on a conversation with herself. I chose a chair farthest away from *The Light of the World* and stared instead at a silver-framed picture of my aunt as a young woman in a feather boa standing alone on a sideboard the size of somebody's tomb. I narrowed my eyes at the inscription scrawled across the lower half of the photograph in a bold masculine hand. "To my dear Emmy, with so Many Thanks, Alicia." Underneath was the date: October 1937.

"I was seventeen when she gave me that," said Emily Hargreaves, bustling in with a trayful of crockery. "Just a slip of a girl, and she was a lovely famous lady at the height of her powers. I helped dress her at Covent Garden, you know. I was so green then, and when she asked if I would travel with her on a permanent basis, I just jumped at the chance. It was the best thing I ever did, but I never dreamed that fifty years on we would still be together. I've been everything to her in that time—dresser, housekeeper, nurse, manager, companion, friend . . ."

I said gently, "And is she still a lovely lady?" She looked at me sharply, clattering a cup as she did so. "Fifty years is a long time," I explained. "I imagine she can be quite demanding in her own small way."

"Anyone with her responsibilities is entitled to be a little difficult at times. It's something one accepts, surely. The only thing that mattered to me was that she was in good health, good voice and protected from disagreeable outside influences." The smile she gave me lit up the whole of her face. "I've been a sort of duenna to her. People have called me a dragon and in a way I suppose I am—I've had to be. She is my responsibility, always has been; my job—my life's work."

The kettle shrieked in the kitchen and she went off to attend to it.

When she reappeared, she carried a teapot in one hand and a plateful of bizarre-looking cream delicacies in the other. "Cakes from Demel's," she informed me. "You cannot possibly resist a cake from Demel's—nobody can. Best bun-shop in the world," she added with a small crow of laughter.

She settled herself opposite me on the rocking chair and proceeded to dispense tea and "buns" with the air of one who has spent the greater part of her life doing just that. The teapot was interred in a cosy disguised as a tabby cat, and her cardigan clashed miserably with an orange cushion behind her.

When in the course of a somewhat desultory tea-time conversation I informed her that I had booked in at the Bristol, I thought for a moment she was about to have a seizure. She looked so distressed that I hastily headed her off and asked instead if she knew in what capacity Madame had requested my presence—as a detective or as a member of the family—a ploy which seemed to restore her status quo.

She gave *The Light of the World* a furtive glance over her shoulder and rocked in gently towards me. "As a detective," she whispered with a small secretive nod.

I returned the nod glumly. I comforted myself with a melting mouthful of *Apfelstrudel.* Mercenary Mitch was going to be disappointed. No hired carpet this year. "What's the trouble, do you know?"

She avoided the question and frowned at the teapot. "She has too many irons in the fire, I know that. Eighty-four she may be, but she doesn't behave like it. Her motto is, Life has to be lived to the full or not at all. At eighty-four it's high time she drew her horns in."

"Maybe that's just what she's doing," I suggested a little brutally. "She looked pretty sick to me."

The dark eyes became suddenly moist. "I refuse to believe that," Emily said almost with petulance. "We've been through all this before—three times. I just won't believe there isn't still hope."

"Nevertheless . . ."

"The last time this happened she was at death's door—at death's very door —and suddenly she rallied. Before any of us knew where we were, she was rushing about the place like a twenty-year-old, hale and hearty as ever. 'I'll go when I'm ready,' she says, 'and not a moment before.' She really is the most determined woman, you must know that."

I shook my head. "I don't know anything about her at all. I've met her twice and heard her sing once. She probably had no time to be anybody's auntie. I'm not blaming her. I know only too well the sort of life she must have led; I've been there myself in the slightly less manic world of the movies. I suppose things were quieter in those days—no jet lag, no bookings three years ahead, not so much rushing about; but the pressures and responsibilities must have been the same. Do you know, incidentally, if I'm her only living relative?"

There was just the slightest flicker of hesitation. "I rather think you must be."

"Then who's that lot upstairs?"

"Friends." She caught the sceptical lift of my eyebrows. "Oh, I know it must look like the gathering of the vultures, but it really isn't. Alice has always held court. When she was in her prime, it was the done thing. After a performance she would never expect to go home to bed—not to sleep, anyway. Friends would come and bring *their* friends and they would sit up half the night, talking, drinking, reminiscing. Oh, she would complain about it from time to time, but only to me, never to them. Recently, of course, it's tailed off—thank the good Lord—but she still has that . . . charisma, I suppose you'd call it. She listens to them, you see; cares about people. She's not egocentric like so many of them; and then of course she has all her outside interests—far too many, as I've said. Do you know that here in Vienna she's almost as well known now as she was forty years ago? When she walks in the Graben, it's like a royal progress." She paused for a second and some of the light left her eyes. "And when she dies, they'll fly the black flag from the Staatsoper."

After a moment I said, "Who is Lorenz?"

She held out a hand for my cup. "More tea?"

"She thought I was Lorenz."

"Lorenz," she said slowly, "is her son."

"Is?"

"Was." She replenished the cup and returned it to me. Her other hand was buried in the tabby cat tea-cosy, which for a moment seemed to take on a life of its own; the head turned eerily and the blind green eyes watched me intently. "He died in the war." She sounded uncertain. "At least . . ." I waited. "Nobody really knows. He was one of those who . . . ceased to exist. He *and* his father. They were taken one night . . ."

"Taken?"

"By the Nazis." She stared at me blankly. "They were Jewish. They were taken off . . . never seen again."

"Ernst Sternberg was a Jew?"

"You didn't know that?"

"My father never mentioned it. I knew of my aunt only through him."

Her voice became suddenly hard. "When she married Ernst back in '26, the people here actually ostracised her. The fact that she was as Gentile as any of them, to say nothing of being British, made no difference. They just couldn't bear the thought that one of their kind could be attracted to a Jew, let alone marry one. The Viennese are dreadfully anti-Semitic, you know. Oh, they'd never admit it, of course, not in so many words, but it's there, deep down inside every one of them. I saw it when Hitler marched in—it was like an eruption, a sort of religious madness . . ." She broke off and was silent for a long time staring at the tea-cosy, caressing it with a rhythmic gentleness as though smoothing the fur of a living animal. "He was nine years old—Lorenz—just nine. Nobody knows what happened to either of them.

"Ernst had realised soon after the Munich crisis that war was inevitable. He had insisted that Alice should accept an American engagement she'd been offered—just to get her out of Europe before the storm broke. But by the end of August '39 we were back in England. She'd heard nothing from him for months and was worried sick about him and little Lorenz. War was only a week away, but that didn't stop her. She came over here to try to find something out about them but was somehow persuaded by his close colleagues—heaven knows how—to return to England almost immediately, taking with her as much of Ernst's stock—and theirs—as she could carry. She risked everything, took a terrible chance—if they'd discovered the diamonds she was carrying, she'd have been clapped into a concentration camp. She only just got out in time." There was another long pause, during which she replaced the tea-cosy, fiddling with it unnecessarily, her mind preoccupied. At last, in a flat tone of abject resignation, she went on:

"When it was all over, Alice came back, raised heaven and earth, and spent a fortune trying to find some trace of them. It was no use. There was never anything concrete to go on, only rumours. Somebody thought he saw Ernst on a train in Poland, another that they'd both gone to one of the Schindler camps, but no survivor ever remembered either of them."

Despondency crawled over me like a pall. Demel's fancy cakes began to lose their flavour. "Is that what she wants me for? To find them? After all these years? It would be hopeless. Besides, the chances are that Ernst would be dead anyway—from natural causes, surely?"

She held up a hand and shook her head. "I can't help, Mark. You must let her tell you herself."

"If she survives the night."

She stared at me for a second almost as if she had forgotten the implications of the room upstairs, then she said quietly, "She'll survive. I know she will." She smiled again and once more I was touched by the warmth of it. "She's not ready to go yet. I can tell." She continued thoughtfully, "Lorenz, funnily enough, has been on her mind lately. She mentioned him a couple of times only last week, quite out of the blue; not in any important way, but the fact that she mentioned him at all was unusual. I thought she'd got over all that, because she hasn't spoken about him for years, certainly not in my hearing."

"Maybe she's just drifting back—elderly people sometimes remember the distant past far more clearly than yesterday."

"If she is, there's no other sign of it. Her memory is phenomenal, always has been. She's always saying, now don't let me forget this or that, but I've never yet had to remind her of anything."

I eyed her curiously. "Whose idea was it to bring me out here? Yours? She's surely far too ill . . ."

She interrupted me. "Early this morning she became restless and, according to the nurse who sent for me, spoke your name a couple of times. She was wide awake and quite lucid when I arrived. She asked me to call you in London, and said you'd changed your name from Sutherland to Savage, and that you were a private detective now, not an actor. Then she said, 'Tell him I need him here, all expenses paid. Make up a room for him. Tell him I'm on my last legs, some such nonsense, so that he'll think it very serious and come. I must talk to him.'" She spread her hands. "And here you are."

I gave her a rueful smile. "I'm sorry about the Bristol. I'll move in here tomorrow if that's what she really wants and if it's all right with you. I'm not usually mad about hobnobbing with clients—they're always breathing down your neck and resenting the way you're spending their money. But this time . . . well, after all, she is my aunt, isn't she?"

CHAPTER TWO

Next morning the sun was shining. Vienna smiled. A pair of trysting collared doves sat on the ledge outside my window hooting at each other like a couple of owls. When I loomed up behind the glass, they blinked at me with ruby eyes and went on with what they were doing.

I paid a king's ransom to spring myself from the hotel and gave the man at the door a twenty-schilling note for bowing at me as I passed. He showed signs of relieving me of my bag and wanted to buy me a taxi. In perfect German I told him I would walk, to which he replied, "Have a good day, sir," in perfect English.

The traffic was thick on the Ringstrasse, and I queued up at the kerbside with twenty others waiting for the little red man to change colour. As I stood there wondering in what condition I would find Aunt Alice, I became aware of a vaguely familiar perfume, a cologne or aftershave, masculine . . . The green man appeared, and I and my fellow pedestrians pounded across the tarmac in a body. It wasn't until I was approaching the far pavement that I linked the scent to a location. I glanced quickly around at the sea of milling faces on either side and at the thick red neck of a man in front. By that time the smell had gone and my own particular group of walkers were elbowing their way through a tight gaggle of American tourists looking at the Opera House.

I was surprised to find that the incident disconcerted me. I have a keen sense of smell and this one, I would swear, was new to me—until the previous evening, that is, when I had encountered it in the shadows of my Aunt Alice's bedroom.

The main doors of the building were open but a second pair, grandly ornamented with an anachronistic-looking electric bellpush set in a brass plate beside them, were fast closed. When I pressed the bell and a voice barked out of the wall at me, I told it who I was; the door buzzed and I pushed it open.

In the diffused light of morning the hallway which last night had looked like something out of *The Merry Widow* now seemed tawdry. Daylight streamed in through high, clerestory-type windows. I could see the joins and the chipped plaster and paintwork; the vulgarity of the cherubs was depressing, their postures obscene, and with the cold light of day glancing from the surfaces of the shiny canvases, the twin rows of portraits were nothing more than a dreary corridor of cracked mirrors. Even the stair carpet had lost some of its crimson glow.

I was being watched. At the head of the stairs, one gloved hand resting on the balustrade, a tall, pale figure stared down at me. I stood for a second, wondering if I were imagining things.

"Mark," said my aunt. "I've been waiting for you. How good of you to come."

Like a sleep-walker I moved to the foot of the stairs. "Aunt Alice?"

"Stay where you are," she said. "I'm coming down."

I watched with dismay as the stately figure moved smoothly down the stairs towards me. Last night she had been dying. Now, trim and elegant in a dove-grey costume and a toque-like hat perched almost humorously on an upward sweep of carefully groomed pure white hair, she was descending upon me like an apparition, a small twisted smile lighting her pale face. "It's a wig," she told me, noting the direction of my gaze. "It comes complete with the hat. Very handy."

I realised why she had seemed so tall up there on the landing; the costume was from another age and reached the floor, the nipped-in waist making her appear even slimmer than she was. When she came to rest two steps up, I realised how very small she really was; her eyes were on a level with mine. The quirky smile still twitched at the corners of her mouth. "Well, nephew, how do I look?"

I put down my bag and shook a bemused head. "I just don't believe it."

She gave a tinkly laugh. "I'm like one of those tiresome ladies who are always giving farewell performances. If I keep it up long enough, no one will turn up at the funeral because no one will believe I've actually gone. Now give me a kiss, there's a good boy, and let me come down to earth."

As my lips touched her proffered cheek, I was surprised at the chill of it; her hand too, through the thin cotton glove, was ice-cold. She smelled of powder and rose-water. "You look really wonderful," I told her. "We are amazed."

She gave a dry smirk, and as she passed me, I had a bird's-eye view of the grey toque and the glittering hat-pin which secured it—if what she had told me was true—to the elegant white wig.

"How do you like my pictures?"

I noticed for the first time that she was carrying a grey leather reticule and that she walked with a slight limp, compensated by a black malacca cane on which she leaned heavily.

She waved the stick at a Klimt-like portrait of Tosca. "I was in love with the man who painted that one. Unfortunately he turned out to be a bounder, made off one night without warning in the direction of Budapest, where I understand he later committed suicide. They are apt to do that over there, you know. Perhaps it's the weather. So I helped myself to his painting—I used to collect them in those days for some reason. Vanity, I expect."

Overtaking her to open a door, I received a smart rap on the ankle with her stick. "I like to open my own doors," she said.

As we entered the kitchen, two startled faces turned towards us, frozen in the midst of altercation. Emily Hargreaves' expression was one of barely suppressed anger; the other face was that of a younger woman, intense with a touch of insolence about it which sat uncomfortably on the wide mouth. I was immediately conscious of her interest in me; the large tip-tilted eyes in which there was the faintest hint of "speak of the devil" regarded me with frank curiosity. When I nodded and gave her what I thought was a friendly smile, she made no attempt to return it; the cool dark eyes remained for a second, still and observant, then shifted to my aunt.

"Good morning, Hedda," greeted Aunt Alice in a tone of studied politeness. "I hope you are well this morning? I don't think you know my nephew Mark. He's the one who came all the way from London yesterday to see me. Kind, don't you think? This is Hedda, Mark, Emily's daughter."

"Miss Hargreaves," I said, swiftly digesting the fact that not only was Emily presumably married but she also had a grown-up daughter. She didn't exactly fall over herself to give me her hand, and when she did, there was no greeting in it.

"I prefer to be called Miss Hartmann, if you don't mind," she said levelly, flicking a glance at her mother. "That was my father's name."

There was an electric crackle in the air which Aunt Alice skilfully defused. "We're just on our way, Emily. Mark has left his bag in the hall. Perhaps you would take charge of it, see that he's nicely settled in somewhere. The Beethoven room is the sunniest, don't you think? In the meantime, I'm taking him for a drive and then on to Demel's for coffee and cakes. You can ring me there if you need me. Mark and I have a lot to talk about." She turned on her heel. "Come along, dear boy." I caught her eye, and this time she did wink. "You do like Beethoven, don't you? Of course you do, you're a revolutionary I'm quite sure . . ."

As I closed the door, I felt the frosty atmosphere in the room beyond begin to warm up.

"I'll tell you all about that some time," she promised, leading the way back through her private art gallery. "Poor Hedda has turned out to be something of a cross. Not her fault, not really . . ." She left the sentence unfinished and changed the subject abruptly—a disconcerting habit of hers, I was to discover. "Do you consider it egotistical of me to have all these hair-raising pictures hanging about the place? I really don't know what else to do with them. Where *can* you put things that size except on the wall? At least they hide the plasterwork. I've thought of offering one or two of them to provincial opera houses to hang in their foyers or bars or wherever they hang dead divas, but wouldn't it be too awful if they didn't want them? Or worse still if they said, 'Alice Who?' I suppose you wouldn't care for one, would you?" she asked brightly. "You could hang it in your office, perhaps. You'd be very welcome to Elektra. She's about the smallest if you haven't a very tall office. It would be so nice to know that she would still be in the family, so to speak."

Mercifully at that moment we arrived at the front door. She paused before it. "This one," she said, "you may open for me. It's much too heavy for me in my state of health. Anyway, nothing's likely to be happening on the other side of it."

"Just fancy," she added rather smugly as we passed out into the blazing sunshine, "two days ago we all thought I was dead."

It *was* a remarkable feat. What I knew about heart attacks bordered on nothing at all. They came in different sizes, I knew that. The one that visited my father had killed him in less than two minutes. For Aunt Alice it had been passover time, and as a member of the family I suppose it was my duty to point out that it would not always be so—that she shouldn't be trudging up and down stairs and rushing off into town the moment she was back on her feet. However, she looked as fit as any eighty-four-year-old can decently look, so I decided to say nothing.

Moored at the kerbside and surrounded by a tight knot of car-fanciers was a majestic vintage Rolls, maroon with brass fittings—or were they gold? Alongside, impeccable and bomb-proof, stood a chauffeur in a matching uniform. On the emergence of my aunt he cleared the way by the simple expedient of opening the door and looking expectant, and the huddle of sightseers fell back to view the vintage owner of the vehicle. If I felt a trifle self-conscious, my aunt didn't. She gave them an indulgent smile, a royal flutter of her hand, and when she turned at the open door, one foot on the running board, I had the heart-sinking feeling that she was about to address them or burst into song. The move, however, was simply to inform me that I had already met Konrad, hadn't I? By Konrad she meant the chauffeur—there wasn't anyone else—and when I peered beneath the overhang of his maroon cap, my operatic driver of the previous evening was clearly visible. No wonder he had refused my money. I nodded affably, and he took my aunt's cane, helped her in, then turned to me, jerked his head happily at the sky and said, *"Es scheint, ja?"*

"He says the sun is shining," supplied my aunt, settling her draperies and regaining her stick. "An unnecessary observation, I would have thought. However . . ." She gave my knee an aunt-like pat as I joined her. "Do you speak German?"

"Brilliantly," I told her with a modest smirk. "But don't tell him that, it'll spoil his day."

Our first stop was Demel's in Kohlmarkt—not, however, for coffee. Konrad alone disembarked and I watched him disappear into the shop-cum-restaurant.

"We're not supposed to be here," said my aunt, "this is a pedestrian zone. But the police are very understanding. And it's never for long." She sounded as if someone had given her the keys to the city. Perhaps they had. I peered out at Demel's display windows.

In one of them was a kneeling reproduction, in sugar I suspect, of someone who looked like Mother Earth with long chocolate-coloured hair fanning out over her lap. My aunt registered my interest and said with a sniff, "That's supposed to be Kundry from the Syberberg film of *Parsifal.* Imagine it! If I'd worn a wig like that when I sang it at Bayreuth, they'd have hooted the place down." She pointed. "Everything in that window is made on the premises; in fact, everything in the place is homemade—even some of the furniture. It is a most remarkable establishment. The man who runs it is straight out of Robert Louis Stevenson—he reminds me of a pirate. He is an extraordinary man with an outrageous sense of humour; I never know whether he's telling the truth or just having me on. But I love him just the same. He should have been an actor. You'll meet him later, I expect; when you do, tread carefully. The bulge at his right hip is a gun—a SIG-Sauer P220, unless I'm very much mistaken. A formidable character is Udo."

"Udo?"

"A derivation of Rudolf, I suspect, though no one ever calls him that. Udo

Proksch-Kirchhofer is his full title and he's the director and general manager. Married, incidentally, to a countess, as one might expect."

A small crowd was collecting on the pavement outside, dividing its attention between Demel's windows and the maroon Rolls-Royce tied up alongside. Several shaded their eyes to catch a glimpse of its occupants. I began to feel like a goldfish in a bowl. Aunt Alice rapped at the window with the knob of her stick and said loudly in English, "Pass along there."

At that moment Konrad appeared bearing a small gift-wrapped package. He shooed away the onlookers with an effective expletive I couldn't quite catch and passed his purchase to Aunt Alice; she stowed it away carefully in her already bulging leather reticule. "Rudolfsplatz, Konrad," she instructed, and a moment later we were off.

"The man we're going to see," said Alice in a tone which indicated that she was now about to tell all, "is one Samuel Meier. Not surprisingly with a name like that, he is Jewish. Also, unsurprisingly I suppose, is the fact that he is a *Textilgrosshändler*—a what's-its-name . . . a wholesaler in the rag trade. Most people in that district appear to be in the rag trade. Sammy is a great friend and something of a colleague—has been for years. We do a little business together now and then which is . . . rewarding in a modest way . . ."

A low-pitched whistle interrupted her, and when she reached for a speaking tube at her elbow I grew quite excited; I had never actually seen a speaking tube except in the movies. I watched her as she listened to Konrad for a second or two, turning her head to peer through the rear window. She muttered something into the tube and returned it to its moorings. She was frowning.

"What is it?"

"We're being followed." She touched my arm as I was about to take a look. "No, don't let them see we're on to them. A grey VW, two men. Konrad's had them in his mirror for some time."

"Who are they?" I asked, mystified. "Why should they be following us?"

"It's not really important," she smiled brightly, "but we may as well lose them. It's always fun for Konrad."

I felt the increase of power surge through the car as Konrad's foot entered the game.

Losing a tail in a vintage Rolls-Royce is an extraordinary and unique experience—at least it was on this occasion. There was no smell of burning rubber, no clanging of metal, no grinding of gears or scream of brakes; we swayed a little, it's true, as we took the odd sharp bend, but there was no sense of flight, no feeling of panic—indeed, until Aunt Alice rolled down the window to let in some air there was not even a sensation of speed if one ignored the fact that people and objects outside were coming and going with remarkable alacrity. The influx of air ruffled my hair and almost unseated my aunt's wig and hat, but she clamped them to her head with the handle of her stick and laughed aloud several times like a madwoman.

All this of course is not to say that the people and things outside weren't behaving quite differently. Our precipitous progress was causing no end of a stir among drivers and pedestrians alike—tram-drivers in particular; they clanged their bells, shouted and shook their fists. But then Konrad had no right to be driving along their tramlines in the first place. In Vienna even a pedestrian takes life and limb into his hands should he be tempted to set foot on them.

I never knew when or where we lost the tail. There was certainly no grey Volkswagen behind us when eventually I took a peep through the window. Konrad braked gently and we continued on our stately way as though nothing had happened. Alice wound up the window and patted her wig in the small mirror opposite her seat.

Konrad glanced over his shoulder with a broad grin. She waved a cheerful hand and immediately sobered up as she caught sight of an approaching tram. "A Number 71!" She might have seen a ghost. "In the midst of life there's always a 71," she wailed.

"What does that mean?" I was bewildered.

"A 71 takes you to the Zentral Friedhof—the cemetery. In this city they even call a corpse a 71. They're a quirky lot, the Viennese. I'm quite sure that tram came along on purpose just to remind me of my mortal state." She turned to me suddenly. "Do you know what they call top hats—the black variety that go to funerals? Anxiety tubes!" She nodded as I grinned aloud. "Yes, you see, it has a certain ring to it, hasn't it?" She sighed heavily. "You know, there's nowhere in the whole world I'd rather live than in Vienna; my happiest days were spent here. And the most miserable . . . most terrible. I have one ambition left . . . to be buried in the Friedhof within chattering distance of Lotte Lehmann and Hilde Konetzni and earshot of Beethoven and Schubert. I'm sure they're all still making music over there somewhere . . ."

She fell silent, morosely watching the traffic as we turned right into the Schubertring and on past the Stadtpark. She took my hand suddenly, pointing. "Look, peacocks." I ducked my head but missed them. Her tiny hand gripped mine. "Dear Mark. It was so truly good of you to come. I have no right to spoil it for you with my stupid melancholy."

I closed my hand over hers. "You have every right. I'm here to do a job, aren't I?"

She frowned down at our hands. "I don't want you to get hurt."

I smiled. "I've been hurt working for worse clients than you, believe me."

She gave a silvery laugh and leaned over to kiss my cheek. As she did so, her reticule slid off her lap and landed with an almighty thump on my foot. Before I could reach for it, she had herself retrieved it and laid it carefully on the seat beside her. I wriggled my foot; it felt as if the little toe had gone. What the hell was she carrying in that thing—a gold bar?

Running alongside the Donau Kanal past the Salztorbrücke we turned left down Heinrichsgasse where every other establishment seemed to proclaim the words *Bekleidung* or *Textilgrosshändel* over their front doors, and so into Rudolfsplatz, tall dusty buildings engulfing a rectangle of fenced-in greenery and a small sandy patch of a children's playground. Alice reached for the speaking tube. "I'll tell him to take a couple of turns around the square—just in case." On the second circuit she said, "Damn," quietly beneath her breath. "They've anticipated us." She nodded. "By the hotel there, tucked in behind the blue van; the grey Volkswagen with the bent fender."

I couldn't see its number but stashed the rest of the vehicle away in my memory bank. The driver's face was hidden behind a deliberate hand; a gold ring glimmered on the third finger and the sleeve cuff was a green loden cloth. Otherwise there was nothing to see. We swung out of their sight and glided to a standstill. We all got out, and once on the pavement Aunt Alice held a solemn parley with Konrad, telling him to stay where he was until we got back.

"They won't get past him," she said as she tucked her arm companionably in mine.

"Who are they? What's going on? Are they dangerous?"

"I'm not really sure. Now come along. All will be revealed, I promise."

The building was tall and yellowish and encrusted with small ornamental balconies jutting from the first and second floors. A couple of doors away the builders were in, the air full of fine grey dust and the sound of hammering; a pneumatic drill clattered behind a swathing of green netting which draped the scaffolding from roof to pavement. From the quick view I'd had of the city that morning, most of Vienna seemed to be in the hands of builders; hardly a *Strasse*, a *Weg* or the smallest *Gasse* was without its quota of green swathing. Everyone's lease was coming to an end, perhaps.

An elevator of about the same vintage as the maroon Rolls but somewhat less mechanically sound lifted us from the ground floor with a couple of bone-grinding jerks, stopped abruptly as if to reconsider, then shot us away to the fourth with a breath-taking whoop, clanking past the intervening floors like an express train clattering over points. When it came to rest, it gave a malignant hiss as if daring us to dismount; I shot a glance at Aunt Alice in time to see her remove the handle of her stick from her hat; she looked windswept.

On the landing an open window stood wide; motes floated in the bright morning sunlight, dust gritted beneath our feet; the plastered walls festered and bloomed where the damp had crawled, dried and crawled again. Paintwork peeled. The green builders' shrouds were long overdue.

My aunt's gloved forefinger was already on the bell-push of a door which said S. Meier on a tarnished brass plate.

The moment I saw S. Meier in the flesh, I knew he was in trouble. He had taken quite a while to appear and when he did, it was in response to a third summons on his bell; he was sweating a little and looked as if he had been doing some unlikely limbering up.

At first the door opened a crack to reveal one large and wary eye which flooded with relief at the sight of my aunt and clouded over again when it descried me lurking in the background. When I made no aggressive move, the door creaked open some more.

His eyes made an almost physical impact upon me. They brimmed with hurt and anxiety and seemed to reflect, in microcosm, the sufferings of an entire people. Somewhere there was a quiet in them too, but you had to look for it. The rest of him was an odd mixture of shambling alertness: big-framed but spare in flesh, grizzled hair and beard, he looked in about his middle fifties but could have been younger. He wore a long green cardigan and black concertina trousers. "Shalom, Sammy," said Aunt Alice rather too heartily. "You look as if you've seen a ghost." She spoke in English, turning to me as she did so and bringing me forward. "I want you to meet my nephew—from England."

The eyes cleared a little as he leaned outwards and took my hand. "I am pleased to meet you," he said in the musical tones of a Russian bass. I didn't think he looked at all pleased; in fact, he looked frightened to death, the more so when he shot a furtive glance over my shoulder as if expecting more of us. His grip was firm enough, but the hand was hot and sticky with sweat. "The lift is working, no?" He pushed past me and reopened the gates I had just closed. "It has misbehave a lot."

He placed a finger to his lips and pointed with significant dread at the floor. "The dust is terrible, huh? Workmen in building next door." In the thin sifting of dust was an outsize set of footprints which belonged to none of us. They entered his front door and were clearly visible on the dark carpeting, tramping down the centre of a wide hallway; it was a one-way set of prints; the feet which made them had not yet departed. Sammy's message was loud and clear, but if Alice was receiving it, she gave no sign.

"Aren't you going to ask us in, Sammy?" He shook his head emphatically, indicating in silence that we should get the hell out of it. She ignored the proposition. "I can't say we were just passing, because nobody just passes Rudolfsplatz, do they? I really wanted you to meet my nephew, Mark. He'll be staying for a few days. I've also brought you some goodies from Demel's. Ah, there—I thought that would get you."

Far from "getting him," the remark seemed to bring further apprehension into Sammy's eye. By this time, however, she was through the front door and marching down the hallway following the footprints, her stick tucked under one arm whilst with both hands she took the Demel package from her reticule. "I've been laid up, you know," she threw over her shoulder, pushing open a door and disappearing into the room beyond. Sammy Meier gave me a resigned look and took off after her, leaving me to bring up the rear.

She was at the window admiring the view—what there was of it. Just the roofs of houses, the tops of trees and a bright blue sky, that was all. "I've always loved this view," she exclaimed untruthfully as we entered the room; she hooked her stick over the back of a chair and peered enquiringly into Sammy's face as he hove up alongside her.

"You like *Kaffee?*" he asked, moving away again, staring pointedly at a half-open door. "Some in kitchen." The wallpaper of the room beyond the door was certainly not that of a kitchen. His eyes met mine briefly. I nodded. Together we closed in on the door in a pincer movement.

Before we could reach it, the door swung fully open and a man stepped out behind it. Enveloped in a tent-like overcoat, he was a formidable figure, big and wide, with a great round head and a flat round sweating face to go with it. All this I might have taken with some show of equanimity; it was the gun which drew me up in my tracks. In the great ham of a fist it looked quite small; it wasn't. It was a huge Colt automatic, nine inches long and weighing two and a half pounds.

"Ah," I said. "Good morning."

I glanced at Sammy, who gave a shrug as if washing his hands of the whole affair.

Having been obliged to reveal himself, the intruder was now plainly at a loss as to what to do next and kept us waiting while he thought about it. With a weapon that size he could afford to ponder the issue.

Alice had remained motionless by the window whilst Sammy and I had pincered ourselves around the room until we stood about a couple of yards apart. We were an untidy target, and I set about making it even more untidy, backing away from Sammy a couple of paces. Not surprisingly, the man snarled and waved the gun at me. What he said was unintelligible, but his intentions were clear. I grew roots.

"Is that a language he's talking?" I enquired in English.

"Hungarian," whispered Sammy.

"What did he say?"

"I can feel my hay fever coming on," put in Aunt Alice promptly, which seemed an unlikely story. "Oh dear," she added and launched herself into a startling series of cat sneezes. "Do you have a handkerchief, Mark dear?" she spluttered through them. "I always do this when I'm frightened."

I made a move towards her; the huge gun swung swiftly in my direction; I froze again as a deafening explosion shook the room followed by a shrill yelp of pain; for a dazed second I thought I had been hit. Then I saw the man's smashed hand, blood dripping, and the Colt suspended from his trigger finger where it hung for a second before thudding to the floor. Sammy lunged forward and took possession of it.

I turned, my head still ringing, and gaped in sheer disbelief at my aunt. A gun smoked in her hand. Somewhere in the room behind me glass ornaments tinkled gently as the waves of sound slowly died away; from beyond the window came the chatter of the pneumatic drill.

At last my aunt spoke, flapping her hand irritably to clear the air of the blue smoke which enveloped her like an aura. I had no idea what she was saying; she was talking to the big man who, in silent stupor, had eyes only for the blood which dripped from his hand on to Sammy's carpet. She spoke in a staccato series of grunts and sneezes which I was prepared to believe was also Hungarian.

The man's eyes were red-rimmed and had tears in them. He was a huge, lumbering and frustrated bear. He looked at each of us for a second, a glutinous tear ambling down his cheek to lose itself in the forest of black stubble around his chin. Slowly he backed to the door, his crippled hand held upright before him as though bearing some precious relic. I moved in a step.

"Let him go," said my aunt quietly.

We watched him leave, Sammy a few paces behind, the huge purloined gun at the ready. In silence we listened to the clash of the lift gates and the rattle of its descent, cut off abruptly as the front door closed and Sammy returned to us looking slightly sheepish. Alice gave a sudden sigh and, closing her eyes tightly, swayed a little, the gun loose now in her gloved hand. Taking her gently by the shoulders, I led her to an armchair. She was trembling violently. Relieving her of the gun, I laid it on the table beside her.

CHAPTER THREE

My mind buzzed like a hornets' nest with unasked questions. I stood indecisive, staring down at the frail figure, obsessed momentarily with the cold glitter of the hat-pin stuck like a solitaire amidst the grey silken excesses of her toque.

It was a whole new ball game. That grand old dependable British institution, The Aunt, was crumbling before my eyes.

"Is there anything I can do?" I enquired belatedly, my mind only then nudging at the possibility of her being on the way to further cardiac arrest. I recovered her stick and placed it beside her.

"Tablets," she muttered. "In my bag . . ."

Detaching the reticule from around her wrist, I discovered why it still weighed a ton: it contained another gun. A second Walther PPK, twin to the one on the table. She was a walking armoury.

I took a deep breath. Her eyes flickered open and met mine. Again that sly droop of the eyelid. "The silver snuff-box," she murmured. I burrowed gingerly in the bag half fearful of what else it might disclose.

Small white pills in a silver box; she took two of them without water, grinding them between her dentures with the resigned grimace of the chronic invalid.

"The gun," she informed me in a whisper, "is for you."

I looked at her with mounting disquiet. "Aunt Alice . . ."

She laid a hand on mine. "Take it, there's a good boy—if only to set my mind at rest."

I placed the Walther alongside the other; they were alike as two peas in a pod. "Can you give me one good reason why I should hump one of these things around with me?" I asked gently. "Or is it mandatory to carry a gun in Vienna?"

"I would have you know," she said loftily, growing stronger by the second, "that Vienna has one of the lowest crime rates in the world."

"Well, let's hope it stays that way."

Sammy Meier reappeared carrying a tray laden with coffee requirements and the recently acquired Colt. I watched him sorting out his cups, cream and bowl of demerara and finally place the huge gun on the table where it dwarfed the two Walthers already there. He didn't turn a hair at the sight of the extra one. He set a chair for me alongside my aunt and seated himself opposite.

I nodded, smiling at him companionably. "Udo has a gun, Alice has a gun, I have a gun, and now you have a gun. Of the half dozen people in Vienna I have met or know about, no less than four of us carry guns."

Coffee pot poised, he frowned at me for a blank moment, then shifted his gaze to Alice to see what she was making of it. Her eyes were speculative as she studied me with the air of an artist deciding on a sitter's best angle. I headed her off before she could make up her mind. "Where did you learn to shoot like that?"

The solemn scrutiny continued for a further second or two, then her eyes suddenly twinkled.

"Mark dear, an opera singer's life is not all deep breathing and *répétiteurs*, you know. Some of us have remarkable handicaps at golf, some of us write our life stories, some of us cook, dabble in computers, visit zoos, have children—Kirsten Flagstad actually knitted. I spent a great deal of my time learning how to shoot straight—aided and abetted, I may say, by my late husband, your great uncle Ernst. In his footsteps too I became quite a dab at archery. He was much lionised for his prowess with the bow. He could shoot an apple from your head at two hundred paces."

Sammy served up Turkish coffee which stood black, thick and upright in the tiny cups. "*Schlagobers?*" He pushed the cream jug towards me.

"Who was that man, Sammy?" I asked abruptly.

His great lambent eyes rested on mine. He said, "Not know. Never see him before."

"What did he want? Why was he here? Did he force his way in?"

Again his eyes shifted in Alice's direction. She was engrossed with her coffee. "He had gun."

I gave a heavy sigh. "Oh, come on, Sammy. He wasn't a burglar, was he? An *Einbrecher, verstehen?* He was after something specific and was prepared to do murder to get it." I glanced sourly at Alice. "He might conceivably have killed the lot of us if one of our number hadn't spent a great deal of her youth learning how to shoot straight."

Alice suddenly threw back her head and laughed. It wasn't the well-bred tinkle I had become accustomed to; this time it was the kind of roistering shout one associates with movie versions of Elizabeth I.

I waited until the gale of merriment had subsided before observing somewhat testily that if that great thing on the table was an example of the calibre of the opposition there was not a lot for anyone to laugh about.

She shook her head at me, a smile still on her lips. "He was a big man with a big gun, that's all. He would have looked silly with a PPK."

"Who is he?"

"I have no idea."

"Didn't you ask him?"

"No."

"Why not?"

"Because he wouldn't have told me." She was being quite reasonable.

"What *did* you say? You said something to him."

"I told him to go and get his hand seen to."

"Was that all?"

"I also told him that next time I'd shoot him through the head."

I rolled my eyes at Sammy, who raised his brows and pulled down the corners of his mouth; he said nothing.

I began again with infinite patience. "Alice, yesterday you sent up a distress rocket and I came running. I sympathise and understand completely about the state of your health. Obviously the last thing you must do is overtax your strength. But . . . if you're fit enough to roar about in fast cars and shoot down complete strangers in cold blood, then in my opinion you are fit enough to sit there quietly and tell me what the hell is going on and why that rocket sounded so urgent. Is that fair or isn't it?"

I thought for a moment she was going to argue about it. There was a glimmer in her grey eyes which flickered in and out like an Aldis lamp advising the submarine not to surface; then it was gone and the eyes were bland again and quizzical at the same time. "You're not at all like your father, are you?" She turned confidentially to Sammy. "His father was an estate agent in Wimbledon, London, you know—where they play the tennis."

Sammy nodded and screwed up his eyes in earnest appreciation of my father's problems.

I found myself wondering, not for the first time, whether my aunt was perhaps ever so slightly unhinged. At eighty-four you can be very unhinged indeed and pass as an eccentric. Her head was cocked as she listened to the clatter of the pneumatic drill next door. "It's strange, isn't it," she murmured half to herself, "how you can shoot a man in a teeming city and no one appears to turn a hair. However . . ." She turned her attention fully upon me. "Dear boy, try not to be cross with me. You have been in Vienna little more than twelve hours, eight of which you must surely have spent in your nice warm bed at the Bristol. A few hours absorbing atmosphere and becoming acclimatised to a place never did anyone any harm. And those few hours haven't exactly been without incident, goodness knows." She fell silent for a moment, then continued quietly. "It's a question of time, you see—*my* time —and how much of it I have left before I board that gloomy 71 to the Friedhof." She gave a wry smile. "We know very little about each other, you and I, and I am to blame for that. My husband and son were my whole family—apart from my career, my whole life. Emily told you something of them last night, I believe." Her eyes lingered over Sammy, who sat foursquare at the table, hands deep in the pockets of his cardigan, moodily studying his coffee cup. "A short while ago Sammy came to me with a story I found almost impossible to believe." She paused again as if waiting for Sammy to chime in and tell me what it was. He made no move.

She went on. "It seems there is a man in Vienna who claims to be Lorenz, my son. Will you go on, Sammy?"

Sammy rocked a little on his chair, then shook his head slowly. "*Nein,* you tell. Easier make him understand."

She spoke suddenly in German, so rapidly that I was unable to keep up with her; only the word *küdisch* sprang out of context. He shook his head and shrugged.

Turning to me once again, my aunt continued in English. "I am sure I don't have to tell you that there is in existence an Israeli faction fanatically devoted to the hunting down of war criminals. While Sammy is not actually one of them, he has occasionally been of assistance to them." She held out a hand. "Sammy, *dein Handgelenk . . . ?*"

Reluctantly he gave her his hand, wrist uppermost. She slid back the sleeve of his cardigan, and I stared soberly at the number tattooed into the pallid skin. Sammy looked apologetic. "Lucky me," he murmured, clumsily repossessing himself of his hand and wrapping it carefully in the voluminous woollen sleeve. "Auschwitz. But over now . . . past . . ."

"Sammy believes there is nothing to be gained by hunting down these men; revenge, he says, is no longer relevant. He also believes there should be a sort of statute of limitations. I wish I could agree with him. He and I suffered the same loss—the people we most cared about in the world. But because he was actually there, sharing their suffering—perhaps his mind has been cleansed of the need for reprisal; two wrongs do not make a right, eh, Sammy?"

He frowned hard at his large hands, then deliberately sat on them. He said nothing.

"In Brazil is a man who calls himself Bronson," continued my aunt. "Rodrigo Bronson, a diamond merchant, as Ernst my husband was. In Jewish circles it is believed that his name is actually Otto Brunner, who during the war was a *Sturmbannführer* in the Waffen SS and *Kommandant* of one of the experimental camps at Mauthausen here in Austria. Not surprisingly he's high on the list of the wanted. So far he's managed to stay out of their reach. He must be quite elderly now, of course—all of them are, aren't they? He's a widower and has a son who, as far as one can gather, now manages the diamond business. Neither of them, it appears, has ever set foot out of Brazil, which is curious in itself because diamond people move around quite a bit if only to keep a weather eye on the market—Antwerp, Tel Aviv, New York, London, Bombay, all the other diamond centres. But not, apparently, Bronson and Son. Is there any more coffee in that pot, Sammy?"

I wondered idly as I watched him replenishing her cup whether she should be drinking coffee in her condition.

"The Jewish contingent—I can never remember what they call themselves —recently picked up the trail of a man who arrived here in Vienna from America. They traced him to the Hotel Imperial where they—er—contrived to lay hold of his passport. It said he was a Lorenz Bronson, diamond merchant, born in Rio de Janeiro. The Israelis maintain that he is Lorenz Bronson the son, in fact, of Rodrigo Bronson—i.e., Otto Brunner. They removed him from circulation."

"Killed him?"

"Kidnapped him. Sammy thinks they intended to hold him as hostage in the unlikely event of his father handing himself over in exchange. They were quite rough with him, I'm told, and finally put him into cold storage in an empty warehouse by the Danube somewhere until such time as one of their number arrived from Latin America to identify him. Under pressure, Lorenz Whoever-he-is denied he was Bronson's son and insisted that his real name was Lorenz Sternberg, that he was born in Vienna on 5 June 1929 and is the son of that well-known and elderly diva, Alicia Sternberg; his father, Ernst, a Jewish diamond merchant, had been murdered by the Nazis in Mauthausen concentration camp early in 1939 . . ."

She broke off. Beyond the windows the pneumatic drill hammered relentlessly; the sickly smell of cordite clung to the walls and furnishings; Sammy breathed heavily and creaked a little somewhere.

Alice said quietly, "*My* son was born in Vienna on 5 June 1929 at four-thirty in the morning. My own investigators, shortly after the war, confirmed that both he and Ernst were taken to Mauthausen in '39, after which they could find no further record of either of them." Her gloved hands clasped and unclasped themselves on the table before her. "I just wonder if . . . whether Lorenz could possibly have survived . . ."

I glanced at Sammy, who stared back blankly. "You know where this warehouse is?"

Sammy opened his mouth to reply but was anticipated by Alice. "He escaped. Which is why they approached Sammy. They wanted him to find out if Lorenz had attempted to contact me. Well, of course he hasn't. He's gone to ground somewhere."

"If what he says is true, and he is your son, he would surely have made contact by now if only to clear himself with them."

"*If* what he says is true. All this happened a fortnight ago, but there's still no word of him. Ever since then I have been followed everywhere. Wherever I go, someone is behind me. They think I know where he is, you see, and will lead them to him."

I thought for a moment. "How would he know the correct date of his birth if he weren't Lorenz?" She was silent. "Was your husband orthodox?" She nodded. "Then Lorenz would have been circumcised?" She stared at me. "That would be enough to convince anyone that he was not the son of a German *Sturmbannführer*—whoever else he might or might not be."

After a moment she said in a small voice, "I wouldn't allow it."

"Allow what?"

She frowned at a memory. "It was the only real quarrel we ever had, Ernst and I. At that time, you see, I was holding on to what little was left of my Catholic upbringing, though if truth be told I never really took to it seriously. It had been difficult enough marrying a Jew in the first place—ethically speaking, I mean—but I would have married Ernst if he had been a Hottentot. I did, however, make a half-hearted attempt to convert him. It's the way of Catholics, you know." There was a wry sweetness in her smile. "But I was just baying the moon. Ernst would have none of it. When Lorenz was born and I was faced with this . . . barbaric and outmoded ritual of circumcision, I stuck my heels in. I was adamant." She leaned in and touched Sammy's arm. "Forgive me, Sammy. I never made much of an effort to understand, I'm afraid. My parents were as strictly orthodox in their way as Ernst was Jewish. I just wouldn't allow it. I couldn't."

I shrugged. "Failing the beard and the ringlets and the big black hat, circumcision seems to be the one proof they all look upon as gospel. God knows why; plenty of Gentiles are circumcised. So the Israelis would obviously have checked him out and found him wanting, which can't have made his story very plausible. So that's it; he is now on the loose and you would like me to find him?"

"I just want to know one thing: is he my son?"

I got up impatiently and prowled about the room in a dither of uneasiness. I met Sammy's eye for a brief second and read there his understanding of my disquiet. I knew too that should the necessity arise, I wouldn't have to spell it out to my aunt.

The war had been over for forty years. The remaining shambles of Nazis and anti-Semites had learned, however ungraciously, to live with the fact that not only did the Jewish race continue to exist but, at the permissive shrug of a handful of guilt-ridden nations, it had established a bastion which it was prepared to defend to the brink of Armageddon itself. To the greater part of the so-called civilised world it was no longer an indictable or indecent offence to be a Jew.

That being so, what had Lorenz Sternberg—if that's who he was—been up to these forty years? If he was now prepared to admit to Semitic roots, why not before? His internationally famous mother had never been further away than a telephone call; that he had not once taken advantage of that fact suggested that he had no burning desire to communicate with her. Only under pressure and presumably to give himself time and save himself from further bodily injury had he eventually acknowledged his origins. But how to prove it? Hardly by the simple expedient of throwing himself into his mother's arms.

"He'd be in his fifties now, wouldn't he? Lorenz?" I was standing now at the window, watching a workman mount an almost perpendicular ladder while carrying on his shoulder a chiselled lump of stonework the size of his head. "Would you know him, do you think—supposing you were to come face to face with him?"

"I would know him. Of course I would know him." Her tone conveyed the slightest hint of outraged motherhood.

"How?" I insisted. "Did he have any peculiarities? Moles, scars, strawberry marks, warts?"

"He had deep brown eyes—like his father's."

"I have deep brown eyes—also like my father's."

"Jet black hair . . ."

I turned back into the room. "Alice, he could be bald as an egg by now. He's lived a lifetime since you last saw him. And if he was taken to Mauthausen with his father, who knows what he was made to endure before he so miraculously survived? He could be tall and beautiful, grey-haired and distinguished; he could also be twisted and shrunken and mentally unstable."

I had gone too far, but it was no time for sentiment. What I had said was true and she knew it and was too intelligent to expect a nine-year-old, four-foot-high schoolboy in a sailor-suit to take belated refuge in her elderly arms.

She broke the silence. "I would know him," she said softly and stubbornly.

Well, maybe she would at that. One would expect some sort of esoteric alchemy to exist between a mother and her son. But Jocasta hadn't known Oedipus; or if she had, she never told.

Aimlessly I gravitated towards my chair and leant over the back of it. "Sammy, what have we got to go on?"

The colloquialism defeated him; Alice translated. He pulled thoughtfully at his lower lip. I said, "Can I meet these men—your friends, the Israelis?"

He nodded ponderously. "Is possible. I fix."

"And perhaps see the warehouse? There might be some sort of lead there."

He hesitated, shooting a worried glance at Alice. "Is more difficult. Could be in hands of Polizei."

"Police? The warehouse? Why?"

"He kill a man."

"Lorenz did? Murdered somebody?"

My aunt said quickly, "It was an accident, I'm sure. He killed an Israeli guard. When he escaped. Someone they'd left behind to keep an eye on him."

"How did he kill him?"

"He strangled him . . . apparently." She waved a dismissive hand.

"Doesn't sound much like an accident to me." Danger flickered in her eye. "Well, does it to you? You strangle someone by intent. It takes quite a time, long enough to revise your ideas if you have a mind to. So the police are after him as well as the Israelis." Both were silent. I eyed my aunt. "And who was that man-mountain whose hand you just shot off? Who did he belong to? Certainly not the police. And he wasn't remotely Jewish. So who was he?"

"I told you," said Alice pedantically. "We don't know."

"He was one of those in the grey Volkswagen, wasn't he?"

"It would seem so."

"They knew we were coming here. One of them remained in the car, and Big Boots, armed to the teeth, came up to confront Sammy . . . or to wait for us. Which would it be, Sammy?"

Sammy again took refuge in language problems. Alice said, "We have no idea, Mark."

"You keep saying that. Just now you said someone is always following you. Who? The Israelis, hoping that Lorenz will contact you? The police, waiting for you to lead them to a strangler? Or this ape-man with his gun and a pal in the car downstairs?" They received the battery of questions in abject silence. "Have the police been asking questions?"

"Not of me, no," said Alice. I looked at Sammy, who shook his head.

"Well, that's one good thing at least. They would have if they'd picked up any connection between any of you." I leaned across her and laid hold of one of the Walthers. I sniffed at the barrel; it was the one she had used. "One more question. Do you always carry this around with you?"

"Not always, no."

"But more so recently?"

It was her turn to sneak a glance at Sammy. "I have taken to it more recently, I suppose . . . yes, I suppose I have."

"Any particular reason?"

Her gloved fingers drummed suddenly and irritably on the table; even her hat trembled; the look she flashed me would have done justice to the murderous Elektra. "Why are you cross-examining *me*, Mark? You are here at my request to discover the whereabouts of someone who professes to be my son —and incidentally your cousin—your great cousin, if there is such a thing. I particularly chose you because you are one of the family and happen to be in this—this detection business . . ."

She made it sound like organised prostitution.

"You're protesting too much," I said, pulling her up smartly in her tracks and handing her a winning smile to offset any offence. I moved around behind her chair, keeping an eye on Sammy, who appeared not to be understanding too much of what was going on. "You two," I murmured tentatively, "are up to something . . . something you're not telling me."

Replacing the Walther, I watched them exchange glances. I picked up the heavy Colt and peered reflectively down its barrel. The look on Sammy's face suggested that he thought I was about to pull the trigger. Had I been in his shoes, I would probably have made a greater effort to deter someone from such a perilous course if only to prevent brains from being splattered over my ceiling. It was in fact Alice who intervened, laying one gentle finger on my elbow. "Don't do that, dear," she said in the soothing voice of one addressing a dangerous lunatic. "It might go off, and then where would you be?"

I slid out the magazine and stared at it for a long time before placing it on the table before her. "You appear to have shot Big Sir's hand off for nothing. It's empty."

It took some seconds for the truth to sink in, and when it did, her eyes registered distress. "How perfectly frightful." She took up the magazine, peered into it, smelt it, shook it and replaced it on the table. "That poor man. Can it be that he meant no harm?"

"I would doubt that," I said drily. "I doubt if he'd have had the courage or yet the intelligence to barge in here on his own with an unloaded gun. What do you say, Sammy?"

He met my eyes boldly enough but caved in pretty quickly, mumbling something beneath his breath. Ferreting around in the pocket of his woolly cardigan, he produced a handful of cartridges which he placed one by one upright on the table until there were seven. He gave Alice a sheepish half-grin.

"Why did you do that, Sammy?" she asked severely. "A gun is perfectly safe in the right hands."

The grin faded. "No gun is safe in anyone's hand," he growled with a small flare of belligerence. "A coward even is brave with a gun in his hand."

Alice sighed and shook her head sadly. "You're a good man, Sammy, a good and peaceful man, but we live in a jungle surrounded by cowards—cowards with guns."

She peered suddenly at her tiny gold wristwatch as if she had just remembered something. She had. "My goodness, we must away or there'll be no lunch for us." She reached for her bag.

I began to feel tetchy. "Aunt . . ."

"Alice," she reminded me.

"We haven't finished yet."

"Oh, haven't we? I'm so sorry." She replaced her reticule and settled back in her chair. "What else was there?"

"For a start, I want to talk to these Israeli pals of Sammy's." I made an ill-advised theatrical gesture and dislodged the upended cartridges on to the carpet, where they dropped slowly one by one like windfalls from an apple tree.

When they had ceased to fall, she said, "You're becoming hysterical."

Sammy and I met head on—literally—under the table. As we scrabbled around for the fallen ammunition, he growled, "Have lunch. I will contact."

"What are you whispering about under there?" demanded my aunt, prodding me under the arm with a sharply pointed toe.

I knelt up, smiling, my chin on the edge of the table. "Aunt Alice, if you are going to question every move I make, I'm not sure I want to work for you."

"And if you're going to make a fuss every time I suggest lunch, then I'm quite certain I don't want you to. You're like a small child."

"Children," I reminded her, "will one day inherit the earth."

Regaining my feet, I took the Colt's magazine, slotted in the seven bullets and slid it gently back into place. I eyed Sammy severely as he too reached an upright position. "Please, Sammy, if you value your life, leave it there. Promise?"

He shrugged, nodded and shrugged again until nobody knew what he meant. Then he added a shy smile which went straight to the heart. Alice, having in the meantime shovelled her gun into her bag, took my hand and slapped the spare weapon into it. "And you, dear nephew, practise what you preach."

I shoved the gun into my waistband, put her stick into her hand and helped her to her feet. "Sammy," she said, "your goodies are over there by the window. Enjoy them."

The smart Demel package lay sweltering in the sun on the window ledge. She looked up into his face and took his hand. *"Mazel un brucha,"* she said solemnly as we walked back and out through the front door.

We watched Sammy's unfashionably trousered legs judder slowly skywards as we clattered down in the lift. "What does that mean?" I asked. *"Mazel* and something."

" *'Mazel un brucha'?* It means 'luck and blessing.' "

"In what language?"

She tilted her head and with an impossibly roguish gesture adjusted her hatpin. "Diamond language," she said.

CHAPTER FOUR

We sat at one of the tiny circular tables in Demel's and watched a privileged section of the world going round making the sort of din one might expect from a school playground at mid-morning break. Eyeing the pink, blue and gold decor of the surprisingly compact restaurant with its impressive pier-glasses, tiled floors and clusters of white electric globes exploding on gilt chandeliers above my head, I reminded myself that Demel's was one of the most fashionable cake-shops in Europe and one would be hard pressed to find a more delectable *Apfelstrudel* or flakier *Milchrahmstrudel* anywhere in the world. At present, however, we were hunched over cold beef Wellington, green salad and iced water.

At Alice's request Konrad had dropped us off at Stephansplatz, and she and I had tacked down the Graben on foot, her tiny hand hooked possessively on my arm, crossing and recrossing the spacious pedestrian precinct a dozen times as one elegant window after another claimed her attention. If we were being followed, our pursuer would be having one hell of a time.

"I just adore window-shopping, don't you?" she crooned, pointing out a fortuitously placed and highly coloured picture of herself as a young diva on the sleeve of an elderly gramophone record.

"Are we being followed, do you think?" I asked her once.

"Oh yes, of course we are," she answered airily. "Someone is always following us."

I had wondered whether she wasn't becoming slightly paranoid about it. My usually alert sixth sense told me nothing of such pursuit, but I could well understand it nodding a little—the confusion of our wayward course had certainly addled my other five senses. Everyone seemed to be looking at us, and an endless succession of well-wishers greeted my aunt's reappearance in public, inclining their heads, raising their hats—a uniform or two even saluted. One or two of them glanced curiously in my direction, but not once did she offer to introduce me.

"Such a bore," she remarked with a tinge of smugness as we had turned at last into Kohlmarkt. "I didn't introduce you, I hope you don't mind. It's far more intriguing to them to be kept guessing."

Now, toying listlessly with my beef Wellington—I rarely eat a carnivorous lunch—and exhausted by our regal progress through the streets, I was fast wearying of the muttered greetings and fluttering fingers directed at us from all sides. I longed to be on my own, making an anonymous progression through the jumble of information which littered the periphery of my mind —"periphery" because, to date, I had no impressive display piece to set in the centre of it. I stared glumly at the rear view of *Parsifal*'s Kundry in the window and wondered with irresponsible eroticism what it would be like to be made of sugar and marzipan.

My eye shifted to the man reflected in the mirror behind my aunt. Small, smooth, well dressed to the point of being dapper, he wore a blue flower in his buttonhole; his head was slick and black like a seal's. He had followed us into the restaurant. I wondered about him.

"You're very quiet," said my aunt suddenly, not having uttered a word since the arrival of lunch. I had expected her to have an appetite like a bird; not a bit of it; she devoured her food, head down, elbows in, knife and fork clashing like the last act of *Hamlet*. She cast a predatory eye over my plate. "Aren't you enjoying your beef?"

A shadow bulked between us and the daylight. I knew who it was before introductions were made. Udo, large and square, his massive shoulders blocking out the view from the window. Alice was right. A three-cornered hat, cutlass and a quarterdeck beneath his seaboots would have become him. Involuntarily my eyes dropped to his right hip. The slightest of bulges beneath his smart blue jacket betrayed the presence of the SIG-Sauer.

He kissed her hand, rumbling away in a subterranean and quite incomprehensible German; when, somewhat surprisingly, she introduced me as her delectable nephew all the way from England, I flinched beneath the grinding onslaught of the hand he offered me. Without a by-your-leave he dragged up a chair and joined us—you can do that if you're the incumbent managing director. The table grew a lot smaller; as he settled in, I repositioned various articles of crockery which seemed to be in danger of dislodgement.

"You not like the beef?" he demanded, eyeing my plate with a frown.

"It's fine."

"You like spinach? I get you a plate of spinach. Make you strong—like Popeye." He raised a large hand to a passing Demeless who drew obediently alongside.

"No, thank you," I muttered hastily, gagging at the thought of a plateful of spinach. "I really don't eat at this time of day . . ."

Alice, immersed in the final act of clearing her plate, said, "Everybody should eat. It's one of the rules of an ordered life. Keeps you up to the mark. Makes you regular." I might have been in short trousers, newly arrived from school for the holidays.

Udo ordered coffee and *Apfelstrudel,* and whilst they exchanged their adult notes about each other's health and well-being, I glanced again into the mirror. I met his eyes; unflinching and expressionless, they were those of a ruminant, blank and blue, giving one the erroneous impression that they saw nothing. I waylaid a covert glance from Alice. Aware of what was in my mind, her eyes strayed over my shoulder. I lifted my eyebrows a fraction. The answer was the slightest of nods. She went back to Udo.

Did she really recognise the man, I wondered, or was she simply indulging her belief in constant surveillance, prepared to place the cap on whosoever's head looked the right size?

Concentrating devoutly on my *Apfelstrudel,* I made a conscious effort to disengage myself from more pressing matters, listening the while to Alice in the toils of what I suspect was the continuing story of the conversion of Udo to opera, a form of entertainment—and he jibbed slightly at the word—in which he professed no interest. She was on a sticky wicket. He sat impassive as a china ornament, bland and smiling, allowing her most cherished and considered arguments to fall about him like biblical seed on stony ground; at one moment her flourishing cake-fork became an offensive weapon as she prodded him sharply on the shirt front to underpin the word "Philistine!" hurled at him with a vigour which brought the restaurant to a momentary standstill.

The blue glaze in the eye of the dapper little man over the way lifted as his attention was surprised by the sudden hiatus. It revealed a very bright blue eye indeed.

An idea began to form itself. Taking advantage of the lull in my aunt's perorations, I said, putting down my fork, "That must be the best *Apfelstrudel* in the world." Udo looked surprised that anyone should find it necessary to mention it. "My aunt tells me you make it on the premises—that you make *everything* on the premises."

He spread his large hands. "Everything. Chocolate, candy, cake, liqueurs . . . everything. Kitchen bigger than restaurant. You like to see? I take you. Show you. Okay?" Fired with proprietorial enthusiasm, he pushed back his chair.

I glanced at Alice. He might have suggested a trip through the sermons of Archbishop Cuthbert; the look on her face was one of utter indifference. "I don't want to see Udo's back parlour," she said. "I've survived this long without knowing what he puts in his cakes. You go, Mark, if you want to."

I picked up her weighty reticule and stared significantly into the mirror behind her. "You'll only get picked up if I leave you on your own—you know that, don't you?"

She met my eye, flashed a comprehending look in the direction of the man with the buttonhole and finally heaved herself to her feet with a theatrical sigh. "I wouldn't worry about him, you know," she muttered, collecting her stick. "He'll still be here when we come back. They're all very patient, these fellows."

The ground floor of Demel's is L-shaped, the long leg, the restaurant proper, lying to the right of the main Kohlmarkt entrance; immediately opposite the entrance is the short leg of the L, on both sides of which stretch display cases and tables bearing a mouth-watering selection of the day's offerings.

Udo led us to the far end of this Aladdin's cave, through a glass-panelled door and into a brightly lit and highly populated kitchen which throbbed like the engine room of an ocean-going liner. White-clad pastry cooks hunched creatively over floured wooden tables and benches; upwards of a dozen technicians and operatives, bakers and cooks, male and female, were occupied at sinks and ovens, working areas and store cupboards. Little or no attention was paid us as we pushed our way into their domain. Someone nodded at Udo; a woman in a white cap eyed Alice with unabashed awe.

When I asked Udo if there was a rear exit to the kitchen, he shook his head, pointing to a black iron door in a corner. "That's the only other way out; a passage leads again into Kohlmarkt. We back on to other buildings."

Alice, indulging in a not wholly credible show of indifference, had become caught up with a man ladling a six-inch thickness of whipped cream on to a two-inch high cake which he held on the outstretched fingers of his left hand; she watched fascinated as he scooped and patted and moulded with a dextrous spatula. Udo joined her.

I stood in a small recess beside the door and waited.

He was so long putting in an appearance that I began to think he wasn't coming, or that Alice was mistaken and he was just another customer with a blue buttonhole. Then the door creaked slightly; the pallid shape of a face hovered behind the frosted glass. The door eased open a crack. From where he stood, he couldn't possibly see Alice; he'd have to do better than that. He did. A round, polished black head appeared cautiously, alert blue eyes quartering the kitchen. I wondered idly how he had broken his nose. Now he caught sight of Alice and Udo, their backs to him, and shortly after became aware of my lustrous brown eyes, not a foot away, fixed hungrily on his. My arm closed about his head and drew it gently into the kitchen.

The man with the cake paused in his work to stare at us with marbled eyes. "Hello," I greeted my captive quietly. "May I help you?"

His head was so well clamped in the crook of my arm, his face so hard against my chest that even had he wanted to take advantage of my offer he would have been incapable of doing so.

The stillness of the man with the cake drew the attention of others and now Alice and Udo turned and stared. Work ceased and silence fell. My captive writhed rewardingly and snarled a little.

Someone shouted a warning—Udo I think it was. As I caught sight of the gun in the man's hand, he jerked away from my slackened grasp and backed towards the iron door in the corner, the levelled gun threatening us all. The kitchen staff froze, only their eyes roaming wildly, seeking available shelter should the necessity arise. The silence, broken only by the heavy breathing of the man with the gun, was intense. Something in an oven was burning.

Alice was the first to move, ferreting suddenly and ominously in her leather reticule. My heart sank. Any moment now the place would become a shooting gallery. When the gunman snarled at her to be still, Udo stepped in front of her with impressive majesty and I lost sight of her completely. Her voice, however, rang through the echoing kitchen with all the defiance of a Fidelio. "Don't you point that thing at me, you silly little man. I need a handkerchief to blow my nose."

To avoid a disastrous shoot-out in the crowded kitchen, Udo wisely kept himself between her and the adversary. I caught his eye; he gave me the slightest of nods. I made a sudden swift move; the gun whipped around towards me, and in that instant Udo's SIG-Sauer blossomed miraculously in his huge hand.

The man swore, ducked and tacked his way across the kitchen, lashing out wildly at whatever stood in his way. With a great flurry of sound and movement the staff dived in a body for their preselected hiding places, several, having chosen the same goal, coming to painful grief as they met head on. Udo yelled at them to stay where they were and keep down.

Now we were all on the move—except Alice, who, riveted to the spot, was drawing a calm and measured bead on the flying figure in grey. I saw him leap for a narrow stone staircase which spiralled away upwards, Udo hard on his heels. Ploughing after them, I skidded on some slippery mess on the floor, thudded heavily into Alice and ruined her aim. "Go home," I shouted crossly. "Go home and lie down!"

I reached the staircase. Udo was blundering up ahead of me, panting and swearing to himself. The sound of two shots in the stone confines of the twisting staircase was like the beginning of the end of the world. From above came a stifled grunt; acrid blue smoke billowed down the stairs followed by the falling, splaying body of Udo. He struck me amidships and I went over backwards, striking my head on the handrail and tangling with him limb for limb as we thudded to ground level.

Willing hands sorted us out.

Shaken by the blow on the head, I clambered to my feet, swayed and stared down at the pallid face of Udo. My aunt, on her knees beside him, picked fastidiously at his blood-stained shirt-front. His eyes jerked open. He clawed at my leg. "There's no way out up there," he growled. "No way . . ."

He made a gallant effort to regain his feet. Alice held him down with what looked remarkably like a half-nelson. She blinked up at me. "Get after him," she said calmly, "there's a good boy."

A young man wearing a chef's hat and a set of eyelashes which would have done Dietrich proud offered his assistance and, reaching beneath his snow-white apron, produced his very own gun. "Jesus," I growled. "Anyone who hasn't got a gun's a sissy."

From behind me Udo croaked, "Take Wolfgang with you. He knows the place . . ."

Wolfgang flung his hat over his shoulder and together we spiralled our way up to the first floor, where a worried overhang of white faces ducked for cover at the sight of our guns. Wolfgang spread comfort and asked if anyone had seen which way he went. All pointed upwards.

"The place is like a bloody lighthouse," I complained halfway up the next flight. "What goes on up here?"

"Offices, more kitchens, workshops and attics," said Wolfgang.

This time we moved more cautiously and met a man in a red shirt who was peering inquisitively from behind a half-closed door. "He went up," he told us in succinct German.

Another flight wound gloomily into darkness. I glanced sideways at the stalwart Wolfgang. "I have the feeling he's going to get away."

"Over our dead bodies," he growled.

"That," I nodded, "is what I'm most afraid of. Would you care to go first?"

But he was already two steps ahead of me, moving with laudable caution, his gun at shoulder level. No flies on Wolfgang.

As I fell in behind, I jabbed his right buttock with my gun. "Do you believe in life after death?"

"I don't even believe in death," he replied promptly, and stopped abruptly in his tracks. We bent our heads to listen. I could hear only footsteps descending the lower staircases.

He went on more slowly, pausing on each step to listen. His eyes were now level with the upper landing. Resting his gun-hand on the top step, he peered along a narrow stone passage, and the next minute had erupted on to the landing, flattening himself against the wall. He was enjoying himself. More than I was. Meeting my eye, he laid his gun to his lips and jerked his head towards the far end of the passage where a door stood slightly ajar, daylight seeping through the narrow crack beneath it; a shadow shifted as the door creaked gently.

I draped myself along the wall opposite Wolfgang, raised an eyebrow and together we crabbed silently along the corridor until we were a foot from the door.

Someone was standing immediately behind it breathing shallowly through an open mouth.

Raising my foot, I glanced at Wolfgang, who crouched low, his gun clasped in both hands. He nodded. I lunged at the door with my foot and dropped to my haunches.

The splintering impact of the door slamming back on its hinges, the ear-splitting scream and the blast of the gunshot were instantaneous. Only a sixth-sense reflex action on our part prevented the girl from being riddled with bullets; neither of us fired.

The small man in grey held her before him, her frail body clamped to his, his gun jammed now into her cheek. His glassy blue eyes glared maniacally over her shoulder as he shoved her bodily between us and, with a shout, drove her before him with a strength and speed which took us unawares. Before we could regain our balance, he had swung violently on his axis, his captive again between us and our useless guns.

Moving backwards along the passage, the girl's dead weight hampered him considerably; the gun gouged her cheek. She shrieked like a bandsaw. He snarled. Behind him footsteps were clattering upwards. Reaching the head of the stairs and realising his danger, he flung the girl headlong down the stairway. For a split second his unprotected back was towards us. Wolfgang and I let fly simultaneously, but he had already leapt for the shelter of the upgoing staircase; the bullets hammered themselves harmlessly into the stone walls.

"We've got him," panted Wolfgang as we chased down the passage. "There's only a loft up there. No way out."

"No windows?"

"Too small."

A shot boomed and echoed around from above. Wolfgang looked startled. "There's a locked store-room where we keep old window displays. Maybe he's blown the lock off the door. It won't do him any good—it doesn't lead anywhere."

We embarked on the final flight. The head of the stairs was in almost complete darkness. Side by side we squatted against the wall, listening. "He's got three shots left," I said.

Murky bluish daylight filtered through a couple of begrimed and frosted dormer windows. The air was hot and stale, reeking of cordite and dust recently disturbed. We were in a spacious loft twenty or thirty feet long and about fifteen wide; the outer walls were barely four feet high, the beamed ceiling sloping down steeply to meet them. Packing cases were piled high against the walls and rubbish strewn about the dusty floor. Through an open door in the opposite wall, I could dimly make out a second similar loft.

Wolfgang touched my arm and we were off again, dust gritting beneath our feet as we sprinted across the intervening space, finishing up at the door, one ranged on each side of it. Wolfgang pointed. The lock had been shot away.

Now we could hear movement, a stealthy creaking sound and a couple of straining grunts; suddenly there came an almighty crash of glass and splintering wood followed by a blaze of diffused sunlight. A dense cloud of dust billowed towards us like smoke, a shadow, looming in the midst of it, monstrously out of proportion.

Wolfgang loosed off a wild shot.

Flame spurted twice from the centre of the aureole of light, and Wolfgang gave a muffled grunt and fell to his knees, swearing lustily in his native tongue. "It's my leg. You go, I'll be all right. He's smashed his way through to the roof."

We were sprawled in a morass of crushed sugar and polystyrene, a severed head wearing a green turban lay disturbingly at my elbow, the sugared almond eyes glinting eerily in the half-light—window-dressing, Wolfgang had said.

I strained my eyes through the flickering flare of sunlight. Frantic animal scratchings and scuffling noises came from the broken window. I began to run, stumbling over the severed head which bounced and rolled before me like a football. I clutched at a beam to steady myself wading ankle-deep through debris. As I raised my gun to fire, the sunlight ceased to flicker.

"He's gone," I yelled, "the bugger's gone."

I waded some more, kicked out at the turbaned head and thrust my head angrily into the hot sunlight—and almost lost it. A bullet clipped a tile not a foot from my ear, spraying my face with needle-sharp splinters. I ducked hastily for cover.

The cavity he had made, no longer recognisable as a window, was too small for me to get through; the lower half of what had once been the frame swung to and fro; glass crunched beneath my feet; a loose tile hung overhead. I struck out at it, smashed it to the floor. Shoving the gun into my waistband, I scrabbled around frantically at my feet; I came up with a short iron stake and, hefting it in both hands, rammed it upwards into the ceiling, shutting my eyes against the avalanche of plaster and tiles and rotten wood which cascaded over my head and shoulders; a hefty lump of the roof fell in on me.

I hesitated for a further second; he had one more bullet up the spout.

Something glinted through the swirling dust at my feet. The ubiquitous turbaned head leered at me. I swept it up and rammed it on to the end of the stake. One of the eyes fell out.

I shoved the head gently through the hole. The bullet tore head and stake from my grasp. Both rattled away down the roof.

I stuck my head out.

He was ten feet away, crouching on all fours, clinging to the steep tiles like a vampire bat, his face glistening with sweat. Fear glazed his eyes. He was in the throes of a nasty attack of vertigo.

Our eyes met. I showed him my gun, smiled at him alluringly, pointed the gun at his sweaty head. He shook the moisture from his eyes and edged slowly backwards.

I felt a sharp tug at my leg. "Stand on my back," muttered Wolfgang, gasping with effort.

I lowered my eyes long enough to plant a foot on his broad white shoulders; when I raised them again, the man had gone. I heaved myself upwards and crouched on the tiles as he had done.

The far eaves of the Demel roof overhung that of a huge flat modern building; he had simply lowered himself on to the roof next door. Further off and against what I assumed to be the rectangular upthrust of a lift-shaft or water tank was an iron fire-escape leading up to a metalled walkway which disappeared depressingly behind the building. He had only to reach that and he would be gone for ever.

I swore loudly. As if in answer to a call his little round head popped up above the slope of the roof. The gun was clutched in his raised hand like a hand-grenade. I ducked instinctively. If he had been playing in the World Series, it couldn't have been a better pitch. It laid open my cheek, I keeled over backwards and embarked on what could only be my final slither into oblivion; handholds were at a premium and I missed them all. I was four floors up and the edge of the roof was coming up fast.

Just above the guttering some far-seeing and Christlike entity had devised a short metal rail to deal with just such emergencies; my head went through but my shoulders balked. I hung precipitously over the edge of the building watching my gun pirouetting languidly into somebody's skylight.

Follow that, I thought nervously.

Clutching at the guttering, I strained backwards to free my head; my ears were the size of an African elephant's. I walked slowly backwards and sideways on my hands.

I took up breathing again. Sweat blinded me. I heard myself groaning loudly.

My quarry was halfway up the metal ladder by this time and labouring visibly. I felt almost light-headed; my gashed cheek was beginning to throb, the blood seeping inside the collar of my shirt.

The drop to the flat roof was no more than a couple of yards. I shambled over to the fire escape, dragging myself upwards, grateful for the handrails flanking the walkway. I lurched between it and the wall like a geriatric recapturing his first waltz.

A heavy woman wearing nothing but a black bra and black satin knickers watched with interest as I weaved my unsteady way towards the balcony of her apartment house. She waggled her fingers at me; maybe she thought her luck was changing; I gave her a drunken flourish.

A sturdy door stood half open before me. I was in time to hear the whine of the descending elevator. Once and for all I knew I had lost him.

I took to the stairs. There was always the chance he would have convulsions in the lift, be sick, faint, drop dead . . .

The building was as tall as the Eiffel Tower. I seemed to go on and on, round and round, down and down until my brain began to addle. When eventually I wound up, panting and distraught, at the bottom, I leaned in at the gates of the empty lift and stared for a long time at a drop of fresh blood which glistened on the floor of it.

"Shit!" I swore impotently. The word echoed derisively up and down the lift-shaft.

I stumbled down some steps into an asphalted and spacious courtyard. The sun, upright in the sky, beat on my bare head, burning into my gashed and bloody cheek like hell-fire.

I zigzagged wildly across the court, eyes clamped to the ground, hoping for one more glimpse of his life's blood. Nothing.

"Shit," I said again.

I wandered forlornly beneath a low arch and out into a narrow street where people ran into me without looking where they were going and blamed me for it in sepulchral German. *"Können Sie mir bitte sagen . . . ?"* I said to one man with whom I had collided.

"Piss off," he said in perfect English as he brushed me aside. He was wearing, I noticed, the old Etonian tie. I suppose I couldn't blame him. I must have looked like the sole survivor in a disaster movie.

So I said "Shit" again and shambled off in what I thought was the general direction of Demel's.

CHAPTER FIVE

The Beethoven room was a nightmare.

To say that it was a shrine to that great and grumbly old master would be to overdo it, since a shrine might legitimately be expected to house a relic or two of so revered a subject. Something worn by him perhaps: a battered hat, a boot, an ear-trumpet. Or a creation of his: an autographed score of one of his more obscure works, an insubstantial WoO perhaps, a Musical Joke for Piano, Mandolin and Eyeglass . . . Even more impressive of course would have been a genuine anatomical relic: a fragment of knuckle-bone or a knee-joint—macabre but rewarding.

Aunt Alice's Beethoven room contained none of these—the city of Bonn and the Republic of Austria would have seen to that—but it had everything that nobody else would be likely to want: pictures, busts, books, a lumpy copy of the death-mask hanging directly opposite the bed where you couldn't miss it; an enormous portrait of Alice as Fidelio wearing an outsize masculine hat and thigh boots; an undoubtedly genuine forte-piano with a ragged score of the *Hammerklavier* Sonata propped open above the yellowing keyboard. When I sampled the tone of the instrument, I found it possessed that authentic honky-tonk twang which Beethoven must have loathed but had to settle for—he was, after all, largely responsible for the forte-piano.

The bed was an immovable sarcophagus in carved black oak, with the rest of the furniture to match. The overall colour scheme—and the phrase is used lightly—was sludge and mauve with an occasional splash of mid-beige.

By anyone's standard a formidable room in which one would normally contemplate no form of occupation other than sleep and then only under heavy sedation.

When Emily Hargreaves had shown me into it, she had watched my reactions with carefully veiled eyes, but all she actually said was, "You should see the Wagner room."

At the moment, unfortunately I was not in the sleeping vein but lay sprawled on the bed naked except for a modest towel draped over the more scary details. It was four o'clock in the afternoon. I had taken an invigorating shower in a chrome-plated bathroom along the corridor, patched up my gashed cheek with some colourless iodine and sticking plaster supplied by a solicitous Emily and was now undergoing the motions and attendant agonies of concentrated thought.

Outside, Vienna hummed and hooted like any other big city. From where I lay, I could see the uppermost corner of the Opera House, with its bronze female on her winged horse about to take off over the Opernring, and though the sky was blue and growing bluer, confusion and depression bore down upon me like the descending baldachin of a four-poster bed in a Vincent Price horror movie.

Earlier that day Alice had pointed out, somewhat peevishly I thought, that the few hours I had spent in Vienna had not been without incident. Since then I had trumped that observation with a running gun-battle through the kitchens and attics of one of the world's most famous coffee establishments and followed it up with a near-fatal gallop across the city rooftops, one of which I had done my best to demolish. And still I had little or no idea of what was happening, or why I was doing it.

My octogenarian client, one-time world famous operatic diva and an eccentric if ever I saw one, was not only the sister of my father's mother and the survivor of four heart attacks, but also an inveterate toter of lethal hardware, a crack shot, and arguably one of the fastest guns in Central Europe.

Pursuit by an assortment of thugs, it seemed, was an everyday occurrence, dealt with quite arbitrarily: you ignored them, outran them or shot them down.

So who were they, these thugs? To date I had been offered no answer to that question other than a puckering of the brow and a shifting focus of those sunken blue eyes. Yet she was aware of the incendiary nature of the situation; otherwise she wouldn't be humping a bagful of guns around with her. I was convinced that she had a pretty good working knowledge of the opposition but for some reason wasn't coming clean.

If they were Israelis whom she hoped eventually to convince of her supposed son's lineage, then she was going about it in a curiously ham-fisted manner, particularly as he was already responsible for the untimely death of one of their number. Blowing their hands off and setting her great nephew at their throats would not, I thought, endear them to her cause. And she was astute enough to realise that. With that in mind I was more than ready to believe that the thugs in question were not of the Jewish faith, but were the disciples of someone else, someone cruder and less subtle—and more dangerous.

All at once I felt put upon—as if I'd been lured out here under false pretences.

She didn't want me to get hurt, she said, but had nevertheless led me directly into the firing line. With the knowledge that I wouldn't be allowed into the country bearing firearms, she had brought one along with her especially for me. Why, to find her son, did I need a gun?

Then of course there was Sammy Meier, a disturbed and frightened man. Disturbed about what, frightened of whom? Certainly not of his own people, with whom he claimed some sort of working liaison. And why, I wondered, had Alice taken me to see him in the first place? He had hardly spoken; what little he had said she could have told me without risking lives and limbs in Rudolfsplatz.

I groaned aloud and eyed Beethoven's death-mask disconsolately.

Then I got up abruptly and stalked about the room, sorting out what remained of my clothes after the excesses of the day. The only presentable garments I possessed turned out to be garishly striped jockey shorts, a blue sports shirt and a spare pair of grey Farah slacks which I'd had the uncharacteristic foresight to fling into my overnight bag. Everything I had donned that morning, with the possible exception of socks and shoes, had died the death up there on Demel's roof. When having landed at street level I had caught sight of myself, torn, blood-stained and reflected in a shop-window, I was not surprised that the old Etonian had told me to piss off—it was just a pity he couldn't have chosen a more erudite word, considering his tie.

When I had appeared at Demel's crowded front door, I was picked up by the nearest Demeless and hustled with the speed of light through the shop and into the back reaches where Udo, in a tearing rage, was busy, it seemed, demolishing what was left of his kitchen. A lot of what he was saying was highly colourful and would have been entertaining had I been able to follow it all.

The police had arrived in force and were marching up and down in their heavy footwear looking important and forbidding in the way that only European police can. A small hapless doctor with a limp and a pair of half-glasses was doing his best to attend to the walking wounded but had been as yet unable to catch up with Udo, who was still bleeding impressively through his shirt-front.

As I stood in the doorway swaying and tattered, a tug at my sleeve turned out to be Aunt Alice making eyes at me like the witch in a pantomime. She gave a jerk of her dishevelled toque and made off in the direction of the iron door. I followed wordlessly into a side passage and so back into Kohlmarkt where Konrad and his Rolls-Royce rode a sea of spectators' heads and badly parked police vehicles.

"Shouldn't we . . . ?"

"No, we shouldn't," said Alice, pushing me head foremost into the car. "It's nothing to do with us if Udo is raided by the police."

"But . . ."

"Don't argue, there's a good boy. It's much too hot. Home, Konrad, please."

Settling herself beside me, she peered into the mirror and set her hat and wig straight. "What a day . . . oh my goodness, what a day." She frowned at my distressing appearance. "You can't possibly go to the opera looking like that. I don't suppose you thought to bring a proper suit of clothes with you?

Never mind. We'll send Konrad out for some. Just give him your measurements and he'll do the rest, he's absolutely a wizard . . ."

"Aunt . . ."

"Call me Alice."

"Alice . . ."

"Yes, dear?" She leaned in sideways, all ears.

I took a deep breath, stared at her solemnly for a second, noting the wild light of excitement in the pale eyes and the fast beating pulse at her throat, and changed my mind. She was having herself one hell of a ball. Why spoil it? I shook my head resignedly.

In no time at all we were back at the house; Konrad, with measurements, was despatched to somewhere exotic in Kärntnerstrasse—"You don't want to go with him, do you, dear? You can trust Konrad's taste."

Emily Hargreaves shepherded me to the Beethoven room and talked me through the intricacies of the bathroom. Aunt Alice herself gently made her excuses and indicated that a "little lie-down" before tea and the opera would be the best possible thing for an ageing ex-prima donna.

"You didn't tell me we were going to the opera," I pointed out as we paused on the stairs.

"Oh, didn't I? How silly of me. It's *Andrea Chénier* with that delicious Spanish gentleman. You must come."

"You're not leaving me a lot of time for sleuthing."

"For what?"

"Detecting."

"Oh, there'll be plenty of time for that." She patted me maternally on the cheek—she was three steps up at the time. "And what, may I ask, have you been doing this afternoon if not detecting? Now off you go and have a lovely hot bath. Nothing like a nice bath when you're fed up and run down . . ." And she had drifted airily upwards and out of sight, disappearing suddenly like Elijah into the Everlasting Arms.

Under the cold shower I had brooded dyspeptically over the time factor. She seemed pretty confident about it. Remembering her condition twenty-four hours ago, I was not quite so sanguine. That 71 tram of hers was never likely to be far away.

The clang of a bell from the street below took me now to the window. I watched a tram, secure on its bland and shining rails, bulldozing its way through the surge of traffic; pedestrians scuttled like coloured bugs across its path. The two little red and white flags on its thrusting blunt nose fluttered bravely in the still air. The bell clanged again. I leaned over the sill narrowing my eyes. It was what they call a J tram. You had to go the Schwarzenbergplatz for a 71.

"I don't believe in death," Wolfgang had said. And neither did I until I found myself looking down the barrel of a gun or into the well of a building from four floors up. Then I believed. Fervently.

Someone down there was playing music, singing. When I leaned out further, I realised it was coming from the open window of a room immediately below Beethoven's. Wagner's, perhaps? But it wasn't Wagner they were playing; more like Strauss—Richard of that ilk. I listened intently . . . *Rosenkavalier*.

I flung on the few clothes I possessed, prinked a little in the mirror and, winking at a large portrait of Beethoven which looked like Winston Churchill in an untidy wig, let myself out of the room and made for the stairs.

The house was deadly quiet, the air hot and musty, too still for comfort. Narrow shafts of sunlight lancing dramatically between the heavy curtains on the stairs supplied the only illumination.

On the landing below I listened for a moment, then moved to the room I judged to be the one immediately beneath mine.

One of its large double doors was slightly ajar. I drew it open.

The room was vast, diminishing even the stature of the concert grand which bulked off-centre on a plain wooden dais. The parquet floor gleamed with polish and was without carpeting; the walls were panelled with lighter wood than the floor; from the intricately painted ceiling hung an elaborate chandelier. A few gilt, straight-backed chairs stood around in no particular order, and against the right-hand wall, built into an alcove, was an impressive bank of hi-fi equipment on the turntable of which revolved the music which had drawn me here. The windows opposite the door were wide open, the street noises more insistent here than upstairs.

The room appeared to be unoccupied, the slightly open door suggesting that whoever had been here had slipped out for a moment. I crossed quietly to the hi-fi and watched the revolving DGG yellow label. On a low table nearby lay an album, an empty record sleeve and the libretto of the opera. I listened to the anguished outpourings of the Marschallin at the inexorable approach of old age: *"Wie kann denn das geschehen?* . . . How can it happen? And if God lets it happen, why does he allow me to watch it with such open eyes? Why can he not hide it from me . . . ?"

With a finger I turned the title page of the libretto. *Die Feldmarschallin Fürstin Werdenberg—Alicia Sternberg.* The voice was young and pure, unmarred by that tell-tale tremolo of the ageing singer.

I moved to the windows and closed them against the noise of the traffic; I stood for a second staring across at the Opera House. "One is here to endure it," said the Marschallin. *"Und in dem 'Wie' da liegt der ganze Unterschied* . . . And in the 'how' lies the whole difference."

Thinking of how Alice had ravished old age and made it work for her, I grinned to myself. Perhaps if Strauss had known her, he would have written a whole new last act for her.

"She knew Strauss quite well, you know," said a voice behind me.

I swung round. Sitting at the piano with her arms resting on its lid, her chin on her hands, was Hedda Hargreaves.

"Hedda Hartmann," she said. "We met this morning. I was rude. I apologise."

I moved in a step. "I didn't realise anyone was here. I heard the music . . ."

"That's okay. Why not?" She rose languidly to her feet and crossed to the hi-fi. "Music is an open invitation." Switching off the machine, she removed the disc from the turntable.

I moved alongside. "Please don't let me interrupt your listening."

She shook her head. "It's okay. It wasn't all that serious."

I leafed through the libretto until I turned up a full-page photograph of Aunt Alice as the Marschallin, looking very like the portrait in the hall below. "Did she really know Strauss?"

"Very well, apparently. But then she's known everyone in her time; worked with most of them, from Toscanini to von Karajan—Gigli to Gobbi—Strauss and Stravinsky."

"She looks incredible, doesn't she?"

She nodded. "She was nearly sixty when she made those records. You must be quite proud of her."

I shook my head. "To be proud of someone you have to see it all happening, live with it, share the traumas. Alice happened before I was born. She's always been just another name to me, like Ponselle or Frida Leider . . . or was until this morning when she . . . erupted into my life."

She laughed suddenly; it was a good sound, and my earlier reservations about her began to evaporate. "She is unbelievable, isn't she? Yesterday she was dead to the world, and now see her. No one can keep pace with her. She is typical of her generation. They are indestructible."

"As is your mother."

Her face darkened. "My mother is twenty years younger. You can't compare them." The rebuke carried a knife-edge. She moved to the windows and reopened them noisily as if to demonstrate disapproval.

She was wearing white jeans and a yellow linen blouse; a studded belt of tan leather encircled her narrow waist; her rear view was slim and boyishly masculine with none of the bulging female buttocks crammed so often and so distressingly into male jeans. Her hair was smooth and dark and cut straight across the nape of her neck in what used to be called a page-boy. She leaned out of the window and stared down into the street. I joined her, and we stood in silence for a time watching the world go by and listening to the din it made.

"When I was a little girl," she said suddenly, "I used to stand here and spit on people's heads."

"That wasn't very nice."

"Little girls are never as nice as they look. Little boys are worse. What did you do when you were a little boy?"

"I took people's front gates off their hinges and piled them up on a green at the bottom of the road."

She gave a little snort of laughter. "What did you do that for?"

"Because it was fun. Even more fun next morning when they were all down there sorting out their gates."

"Did they know it was you?"

"I expect so. They're a shrewd lot where I come from."

"Where's that?"

"Oxford, then London."

"Alicia comes from Darlington, doesn't she?"

"Ay, a Yorkshire lass."

After a pause she said, "I've never really seen England properly. A couple of holidays with mother and that's all. My father wasn't English. He was a violinist, you know—in the Philharmonic—over there mostly." She nodded towards the State Opera.

"Your English is remarkable."

"Thank you." She gave me a wry smile. "I teach it."

I made a face. "Sorry, I didn't know that."

"Only in my spare time. I speak it all the time when I'm with my mother. Like most English people she can't be doing with languages and hates German most of all. She was brought up in the shadow of the First World War. Father quite approved of a second language and spoke English very well himself. I also went to the best gymnasium in Wien—and I don't mean parallel bars and vaulting horses, as you well know, so you can remove that smile from your face."

"Is your father still with us?"

She shook her head. "He died."

His spirit flitted uneasily between us for a second or two. "Are you musical?" I asked, to lay the ghost.

"I sing a bit," she said. "Also over there."

"At the opera?"

"In the chorus."

"We're supposed to be going tonight."

"Then you'll see me—if you have a quick eye. In the first scene I am a pink and white blancmange with a Harpo Marx wig and fan. The rest of the time I'm a dirty and elderly revolutionary with a tricolor on my hat. It's a good show, you should enjoy it. Carreras is fabulous as Chénier."

"Can you clamber up to bigger and better things from the chorus or are you there for the rest of your days?"

"Depends on the voice. Alicia once thought I might have one somewhere and started looking for it—just for fun, I think. I soon disillusioned her. I'm probably a great disappointment to her. I've stood in a couple of times as an understudy and have sung the odd small role, but nothing important. In Vienna once an understudy always an understudy, you know? I'm not sure I really like the Viennese."

"Aren't you Viennese yourself?"

She flicked a quick look at me. "I think of myself as German. My father was German bred and born. A Berliner. Pure Aryan. One of the Master Race."

It was more than a statement of fact. The words shouted with capital letters and, levelled at me as a challenge, hacked a sizable rift between us. She straightened up and leant against the window-frame, half facing into the room. I stayed where I was leaning out of the window, my hands on the sill. I knew she was watching me and for some seconds refused to be drawn. Then I too straightened slowly and set my back against the opposite frame; we stood there staring at each other like a couple of caryatids holding up the building.

I said slowly when the silence had gone on long enough, "What does that mean?—'One of the Master Race.' That he was a Nazi?"

"He was never a Nazi—not as you would define a Nazi—concentration camps, torture chambers, crematoriums and the black uniforms. My father never wore a uniform. He was a musician. One of the people. A true German. Just one of the millions and millions who believed in the Third Reich."

"And never thought to question its policies," I put in sourly.

"The Third Reich and its policies were the people's choice; we voted for them."

"And Hitler?"

"Hitler *was* the Third Reich."

I held her eyes for so long that eventually and surprisingly they succumbed to mine. I moved away into the room, gravitating towards the piano. I sat down on the square leather stool and stared morosely at the keyboard. I glanced back at the window.

She hadn't moved. Her eyes were fixed on something in the street, her head slightly bowed. Her shadowy profile was devastating. There was something of Garbo about her.

"Hedda," I said softly. "You said 'we'—'we voted for them.' " She turned her head slightly. "You never saw Hitler," I said, "you never lived under the Third Reich. You weren't there. You weren't born."

"Were you?"

I said mildly, "The war's over, Hedda."

She turned on me. "Hitler was a great leader."

"So was Genghis Khan, by all accounts." I ploughed on hastily. "He was a clever man. He put Germany back on its feet; even the British admit that. But as God Almighty with the divine right to decide who shall live and how many millions shall die . . . ? Never—not on your Nelly. For what it's worth, I'd say he was a flawed genius. A *dead* flawed genius."

She was moving swiftly towards me. "Because a leader is dead does not mean his cause is dead. Jesus Christ *died*, but what he preached is still gospel to some people."

I stared at her for a second. "What is it with you? A holy war?"

She slammed a hand down on the piano; the strings buzzed like a hive of bees. "I don't want to talk religion," she shouted.

I raised both hands. "Neither do I. What *shall* we talk about?"

That was the moment when any self-respecting and right-minded fanatic should have flattened the adversary or flounced out and left him to the pathetic puerility of his dream world. She did neither. She glared down at the piano, thumping at it gently with the flat of her hand. She flashed me a frustrated glance from beneath her lashes and swung away again to the open window, thrusting her hands deep into the pockets of her jeans. She was breathing heavily, as if she'd just completed the hundred-metre sprint.

I stared glumly at the keyboard and suddenly struck an A. There, I thought, now we can tune up the band.

She spoke quietly, making no effort to be heard above the street noises, as if she didn't care whether I heard or not. "I don't even remember my father, let alone Hitler." Perhaps she was capitulating, hauling down the scarlet and black flag for an uneasy truce. "Sometimes I used to look at the photographs mother had of him—tall, she said, blue eyes, fair hair. I could remember nothing of him, not the sound of his voice, his laugh, the touch of him . . . nothing. You would think, wouldn't you, that looking at his pictures would have revived something, stirred some sort of memory . . . ?"

"What happened to him?"

It was some time before she answered. "You know the Pestsäule in the Graben—the Plague Column?" I nodded. It was one of Vienna's most impressive monuments, built to commemorate the city's liberation from the Black Death. "He was found hanging from it—a Nazi dress dagger in his stomach." Her voice was calm and matter-of-fact, as if she were taking someone on a guided tour.

"When was this?"

"Oh, quite some time after the war—'49, early '50s—during the occupation. No one ever found out who was responsible, of course. Things like that happened every day. Some people thought he might have been killed as a reprisal for something—they never said what. He had plenty of enemies, I'm sure. Others thought the Russians had killed him, which was much more to the point. They'd have killed him simply because he was German. But no one will ever know, and it's not important anyway."

"To you it is."

"Not even to me. I was two years old when it happened, traipsing around after mother and Alicia on one of those endless American tours of hers."

"How did your mother take it?"

I watched her wandering aimlessly about the room, stooping to pick up a sheet of manuscript music which had escaped from a fat file on a chair. "By that time I don't think she cared any more. When the war finally came to an end, she raced back here as fast as she could, hoping, I suppose, to pick up their marriage where it had left off. From all accounts they seemed to get along together happily enough—enough to conceive me in the rapture of it all. But the euphoria was short-lived. Vienna was in ruins and so was their love. As you know, mother's terribly British, and as time went by she just couldn't live with the fact that during the war her husband had been on the wrong side. He was a German, for God's sake, and responsible for all those dreadful atrocities in the camps. And anyway, his Teutonic charm had worn thin, to say nothing of the fact that he had other, more nubile, feminine strings to his bow. Not really his fault; after all, he hadn't seen her for seven years. So it all collapsed, slowly and painfully. My coming brought them closer for a time, but even *my* charm wore thin—and that was that. They separated. She dropped her married name and went back to Hargreaves, her maiden name." After a pause she went on: "The mistake they made was getting married at all—mother being who and what she was—it would have been much better if they had just lived together. According to Alice, it was a love match gone wrong—and nothing can go more wrong, it seems, than a love match . . ."

She looked at me for a moment, then, pulling up one of the chairs, sat down. "Now it's your turn," she said abruptly. "You were once a film star." She sounded like a newspaper reporter.

"So they said."

"I've seen you many times on the screen."

"That's living dangerously."

"But now you are a detective?"

"An investigator."

"Which is why you're here?"

"I'm here because Aunt Alice asked me here."

"Why?"

"For all I know, she wants me to set her affairs in order and then leave me all her money."

"*After* you've found Lorenz."

I met her eyes steadily. "If Lorenz is to be found."

"And if he *is* found, and *is* Lorenz?"

"Then I'll have to go home again and live on my earnings."

"Will you tell me something?"

I smiled. "I'll do my best."

"Is Alicia in danger?"

I hesitated. "With a heart like hers she's always in danger."

She shifted impatiently. "She's taken to carrying a gun."

"Since what's-his-name raised his ugly head? Lorenz?" She nodded. "If he is her son, why would she need a gun, do you think?"

"Do *you* have a gun?"

I raised my hands to shoulder level. "Not guilty."

"But you have one."

"Never use one."

She stared at the sticking plaster on my cheek. "That's not what I heard."

I studied her now cool eyes. "News gets around."

"You only have to smile at someone's dachshund to set Vienna on the buzz." She hesitated for a moment, then asked again, "*Is* she in danger?"

I frowned at the keyboard, then at her. She was leaning forward, her hands gripping her knees, face intent, eyes earnest and appealing. Again I was struck by the haunting quality of her features. In the generally accepted sense of the word she was not beautiful; you wouldn't find her picture on a chocolate box, but you might on a record sleeve of *Rusalka* or *Swan Lake*—a being caught between two planes, physical and ethereal, drawn to both, uncertain of either. I wanted to trust her, needed an ally, someone who knew the Vienna ropes, on whose perception and opinions I could rely. But the dark glimpse she had given me of herself had got me walking backwards. On the other hand, as I had so glibly reminded her a couple of minutes ago, the war was over.

I came to as she repeated yet again in a more peremptory tone, "Is she in danger?"

I met her eye squarely. "I don't know, Hedda, I really don't. I'm sure she *thinks* she's in danger of some sort and irrationally seems deliberately to go out of her way to court it." I paused for a second and then asked, "Is she mixed up in anything political?"

Her eyes wavered a fraction. I waited. "Isn't that something you should ask her yourself?"

"Probably, but I doubt if I'd get a straight answer." I waited again.

She pursed her lips. "There's a rumour . . ."—she gave a colourless smile —"a rumour that . . . Israel is her favourite charity."

"What does that mean. That she donates money to them—to the State of Israel?" She turned away. "For any particular cause?" She was silent. Her face took on a sudden stubborn grimness. "Like hunting down war criminals?" She gave an untidy shrug and still said nothing. "Is this purely surmise on your part, or do you really know something?"

"I've told you." She moved impatiently to the window. "It's hearsay. Why should she confide in me? She doesn't confide in anyone. She plays her cards —how do you say?—close to the chest." After a short silence she added slowly, "Considering what happened to her husband and child, she might well be willing to finance something of that sort. Ask Laverne Wayne, he'll know. Sammy Meier too. You've met Sammy Meier, haven't you?"

"Who's Laverne Wayne?"

"He's by way of being . . . her business manager. He deals with most of her affairs, engagements, accounts, doctors, decorators, wig-makers . . ."

"But not, apparently, private detectives."

"Apparently not."

"Where can I find him?"

"Oh, he's always around somewhere. He'll probably be at the opera tonight—you'll see him there I expect."

"Is he an American?—a name like that? Laverne? I thought that was a girl's name."

An amused glint appeared in her eye. "I think it is. You'll find he prefers to drop the 'La.' 'Just Verne will do,' he always says. He's okay. You'll probably like him. At least he's loyal to her."

I got up and joined her at the window, my heels clacking on the parquet flooring. "Talking of business management, does she actually earn anything these days?"

"She teaches occasionally, coaches a little when someone needs it, but that wouldn't do much for a bank balance."

"So everything she has in the way of assets must be stashed away somewhere in stocks and shares, bonds and the like—vaults perhaps—a numbered account in Switzerland perhaps. What I'm getting at is that to be solvent after all these years she must have put a hell of a lot into cold storage."

"Well, she *was* the highest-paid singer on the circuit—and that means the world." I stared thoughtfully at the great bulk of the Opera House across the way.

"Vienna's 1st District must be one of the most expensive places in the world to live. If she's not earning, she's living on capital and has done so presumably for the best part of thirty years. That's a long time. Her farewell performances were way back in the fifties."

"Her farewell to opera," Hedda pointed out. "She went on working long after that. Concert tours, lieder recitals, public appearances, all highly paid, and when eventually she retired from singing altogether, she opened a full-time opera studio here in this building. This was the music-room—still is."

"But the studio no longer exists?"

"Not as such, no."

"Was it expensive?"

"For those who could pay, yes. She was the most sought after singing teacher in Europe. But if someone came to her with a future and no money, she wrote off the fees. In some ways she's very generous."

"And in others?"

She peered at me sideways, with a little smirk. "Very shrewd."

"What you have not mentioned," said a neutral voice behind us, "is that my late husband was in the diamond business."

We turned to face her. Leaning heavily upon her stick and dwarfed by the lofty doorway, she looked frail and vulnerable. Hedda and I exchanged sheepish glances.

Alice limped slowly into the room, head raised, nostrils twitching like a horse scenting the stables. "This room has a smell all its own," she mused half to herself, making a beeline for the piano. "Floor polish, gramophone records, ancient sheet-music and the interiors of pianos. The smell of success is here, too. And sweat—the sweat of endeavour. Go away," she added mildly as I stepped in to give her a hand. "I can manage." She alighted on the piano stool and parked her stick alongside.

Her floor-length gown appeared to consist of several layers of some diaphanous material, each of a different shade of pastel blue, pink and silver, which shimmered like moonlit water. Pale elbow-length gloves matched elegant leather slippers; a neat white head-hugging wig was an improvement on the one which came complete with hat. Her jewellery consisted of tiny diamond stud ear-rings, a narrow choker, bracelet and wristwatch, all set with diamonds. I came to rest in the bend of the piano, which detractors suggest is moulded for the accommodation of overweight sopranos. I eyed this particular soprano critically. "You've been eavesdropping."

She met my gaze coolly. "And why not? In this city listening in on other people's conversations is a national pastime."

"How long were you there?"

She blinked at me like a smug mother hen. "I came in the first place, dear boy, not to eavesdrop but to inform you that Konrad has returned from the shops with your new finery. I have instructed him to place it in your room. Now you were discussing my financial affairs . . . How do you like the Beethoven room, by the way? A little grimmity, isn't it? I hope you'll be comfortable there. Feel free to remove the death-mask should it disturb you . . . Where was I? Oh yes, as I pointed out, Hedda overlooked the fact that my husband was a successful diamond merchant. By successful I mean that his goods were not, as they say, all in the one basket. The Nazis, true to form, snatched everything they could lay their grubby hands on, never realising that the diamond business is like an iceberg—only the tip of it shows." She fingered her glittering bracelet. "Those we wear and those we exhibit. Underneath is a great flowing river of wealth unseen by all but those who buy and barter. Hence my ability to maintain myself and my household in the manner to which we have all become accustomed. Does that answer your question?" Her gloved hand wandered caressingly over the keyboard. " '*Vissi d'arte, vissi d'amore* . . .' " she whispered in a pale quavering voice. "Do you know *Tosca?*" Her eyes were on the keys. " 'Love and music, these have I lived for . . .' " Her hands had become still. She frowned at them. "Now go and take a look at your new clothes, will you?" She consulted her watch. "Do you mind eating after the opera? If I eat before, I am apt to nod off in the third act, occasionally with embarrassing consequences. Black tie, I think, don't you?" She gave me a quick smile of dismissal. "And Hedda—stay for a moment, will you; I'd like a word with you."

I had the uncomfortable feeling of having been discovered by the headmistress in the junior girls' cloakroom, exposed and trouserless, about to compromise her favourite pupil.

I exchanged a covert glance with Hedda which proved not quite as covert as I had intended. "It's only a word I want with Hedda," said Alice drily. "I'm not about to send her down."

Hedda was right: she was as shrewd as they come.

I moseyed reluctantly to the door, pausing with a hand on the knob. "Aunt . . ."

"Alice," said Alice.

"Are you trying to tell us that on top of everything else you are also a diamond merchant?"

She gave me a bland smile. "Indeed not; that wouldn't be true. I'm a smuggler. A diamond smuggler. If you see Emily, would you mind asking her if we could have tea in the withdrawing-room in fifteen minutes? And close the door as you go out, will you, dear boy?"

CHAPTER SIX

Suspension of belief and a naive trust in good and evil are the prime ingredients for the understanding and enjoyment of opera, though a working knowledge of the music helps, of course.

Handsome and bedworthy though the baritone may be, it is the tenor who will eventually wind up in the soprano's bed—if he lives that long. The unstable bass, usually the heroine's father, may be relied upon to disown his offspring before the first act is out, often expiring with a paternal curse on his lips, having been accidentally and fatally wounded by his daughter's clandestine lover, the tenor—who else?

Discontented wives, hallucinating mothers and vindictive homicides are the exclusive property of the mezzo-soprano. Only upon the heroine can one reasonably expect to pin one's faith, but even she, lacking the necessary understanding of the plot—and who can blame her?—may fail, fall, betray, kill and, if honour demands it, go up in self-kindled flames.

It was all food for brooding, I thought, glooming over my programme in the director's box at the State Opera. I had long since given up trying to make sense of opera, and that same despair now included one of its most worthy exponents—my elderly and eccentric relative who, back again on her old stamping ground and surrounded by the trimmings of a lifetime's glory, still reaped the adulation of a loyal public.

If her reappearance on the Graben had been spectacular, her arrival at the opera was overwhelming. Had I been escorting a reigning monarch to a gala performance, I could have expected no more effusive courtship than that paid to my great aunt Alice. Clinging like a limpet to my arm, she took it all in her considerable stride, interposing the proffered felicitations with smiles and waves and gracious inclinations of the head.

Speculation as to the identity of her escort was rife—anyone with half an eye could see that—but having been in Vienna for the best part of twenty-four hours, I couldn't believe that most of those who really wanted to know were not only aware of who I was but also what I was doing here. Considering the stir I had created in Demel's that morning, I could hardly be surprised; what did surprise me was that as yet I had received no official recognition of my exploits; the Polizei appeared to be keeping a suspiciously low profile. Somebody must surely have mentioned my unorthodox performance in the kitchen—Udo, Wolfgang . . . Unless of course they had been sworn to secrecy, or Alice had bailed me out before the hands of authority could be laid upon me; I wouldn't have put it past her.

A diamond smuggler! An eighty-four-year-old diamond smuggler! And if that wasn't enough, a crack shot to boot.

I stole a glance at her sitting bolt upright beside me. She was peering inquisitively through her opera-glasses at the occupants of a box on the far side of the great horseshoe. They obviously caught her at it, for presently she fluttered her fingers and nodded amiably in their direction. "That girl is far too fat," she muttered half to herself. "They'll never get her married off while she's that size."

I leaned over the padded edge of the box to watch the milling crowds below seeking out their seats. I thought of Hedda spitting on passing heads when she was a little girl, and of myself when young removing gates from other people's hinges . . .

"Why are you groaning like that?" asked Alice.

"What?"

"You were groaning like a sick animal."

"I've probably got distemper."

"Distemper?" The voice was packed with dismay and concern. "Why are you distempered?"

"Perhaps because my great aunt's turned out to be a crook."

She bowed at some smart people who were slotting themselves awkwardly into the box next door. She lowered her voice. "Who's a crook?"

"You are."

"I'm nothing of the sort."

I crossed my eyes at the huge circular chandelier in the roof. She leaned in and hissed at me. "Diamond smuggling, I'd have you know, is by way of being a tradition, an honourable and well-thought-of institution."

"Among thieves and law-breakers, I expect it is," I muttered unhappily, glaring at the orchestra, who were practising with loud discordancy in the pit. I leaned in even closer to her until I was breathing in her ear. "Why couldn't you have told me about it before?"

"You never asked. In any case I fail to see what possible bearing it could have on the whereabouts of Lorenz. That's what you're here for, you know, to find Lorenz, not to interfere in my private affairs. My little smuggling business is my private affair and, incidentally, quite legitimate."

I stared confounded at her diamond ear-ring.

The scraping and grunting from the orchestra was settling down to a steady wail; most of the audience had taken to their seats and things began to look more promising.

Aunt Alice leaned back in her chair with a great sigh, her eyes straying lingeringly over the clean bright lines of the auditorium, and as if erasing every word of our conversation, said in a whisper, "What a lovely house this is. It must be one of the most elegant in Europe. The Americans bombed it, you know, razed most of it to the ground. The whole place was rebuilt, faithfully and with love, to the original plan." She laid a light hand on my knee. "I sang my very last performance on that stage. The Countess in Strauss's *Capriccio.*" She sighed again. "It was a good end."

The sadness in her voice overwhelmed me. I took the tiny hand in mine, squeezed it gently; she was every time a winner.

As the fading lights ushered in the conductor, so the applause for him brought Emily Hargreaves into the box, loudly apologetic for her late arrival and stumbling heavily in the dark, to be fielded by a tall shadowy man she had brought with her and didn't bother to introduce.

I offered her my seat next to Alice, but she waved me down and took the chair on my left, so that I was between them. The shadowy man she left to his own devices. I could hear him creeping about behind, arranging his chair and preparing to watch the upper corner of the proscenium arch, which was about all he'd be likely to see from back there; boxes at the opera are notoriously the worst seats in the house. Emily smelled of rose-water and camphor and rustled her taffeta dress into submission until I could have struck her. She handed me a small box of chocolates, signing me to pass it on to Alice. As I shoved it along the ledge, I noticed it bore the name of Demel. Alice gathered it up with a nod and placed it carefully alongside her programme.

The curtain rose on a smart aristocrat's salon on the eve of the French Revolution.

Any preconceived notions I may have had with regard to the normal progress of opera were immediately exploded by the baritone, who, secretly in love with the soprano and unable to do anything about it because he was only the butler, confidently addressed his first big aria to an outsize sofa set down centre with its back to us. Inanimate objects are not usually the target of operatic outpourings—so it was original if nothing else. When the chorus trooped on a few minutes later, I searched for a pink and white blancmange with a fan, and found five, none of whom bore the slightest resemblance to Hedda.

At this juncture I became increasingly aware that the shadowy man behind was wearing that same pungent aftershave I had registered twice before—in Alice's bedroom and outside the Bristol that morning. It crept over me and hung around like mustard gas and put me on the defensive, a state relieved only by the intrusion of Chénier's *Improvviso*, executed superbly by Carreras, applauded by the packed house and cheered to the rafters by his fan club, which had wedged itself into standing-room-only behind the stalls. I took the opportunity of the respite to have a look at the tall stranger behind. He was applauding with the rest of us and, seeing me turn, flashed a set of teeth which lit up the encircling gloom like a beacon. Even if he couldn't see anything, he appeared to be enjoying himself. As the applause began to fade,

I leaned in towards Emily. "Who," I enquired in a whisper, "is the gent behind?"

In the hiatus which occurred between the collapse of the applause and the resumption of the music, Emily said quite loudly, "Laverne Wayne," causing several heads to turn and bringing a petulant "Sh!" from Aunt Alice.

When the interval arrived, Wayne and I were formally introduced. He looked like an ageing American film star from Hollywood's Golden Age. Tall, clean cut and wearing a tan like a second skin—ultraviolet, I suspected, rather than solar—he boasted a full head of snow-white hair; a well-mani-cured pencil-thin white moustache offset a perfect set of wrap-around Ameri-can dentures which were on almost permanent display owing to the fact that his mouth was too small. His clothes were immaculate, draping his spare and slightly stooping frame with expensive care.

Emerging from the box, Alice and Emily departed for the Ladies', leaving Wayne and I marooned on an island of mutual indecision.

I could see now why he stooped, he was too tall and too conscious of it. Offering me a cigarette, he loomed over me like a friendly giraffe. "I don't," I told him.

"Drink?"

I hung my head. "I don't do that either." He looked crestfallen. "I have a past history," I explained, and told him I had nothing against watching him drink. At that he whipped out a silver brandy flask and, turning guiltily into a corner, knocked back a couple of short ones. He seemed to grow even taller.

"Hate theatre bars," he grinned. His voice was deeply attractive, with only the slightest American flavour.

"So . . ." he said, then smacked his lips and fell immediately into a silent reverie.

"I hear you're Aunt Alice's right-hand man?" I helped out after several moments.

"She's a great lady, a great lady."

"She is that."

"Let's—er—why don't we move into the Tapestry Room. Alicia will want to promenade . . ."

We shoved our way through the opulent loggia with its glittering chande-liers, mirrors and grim busts of the composers peering critically from their niches above doors and windows.

Wayne pointed out the von Karajan bust, and we lingered for a moment over Rodin's Mahler on its marble shelf. In the mirror behind I caught sight of myself and thought I looked rather trim; I really should have stuck to acting. Konrad's wizardry had been justified; the dinner suit he'd picked off the peg was a dream of sartorial craftsmanship and made me look like a well-heeled stockbroker on the spree. The obliquely placed sticking plaster on my cheek added a certain buccaneering charm. I met Wayne's amused eye in the mirror. "How *is* the face?" he asked, indicating not only the plaster but also his knowledge of how it came to be there.

I gave a non-committal grunt and we moved on.

Traditionally the centre of the long and spacious Tapestry Room was reserved for those who wished to "promenade," an old Viennese custom. If you want to talk, you stand by the bar or study the tapestries which adorn the walls and depict scenes from the operas of Mozart.

Here we gravitated to await the reappearance of the ladies, Wayne leading me to the only quiet corner, where he helped himself to a further shot of brandy. As he threw back his head, his aftershave hit me like a wave. While he was still in mid-swallow, I asked casually, "Why were you tailing me this morning?" It was an excellent ploy; the alcohol went down the wrong way, and I stood by watching blandly until he got his breath going again.

"What did you say?" he heaved at last, dabbing his lips with a handkerchief and stowing the flask away.

"You heard me."

He did his best to stare me down, but I wasn't having any and he knew it.

"I wasn't exactly—er—tailing you."

"What were you doing?"

"Keeping an eye on you."

"Why?"

He put his weight on the other foot, decided against it and swayed back on to the original one. "How did you know I was there?" I gave him my inscrutable look. He nodded, slightly abashed. "I stick out in a crowd, don't I? There's six feet two of me in my socks. That's a terrible disadvantage. Listen, Mark . . . may I call you Mark?"

"I wish you would."

"And if we are to be friends, and I trust we shall be, won't you please call me Verne. Forget the 'La.' I just hate it." He lowered his voice and bent lower. "I need to talk in private, okay?"

"Sure."

"Something to eat after the show, perhaps?" He anticipated my objection. "Alicia never eats late. She'll want to go straight home. We can drop her on the doorstep. A date?" I nodded. "Do you eat Chinese?"

"Only if they're young and tender." I grinned. "I eat anything except spinach, mushrooms and a Yugoslav soup I once nearly died of over in Dubrovnik. What's your next question?"

He laid a solemn hand on my shoulder. "I'm mighty glad you're here, Mark."

"Take your hands off my nephew," said Aunt Alice, creeping up behind as usual. "Mark, let's promenade."

And solemnly and sheepishly I promenaded, the talking point, I suspect, of a good number of those present.

*　　*　　*

Locked irrevocably in each other's arms, hero and heroine eventually jolted off into the sunrise, their tumbrel bound for the Place de la Révolution and the guillotine. The house fell in about our ears as all good opera houses should. The fan club burst its bonds and howled down the centre aisle like a pack of hounds in full cry. We in the boxes, somewhat more restrained, managed to demonstrate our appreciation without actually casting off our clothes, but when Carreras took his solo call, even Alice allowed herself a couple of hooting bravos—she was clearly smitten with him—and shouted excitedly over her shoulder in a language I didn't understand—Hungarian probably.

When the shouting was over, I helped her gather up the various belongings she had strewn about the place. "Somebody pinch your chocolates?" I asked as I handed her the glasses and looked around for the Demel box. I had to repeat the question on account of a sudden attack of deafness on her part.

"It's all right, dear, I have them here." She waved her tiny evening bag.

Having deposited her and Emily on their doorstep—they appeared delighted that Wayne and I had got together so amicably—he and I made off for Jasomirgottstrasse where he had a pet Chinese restaurant he thought I would like.

The night was moonlit and balmy. As we strolled along Kärntnerstrasse in the direction of Stephansplatz, he nattered on about *Andrea Chénier* and the French Revolution, comparing the latter with the Russian Revolution and the former with Thomas Paine and his epic *The Age of Reason,* a tome which Mitch would doubtless know about but which I had never felt called upon to investigate . . . It was about here that I lost his drift altogether and withdrew stealthily from the conversation, wondering instead how I could separate from the herd whoever it was who was following us.

Leaving Wayne to carry on talking to himself, I pulled up abruptly at Dobrowsky the jewellers and stared blankly at the window, hoping for a glimpse of someone caught up in his tracks. There were too many people about—trees, lamp-standards, open-air restaurants—too many shadows. I muttered crossly to myself. The hairs on the back of my neck told me someone was there. The only way to get him in the open was to lure him down some unfrequented alley-way.

"I found myself talking to a completely strange woman," complained Wayne, rejoining me without malice. He peered with interest at the jewellery in the window. "Seen something you fancy?"

"Sorry, no . . . I was just keeping an eye open . . . I never mind being tailed so long as I know who he is, where he is, and why he's doing it, but this just makes me plain mad."

He pointed to a heavy gold wrist-watch. "I'd go for that one if I were you." Without changing his tone he said, "Pronuptia de Paris over the way a little further up. He's admiring the wedding-gown in the window. Young, blond, dark glasses, grey pants, blue blazer . . . Got him? He's got us reflected in the window."

I pointed back the way we'd come. "We've just passed a Chinese restaurant back there. What's the matter with that one . . . ? Are you sure it's him?"

"He's one of them. I do a rearguard job sometimes when Alicia's on the prowl. I could lay my hands on three of them by sight. They work in shifts."

"Who are they?"

"That's one of the things I'd like to talk to you about."

We continued on our way. The man in the dark glasses studied the frothy nuptial garments with intense care as we passed not a yard behind him, Wayne saying in a loud voice, "If she wants a watch, I really wouldn't get it here, you know. You'll pay twice as much in Kärntnerstrasse as you would anywhere else . . ." He lowered his voice. "He's away again. Do you want to lose him?"

"We're only going to eat, for God's sake. Let him sweat. We could have some fun later if you're game. And sober."

We exchanged looks. He flashed his great white teeth at me. He was another I was beginning to warm to.

The cathedral was like a great ship at anchor in a moonlit sea. We paused to stare up at the towering spire spearing the deep blue darkness like an icicle. Our tail chugged negligently across our bows, pausing to read a boring notice stuck on the church door. While his back was turned, we doubled down Jasomirgottstrasse and into the Chinese restaurant, giggling like a couple of school kids playing hooky.

*   *   *

"She's a crook," I told him later, ladling more fried chicken on to my plate.

He frowned heavily and gave a reluctant nod. "I suppose you could say that." Then with a wry smile he added, "Though I guess you'd have difficulty convincing her of it."

"I've tried."

"With what result?"

"Diamond smuggling is an honourable profession and her particular operation quite legitimate."

He grinned broadly. "You can't argue with that, can you?"

"I know some who'd try. How in hell does she get away with it?"

"You know the sort of life she leads. She's everyone's idea of the Queen Mother. It would be unthinkable to run her in or shut her away on account of a couple of tax evasions." He registered my sagging jaw and gave his chopsticks a flourish. "Well, *several* tax evasions . . ."

"Have you tried to dissuade her?"

"Frequently."

"And?"

"It's like trying to persuade NASA that there's no future in air travel."

I chased a piece of chicken around my plate with inept chopsticks. "Is it a large operation?"

"Oh Lord no, not now it isn't. It used to be, but it's pretty one-horse now.

The pipelines have to be kept open and manned, of course, however small the operation: source contacts, the mines themselves, market-places and so on; then there are cutters, polishers, couriers and not least the buyers. Over the years I imagine they've all changed quite a bit—sources dry up, companies merge, go bust, people die . . ."

"But Alice goes on for ever."

"Let's hope so. Ernst, her husband, was to blame in the first place—your uncle—a highly respected *diamantaire*—one of the greats. A *diamantaire*, she tells me, is only as good as his knowledge of gemmology, so he must have been pretty expert. How much of that expertise he was able to pass on to Alicia I don't know. Very little, I'd say. She'd have been much too busy knocking her own career into shape to take in the complexities of the diamond business, which is, I gather, a way of life rather than a profession."

He took time off to concentrate on his food for a bit. He was more useful with chopsticks than I. Brooding over the present frailty that was Aunt Alice, with her wigs and stick and diamond hat-pin, I did my best to adjust my mind not only to the shadowy image of the one-time reigning *diva* of the opera, but also to the swashbuckling, sharpshooting heroine of the smuggling saga which was emerging with every word Wayne uttered.

"Being a prima donna, of course," he went on eventually, "she was always on the move—New York, London, Berlin, Paris, Milan . . . so Ernst, being no better than the next man but possibly less ethical, suggested one day to his young and famous wife that it could be quite profitable to them both if she would occasionally carry a diamond or two through customs without actually mentioning it to anyone. Well, you know Alicia—and she hasn't changed any over the years—it was exactly the sort of hairy scheme she would jump at. As a world-renowned opera singer with everyone at her feet, customs' officers included, she could have worn the bloody things on her hat and no one would have questioned it. But not Alicia, oh no . . . she had to have special shoes made, didn't she?—with hollow heels! She stuffed diamonds into pots of cold cream, into sticks of make-up, sewed them into her corsets, on one occasion into her knickers—bloomers, she called them—she never tried that again; they broke loose apparently and she had to sit on them for several hours. For *Tosca* she toured her own tiara, diamonds sometimes replacing the theatrical junk. As Turandot she wore a head-dress like a Christmas tree stuck all over with glitter—twice it was worth a million dollars, give or take a couple of cents. Fans, lorgnettes, hat-pins, nothing was sacred . . . I tell you, Mark, that lady is one on her own."

I finished the fried chicken and rice and sat back looking gloomily at my empty plate. "So what can any of us do about it?"

"She was at it before you were born, Mark dear, and she's not going to stop now." He met my eyes. "It'll end when she ends, not before." He looked at me as if he thought I had lost my sense of humour—which I had.

After a moment I said, "Since her retirement there can't have been much going on surely?"

He shook his head. "As I said, she rarely moves out of Vienna now. It's only a trickle to what it was. She said once it's what the English would call a hobby."

We ordered jasmine tea and huddled over the tiny cups like oriental conspirators. "When Ernst . . . disappeared," I said slowly, "and the war came, what then?"

"You'll have to get the full story from her. The Nazis seized everything. Most of what they found was just window-dressing. He had seen the writing on the wall. God knows why he didn't get out, there was plenty of time; others did—I suppose he just didn't believe the Anschluss would come. Alicia knew what provisions he had made in the event of such a catastrophe, and two days before Britain declared war, she snuck into Vienna, not without a great deal of courage, I may say, picked up the options or whatever they were and got out of Austria by the back door with millions of dollars worth of goodies spread about her person—not only Ernst's property but that of some of his fellow merchants who also wanted their stock out of the country before the Nazis got at it. She arrived back in England on September 3, two hours, she said, after war was declared."

"And when it was all over, she came back and set up the search for Ernst and Lorenz, right?"

He nodded. "Exactly. She was a rich woman, money no object; she literally turned the place over. If they'd been alive, she would have found them. I'm certain of that."

"So you don't think it's Lorenz out there?"

He stared into space. "No, I don't." A waiter replenished his cup. "Those who survived were eventually rehabilitated. Even if their names were lost, their identities gone, they were there, somewhere, to be seen and questioned by relatives and friends. She went everywhere, visited every camp, every rehabilitation centre. Nothing. Rumours there were but no facts. But Mark, millions . . . millions just vanished. I don't have to tell you that. No records, no memories—just ashes in the wind . . ."

A clock was striking somewhere, brazen and ponderous. I counted the strokes, looked at my watch; it said eleven thirty-five. I gave up counting. The knell went on . . .

He continued in a hushed voice. "Seeing what she saw, firsthand, travelling to those places, trying to communicate with men and women who might have come from an alien world, crippled people, whose eyes, she said, remembered but could not see, she became obsessed with the need to help, make them well, return them to wherever they'd come from. She organised charity performances, concerts, recitals, launched various programmes to aid the victims of the horror camps. But however much she was able to give of herself and her money, it was a drop in the ocean to what was needed. So she concentrated on Jewish needs alone—as a gesture to Ernst and Lorenz, I suppose. When the State of Israel was created in 1948, she offered assistance to the Israeli version of the Save the Children Fund and that still goes on—

even today after all these years. And that's all above board and legitimate. Her 'submarine goods,' as she calls her smuggled diamonds, are there for the sole purpose of rooting out war criminals and bringing them to trial. She has an ungovernable hatred of the Nazis and what they stood for . . . or perhaps I should say 'stand for,' because they're still around. The proceeds from her smuggling racket have helped the Israelis to expose quite a few ex-Nazis, which is why I imagine she calls her trade legitimate. Because if you look at it in the right light, it *is* legitimate. It *is* lawful to bring people like that to justice." He eyed me sombrely. "Or don't you think so?" He signalled to a waiter for the bill and more tea. "Or are you too young to care?"

He watched me closely as he put a match to a cigarette and blew the smoke away from me over his shoulder. I pushed an ashtray towards him. "When I was born, it was all over," I told him. "History. But the State of Israel and myself are of an age. So no . . . I'm not too young. I can still work up a lather about King Herod and the Massacre of the Innocents. There are enough guilty people about without starting in on the innocents. Which is why I'm not overfond of terrorists." I nodded slowly. "Oh yes, I'll fight Nazis any day."

He gave me a strange look and then turned his attention to the tip of his cigarette. "In that case," he said quietly, "you've come to the right place."

That bell, or whatever it was, was still tolling.

"Vienna?"

He gave a slight shrug. "Why not Vienna? They're everywhere else. In Latin America they're quite open about it. The Fraternal Order of Nazis, they call themselves, I believe. They play a waiting game, but they're here."

I looked at him curiously; he stared back wide-eyed, almost challengingly, and though his teeth were visible, he was not smiling. "Who are you?" I asked. "*What* are you? A Nazi hunter, CIA, double-O-something? What?"

Now he smiled, slowly, like a drawl. "I'm far too old for any of those things, but thank you for the thought. I'm simply Verne Wayne and exactly what I've told you. I belong to your Aunt Alicia hook, line and sinker. Our paths met in the States years ago when I was a hard-working concert agent organising a Stateside tour for her; she asked me if I'd be her personal manager. And that's what I am still, I guess, though I figure somewhat less in the general pattern of her life now she's retired. She no longer needs me to manage and guide her career, but there are still plenty of things to keep me occupied." He smiled. "Her coming of age has not diminished my responsibilities or my anxieties. On the contrary. Now I've come to a point where I need to share those anxieties with a younger and more agile brain—to say nothing of a younger and more agile body. Someone who can be loyal to her as I am—as Emily Hargreaves is and Konrad. Your Aunt Alicia has a great capacity for inspiring loyalty."

I gave him a glassy grin. "I can't say I've noticed it. She's been giving me the run-around ever since I arrived. She's impossible to pin down; she doesn't tell me a bloody thing—or if and when she does, it's already a *fait accompli.*

I've been cursing her soundly for the best part of twenty-four hours. 'Frustration' is the word, not loyalty."

"Nevertheless you're here."

"For the money. And because I am her only living relative. I thought maybe I might even figure in her will. I'm your common or garden vulture, okay?"

He suddenly threw his arms wide and laughed; only by a swiftly and superbly executed side-step did an imperturbable Chinese waiter, passing at the time with a shoulder-high tray of crockery, avoid calamity.

Then suddenly the laughter had gone. He leaned across the table. "Now listen to me, please listen . . ." He was deadly serious, speaking with low urgency. "Ever since this Lorenz business began, something nasty and sinister has been lurking just around the corner. I scent it like a hound-dog. Whatever it is, I think it's dangerous—to Alicia. She thinks so too but wouldn't bloody admit it if her life depended on it—as well it might. All she wants is to find out the truth about Lorenz—is he or isn't he? So yours truly began to drip *your* name into her ear like poison. She wouldn't listen, of course. But who better, I insisted, to seek out a long-lost son but that son's own cousin, who as it happens is also a clever private investigator. I even threatened to get you over here under my own steam, but she still wouldn't hear of it, pretty well put me on my honour not to attempt it. What she's really been hoping for is that Lorenz comes to her of his own volition—as he should have done, of course, if he really is her son."

"I wonder. He's killed someone, remember?"

He nodded. "That's true. Anyway, that last attack of hers frightened her out of her wits, I think, and it was that which finally forced her to make contact with you."

A waiter glided up with the bill and a fresh pot of jasmine. I watched with wry amusement as Wayne checked over the damages, totting up the individual amounts with a concentrated frown on his face. Satisfied, he scrawled his name across the paper with a gold Parker pen. He caught my eye and grinned. "That's why I am a business manager."

I poured tea. "So to recap—I'm here to track down a Lorenz who doesn't exist."

He raised a cautious finger. "*Someone* exists, and to set all minds at rest you're here ostensibly to find out who it is. But—and here's the problem— there's this other band playing in the park." He jerked his head at the street outside. "That one out there."

"Which hasn't got a name?"

He held his cup delicately between forefingers and thumbs and inhaled the scented contents. "One day they just came up out of the woodwork and latched on to Alicia."

"The day Lorenz got away?"

"Yes. Konrad was the first to spot them; he complained about the grey VW which always seemed to be in his driving mirror. After that we all began looking for them. I got Alicia and Emily to venture out on dummy shopping expeditions and hung about a long way behind, eventually picking them up. As I said, there are three of them I recognise. The one out there now, your man from Demel's and the one in the car, who's now got his hand in a sling. I've never actually seen the other, the one who drives. The odd thing is, they don't seem to care whether they're spotted or not. I mean, they don't change their suits or put on false whiskers; they don't even get another bloody car. It's almost as if they want us to know they're there."

"Perhaps they do."

"Why? It can only put us on our guard."

"Against the enemy you *see*, yes. But it could be the old flanking strategy —like on the battlefield. You're so busy looking at one lot you don't see the others until they're on you and it's too late." He looked doubtful. "It's done all the time. The theory being that even Homer nods. Once the pursued thinks he's lost his tail, he's apt to become careless and lead the second lot directly to where they want to go."

"Which is where?"

"To the elusive Lorenz. He says he's Alice's son; the current belief is that he's making a home run to prove his point, but he can't do that because the Israelis and/or the police will be waiting for him. Now the Israelis believe he's the son of an ex-Nazi living in South America. So let's suppose for a moment that's who he is and he has come over here to contact someone . . . Who? . . . Let's say for the sake of argument—the Nazis you're so keen about. How does that grab you?"

I paused for thought rather than for an answer, but in the lull he came up with the observation that if Lorenz was here to contact the Nazis, why the heck hadn't he already done so?

"Perhaps he has."

"There you are then. If he's already home and dry and the Israelis are coming out into the open to meet you, whose little nest does your Demel bird come from? And our friend outside in the dark glasses—to say nothing of the contents of the grey VW?"

"Oh Jesus, do shut up Verne," I growled.

It would have been nice to get up and stamp around the restaurant for a bit if only to ease my shot-up brain, but I stayed where I was and took it out on the tablecloth instead with a didactic finger. "We don't really know yet, do we, whether the Israelis are willing to co-operate with us? Sammy only said he'd *try* to fix something. So at a pinch it could be them outside, couldn't it?"

"Sammy's one of them, for Christ's sake. Why should they bust in on *him* with a bloody great shooting-iron? He's their own man."

I raised my hands in surrender. "Okay, okay . . . I was only trying it out for size. You're so passionate."

A lengthy silence ensued during which I slurped miserably at my jasmine tea.

"I think . . ." he began at last, slowly, as if he too were trying something out for size. "I think . . ." I waited an unconscionable time.

"What?" I asked patiently when I couldn't stand the suspense any longer. "What do you think?"

"I don't think . . ." he tried again, adroitly revising his original plan. "I don't think he has made a rendezvous with the Nazis or whoever. I think he's on his own somewhere, holed up. I think he's gone to ground."

I nodded with relief. "Well said that man. That's what I don't think too."

I entered a state of trance for a minute or two. Wayne watched with stoic calm. Then I looked at my watch.

"Twelve-twenty," he said.

"Do you think they ever go off duty out there? Or do they see us all home and tucked up in bed first?"

"You have a plan?"

I thought for a further minute. "Do you have a belt?"

"A belt? No."

I leaned in towards him and with a finger drew aside the elegant hang of his dinner jacket. "If you took off your braces, would your trousers fall down?"

"My braces?"

"Suspenders, sorry."

"I know what braces are."

"Well, would they? Fall down?"

"Why?"

"Because I haven't got any. Konrad didn't buy me any. And I haven't got a belt either, only a cummerbund and that won't do."

"For what?"

I smiled. "For what I have in mind. May I borrow your braces?"

"Now?"

"If you would be so kind."

His hands were busy below the table. I glanced around cautiously. A Chinese waiter was watching with flat incurious eyes; they shifted slightly and met mine. I raised a pair of questioning brows. He looked away.

The braces were off. Wayne was panting slightly. He rolled them up neatly and passed them in a closed fist over the table. As I took them in mine, the Chinese and I exchanged another glance. I smiled slyly. The oriental inscrutability slipped a trifle as he turned on his heel and disappeared into the shadows.

"What are you up to?" asked Wayne.

I pocketed the braces. "Nothing probably—it may not come off. If it does, it may save us further heart searching."

"Am I coming?"

I shook my head. "Like you said—a younger and more agile body. No offence meant."

"None taken." He looked pretty down in the mouth for all that.

"I'll walk you home, and if he's still with us, I'll take it from there. If he's not, you can walk *me* home—and have your braces back."

CHAPTER SEVEN

Jasomirgottstrasse was almost deserted when we stepped into it and stood for a while to accustom ourselves to the change of atmosphere.

The moon was enmeshed in a wraith of pale cloud, the bright edges of its beams blunted, the sharp shadows smoothed to a shifting blue.

My spirits took a dive as I peered furtively and in vain for a glimpse of the man in the dark glasses. Having at last formulated some sort of plan, it now looked as if I was about to be cheated of its fulfilment. Not that I could blame him if he'd gone home to bed. Who the hell wants to hang about half the night waiting for a couple of opera-sodden plutocrats to lay down their chopsticks and finish their dainty cups of jasmine tea.

Wayne sensed my frustration. "Not to worry," he comforted, "he'll show up." He turned away from St. Stephen's looming eerily at the far end of the street and moved off in the opposite direction towards the Peterskirche. "I live five minutes away in Brandstätte," he said. "Over a furniture shop." He lowered his voice. "He's a professional. He wouldn't be fool enough to opt out even at this late hour. After all, if we intended to call on Lorenz, what better time than half past midnight? I just hope they're paying him well, that's all."

"Who's 'they'?" I asked, grinning into the darkness and falling in alongside him. "Incidentally," I added, "and while I think of it, any news of the Demel Diehards—Udo and Wolfgang?"

"Emily and I called in on our way to the opera—hence our unpunctuality. Udo's breathing fire and vowing vengeance. And will live. You'd need a dumdum bullet to make an impression on that iron constitution of his. It was a flesh wound, a ricochet, I'd guess. What got his goat was falling downstairs in front of everybody. Wolfgang has to lie up for a few days. They carted him off to the *Krankenhaus* for some X-rays. The bullet seems to have chipped a bone, but they're not worried. Neither is he, apparently. I'm told he's reliving the experience blow by blow and will probably write a book about it. He'll be out of there tomorrow, and since he lives right next door to Demel's, he won't have to do a lot of walking."

As we crossed Bauernmarkt, my built-in antenna gave a sudden jolt. "We're not alone," I muttered, my hair on the bristle. "He's with us again." "There," grunted Wayne, "what did I tell you?" In Brandstätte we came to a halt outside a classy-looking furniture shop. He pointed to the first floor. "That's me up there. You must come and visit some time—if you survive the night." He looked at me quizzically. "Will you be all right?"

I smiled. "I'm like Wolfgang. I want to write the book." He sorted out a large bunch of keys. "When do I get my braces back?" "You've already waved them goodbye." He grinned. "They'll go on the bill." He turned at the door, key in the lock. "Keep your head down, Mark, right?" "Right," I nodded. *"Deo volente."* "I'm sure He will be." He raised a hand, closed the door gently and was gone.

A young couple in jeans and sweatshirts locked in each other's arms whispered and laughed together as they ambled by.

I stood for a moment peering back the way we had come as if probing the shadows for possible pursuit. I had to alert him. I needed his co-operation. As if satisfied, I moved off, ostentatiously consulting my watch as I passed beneath a street lamp. I walked briskly as if to keep an appointment. Twice I looked back over my shoulder. He was good, I have to admit—a professional, as Wayne had suggested. Not once did I catch him on the nod. I didn't know where he was, which side of the road, how far away. I just knew he was there.

Vienna, like any other elderly city, is a confusing place to be at large in, even more so at night, and particularly when one is not all that familiar with it. With the cathedral and the Peterskirche at my back, I moved northward away from the city centre and towards where my bump of locality told me lay the Donau Kanal.

I had no idea where I was going, and wouldn't until I actually got there. I needed a particular kind of locale: narrow streets, alleyways and a general lack of street lighting; open doorways and few pedestrians on the prowl would be acceptable.

Kurrentgasse, Judenplatz, Fütterergasse and Wipplingerstrasse were a few of the street names I slotted away into my memory. Now the pierced stone cupola of Maria am Gestade, a landmark I recognised, loomed ahead . . . narrow cobbled streets, darkened doorways, dim lighting . . .

I slackened my pace and made a great play of appearing to search for a particular house. Once I thought I heard him stumble. He was not far behind.

Presently I found what I was looking for: a low arched doorway from which the doors had long since departed, opening on to a one-time paved but now neglected courtyard; broken and overgrown stonework crumbled in the centre of it. Stepping carefully, I almost came to grief over the remains of what looked like a perambulator lying on its side half buried in weeds and rubbish.

A small animal scurried through the undergrowth. From somewhere I could hear the continuous thudding of pop music.

Although the whole place looked sick and abandoned, a curtained glint of light from a couple of upper windows indicated occupancy. A narrow entrance hall to one of the buildings huddled about the yard was also lit, but only dimly by a single electric bulb which flickered like a candle in a draught.

Moving towards it, I found myself in a narrow noisome passage smelling of decay and urine from which a stone staircase led to the upper floors. The steps were uneven and gritty with dust, the flickering lamp no help at all. On the first landing a streak of pale light glowed beneath a closed door. Behind it I heard voices—a man and a woman arguing—a television perhaps. You never could tell. Beside the door a sink jutted from a shallow recess in the wall. It would have to do.

I buttoned my dinner jacket, turned up the collar and folded the lapels over my white shirt front. Edging into the recess, I turned my back on the lower stairs. It was from the floor above that the music came. Through a grimy window set high in the wall between landings filtered what little was left of the moonlight.

A small stone was wedged beneath my foot; I picked it up and palmed it. I waited.

From the courtyard came the stealthy crunch of a footfall. I stood rigid as the walls about me. Someone was whispering. I strained my ears. My heart sank. More than one of them . . . ? The light below flickered miserably for a second or two longer, then went out altogether . . . More than one and the plan was a dead duck. Me too, probably.

I pitched the stone on to the upper landing. It was only a small stone—no more than a piece of gravel; it sounded like the cave-in of the walls of Jericho.

The music thudded away upstairs. Why do we call it music? An off-key raucous voice joined in the racket. Someone thumped lustily on a wall; the voice was stilled.

I knew he was standing in the doorway downstairs. He had heard the stone. His feet gritted as they slowly mounted the stairs. If he had a gun . . . Why should he have a gun? He was a tail, that's all he was, employed to follow, check my whereabouts, find out who I had come to see . . .

The gorilla in Rudolfsplatz had a gun. A big one. Everyone else I knew had a gun.

He halted at the door behind me, barely a yard away. I stopped breathing and concentrated on balance, the way I had been taught. I could almost hear the voice of my ancient Sensi, the saintly Hu Shiy, frail and mesmeric, instructing me. *Shuto.* I folded my right thumb firmly across the palm of my hand.

His breathing was steady and unhurried. I knew his ear was against the door. Then he was on the move again, gliding past me like a shadow. He must surely be blind. He would sense me, smell me. A yard in front of me he stopped. The slightest glint of light filtered through the lens of his glasses. His head ducked. He was whispering again.

With the side of my hand I chopped, clean and hard. *Shuto.* He went down slowly like a felled tree, buckling at the knees with only the slightest of grunts. Something metallic clattered to the stairs.

I waited for a door to open, prepared to run. Nothing—only the radio thudding on its dreary way . . .

I felt for the pulse at the base of his throat. He was alive and as well as could be expected; with any kind of luck he would remain that way for the next twenty minutes or so. Taking Wayne's braces from my pocket, I strapped his wrists behind him, stretching the elastic so that it bit hard into the flesh. I heaved him over on to his back. The glasses were dislodged and scrawled across his face like a comic turn. The skin around his eyes looked puffy, as if he'd been crying. I undid his tie and with a masterly assortment of original knots secured his ankles.

The inside breast pocket of his blazer rendered up the *raison d'être* of the exercise. A wallet and two letters. Perhaps he wasn't that much of a professional after all. I squinted closely at the envelopes. It was too dark. I slipped the wallet and the letters into my pocket. I let him keep his cigarettes, took his lighter and relieved him of the bunch of keys in his trouser pocket.

Rolling his handkerchief into a ball, I stuffed it into his mouth and for good measure tied my own handkerchief as a gag between his teeth to keep it there. His leather belt was a bonus. Wayne could have kept his braces. Man-handling him into the recess under the sink, I threaded the belt through his wrists and buckled it around the waste pipe.

He was breathing heavily, almost a snore. I propped his head against the sink; it quietened him a little but not much. "Shut up," I hissed. "You'll wake the neighbourhood."

Now that it was done, I was beginning to feel slightly light-headed. As I got to my feet, I remembered the falling metallic object as he had hit the deck. It was standing upright against the rise of the first step. A short-wave transmitter.

My head grew a little heavier.

He had been broadcasting his whereabouts. They would know exactly where he was, were probably on their way right now, already outside perhaps, ganged up in the courtyard, eager to discover why he had gone off the air without saying goodbye. I stowed the transmitter into my pocket and moved swiftly downstairs.

After the darkness and stench of the stairway, the outside air was pure and fresh. The moon had gone. I hung about in the doorway quartering the courtyard for a sign of movement. Except for the pop music the place was as quiet and still as a grave.

I doubled across the courtyard, lifting my feet like a hen on the run, hesitating only for a second beneath the arch before sprinting healthily down the road, keeping to the shadows and using the tower of Maria am Gestade

to guide me. In the close vicinity of the church I slowed down, skirting the
gaunt black building and making for the steeply descending steps known as
the Fischerstiege—the Fishermen's Steps.

It was apt enough, I thought. I'd cast a fly and landed a trout. All I needed
now was time, luck and the assurance of the deity who watched over people
like me that my trout wouldn't flop back into the stream before I had done
what I had to do.

Augmenting the dim light of a street lamp with the stolen cigarette lighter,
I studied the envelopes. Both were addressed in dissimilar handwritings to
the same person: one Herr Hans Schmidt. That was a laugh for a start. Mr.
John Smith. However, we must manage with the materials offered us. Oddly
enough the address was Trautsohngasse. Although I was not gullible enough
to believe that *Trautsohn* meant the "son of the trout" (according to Schubert, the German for "trout" is *Forelle),* I might perhaps be excused the
fleeting hope that an omen might be around somewhere.

A cab dropped me off at the corner of Trautsohngasse. I was startled to
read on a plaque alongside the nameplate of the street that in that very
house, Number 2, Beethoven had written the *Credo* of his *Missa Solemnis.*
That couldn't be bad. Another omen perhaps?

I genuflected to Number 2 as I passed on my way up the street to find the
abode of Herr Hans Schmidt. His name and the number 5 were alongside a
bell-push which I ignored. From the bunch of keys I had lifted, I chose the
one that looked most likely and in thirty seconds flat was outside a door on
the second floor which had a 5 on it. No light shone through the frosted glass
fanlight above it. If he had a wife and three children, they were in bed and
asleep. I had to risk it; I had no inclination to knock or ring the bell in case
the neighbours came running.

A Yale key on the ring fitted the lock. I closed the door noiselessly behind
me. The place smelled of cigarette smoke and gas. I flicked on the lighter. A
small entrance hall; a coat rack housing only masculine garments—a light
overcoat, a couple of leather jackets, a green Klepper raincoat and a natty
Tyrolean hat; the portents suggested that neither wife nor children were in
residence.

Three doors led off the hall, one on either side and the third at the end
facing the front door. To the right, sitting-room-cum-kitchen, left, a bedroom
and the third, bathroom and lavatory. And that was it. What had once been
a well-proportioned house had been vandalised and divided up into apartments. Elaborate ceiling cornices ended abruptly and unfinished at most of
the walls, to complete themselves presumably on the other side in somebody
else's apartment. The windows were all at the rear overlooking the backs of
other houses.

With a possible hasty retreat in mind I hung out of the bathroom window
and studied the lie of the ground below and an adjacent drainpipe. As an
emergency exit it was just possible. I left the window ajar.

I began with the sitting-room, which stank of fish, smoke, beer and grease, in that order. I closed the curtains and switched on the light. He had neither wife nor children, or if he had, he'd driven them out long since. He lived in a masculine pigsty. At first I thought the place had been turned over, but no one could have achieved such built-in havoc in anything less than several months.

I worked swiftly and systematically. Time was not on my side. It couldn't be long before he recovered consciousness, and even if he hadn't already been discovered and released, he would have little difficulty in rousing somebody. After that it would only be a question of minutes before he woke up to the loss of his keys and came howling at my heels.

Judging by the posters and pamphlets and the rest of the junk plastered about the walls, he was anti whatever establishment happened to be on the go at the moment. Pictures of ill-dressed and ungroomed revolutionaries glowered and gesticulated from all sides; fingers pointed, flags and banners unfurled, mouths gaped; exclamation marks and blood-red question marks peppered the incitements to rise against the oppressor; hammers, sickles, swastikas, skulls, cross-bones, SS lightning flashes, they were all there making depressing viewing.

On the mantelpiece in an ashtray I found a swastika badge of the kind once worn in every good Nazi's buttonhole, but in view of the abounding wall decorations it probably meant nothing; doubtless he had a boxful of similar mementos from the world's more dangerous dissidents. The rest of the mantelpiece was taken up with cans of beer, packets of unwholesome-looking biscuits, some loose potatoes and an unopened half-kilo of sugar.

In a drawer of a sideboard, jammed in among a riot of ties, socks and sex books, I turned up a loaded Luger pistol with two spare magazines and a box of bullets. I shoved the pistol into my waistband—Aunt Alice could practise with it—and the rest of the stuff into my pocket. An assortment of various other offensive weapons was in an adjacent drawer including what looked mighty like a live hand-grenade. It could have been a phony, but I didn't bother to remove the pin in case it wasn't.

He obviously had a cat. I trod in a plateful of smelly fish and later in the bedroom kicked over a saucer of milk. My ex-wife used to complain, not without cause, that I was the untidiest person she had ever come across. She hadn't even begun to live, poor dear; she would have fallen in love with me all over again if she could have been with me now. Cigarette stubs, over-loaded ashtrays, newspapers and the occasional empty beer can littered the floor. No sign of books anywhere—other than the porn and a couple of comics; pictures were easier.

One corner of the room was taken up with what passed for a kitchen and the less said about the state of his gas stove and what few utensils he possessed, the better.

I began to feel hung-over with the sheer squalor of it. I almost heaved when I saw what the kitchen sink contained.

I put out the light and departed hastily for the bedroom.

A life-size blow-up of Charlotte Rampling in the concentration camp sequence from *The Night Porter* dominated the wall at the foot of the unmade bed . . . the rakish SS cap, the swastika arm band, the riding whip, the expanse of naked leg . . .

He was a hypochondriac. The bedside table was littered with bottles and boxes, packets and tubes of all shapes and sizes, every one of them containing pills and patent medicines of the type which can be bought from any local chemist; nothing, so far as I could see, had been prescribed by a doctor. I saw no indication of drug addiction, but it could have been stashed away somewhere out of sight of prying eyes like mine.

A large wardrobe contained his clothes, all surprisingly neat on individual hangers. I went hastily through some of the pockets: tram tickets, the odd few schillings, the photograph of a youngish-looking man in a beard and a raincoat. I pocketed it for future reference. My fingers contacted something metal beneath the lapel of one of the jackets—another badge similar to the one in the ashtray.

I stood for a further second or two staring around me, depression lapping at my toes like a rising tide. I glanced at my watch; time I was away. I could do without a show-down with a vengeful sex maniac who wore Nazi badges and kept a drawerful of weapons of which any punk would be proud.

An old-fashioned wash-stand stood resentfully in the corner behind the door, dog-eared photographs stuck into the frame of its blotchy mirror. They were not enlightening; snapshots mostly, presumably friends—if they had him for a friend, they wouldn't need to worry about enemies; people wearing funny hats and making comic faces for the camera; a Christmas tree with an elderly couple sitting beside it, hands quietly crossed in their laps—Mum and Dad, perhaps? A buxom girl in a swim-suit looking embarrassed; a group of pale-faced surprised-looking people snapped by flashlight in a red and green restaurant, one of them in dark glasses looking suspiciously like Hans Schmidt, his arm draped around a girl's shoulders. I decided to take them; they could be useful; Wayne might know some of them . . .

I was staring at the woman next to Schmidt—not the one with his arm around her, the one with her hand touching the other man's bearded cheek. The man with the beard was the man in the photograph I had found in the wardrobe. The woman touching his cheek was Hedda.

My stomach twitched.

Hitler was a great leader, she had said. Well done, Adolf! The shouting matches at Nuremberg were over; the torchlit processions, the blazing arcs, the scarlet and black banners and the whole blood-boltered muck heap of the Third Reich had been bombed and bulldozed out of existence, and places like the one in which I now stood knee-high in shit were its heritage and monument. And Hitler was a great leader?

I gloomed over the photograph. How deeply was she into this? And who was the man with the beard? Was he the initiator of her outmoded beliefs in the Master Race? Poor though it was, the photograph suggested not only an intimacy between them but also a friendship for the man responsible for the insanitary shambles now surrounding me. The uneasiness I had originally felt about her, and subsequently disregarded as I had warmed to her, seeped back as her involvement with both camps bore in upon me. She was a fifth column all on her own . . . Or maybe she was just the daughter of a father she could not remember, who had been stabbed by an unknown hand and hanged on the Plague Column in the Graben.

I heard the slam of a car door some seconds before I responded to its implications. It was the short peal of a distant doorbell which eventually brought me to my senses. I had lingered too long.

On my way in the taxi I had devised a course of action likely to be taken by him on awakening to his dilemma. Realising his assailant had got both keys and address, he would assume that he had gone to the apartment to have a snoop around. Had I been in his shoes, I would immediately make tracks in that direction in the hope of catching him at it, ring someone else's bell, get him to open the front door and then do the best I could with my own door . . . By which time the assailant would be out of the bathroom window and home and dry.

The results of my divination had not included the movements of possible reinforcements which may have come to his aid on the interruption of his broadcasts. If he'd brought with him what was left of the Third Reich, then considerable rethinking on my part might well be necessary.

A grumbling voice and reluctant footsteps making for the front door decided me it was time for departure.

I dowsed the bedroom light and scuttled to the bathroom window, dropping his keys down the lavatory as I passed—a mean thing to do because he wouldn't have a hope in hell of recovering them—not without the help of a plumber. I know. I once lost my wallet down there. It isn't just a question of your common or garden U-bend; in Austria it's all much more complicated and time-consuming.

Elbowing my way through the window, I crouched on the sill for a second to get my bearings. The drain-pipe was further off than I had hoped, but it wasn't impossible. Closing the window as best I could, I edged to my feet. The Luger stuck down the front of my trousers didn't help. Pressing my face against the wall, I grasped the pipe.

To an erstwhile stuntman a drain-pipe was a piece of cake; in the movie world, however, since dead film stars and crippled stuntmen can embarrass the budget, all drain-pipes are carefully scrutinised and reinforced. In real life they receive no such attention, the present one being no exception. When it was treated to my full weight, it positively reeled and let out a groan which must have been heard in Budapest. I hung for a hideously expectant second, but the pipe recovered itself and because it is never wise to hang about, as it were, on such occasions, I made it to the ground in record time. And only just in time.

The window upstairs burst open, and I rolled myself into a hasty ball inside a rhododendron bush. An upward peer through the overhanging leaves revealed his head silhouetted against the dark sky; we seemed to stare directly into each other's eye; it went on for some time, then he gave up, withdrew his head and slammed the window. To look for his keys, I hoped.

I climbed a wall, shinned up a tree and hung over somebody's greenhouse, wriggling out on a limb to avoid coming to earth in the middle of it. Roosting pigeons fluttered and hooted irritably, awaking a dog who added some barking to the general uproar. No humans, however, appeared on the scene, and at long last I found myself in a yard not unlike the place where I had clobbered Schmidt, except that this one was well cared for and had a spry little tree growing in the middle of it. An archway with double wooden doors barred the exit, but a wicket gate set in the midst of one of them was secured only by a Yale lock.

Caution was at my back and I was glad of it, for the first thing I saw and heard as I released the catch and peered tentatively into the street beyond was the grey VW with the damaged rear fender cruising by like a police car on the prowl. Reinforcements had been contacted and were on the job. As I watched it move away, I realised I was on familiar territory. On the far side of the cobbled street and fifty yards away was the English Theatre on whose stage many years before I had perpetrated Checkhov's *Sea Gull.* I gave a sigh of relief; at least I knew where I was.

Waiting until the red glow of the VW's rear lamps had disappeared around the corner above the theatre, I sprinted in the opposite direction out into and across Auerspergstrasse towards the Parliament Buildings, where I picked up a late cab.

Sprawled on the back seat, I unloaded the Luger, transferred it to the inside breast pocket of my dinner jacket and, closing my eyes, consigned them all to hell. I didn't even bother to check whether they had caught up with me again. I suppose I didn't really much care. If they wanted me, they knew where to find me.

Which was no less than the truth, for as I was paying off the cab, the grey VW pulled wearily around the corner, squeaked to a standstill and sat there staring at me through baleful headlights. Nobody got out. There was no need. I had the uneasy feeling that the cold war was over and the shooting war about to commence.

At the door I turned and waved them good night.

CHAPTER EIGHT

The morning was beset with the doldrums. Across the way, like a great square-rigged vessel, the Opera House wallowed against a jaundiced sky; everything was warm and damp to the touch; no discernible breath of air stirred; the traffic moved on felt-covered wheels.

I had spent a bad night disturbed by intricate and incomprehensible dreams in which I fell endlessly into space and ran with frantic endeavour but made no progress; I stood on a dark stage in a black uniform watching a silent audience watching me; I lay spread-eagled on a bed bound and gagged whilst a monstrous tarantula with diamond eyes crouched on my naked chest . . .

Between the dreams I sweated profusely and prowled the room, my mind plagued with questions to which there were no answers. On both planes, waking and sleeping, the sense of danger predominated.

The pale morning light glanced across the ashen face of the dead Beethoven brooding on the wall. I stared back disconsolately.

Last night I had stirred up a hornets' nest, and had done so deliberately. Someone had to make a move, or we'd never get anywhere.

According to those concerned, Alice and her ménage had been dogged and spied upon for several weeks—no one appeared to have been dismayed; no one had done anything about it. Until yesterday, when I became one of the fixtures and fittings, there had been no overt acts of aggression or threats of violence—on either side. And then, out of the blue, comes this great Hungarian knucklehead erupting into the gentle Sammy's life, uttering dire imprecations and waving his huge gun about. In the next act it was my turn to become a star performer, playing opposite the character man with the blue buttonhole and demolishing half the Demel establishment in the process. The final sequence of the day had been a monologue intended by me as a sort of getting-to-know-your-enemy number.

I wandered back to the forte-piano on whose lid I had displayed the gleanings of last night's escapade, the property of Hans Schmidt; one Luger pistol with ammunition for the use of, one cigarette lighter, one swastika badge, a clutch of photographs, a couple of letters in envelopes, a wallet and a handheld transmitter and receiver set.

The letters, apart from supplying his name and address, were otherwise unedifying, one from Father in Frankfurt relaying local news and colour, the other from girl-friend Lili, regretted that owing to the fact that she had developed a *Furunkel* on her bottom she would be unable to meet him on Saturday for the Spring Festival. I wondered whether she was the one in the photograph. I was sorry about her boil, but if she chose to hobnob with Hans, it could have been the result of divine intervention.

Disappointingly the wallet too revealed nothing of interest—a few hundred schillings, some postage stamps, and a couple of unused *Strassenbahnfahrkarten* (German for "tram tickets").

I took the photo which included Hedda to the window and examined it again in the cold light of a new day. The crude flash lighting threw the classic bone formation of her face into sharp relief, giving it an almost predatory look. The man in the beard was round-faced and smooth, with small closely set eyes, undeserving, I thought, of the hand on his cheek. On the table before them lay what looked like an outsize menu card bearing presumably the name of the restaurant. I turned the photograph upside down and carefully spelled out the word, letter by indistinct letter: Kékszákallú. Were we in Vienna, I wondered, or Hungary? Budapest wasn't all that far away. *Kékszákallú* . . . somewhere in the echoing recesses of my mind a bell was ringing . . . the word was familiar.

At that moment there came a discreet knocking at the door.

"Who is it?" I moved to the piano and flicked the corner of its Spanish shawl over the exhibits.

It was Emily Hargreaves with a tray. "I heard you moving about, thought you'd like some tea. Good morning." I looked at my watch; it was not yet seven.

"You're a treasure, Emily, thank you."

I took the tray from her, but she followed me resolutely into the room to draw back the curtains fully. "Did you sleep well?" She caught sight of my rumpled bed. "Oh dear, was it you or the bed?"

"I'm not good with strange beds."

"And this *is* a strange one, isn't it?" She glanced slyly at the Beethoven mask. "Now, have your tea and a shower and I'll get you a nice breakfast."

As she bustled out, she gave a tweak at the corner of the Spanish shawl to set it right and in doing so revealed my secrets. "Oh goodness . . ."

I was at her side gathering up the photographs before she could get them into focus. She was eyeing the Luger.

"Isn't that an ugly-looking thing?"

Privately I've always thought that the Luger has a touch of elegance, but I said, yes, wasn't it and whipped it up to put it somewhere else, found nowhere and replaced it.

"My husband had one. It's a Luger, isn't it?" Now she had the Nazi badge in her hand. "One of these too . . ." She turned slowly, her eyes full of mistrust. I took the badge from her. "No, Emily, it's not mine. I . . . picked it up last night"—I grinned—"doing a bit of detecting."

I was shepherding her to the door when she stopped and looked at me squarely. "Does this business concern *them?*"

"Them?"

"The badge."

I smiled reassuringly. "They all went up in smoke, Emily, you know that."

Her face was grim. "Not all of them." Her voice was quiet. "Some of them are still alive. And they pass it on to others—young people who don't understand; who never saw that . . . *thing* everywhere, on flags and banners, armbands . . . everywhere . . ."

I took her gently by the hand. "Emily, it doesn't mean anything any more. Back in England the kids have it painted on their jackets, girls wear swastika ear-rings—boys too if it comes to that. They flaunt it around because they think it riles people—and it probably does—some of the older people. It's a pathetic attempt to look tough, that's all . . ."

"England!" She was full of contempt. "What do they know about *anything* in England? It's here that it happened. And I'm not talking about the people who *flaunt* it—it's the ones who *don't*—they're the ones who frighten me." She blinked up at me. "You can't kill off that sort of vileness in a generation . . . it's in the blood . . . it's a disease . . ." She hesitated for a second, was about to add something more, thought better of it, turned and left abruptly.

I watched her tramping down the corridor. I called quietly, "Emily." She stopped. "How is my aunt this morning?"

She turned. "I'm letting her sleep in a bit. She was dead tired after yesterday. She did much too much. I tell her, but she won't listen. Perhaps you could have a word. She might listen to you. Bacon and eggs in the kitchen whenever you're ready." And she was gone.

I returned slowly to my room and glared at the loot on the piano lid.

I pondered over the walkie-talkie for some little time. If still in working order and set on a preselected wavelength, it might well open up the channel between "them" and me; we might have some interesting words to say to each other; an intriguing idea but one not to be squandered by hasty judgment or an irresponsible desire to get a rise out of them. I packed it away with the Luger in my overnight bag. The rest of the stuff I distributed among the pockets of the new oatmeal linen jacket Konrad had picked out for me.

I showered, shaved and squirted Houbigant liberally over my face, which usually improved the outlook but this morning only made me smart, then I went down to breakfast.

*   *   *

Upright and wizened in that formidable four-poster, packed in and propped up with cushions and pillows, her silver-topped stick at rest beside her, she was engrossed in *The Times* crossword puzzle. I almost genuflected. She presented me with a withered cheek and tapped me on the chin with her gold pencil. "You've taken off your plaster. Is it better?" She squinted closely at the red scar.

"I've just set it alight with after shave; I'm now letting the air get to it, as they say."

"And I'm being kept in bed," she complained darkly. "Have you breakfasted? Emily tells me you didn't sleep well."

"I've had breakfast and better nights." I peeked at the puzzle, which she immediately held close to her bedjacket in protective custody, as is the wont of crossword addicts. "I didn't know you did *The Times.* How's it going?"

"Like constipation," she grumbled. "It's never been the same since they had that silly strike. Pull up that chair where I can see you. Now tell me what you've been up to."

I gave her the briefest outline of the night's happenings.

"How exciting." She all but clapped her hands. "I wish I'd been there."

"The drain-pipe was a trial."

"But you did find out something?"

"Not a lot, no, but let me show you this."

I produced the restaurant picture. She adopted a severe expression as she regarded it intently through narrowed eyes. "It's Hedda."

"And?" I prompted. "Who's that with her?"

"Oh . . . that's someone from the opera—what's his name? Karl? Kurt? He's an up-and-coming baritone . . . Dieter, that's it, Dieter somebody . . . *Moll.* Dieter Moll, that's the boy." She continued to stare critically at the photograph. "His eyes are too close together. His nose only just got in, didn't it? Who are the others?"

I pointed out the one in the dark glasses and told her who he was. She gave me a sudden startled look. "What's Hedda doing with him?"

"Exactly."

She frowned. "Oh dear. That's worrying, isn't it? You haven't shown this to Emily?" I shook my head. "Better not, eh? Might upset her. Oh, that girl, that girl . . ."

"What do you know of the Kékszákallú?"

"What do I know of it? You mean have I sung in it?" I looked my confusion. "*Kékszákallú* is Hungarian for Bluebeard," she explained patiently. "Bartok wrote a one-act opera called *A Kékszákallú Herceg Vára—Duke Bluebeard's Castle.*" She looked at me curiously. "You really are being most confusing, Mark dear. What has this to do with Hedda?"

"The name on the menu card there on the table in front of them is Kékszákallú, so at a guess I'd say they're in a Hungarian restaurant. Do you know of any such restaurant?"

She shook her head. "There are so many Hungarian restaurants; I never go to any of them; Hungarian food doesn't agree with me. Konrad will know. There's not much about Vienna he doesn't know. On the other hand, of course, it could be over the border, couldn't it? Budapest or somewhere."

I nodded. "That had crossed my mind. I'll look it up in the telephone directory. It could be a lead; they may hang out there, whoever they are."

"And no news of Lorenz, I suppose?" I shook my head gloomily. "Well, *nil desperandum*, dear. You've only been here a day." She returned the photograph, a worried frown on her face. "What *is* that girl up to, I wonder? Did she tell you anything about herself yesterday?"

"A bit, yes."

"Illuminating?"

"Very."

She pointed. "In the bottom right-hand drawer of that dressing table you'll find some photograph albums. Be a dear and bring me the blue one." Whilst I complied with her request, she went on: "I've never had any real doubts about Hedda, but she's headstrong, you know, a rebel. She and Emily don't get on. Hedda's as German as Emily is English; a peculiar relationship, and I suspect dear Emmy is mostly to blame. She can be suffocatingly English, a situation never helped by that husband of hers who turned out to be something of a rotter. Oh, he was quite a charmer in a Teutonic sort of way—a heel-clicker, you know, but then they all were in those days. Emily was swept off her feet. It was love at first sight and as star-crossed as ever love was. The coming of the war destroyed it, of course, as it did so many others . . ."

She was leafing through the thick pages of the album. "There he is, that's him . . . Do you know, I've completely forgotten his name . . . Come and sit here on the bed." She turned a page. "And that's Hedda as a little girl. Isn't she pretty? She must have been about fourteen then." She turned back a page. "Let me show you now . . . there . . ." She smoothed out a page gently. "Lorenz." Her fingers trembled. A small boy in a sailor-suit, like every other small boy of the period, the ship's name on the ribbon of the cap in gold Gothic. "Isn't he beautiful?" she whispered. "Lorenz . . . that was taken on his eighth birthday—a year before he . . . Doesn't he look grown up? Black hair and those dark, dark eyes . . . He's *not* dead, you know. You'll find him, I know you will."

I avoided her eyes and stared instead at the delicate young face in the yellowing photograph. I remembered what Wayne had said about her tireless search after the war, and how if Lorenz had been alive there would surely have been some record or proof of his continued existence.

Once again she smoothed gentle fingers over the photograph and once again turned back the pages. "And there's Ernst, my husband," she smiled up at me, "your great uncle. Isn't he a terrible heap? I could never get him to look tidy. That awful old jacket, it must have been a hundred years old . . . how well I remember it. Mind you, when he was off on business somewhere he could look really sharp."

There was nothing Semitic about the face in the photograph, I thought. He was an ordinary good-looking man of about forty in a baggy tweed jacket and knickerbockers; short-cropped hair threw into almost comic relief a large drooping moustache. Dark limpid eyes gazed with fondness at the camera.

"He doesn't look like a *diamantaire*."

"And how should a *diamantaire* look?"

I shrugged. "Like Diaghilev, or Puccini . . . Mahler even. They all look as if they might have had something to do with diamonds."

She gave a sudden snort of amusement and pointed a bony finger at Ernst. "That man knew more about diamonds than anyone in Europe. Even Ernest Oppenheimer had to admit that, and he was Mr. Diamonds himself—chairman of De Beers. People used to come from all over to consult with Ernst. To watch him sorting stones was an education. *I* could never see why he chose one particular stone instead of another. It was never because it looked more beautiful than the others, nor was it because of its weight; a good half carat could be worth much more than a poor one carat. He used to say a diamond was a living thing, and if you listened, it would talk to you." She shook her head in fond reminiscence. "We were married eleven years, eleven desperate and happy years. On each anniversary he presented me with a perfect diamond. 'Keep them by you,' he said. 'Lock them away. One day your beautiful voice will be no more . . .' And every now and again he would say, 'Have you still got the goods?' They call diamonds the goods in the trade you know—what a crude word for such beautiful things. When I nodded, he would say, 'I don't want to know where they are—so long as you've got them and keep them safe.' "

"And have you still got them?" I asked, adding hastily with a laugh, "I don't want to know where they are either."

The pale eyes regarded me steadily for a long quizzical moment. "I've still got them . . . eleven of them . . ."

"Safe?"

"Safe enough."

A second or two went by in silence. I got up and went to the window while she continued her trip down memory lane with her photograph album.

She said suddenly and without preamble, "Mark dear, we have not yet discussed money. Apart from board and lodgings, what am I to pay you for your professional services?"

When I mentioned my usual expectations, she gave a rude snort. "That's quite ridiculous; that won't even buy you a seat at the opera."

"I wasn't actually thinking of going to the opera."

"You do like the opera, don't you?" She sounded severe.

"I love it, all that shrieking and banging about, it's food and drink to me; sets me up for weeks on end."

She looked doubtful. "In the drawer of the bedside table there you'll find an envelope containing your expenses. I'll make up my own mind about the rest of it and you'll take it whatever it is, otherwise I shall send you straight back home. Is that understood?"

"Yes, aunt," I grinned.

"Alice."

"Yes, Alice."

Beneath a bulky envelope lay a gun—not the Walther she had used in Demel's but an elderly little Beholla, a self-loading affair, one of the smallest military pistols on the market—if indeed they were still on the market— dating back to before World War I.

I shoved the envelope unopened into my pocket—I wasn't going to argue with her—and closed the drawer.

"Alice," I said tentatively. "Will you tell me something?" She didn't say whether she would or not. "Why do you always have a gun within easy reach?"

"I like guns," was her unsatisfactory reply.

"Are you afraid of something? Someone?"

"Why on earth should I be afraid?"

"Alice, will you kindly stop fencing with me. If you believe you are in some sort of danger, then I would like to know *why* you believe it."

She closed her book carefully. "I have never said I was in danger." She sounded tight-lipped.

"Ever since you heard that Lorenz might be alive and in Vienna, you have carried a gun. Why? Does the possibility of a live Lorenz carry a threat with it? If it does, then it might not be a good thing to go out looking for him."

She came back at me forcefully. "It's Lorenz who's in danger, don't you see that? Others are looking for him. Brutes like the man in Sammy's flat yesterday—brutes with guns. How can an unarmed boy hope to stand up to a lout like that?"

"The unarmed boy," I interrupted her a little wearily, "is fifty-three years old if he's a day and is, if what Sammy told us is true, quite capable of taking care of himself—even to the point of murder."

What little blood there was in her face seemed to drain away; her hands clenched and began to tremble. I moved quickly to the bed, sat beside her, taking her hands in mine and cursing myself for my tactlessness. "I'm sorry, that was unforgivable of me." Tears were on her cheeks; she clung with awesome strength to my hands. With my arm around her shoulders I held her close, her head against my chest. I felt the dampness of her tears seeping through my shirt, smelled the stringent cleaning fluid on her wig—did she wear a special wig for bed, I wondered . . . ?

She wept with little hiccuping noises, small birdlike sounds like the flut- tering of young feathers in a nest. "Why hasn't he come?" she whispered in the midst of it all. "Why hasn't he come?" over and over again, an endless threnody of despair.

When I felt it had gone on long enough, I eased her from me gently, murmuring comforting phrases and wondering how long that treacherous heart of hers would stand up to this sort of treatment. Eventually she quiet- ened and lay back on the pillows, desperately and dangerously spent, her face drawn and pale, the skin strangely fluorescent and faintly bluish in colour. The lids heavily drawn over the deep-set eyes reminded me of the death-mask upstairs . . .

As if she sensed the rising panic in me, she laid a hand on my arm. "I'm all right . . . I'll be all right." I watched her taking deep deliberate breaths. Her hand sought mine, gripping it hard. I stared down at the little twisted claw which had so much strength in it; blue veined and blotchy with age, it lay in mine twitching like a dying animal. On the third finger glittered a large diamond, a cold and watchful eye. A diamond is a living thing, Ernst had said; if you listen, it will talk to you . . .

I looked up, sensing her eyes on me. Her cheeks were wet with tears. I reached for some tissues on the side table, gently dabbing away the dampness and placing some clean tissues in her hand. The unanswered and unanswerable question rankled deep in her eyes.

"Why hasn't he come, Mark?"

I shook my head helplessly. "I don't know, darling. I wish I did. You really must let go, you know, and stop brooding; it can do you no good at all. My mother used to say, 'Let go—let God.' For what it's worth."

She smiled through a half-frown. "I don't believe in God any more." I made a face at her. "Do I know your mother?" she asked a second later.

"I don't think you ever met. And you won't now because she's dead."

She closed her eyes wearily. "I too, Mark dear, I too. Sometimes I wonder what keeps me going. Obstinacy, I suppose, sheer obstinacy. Just look at my hands—I noticed you were a moment ago—bruised, discoloured, arthritic, like monkey's paws. They're not usually on view. That's why I wear gloves; I hate them so much. Wigs too . . . without a wig I'm a crone." She raised my hand to her lips. "Never grow old, Mark; it's not worth it. And don't believe them when they tell you old age has its compensations."

I began to think it was time to go. I was well out of my depth. I couldn't bring myself to tell her that she didn't know what she was talking about, because she did. It sickens me to hear people buttering up the elderly, telling them they'll live to be a hundred and get a telegram from the Queen, all that crap. The elderly know what day it is.

I gave her hand a squeeze. "I must go. It's getting late and no smoke up the chimney."

As I rose, she held on to me. "He hasn't come because he isn't Lorenz . . . that's what you think, isn't it?"

I stared down at her earnestly. "If he *is* Lorenz," I said carefully, "he *should* have come, that's all I can say."

"But why"—she paused—"why should a . . . stranger choose me for a mother? Why? And *how* should a stranger know the name of my child and the date of his birth?"

I took both her hands. "Whatever else I may or may not be able to do, I promise I'll bring you an answer to that question."

The telephone on the bedside table mercifully chose that moment to give a seductive purr. I passed her the instrument. She grunted into it and listened intently. "All right, Emmy, I'll tell him. And will you come up, dear? When you're free, no hurry."

I took the phone from her. "Sammy wants you to meet his friends this morning—the Israeli crowd. At the Kunsthistorisches Museum—do you know it?" I nodded. "The Breughel Room at ten. I imagine they think it's safer to meet in a public place."

She drew a deep breath, exhaled loudly and, taking a tissue, blew a resounding D flat on her nose with formidable resolution and perfect pitch. She shook herself like a dog emerging from a pond and smiled up at me, transformed. "There, that's better. A good nose-blow clears the tubes and gets you on your feet again."

"You," I said, stooping and kissing her on the top of her wig, "are a great lady."

* * *

Purposefully I strode back to the Beethoven room, unearthed the walkie-talkie and stood for a second or two, my thumb hovering over the send button. The scene with Alice had convinced me that neither time nor opportunity were to be lost if the truth about Lorenz was to be disclosed before my aunt underwent that final and fatal stroke; even collaboration with the opposition would be preferable to a return to her bedside empty-handed; whoever they were and whatever they wanted, they had to know more than I did. It was unlikely they would know less.

I switched on the transmitter. Static. Did they have a call sign? A code word? My thumb jammed down hard on the button. I held the thing close to my mouth.

"Listen," I said in German. "If there's anyone there, I want to talk. Understand? Over . . ."

I released the button. More static, loud and long. Again I depressed the button. "My name is Mark Savage. I want contact with you. Over . . ."

I waited while the static seemed to go on for ever. Then a voice spoke in English, loud and clear, almost as if it were in the room. "Speak. Over . . ."

"I want to meet and talk," I told him. "Do you understand? Meet and talk. Over . . ."

"Understand. Over . . ."

"Where and when? Over . . ."

A long pause; then the dry metallic voice said, "Wait."

I waited. I stared up at the Beethoven mask. It seemed to brood depressingly over everything I did.

The voice burst into the room, cold and impersonal. "Will contact you. Over and out . . ."

"Wait," I shouted. "When? *When* will you contact me? Over . . . Listen! When will you contact me?"

Nothing but crackling static.

"Listen to me." I was beginning to snarl. "I am not lugging this bloody machine around with me, so if you want to make a date, you'd better make it now, understand. *Right now.* Because I'm not going to try again. Over."

He had gone off the air. He could hear me, I was damn certain of that, but he just wasn't answering. Okay, so I'd tried. I pressed the send button once again and said the rudest thing I could think of in German; it gave me no satisfaction except that it sounded even worse in German than it did in English. In my job I am always being asked to do the impossible; let him try it for a change.

CHAPTER NINE

Vienna is an immaculate city, remarkable for its shortage of litter and graffiti. Time and a change of generation will doubtless alter all that—vandalism will catch up with most of us sooner or later. But on this particular breathless morning I was prepared to concede that it was just about the least be-smirched city I knew, and the sense of danger and frustration which had possessed me since my arrival now began to recede as I legged it down Nibelungengasse on my way to the Kunsthistorisches Museum.

Also responsible for the growing feeling of euphoria was the almost certain knowledge that I was not being tailed. My inbuilt antenna sat immobile at the back of my neck and said nothing.

Alice had revealed the presence of a back door to her building which led into a courtyard from which there were four exits, one into a main road, the other three into side streets. I had chosen one of the latter and so far all seemed well. Presumably the usual pursuit had become accustomed to Alice and her entourage emerging grandly from the front entrance to acknowledge the bobs and bows of the populace and had made no provision for wily old private investigators like me.

Since my previous visit they'd done a cleaning job on the massive structure of the museum and it now looked crisp and pristine as a birthday cake. No such consideration had as yet been paid to the Empress Maria Theresa who sat enthroned in the middle of her *Platz*, begrimed and uncared for, surrounded by her pigeon-bedaubed equestrian generals and sober-suited counsellors.

The marbled entrance hall and staircase rang to the chatter of a crocodile of schoolgirls who trailed off dutifully to view the Imperial crown jewels and Cellini's salt-cellar whilst I trudged up the impressive centre staircase, said hello to Canova's *Theseus and the Centaur* and went in search of the Breughels—Room X.

The room was in the sole possession of an elderly man with a monocle and a scatty looking female in a red hat who clutched at his arm as if afraid of mislaying him, and stared at him with unabashed admiration as he held forth about the pictures with magisterial omniscience.

I sat on the padded bench in the centre of the room and renewed acquaintance with *The Peasant Wedding*, spending the usual few minutes worrying over the problem of the man with three feet in the foreground of the picture. Know-all with the monocle then came and parked himself close to the canvas to demonstrate his version of exactly *why* the man in the foreground had an extra foot. An invisible public-address system barked at him loudly, informing him that it was *verboten* to approach the pictures and would he kindly remove his finger from the canvas. He fell back as if he'd been shot.

I eyed the television camera tucked away high in the corner of the room and wondered at the wisdom of a projected gathering of foreign agents immediately under the eye of an alert security system.

At that moment Sammy Meier, wearing a long flapping black overcoat and a round black hat, arrived on the scene trailing behind him a group of three on what looked like a conducted tour of the gallery. They were making a considerable amount of noise and were frowned upon by The Monocle and his lady companion, who shortly afterwards took themselves off with a meaningful glare at the camera.

Sammy overdid the performance of unexpectedly running into an old friend of the family by holding me to his chest and smiling too much. He probably knew he was on television and was making the most of it. A completely different Sammy Meier from the bashful and careworn individual I had yesterday despaired of, he introduced his companions: a dark handsome girl in her late twenties with straight black eyebrows, straight black hair and a luscious mouth, who went by the name of Ruth, stood to attention when she took my hand in a vice-like grip and ducked her glossy head in salute. "And you remember Milo and Albert, of course?" clucked Sammy loudly.

"Of course," I clucked back. "Nice to see you both again. Amsterdam, wasn't it? And how's your poor mother, Milo?"

If Amsterdam and Milo's poor mother took either of them by surprise, neither let on. We all shook hands and stood around for a second or two smiling vacuously at each other. I wondered what the museum's security force were making of this chance meeting of old friends. I doubted whether they were wired up for sound as well as vision, but Sammy was taking no chances.

Milo was undersized, bald and myopic, his pebble-lensed glasses magnifying his eyes and lending him the oriental look we have come to expect from too many B pictures. Albert was aloof and mainly silent, with crinkly blond hair and a black T-shirt. He wore frayed and bulging blue denim shorts from which grew narrow stick legs ending in enormous dirty white tennis shoes.

As Sammy drew us together in a tight huddle in front of *Hunters in the Snow*, I gave Ruth a friendly wink, which went down like a lead balloon. The favoured language was German with which, of necessity, I was making laudable headway. Sammy, indicating the ice skaters in the picture, said in a low voice, "My friends have, I regret, nothing to report. Ruth believes Brunner has left Vienna; the others don't agree. By Brunner, of course, I mean the man who now calls himself Lorenz Sternberg; the man who killed Friedrich, their colleague."

We stared with intense concentration at the canvas for a silent second or two. I made a vague gesture at the dogs in the foreground. "Do we know whether the police have made any progress?"

"Police!" The girl spat the word. "Why should police be interested?"

"Why should they not be?" I asked mildly.

"Because Friedrich was a Jew, that's why. Why should the police care about a Jew?"

I looked at her briefly. The lovely mouth was sour. "I can't believe that's true," I said shortly. I turned my back on her and moved on to the next picture, the three men trailing after me; as I came to a halt, I noticed she hadn't moved; I could see her jaw muscles working.

Milo said quietly, "Friedrich was her brother."

"Oh Christ no," I groaned. "Not bleeding hearts! Why the hell haven't you sent her home?"

"This is her home."

Another small group of art lovers had idled into the gallery and with the unerring herding instinct of the human races were gravitating in our direction. I moved off abruptly, Sammy at my heels. "They have a photograph of Lorenz brought over from Brazil; a recent one."

"Good. That could be useful." Milo and Albert had joined up with Ruth and for a moment Sammy and I were isolated. "Is it true what she says about the police here?"

He shook his huge head. "A murdered man is a murdered man, an embarrassment to any police force. You must excuse her."

"To hell with her. Why must I excuse her? She's just another fanatic, and I loathe bloody fanatics."

He gave a placid shrug. "They're all fanatics, Herr Mark. Why else are they here?"

I glared crossly at *The Massacre of the Innocents*. "If she goes off at half cock she'll bugger up everything." I couldn't think of the German for "half cock" and "bugger" so I said it in English, which Sammy found highly amusing.

Milo appeared at my elbow. He wasn't much taller than my elbow. "Sammy tell you about the photograph?" I gave him a distant nod. "The man who brought it said also that Otto Brunner, the father, is ill and likely will die."

"May in fact already be dead," added the taciturn Albert, ranging up alongside, his tennis shoes squeaking on the polished floor.

We stared morosely at the *Massacre*. I said, "If he's already dead, then your job here's finished, isn't it? You won't want the son now, will you?" They exchanged looks. I added abrasively, "Well, will you? Your war is with the father, not the son."

From behind came the taut voice of Ruth speaking in perfect English: ". . . and visit the sins of the father upon the children even unto the third and fourth generation . . ."

Something snapped in me. I swung on her. "Don't quote your bloody scriptures at me," I snarled, riled by her sudden smug bigotry. "We can all of us hide behind the bloody scriptures, and when we do, it's usually because we're on the defensive, because we have other motives—nastier motives."

Albert flashed her a warning look as she was about to return my fire. He muttered placatingly in German, "We wait. We see what happens. In the meantime we hunt the son."

"To what end?" I demanded, my rising voice echoing in the hallowed silence. "What are you after, for Christ's sake? Glory? Bounty? What do you want, a living sacrifice to take back with you?" Sammy laid a restraining hand on my arm; I threw it off. A man in uniform had come in to watch and was hovering uncertainly in the doorway.

The girl's face was suffused with blood. "We have a job to do and we'll do it whether you like it or not."

"Listen." I moved in a step and shoved a finger halfway up her nose in my excitement. "Lorenz killed your brother *after* you had kidnapped him, *after* you had tortured him." I turned from the black fury in her eyes to the sullen faces of her two companions. "Do you know something? Until this morning I believed there might be some sort of common ground between us, a shared sympathy perhaps; you know the sort of thing, you scratch my back and I scratch yours . . . Well, I was wrong, I'm sorry to say. As far as I am concerned you can all go and get stuffed—and I hope it hurts . . ."

And I swept out in search of fresh air, touching Sammy gently and apologetically on the sleeve as I passed. The man in uniform sprang aside with respectful haste as I bore down upon him.

I had gone too far, I knew that. Such an outburst was not typical of me, but I was tired of the whole damn world being run by fanatics and terrorists and anarchists who didn't give a damn about anyone or anything other than themselves and their own shabby little beliefs. Anyway, I had enjoyed it while it lasted, so sucks to them all.

I was ploughing through the entrance hall when Sammy caught up with me, breathing heavily and sweating profusely into his huge black overcoat. I didn't slacken my pace but barged through the massive doors like a bat out of hell, out into the open air, coming finally to rest at the top of the steps, where I stood glaring across the square at the rectangular mass of the twin museum opposite. I gave a loud growl. Several people paused to look at me and probably wished they hadn't when they encountered my eyes.

"Sammy, I'm sorry," I mumbled at last. "I can't talk to the silly sods. Why are they always on the defensive? Why do they kick and spit and make everything impossible for themselves and everyone else? Hedda's on the same wavelength too, except that she's on the other bloody side. She thinks Hitler's the greatest thing since Guy Fawkes." I grinned at him. "P'raps we ought to lock 'em up in the same room, let 'em fight it out between themselves like they used to settle wars in the good old days. Torch-carriers make me want to vomit."

I took him by the arm and piloted him down the steps and over to a vacant bench where we sat for a moment in neighbourly silence watching someone's dachshund peeing up against someone else's plinth.

"It's your turn, Sam," I told him, feeling vastly apologetic. "The soap-box is yours."

He gave a gentle smile. "I think there is no more to say. Like you, I find no answer to their problems. I think of myself, falsely perhaps, as a man of peace. Sometimes I believe I am unworthy of my faith because I see no sense in such missions as theirs; none of them can penetrate the sufferings of those they claim to avenge. They speak of religious and patriotic commitment, but I doubt their sincerity; the banners of both reek with the blood of personal vendetta which has nothing to do with either." He fell silent. The dachshund pottered over to snuffle at our feet; Sammy stooped to tickle him behind the ear; the animal retreated a wary inch, eyeing him with suspicion, tail alert and a-quiver, then cantered off with a falsetto bark.

Sammy straightened up with a grunt. "I tell you a thing I have never before told anyone." He removed his round black hat and studied it earnestly as if seeking inspiration in its worn crown. "The Torah frightens me. It is full of blood and slaughter and disregard for human life; so many of our kings and heroes were rogues and liars, adulterers and killers—even our God calls himself jealous, and though I prefer to think of the word as meaning 'vigilant' or 'watchful,' so many of his pronouncements are reprehensible—at least they are to the ears of the twentieth century—or should be." He added hesitantly, "Who can blame those children for behaving the way they do? Life for life, eye for eye, tooth for tooth, hand for hand . . . etcetera, etcetera . . . So says the book of Moses upon which our thinking and our state are built."

He raised his head slowly and looked up, blinking a little at the lowering yellow sky. "I *am* unworthy," he said simply. "It is enough." He replaced his hat and began rooting around in the various pockets of his unfashionable overcoat, bringing to light a crumpled eight-by-ten photograph which he ironed out on his knee.

Nearby a child was playing, its laughter mingling with the ripple and splash of a fountain.

Sammy passed the photograph to me. "Lorenz," was all he said.

If the face which stared up at me had ever borne any resemblance to Aunt Alice, it was no longer there. To say it startled me would be an understatement. The coarse grain of the print indicated that it was a blow-up, possibly from a 35-mm snapshot. As an example of photography it had nothing to recommend it; as a portrait of a man it was riveting.

The carriage of the head suggested that he had been caught unawares, that someone had called to him, the picture taken as he had turned questioningly into the lens. A man in his fifties, he was squarish of face, clean-shaven, with heavy black eyebrows contrasting with a thick mane of wiry grey hair which whitened dramatically at the temples. The nose was straight and impressive, with a contentious flare to the nostrils from which heavy lines bracketing a sensual mouth radiated further lines denoting a quick and quirky sense of humour; parted lips revealed strong-looking uneven teeth. The chin was firm and square.

The dark eyes had narrowed against the sudden glare of sunlight, at least one of them had; the other was false and glittered with an unnerving malignancy from the sunken darkness of an otherwise empty socket. The origin of the disfigurement was an oblique and deeply scored scar which ran from temple to cheek and gleamed bone-white against the tanned skin.

I frowned at the portrait for some time in silence. It was not the sort of face I had expected. I had not much cared for what I had heard of Lorenz the killer and probable offspring of a Nazi war criminal; I also knew that I had never really entertained the possibility of his being the long-lost son of my great aunt Alice. Yet now, faced for the first time with proof of his existence and a pretty vivid idea of what he looked like, my mind was clicking away like a Rubik's Cube, restlessly revising ideas and impressions and wondering whether there could be any truth in Alice's pronouncements. For somewhere, deep down, hidden in the non-existent third dimension of that photograph, there lay a shadowy insubstantiality which reminded me of my father.

I asked softly, "What happened to him?"

"The eye, you mean. Nobody knows. When they picked him up, he was wearing dark glasses, which were smashed in the . . . argument. In his pocket he carried a black eye-patch."

I peered closely at the picture. "Looks like someone swiped at him with a knife and took his eye out on the way. A long time ago, I would guess."

The child's laughter had ceased; only the fountain played on. I looked up. A small boy bore the body of a dead bird to his mother close by, his face stricken, eyes large and questioning . . . Almost furtively I glanced at Sammy beside me. He too was watching the child, hunched forward on his seat, hands spread on splayed knees.

"Anything else in his pockets?" I asked.

He straightened up slowly. His face glistened with sweat. "They say not. Nothing of importance. I think you can depend on that. They're unlikely to have overlooked anything."

"He had money, of course?"

"Plenty. Which they did not touch." He was mopping his face with an outsize handkerchief.

"Why don't you take that bloody coat off?" I asked with sudden irritation. "You must be baking."

"I am," he said, and took off his hat; the coat remained where it was. "What about the photo?" he asked.

"What about it?"

He ran patient fingers through his beard, eyeing me narrowly but saying nothing.

I shrugged. "The eye is a dead give-away, poor sod. Short of wearing a mask, there'd be no way of concealing it. He'd be easily recognisable if we could get him into the open."

A stubby forefinger rested firmly on the right eyebrow of the man in the picture. I looked at him questioningly. He said, "The way the eyebrow is lifted . . . a family characteristic perhaps?"

"So?"

"You have it too," he said almost casually. "And the set of the eye—tilting slightly upwards at the outer edge . . . you too have that."

It was a long time before I spoke again. I stared blankly at the picture. Having been vaguely conscious of something tentatively applicable to the memory of a dead father, I could now see nothing of him at all—and certainly nothing of myself. The face was that of a stranger and began now to assume the jigsaw zigzags of an Identikit mock-up . . . *Wanted for Murder . . . Have You Seen This Man?*

"Has my aunt seen this?" He shook his head. "I think perhaps she shouldn't." He was silent. I held the picture at arm's length. "Looks a bit like Lenny Bernstein." I became impatient. "There are bits and pieces of everybody in any face you like to look at—eyes, nose, mouth, eyebrows . . Hasn't anyone ever said to you, 'I saw your double today'? People used to say that I looked like . . ." I pulled myself up. "*Is* there a family likeness? Or are you just looking for it, hoping for it?" I looked at him earnestly. "I've got to find him before they do, Sammy, otherwise he'll be dead meat. And if I do find him, I'll fight them off with every dirty trick in the book." I thought for a moment. "If Brunner senior dies, will they go on hunting Lorenz?"

He met my eyes. "Ruth will. For her own gratification if for no other reason. She's head-hunting. Eye for eye, tooth for tooth . . . all that."

"He really did kill her brother, I suppose?"

A wealth of sadness glinted in his eyes. "Of that there can be no doubt."

A large woman in a voluminous black apron and wrinkled black stockings tucked into cut-down red rubber boots was listlessly sweeping up newly cropped grass on one of the lawns. After a couple of languid strokes she would pause, rest on her broom-handle and survey the future with vacant, bovine eyes. I knew how she felt.

"Sammy," I said desperately. "I'm at sea. I'm lost. I'm no further on than I was yesterday. I *know* a lot more, but I've *learned* nothing."

The child approached the woman, the dead bird on the flat of his open palms, offering it to her like a precious gift. She stared at him blankly, took the bird between finger and thumb and flung it into her wheelbarrow. The little body thudded hollowly against the metal. The boy moved away from her slowly, stepping backwards cautiously, over the new-mown grass, his eyes never leaving her face.

"There's a Hungarian restaurant or night club called the Kékszákallú," I said, "up near the Danube somewhere—according to the directory. District 20. There could be something going on up there. You don't know anything about it, I suppose?" He shook his head. "That gorilla who busted into your apartment yesterday—he was Hungarian, wasn't he?" He nodded. "What was he after?"

He thought for a moment. "Lorenz?"

"In your apartment?"

He hunched his shoulders. "Madame visits me occasionally; maybe they thought I was harbouring him."

"How occasionally?"

He looked wary, spread his hand. "She is an old friend."

"And business associate?" He said nothing. "You're one of the flies in her homespun smuggling web, aren't you?" He almost dropped his hat. "I'm her nephew, Sammy. Working for her. She mentioned her smuggling activities yesterday afternoon when she was ordering tea. How long has it been going on?" He shook his head. His lips were sealed. "Sammy," I persisted, "I don't give the German equivalent of a tinker's cuss for what either of you do in the way of business, illicit or otherwise. You can smuggle out the crown jewels for all I care. What does concern me is the security of your network and the danger involved should that security break down. Madame yesterday tossed off that information quite casually, as if it were something she had forgotten to tell the cook."

"You are her nephew, she trusts you."

"And Hedda? Does she trust Hedda? She was there too."

"Hedda is part of it."

I stared at him. "The smuggling?" He nodded. I gave a heavy groan.

He leaned forward, elbows on knees, turning his hat clockwise between large and gentle hands; he spoke in a low voice which I could hardly hear, choosing his words with care.

"There are two 'runs'—we call them 'runs'—one to Tel Aviv in which I am the first link, and one to Berlin for which Hedda is responsible. We know little of each other's work. It is better that way. I know of only one contact and that is a boat not a person. The submarine goods Madame sends to Tel Aviv are a gift—she receives no payment for them. She likes to think of them as part of a legacy from her dead husband to the State of Israel and that part of it which is responsible for—bringing crimes against humanity to justice."

"And you aid and abet that kind of operation? I thought your motto was, Let bygones be bygones."

He looked downcast. "I am of my people. A taxpayer if you like. And taxpayers the world over—peace-loving individuals—are subsidising the weapons which one day will destroy them."

"Taxpaying is hardly a matter of choice."

"Nor yet is loyalty. I owe my life to Madame. While she lives, I serve her."
He smiled suddenly. "We *could* send the goods by post, of course, it would
be a lot cheaper. Customs duties on diamonds exist now in few countries—
certainly not here and in other Common Market countries, or America. It's
the local taxes which cripple and are to be avoided—VAT, profits taxes . . ."

"Then why the cloak-and-dagger stuff?"

His smile was broad. "Madame is a theatrical."

"Madame," I said tersely, "is also an irresponsible eccentric. And Berlin?
What about Berlin?"

"In Berlin she sells for profit. Berlin pays for Tel Aviv. The rough goods
come from all over: South Africa, Botswana, Sierra Leone, Venezuela, and are
channelled to Antwerp or Lucerne for cutting and polishing and then on
here to Vienna."

"How?" He raised his eyebrows. "How do they come? By post?"

He smiled. "Sometimes, yes, surprisingly enough. Occasionally by courier
who happens to be on his way through—an airline pilot perhaps; sometimes
they come in a wig-box—she has a wig-maker in Antwerp . . ."

"And how do they leave here?"

"She has used many ruses over the years, and changes them frequently."

"And you're not going to tell me?"

"She will tell you if you wish to know."

He fell silent.

It all seemed to me a remarkably amateur affair. "Diamond Smuggling in
Three Easy Lessons." Correspondence Course Forwarded on Application.
How could a woman of eighty-four run a viable diamond business? Not a hat
shop or a bun shop, oh no, an international diamond concern! True, her
mentor had been the highly respected Ernst Sternberg, one of the great
diamantaires of all time, who having laid the tracks had presumably left
behind him a well-oiled and efficient network over which the contraband
traffic could be relied upon to roll smoothly for just so long as security and
maintenance remained alert and responsible.

"Sammy, I take it you talk very little about all this?"

He looked at me with pained surprise. "I don't talk about it at all. Only to
you have I talked." He placed his hat solemnly on the seat between us as if in
earnest of his incorruptibility. It sat there looking like a sacrificial offering
about to burst into flame.

"Has anyone ever questioned you about it?"

He shook his head.

"So who else knows? *Your* contact you tell me is a boat. You never see
anything on two legs? You just leave the stuff in an appointed place, the boat
sneaks in, picks it up, and that's that, right?" He nodded and was about to
enlarge upon it when I laid a hand on his hat. "I don't want to know where.
Not yet anyway. So . . . Who's Hedda's contact?"

"Someone at the opera."

"Why does she trust Hedda? Doesn't she know about her pro-Hitlerism?"

He shrugged. "She knows. She trusts."

"Who else? Emily Hargreaves?"

He shook his head emphatically. "Madame has always insisted that Emily would never understand."

"And Madame is probably dead right. However, if she fondly imagines that Emily doesn't know anything about anything, then she's deluding herself. Emily has been devoted to her for fifty years. She couldn't possibly *not* know something about it, even if she doesn't know all the details. Laverne Wayne, of course, would know in his capacity of business manager. Who else?" Sammy looked blank. "Sammy, there's got to be a whole bloody army of people in the know: sellers, buyers, cutters, polishers, couriers . . . wigmakers! Every one of them must have a pretty shrewd idea of where the goods eventually land up, and any single one of them, subjected to the right kind of persuasion, could cave in."

He looked suddenly prim. "Diamond smuggling," he growled, "is a family business. Everyone respects everyone. No one 'caves in.' "

I shook my head patiently. "I'm not doubting anyone's loyalty, Sammy, but there's a saying in the movies: 'We have ways of making you talk'—and it's usually uttered by nasty-looking individuals with black uniforms and pale blue eyes who happen at the time to be in charge of the thumbscrew. Even your lot is not exempt on that score—Lorenz will vouch for that. I have a gut feeling which says that these illicit business affairs of yours are at the bottom of Lorenz's sudden appearance, to say nothing of his equally sudden disappearance. *He* is in diamonds—*Madame* is in diamonds. It can't be coincidence. I suppose you wouldn't know if she's ever dealt direct with the fatherfigure of all this—what's his name, Brunner? Otto Brunner?"

He thought for a moment. "Some of the rough goods come from Venezuela; to the best of my knowledge that is her only trade with Latin America. But in the world of diamonds Venezuela and Rio de Janeiro are only a stone's throw apart."

At that moment a gaggle of leggy, teenaged Nipponese students descended upon us. Hung overall with cameras and sketch-blocks, writing-pads, sandwiches and multicoloured carrier bags, they thronged around us like a lynching mob, babbling and chattering in a language which I, for one, privately believe to be invented on the spot for the confusion of foreigners.

Sammy grabbed frantically at his hat to prevent its being mangled beneath a pair of female tennis shoes whose wearer, camera in hand and quite oblivious of us, leapt on to the seat for an uninterrupted view of the museum behind us. I stared idly up her miniskirt and had an uninterrupted view of her bottle green regulation school knickers. I was surprised that the Japanese wore regulation school knickers.

It was time, I thought, for Sammy and me to leave.

Thrusting the photograph into an inside pocket, I got to my feet, and together we breasted our way through the surge of foreign bodies, almost falling over the working woman's wheelbarrow. She looked at us severely, but when I grinned and Sammy raised his hat, she smiled and waved her broom in friendly fashion.

"Did you see that girl's knickers?" I asked Sammy.

"Girl?" He sounded startled and looked back at the woman in the black apron.

"The girl on the seat. She was wearing green knickers."

He gave me an uncertain sidelong glance which developed into a broad grin and finally into a grainy laugh; he also dug me hard in the ribs, which almost capsized me. It was only when he asked me what the English for *Schlüpfern* was that I realised I had spent most of the morning speaking passably good German.

" 'Knickers,' " I told him, a word which seemed to delight him, for he repeated it several times in a loud voice. I asked him to desist as we passed the Empress Maria Theresa, who was having her photograph taken by a tall, horse-faced English woman with a disconsolate husband at rest against a nearby plinth.

"She's *so* like Queen Victoria," she was saying, peering through her view-finder.

"That's because she was Queen Victoria's grandmother," her husband told her.

"I never knew that," I told him *sotto voce* as I strolled past. He crossed his eyes at me.

"What did that man say?" demanded his wife.

"He said he'd bought himself a new hat, dear."

I glanced over my shoulder. He gave me a huge wink.

CHAPTER TEN

Parting with Sammy at the Hofburg, I loitered through the War Memorial Arch to be met by coachloads of tourists shuffling and clamouring across the Heldenplatz, shepherded and shouted at by a battery of loud-mouthed guides. Appalled by the sheer volume of sound, I stood for a second whilst representatives of most nations of the world, bowed beneath shoulder-bags and plastic bundles of wet-weather wear, tramped doggedly past me deter-mined to "do" Vienna in a day. On the pedestal of Prince Eugene's eques-trian statue a burly American in a Texan hat, irretrievably lost and already the worse for drink, bawled plaintively for someone called Millie.

Vienna was filling up with a vengeance for the coming Spring Festival, which this year, announced the publicity, was celebrating the city's liberation from the Turks. Some people will do anything for a firework display, and the occasion of a Turkish defeat three hundred years ago was, I suppose, as acceptable as most. It was quietly ironic that the group of dusky-looking young athletes who were doing their best to liberate the beleaguered American from his perch wore the Turkish crescent on the breast pockets of their blazers.

The relentlessly surging crowd, hellbent on culture, and bearing me along with it like a leaf on the waters, funnelled its way into the tunnel beneath the Hofburg cupola, and only by dextrous use of elbows and an occasional well-placed knee did I avoid spending the next half hour viewing the State Apartments in the company of an Italian football team. Emerging into the comparatively deserted Michaelerplatz was like coming home after a day of Christmas shopping.

I was in need of rest, refreshment and time to think, so I headed for Demel's, where business appeared to be booming.

I found a corner table, was eyed uncertainly by a couple of pretty young Demelesses, one of whom shied away like a frightened mare, whilst the other, of sterner stuff, took my order and sent me off to choose a cake. While I was in that part of the world I stuck my head through the kitchen door. Everything was in order and humming industriously, with nothing to show for yesterday's unrest. I was about to duck out again when I caught sight of Udo gesticulating loudly into a telephone. He saw me at the same moment and held up a large square hand like a traffic policeman. I slid inside and stood somewhat sheepishly in the doorway; several of the kitchen staff glanced at me with apprehension, their eyes sliding to right and left in search of possible corners of refuge should necessity arise.

Udo finished his conversation, handed the telephone to a passing minion and bore down upon me with a smile. Around his neck he wore a looped scarf of dramatic red silk which I assumed to be a sling but which was unoccupied at the moment owing to the fact that the hand it should have housed was outstretched in my direction.

"You are still alive," I greeted him, my grin petrifying as he crunched my living hand in his.

"Nothing serious," he said, tucking his hand nevertheless into the red silk sling. "How do I look?"

"Like Nelson."

"Nelson who?" He frowned. "Eddy?"

"How is Wolfgang?"

"All well. He is home today. X-rays fine. Tomorrow he hobbles back to work—he says."

"What happened about the police?"

"I told them a customer went berserk. They are looking for him."

"And me? What did you tell them about me?"

"You?" He smiled broadly. "Nobody mentioned you. Just Wolfgang and me risk our lives to save the shop. Better, Alicia thinks, you are not—er— entangled with Polizei. Correct?"

"Very correct. Thank you."

He waved aside my gratitude. "I have something for you." With his back to the kitchen staff he unlocked a drawer and produced a gun which looked very like the one I had dropped off the roof the day before. "It smashed my neighbour's greenhouse and wrecked two valuable plants." He gave a wry smile. "He ask me not to do it again." He passed the weapon to me. "Please do not flourish it before the staff." I tucked it into my waistband. He gave me a nod. "You stir up the trouble. I think perhaps you have not seen its end yet." The telephone rang; he stepped over to it. "I see you. Take coffee before you go . . . *Wiedersehen* . . ." He picked up the phone. "Mark . . ." I turned. "How is Alicia?"

I shrugged. "She did too much yesterday. Today she is staying in bed."

He nodded, frowning. "Keep her there," he said, and raised a hand in farewell.

It was only when I was searching for the odd hundred-schilling note to pay the bill at Demel's that I found the message in the right-hand pocket of my jacket. Yellow-tinted paper, folded, with the words *"Mölker Bastei. 22 Uhr. Allein"* written in capitals with a ball-point pen. No signature, no date.

Had my performance in *The Case of the Missing Diamond Merchant* been anything other than it was, I would have said that I was slipping; it was just another example of Homer on the nod. I took comfort from the fact that had the note been parked on me during the struggle through the tourist horde at the Hofburg, then Argus himself wouldn't have noticed it. If it had happened anywhere else during the morning, then I was ready to hang up my deerstalker.

I smoothed out the paper on the table, stared at it intently and peered closely at the reverse side for all those clues which people like me look for and never find. I was to be at Mölker Bastei at ten o'clock. Alone.

I remember thinking quite irritably that Ludwig van Beethoven was fast becoming my own personal *Doppelgänger*. Unsurprisingly Mölker Bastei had been one of *his* hangouts. In the thirty-five years he had lived in Vienna, he'd had no less than thirty-three different addresses—seventy-one if you care to include the thirty-six summer bolt-holes on the outskirts of the city. So a plaque on the wall which said that L.v.B. had lived there was news to nobody; what he did there was much more important—apart from being thrown out by the landlord for dirty habits and making too much noise. Number 8 Mölker Bastei was where he had written his third symphony, one of the *Leonoras* and thought a lot about *Fidelio*.

"Alone," said the note succinctly.

I was beginning to wish I had not been quite so headstrong. A man could get hurt that way. A man could get killed.

I thought of the smooth little man with the blue flower in his buttonhole who wouldn't be averse to a return match; and the one in the dark glasses and the blazer, the one who lived in a pigsty; he was probably sorting through his drawer of offensive weapons at this very moment, mooning and crooning over their destructive merits. Were I in his shoes, I would be tempted to bring the lot. Then of course there was the gorilla whose hand Alice had incapacitated.

Which brought me to timely consideration of my own defences. There was of course no shortage of guns; in Vienna they grew on trees. I had one in my waistband, another in my overnight bag; Alice had a Beholla tucked away in the drawer of her bedside table which she would surely hire out. On the other hand, the first thing they would do on my arrival at the rendezvous would be to turn me upside down and shake me to see what fell out. I needed something small and sharp which wouldn't fall out of anything.

On the spur of the moment I decided to look in on Laverne Wayne. He was an American. He would know all about devious weapons; he would have seen all the films and with a name like Wayne would surely know how to use them.

He was something of a disappointment. He didn't even possess a gun. He looked at me as if I were something slightly vulgar when I asked him what means of self-defence he had at his disposal.

He wandered into his kitchen—an enormously glittering affair full of chrome and porcelain with everything fitted and fitting like a television advertisement—and drawing open a drawer with one effortless finger, disclosed a collection of slim silver meat skewers dating back to the days when barons meant meat as well as elderly gentry. I didn't even know what they were until he told me. They looked like stilettos; each was more than a foot long with a flat blade narrowing to a nasty point; where the hilt should have been was a round hole into which, presumably, you stuck your finger to pull the thing out of the baron—the meat variety, of course. I was greatly taken by them and wondered whether it would be worth borrowing one to stick down my sock. He had nothing else to offer other than an alarming selection of carving knives and kitchen forks, none of which appealed to me. Of blunt instruments he had none.

Over a splendid green salad and a bottle of cool Italian wine, I told him of my escapade the previous night. He seemed as delighted as Alice had been and wished he had been there. I also gave him a quick run-down of the events of the morning and why I was now on the look-out for lethal weapons. When I showed him the note from the enemy, he did exactly what I had done—read it through several times, looked at the back, held it up to the light, he even sniffed at it for some reason. It obviously told him nothing more than it had told me. He returned it reluctantly.

"I think I should come with you."

"It says '*allein.*' "

"No one expects such instructions to be complied with."

"I do."

"They'll never see me," he persisted. "I'll merge into the background and not show myself until you send up a distress rocket."

I grinned at him. "We're fresh out of distress rockets," I drawled in American. "No, Verne, thanks all the same, but forget it. *My* pigeon, not yours— I'm the one who's being paid. Ring me up at Auntie's in the morning; if I'm not there, I'll be on the missing list and a search party will be appreciated."

"You could be at the bottom of the Kanal."

"Then tell 'em to wear their wet-suits."

As a climax to the performance I then produced the photograph and slid it over to him, watching him closely.

He stared at it for a long time in complete silence, his face expressionless. "This is Alice's Lorenz?" he asked at last. He raised his head. I nodded. "What happened to his eye?"

"Nobody knows."

His eyes returned to the photograph. "I see nothing of Alice there." I made no comment. He placed a hand over the lower half of the picture. I waited. Again he raised his head, slowly, examining my face minutely through narrowed eyes. "Curious . . ." he murmured. Still I said nothing. "The wound has disfigured the left brow . . . If it hadn't, the upper half of the face . . . there's something of you there. Do you see it?"

After a moment I said, "Sammy pointed it out."

"Do *you* see it?"

I said reluctantly, "It occurred to me that there was some—resemblance to my father, somewhere . . ."

I had the odd feeling that he was holding himself in; when I saw his eyes again, I was baffled by the expression in them: distress, despair, a sadness— defeat even . . . they were all there interlocked, confused, inseparable. "He could in fact be Lorenz?" he said quietly.

I didn't answer that. I sat staring at my plate wondering about that expression.

Then abruptly I picked up the photograph and stowed it away.

"May I borrow one of your skewers?"

"Pardon me?" I repeated the question. "Oh yes, surely." I watched him make an effort to throw off his preoccupation. "But be careful, will you, as a favour to me, huh? Please don't use it unless you have to; I would just hate to have you on my conscience either as killer or victim, okay? Remember it was I who prompted Alice to send for you."

After lunch I trailed after him to the kitchen, where I selected a likely-looking skewer. "I shall tape it about my person," I told him. He looked amused and disbelieving. "If you know what I mean," I added with a grin.

In his bathroom just before I departed, I ran down his pungent aftershave lotion. It was called Ikon and was emerald-green in a phallic-shaped atomizer. I resisted the temptation to give myself a quick squirt.

At his front door I made Wayne lay his hand on his heart and promise not to lurk uninvited around the Mölker Bastei that night.

"Take care," he said, giving me an avuncular pat on the shoulder.
I gave him fervent assurance that I would.

*   *   *

I was peering at the photographs outside the Opera House when a shapely
fingernail was placed carefully on the protective glass six inches from my
nose. "There," said a hoarse voice in my ear, "there I am." It was Hedda
wearing a grey fur hat and a smile. I narrowed my eyes at the amorphous blob
of pink and white she had indicated and shook my head. "You're very small."

"It's a very small part."

I turned to her. She looked delectable—Garbo in *Anna Karenina.* "Are
you snooping on me?"

"I've just been let out. I've been rehearsing. Saw you worrying over the
pictures and thought I might help." She smiled. "What are you up to—apart
from staring at photographs? Have you had lunch? Why don't I take you to
some low dive for a snack?"

I explained about the green salad with Verne but said a low dive might be
nice. She considered for a moment, then said, "Why don't we settle for
Vienna in the park? Tea and cakes on the terrace with Strauss and Lehar.
Would that do? The Kursalon. Silly and romantic but better than a dive."

She linked her arm through mine and drew me away, stopping again to ask
abruptly, "Or are you in the middle of detecting something?"

When I shook my head, we were off again and plunging down an escalator
before I could draw breath. Battling our way through the crowded
Opernpassage and making for the escalator that led up to the Kärntnerring,
she held on to me tightly—an unexpected and rewarding experience. This
was a different Hedda from the one in the music room yesterday, not exactly
a clinging Hedda, but one in search of companionship and conversation.

The Kursalon terrace was overflowing with tourists, but we ran down a
vacant table, ordered tea and flagged down an itinerant waitress supervising a
trolley-load of delectable-looking pastries. The orchestra was pounding out
Strauss's *Voices of Spring,* God appeared to be in his somewhat murky
Heaven and all was suddenly very right with the world.

I watched her face animated in conversation, the smile ready on her lips,
the elongated eyes always on the brink of laughter. It seemed to me that we
became drunk on tea and cakes, for suddenly we were holding hands across
the table, our bodies swaying stupidly to the gentle rhythm of the waltzes.

"How was Verne?" she asked suddenly.

I made a face. "Aching to be in on all this, but I'm doing my best to fend
him off—I'd sooner be on my own. And," I followed up, "how was Alice?
When I left you together in the music room, I had the feeling my slip was
showing."

She gave me a quirky smile. "Your Aunt Alice thinks you and I should get
married."

"My Aunt Alice is a busybody," I grinned, and stared at the back of her hand for a couple of minutes.

She smirked. "She probably just wants to keep the diamonds in the family."

"Very like, very like."

The cry of a peacock screeched like a warning above the orchestra. The huge bird was preening itself on the terrace behind Hedda. I watched it for a second in silence, then said, "I imagine she's tied all that up neatly in her will?"

"Verne will have seen to that. He's her executor. He won't have left anything to chance."

"If Lorenz turns up, there'll have to be some hefty rejigging in that quarter. She won't have any time to let the grass grow under her feet. Still, that's not our problem, is it?"

Our problem took the opportunity at that moment to lour over me. The photograph of her lolling at a table in the company of Hans Schmidt was burning a fair-sized hole in my pocket. I toyed with the idea of producing it and demanding an explanation but in the light of the coming evening's escapade resisted the temptation—such a revelation might well capsize the boat. Later, perhaps . . . *domani* . . . If she was on their side, she would know about ten o'clock at Mölker Bastei anyway.

I met her eyes, grave and quizzical. *"Have* we a problem?" she asked quietly.

I gave her a sheepish grin and shrugged. "Ideologically I suppose we have, but don't let's start that again and spoil a perfectly good afternoon."

She smiled. "Politics and religion should never come between friends."

"But always do."

She nodded. "It won't happen again, I promise. As I said, I wasn't even born—and neither were you."

I stared into her long dark eyes, the grey fur hat perched like a pillbox jauntily over one of them belying their gravity. The orchestra was playing something lurchingly romantic, the chestnuts were in blossom, the grass was green and tulips nodded brightly through the trees. It would all be so easy . . .

"Another cake?" I asked.

Glancing at her watch, she shook her head. "I must away. I'm due back. I have a fitting at four. At the theatre. We could stroll back if you're game?"

I signed to the waiter, plunged my hand into an inside pocket for money and speared my finger on the point of Verne's meat skewer, which I had stupidly stood upright in the pocket for want of somewhere better to put it. I sucked diligently at the finger and wrapped a clean paper napkin around it. "I've drawn blood," I said before she could mention it. "A lethal fountain pen I keep in there. It's always biting me."

Another reminder that dalliance was not to be the order of the day. I shivered with sudden chill.

She went off to the *Damen.* Loitering in her wake, I browsed among the merchandise of a souvenir stall tucked into a corner of the building and bought her a blue silk scarf printed with pictures of the Spanish Riding School. I wondered if she liked horses. She seemed delighted with it and folded it with a hint of sensuality about her throat inside her coat. Her lips were cold on my cheek.

As we strolled away from the park hand in hand, the distant orchestra launched into yet another Strauss waltz—there was no end to them.

"Which one is that?" I asked after a moment of trying to place it.

We walked in step as she listened and considered. Eventually she said, *"Wiener Blut."*

*   *   *

The doctor was with Alice when I returned to *chez* Sternberg. Emily had decided he ought to take a look at her. "She seemed so spent last night." She looked at me accusingly as if it were my fault—which of course it was.

I talked to the doctor. He was a gentle, sloe-eyed, bearded individual who looked like every film producer's idea of a psychiatrist. He had obviously given up worrying about his operatic patient years ago and was clearly puzzled by her continued existence. "She should remain quiet and unexcited," he told me with a doubtful shrug of his shoulders. "I have learned to expect nothing from her other than disobedience." My heart bled for him. "Perhaps you," he added, "as a close relative may have some influence." He hurried on as he saw my face begin to open up. "Do your best," he said in a high panic-stricken voice, "that's all anyone can ask. Eighty-four's no age nowadays; she could live another ten years; she could live to be a hundred. On the other hand . . ." He stopped on his way to the front door, peered up at the enormous picture of Tosca towering over him from the wall and gave a visible shudder. "This is a corridor of ghosts," he muttered, then went on with his previous thought. "On the other hand, she could go tomorrow—just like that," and he snapped his fingers the way they do. Pausing at the front door for a rethink, he said, "This afternoon she could go." I snapped my fingers enquiringly. He nodded, hesitated, frowned at me suspiciously and departed bearing his black bag before him like a badge of office.

She didn't look at all well, I had to admit. When I tapped my way cautiously into her bedroom, her eyes were closed and to all intents and purposes she was fast asleep; I was about to withdraw when she told me to come in and close the door. She hadn't even looked at me. Perhaps I too carried my own peculiar scent around with me, like Verne Wayne.

"Come and sit," she said. "I won't keep you long . . . just a few minutes." I pulled up a chair. "News?" she asked.

"None."

She gave a single resigned nod. "I ask the impossible."

I put a hand on hers. "You mustn't give up hope."

The heavy lids lifted for a brief moment, the eyes weary and unfocussed;

they fixed themselves finally on my face. "Don't think harshly of me, Mark dear, will you?" She smiled, patting my hand gently. "Diamond smugglers are not freebooters, you know. Nor yet pirates. We have incomparable taste. When I die, the whole thing will die with me anyway; it's all tied up in my will . . ." Her eyes drifted away; she forced them back again. "Dear Mark, I have as yet made no provision for you—except of course you are to have one of my pictures; the Salome, we said, didn't we—but you shall not go unrewarded, I promise." She frowned at me with sudden mock severity. "How, I wonder, have we managed to avoid each other all these years? We could have become such wicked friends . . ." Her voice trailed off into a whisper.

Her eyes were smiling, but a large tear coursed down her cheek. "Sometimes I wish it were all to do again. But then one became so weary of it all, and so—panic-stricken, especially towards the end when one began to reach for the notes instead of looking down at them." Her eyes were now quite bright. "That's when you know it's time to hang up your tiara . . ."

"And concentrate on smuggling," I added with a smirk.

She gave a faint snort. "I've been smuggling for fifty years *and* enjoyed every minute of it. It's a great life. I just hope I'll be able to pull the wool over old St. Peter's eyes when and if ever I get up there; he'll be the first and only customs' official I'll not be able to flirt with."

"You tell him he's going to have to wait a bit," I told her firmly. "The doctor says you could battle on for another ten years."

"Then he's an idiot. And if you believe him, so are you. Good heavens, another ten years of this would kill me."

Suddenly she gripped my hand tightly and I wondered again at the strength in those tiny hands. "Give me some good news about Lorenz and I'll leave you in peace—quite happily."

For a few seconds I was sorely tempted to show her the photograph of Lorenz. She had every right to see it. After all, the identification of the man in the picture was the whole purpose of the exercise.

I pulled myself up. The whole purpose was to bring Lorenz here to this room in person and stand him before her, alive and well. What happened after that would be up to the pair of them. If he were her son, there would be no difficulty in proving it. If he weren't . . . Could he hoodwink her into believing that he was? If he'd prepared the ground and knew his lines, yes. She was a rich woman on the point of death; a new will could be drawn up in a matter of minutes; he could inherit all she had. If that was his objective, why hadn't he come before, years ago? Why hadn't he come two weeks ago, after he had slipped the Israeli hook? And if he couldn't make it in person, what in hell was wrong with the telephone? "Hello, Mum, this is Lorenz . . ." So simple. If he were genuine, it would have been the natural thing to do; if he were false, and after her money, the most obvious; essential if he was to get at her while she was still capable of altering her will.

"What are you thinking?" Her pale eyes were watching me intently.

I let out a great theatrical sigh. "I was just wishing I could be of more help.

However, tonight I'm meeting some people who might throw some light on the subject. Apropos of which," I added, producing the Walther from my waistband, "I wonder if you'd be willing to trade in your little Beholla for my Walther. I need something smaller, something I can tape to the inside of my leg if need be. How about it?"

She took it like a man. "Will it be that dangerous?"

I shrugged. "Could be. I'm going on a sort of pocket Battle of Balaclava, charging the enemy's guns and all that, and I'd just like to have a trick or two up my trouser-leg, that's all. Everyone of them humps a gun around; I'd just hate to be the odd man out." I was weighing the little Beholla in my hand.

"It's loaded," she warned. "And if you have to use it, get in close; it's only a .22."

I placed the Walther in her drawer. "That," I told her, "is also loaded." I grinned broadly. "Most people wouldn't believe this conversation between a great aunt and her nephew." I leaned in and kissed her cheek. " 'Bye for now."

"Stay out of danger, won't you?" Her cold finger touched my hand. "You are my responsibility; you will try to remember that, won't you?"

I winked at her. "Not to worry. I'm the original coward." When I turned at the door to take a last look at her, she was staring at me wide-eyed as if expecting never to see me again. Then she fluttered her fingers and smiled brightly and the moment was gone.

CHAPTER ELEVEN

They were there before me. I was early, but they had already tucked themselves away in the woodwork—two of them, one at the upper end of the Mölker Bastei in the doorway of the house on the corner, the other some way down towards the steps. On my arrival I had walked the short length of the street pinpointing their whereabouts; my hair had pinged like asdic as I had passed through their particular fields; I could almost smell them. They made no effort to show themselves.

It didn't bother me; if they wanted to play games, that was their business.

What did bother me was the weather. The rain which had threatened most of the day had finally decided to let itself go; it was a drizzle rather than a downpour, but beyond the spires of the Votivkirche the horizon flickered and muttered like distant gunfire, presaging a storm.

I hunched myself damply into what little shelter the doorway of the Pasqualati House, Number 8, afforded and spent the time imagining the burly figure of L.v.B. stumping noisily through that very doorway after a night on the tiles and up to the fourth floor where he had lived, pausing on each landing to try out the early drafts of his *Eroica* Symphony on the shrinking ear-drums of his neighbours.

Opposite loomed the bulk of the university, a few lights still burning in its windows; below and out of sight beyond the rampart walls, the never ceasing traffic rattled and rolled along the Dr. Karl Lueger Ring.

I listened to the clocks striking ten.

The temperature had dropped considerably and was now somewhere in the middle forties. I was beginning to freeze. It would have been comforting to stamp my feet to bring some life back into them; I didn't because of the pound and a half of Beholla pistol taped to the inside of my left thigh; the tape was easing the hairs out of my leg one by one; further down on the other leg, just below my right knee and inside my sock, Laverne Wayne's meat skewer was also taped.

The Luger stolen from Trautsohngasse the night before was stuck into my waistband; when they found that, maybe they wouldn't look any further. A hand-grenade would have been nice.

The soft scuff of approaching feet—I leaned back against the door and looked nonchalant—like I was half asleep.

A figure, hands thrust into the pockets of a glistening waterproof, hove up and stood silently in the rain. My heart sank. His rainwear wasn't the only thing that glistened: the dark glasses gleamed as if there were light behind them. Hans Schmidt, the owner of the Luger, he with the drawerful of thumbscrews and knuckledusters. A second later the other appeared, a tall black silhouette in a black hat and a long overcoat.

"And about bloody time," I growled in English. In German I said, "You're late."

Neither of them seemed to care about that; they closed in on me quietly, and whilst the silhouette held my arms away from my body, Hans frisked me inexpertly, giving me an almighty jab in the groin as he did so in part payment for last night's escapade; I can't say I blamed him.

He found the Luger, of course, checked to see that it was loaded and rammed that, too, playfully into my crutch. I had the sick feeling for a split second that he contemplated squeezing the trigger. For fun. He looked up saucily, the glasses glinting with amusement.

"Later, pretty boy," he promised in a voice which sounded like Donald Duck's.

In his excitement he missed both the Beholla and the meat skewer, an oversight, I thought nastily, he might well live to regret.

He jerked the Luger at me. *"Komm,"* he snarled.

"Listen, meathead," I said before everything got out of hand. "I'm here of my own free will, so you can stick that thing up your jaxey or I shan't come at all. Understand?" I didn't know the German for "jaxey," so I used *Arschloch* instead, which was worth twice as much and went down quite well. I thought he was going to hit me, but the raised gun was caught by his colleague, who told him in a grumbly sort of voice that there would be plenty of time for that sort of thing.

They shepherded me to the upper corner of Mölker Bastei and down the cobbled alley-way to the steps, Hans rustling ahead in his gleaming raincoat, the black silhouette bringing up the rear. I turned my head. "I didn't quite catch your name," I said, not expecting an answer. He replied quite civilly, "Johannes Brahms." It was like me saying I was Edward Elgar.

I let it go.

In Schottengasse awaited the grey VW. Johannes Brahms clambered into the driver's seat, leaving me to share the back with his friend, who, divesting himself of his mackintosh, settled himself beside me, the Luger, buried in the wet folds of the waterproof, pointing resolutely at my stomach.

Brahms sorted out his boxful of gears, and we jerked off into the night, the windscreen wipers making nearly as much noise as the engine. I glanced at my watch: 10:12. We turned right into the last remaining section of the Ring, heading towards the Kanal.

"Incidentally, Hans," I said, staring mildly into his glasses, which flashed on and off like morse code signals as the street lighting sped by, "I have several of your belongings at home. If you'd be good enough to drop me off on the way back, I'll let you have them: couple of letters, walkie-talkie, and of course your Nazi badge. No good Nazi should be out after dark without his badge."

Any excesses he might have been contemplating were cut short by Johannes Brahms swinging the car left into Franz Josefs Kai and muttering something I didn't catch over his shoulder. Next minute the wet raincoat was flung over my head and I couldn't see a bloody thing. I put up a bit of a struggle, but he jammed the Luger hard into my ribs and with his other hand twisted the coat around my throat. I felt the car turn abruptly to the right, which meant the Augarten Bridge, across the Kanal.

"I can't breathe under this bloody thing," I complained loudly. "Haven't you got a blindfold or something, for God's sake?"

Another jab with the gun and a slight loosening of the rubbery folds; I wriggled around for a second or two and came up with an unexpected air hole; my head was stuck halfway up the armhole, my nose and mouth close to the underarm vents; not a situation to be recommended, but at least I could breathe, and if I narrowed my left eye, I could almost see what was going on outside. So I cut my losses, ceased my complaints and watched the lights going by, picking up the sounds of the night traffic and the occasional homely clang of a tram bell.

Vienna this side of the Kanal was a closed book to me. All I knew was that we were moving in the general direction of the Danube, a river I hadn't trusted since discovering that it was precisely the same colour as Old Father Thames—a sludge brown.

A few minutes later I became aware of the clink and clank of trains, hysterical toots, slamming of doors, public address announcements, and smooth metal wheels rolling on steel rails. A large terminus. There was only one such in these parts: the Nordwest Bahnhof, little more than half a mile from the Danube. The announcements were in gobbledygook and didn't tell me anything; like railway station announcements the world over they were intended only to keep passengers on their toes.

Johannes took an abrupt turn to the right into a side street, murkier and without traffic; fifty yards or so, another turn, this time to the left, and into what was obviously a garage. The squeal of brakes, the headlights dowsed and the engine stilled. Complete darkness. Above the soft ticking of hot metal I heard the mournful baying of a ship's siren. The Danube. We were somewhere between the station and the Danube. I would later be able to pinpoint the place to within a square half mile.

My thoughts wandered wistfully over the possibility of Verne Wayne betraying his hand-on-heart promise not to tail me from Mölker Bastei, but I couldn't think of any reason why he should. A heavy hand was laid on me with the intent of bundling me out of the car. I threw it off, tore the raincoat from my head and inadvertently kicked someone in a sensitive spot. The snarl of displeasure came from Hans' lips, then he was on me like a maddened animal, clawing at my face in his effort to get at my eyes and throat. He was as fed up with me as I was with him.

"For Christ's sake," I yelled in English, grabbing at his hands. "It was an accident, you stupid sod."

I didn't know what had happened to his gun; he didn't have it with him and I wouldn't have cared even if he had; I could take him easily—in the dark and the confined space he was a piece of cake. I jockeyed him into some sort of position, and when I was ready gave him everything I'd got with my left knee; as he fell backwards through the open door, I jabbed at his throat with the extended fingers of my right hand. Something went; I suspect it was his larynx; it felt nasty, but by the time I had regretted the attack, it was too late and I had stumbled back into the car, discovering the whereabouts of his fallen gun as it dug itself into my left hip.

Someone touched a switch and there was light. I shut my eyes against it, scrabbling crazily for the Luger beneath me. When I opened them again, I was looking down the barrel of yet another gun, a black-gloved finger on its trigger. Framed in the doorway, and straddling the stricken Hans on the floor of the garage, loomed Johannes. Except for the glitter of the eyes beneath the brim of his hat, he was still no more than a featureless silhouette. The gun was less than a foot from my face, much too close. On the other hand, he had no room to manoeuvre; half in and half out of the door, with a blank brick wall immediately behind him and Hans bubbling and thrashing about

on the floor between his legs, he was sufficiently *distrait* for me to risk a
follow-up. My left hand had closed over the barrel of the Luger beneath me.

"Out!" he yelped. As he began edging his bulk out of the car, I brought
the Luger up with all the force I could muster. Its butt struck the barrel of
his gun. I felt the heat of the explosion, saw the flame, heard the bullet
ripping through the roof of the car and thud into the ceiling. Worst of all was
the blast. My ear-drums gave up. I was quite deaf as I wrestled myself from
the floor, twisted on to my knees and, before he could recover himself, butted
him hard in the stomach with my head. Off balance, he staggered back and
splayed himself against the wall; his head thudded sickeningly on the
brickwork. He slid, senseless, down the wall, hat tipping slowly over his eyes
and covering his face as if he were already dead.

I clawed my way out of the car, choking in the heavy fumes. Waves of
sound pulsed painfully into my ears. I felt suddenly and overpoweringly ill.
Unerringly, and again inadvertently, I planted my foot on one of Hans'
thrashing limbs. The sound he made was straight out of a horror movie.

With a muttered apology I lurched drunkenly on to the wall, dislodging as
I did so the sleeping Johannes, whose hat slid slowly from his face and
toppled into his lap. Propped against the wall, I stood and stared at the lolling
body with blank-eyed disbelief.

It wasn't Johannes Brahms I had clobbered. It was Verne Wayne.

CHAPTER TWELVE

I didn't have a lot of time to mull over the revelation—a couple of seconds
perhaps, no more; then two ominous metallic clicks from behind added
themselves to my already badly shaken status quo. I knew what the clicks
were before I turned, still holding the wall up. The twin black eyes of the
double-barrelled shotgun stared back at me with unflinching malignity.

Rule One of the Private Investigator's Handbook of Practical Detection:
Never tangle with a double-barrelled shotgun.

I squinted stoically over the barrels into the eyes of the man who wielded
them; they were almost as close-set as those of his weapon, twice as mean and
were the least savoury features in a wholly unsavoury ham-sized face I had
seen before. I checked on the grubbily bandaged right hand and the general
contours of the gargantuan edifice which stood on a couple of steps in an
open doorway. My heart sank to a new low. Even in my distracted state of

mind I could see that he bore a grudge which weighed heavily on him. I eyed the bandaged hand which supported the cumbersome weapon; the left hand looked awkward on the triggers.

Rule Two of the P.I.'s Handbook: *Never ever tangle with a double-barrelled shotgun.*

"Hello again," I greeted him in English, smiling glassily through clenched teeth and leaning heavily against the wall because I wasn't sure I could do without it. Behind me Hans, gurgling loudly and making odd bubbling noises, was making a sterling effort to get to his feet. I half turned to keep him in my eyeline; larynx or no larynx, he still had hands and feet.

He had mislaid his dark glasses—as a matter of fact he had fallen on them and smashed them—and for the first time I was able to see his eyes, pale blue, red-rimmed and full of tears. He looked curiously immature and rudderless. I almost felt sorry for him. I braced myself as he stepped over the supine figure of my erstwhile friend, but so concerned was he with his own troubles that he passed me by with barely a glance, stumbled up the steps, shoved past Gorilla Face and disappeared into the house. The second or so when his body had stood between me and the twin barrels was the second or so when any P.I. worthy of his hire would have leapt forward, stormed the gun, smashed the Gorilla's face in and made a break for it. Fortunately I hadn't a leap left in me. Not even Action Man could have done it, and if he had, they'd have scraped him off the walls.

Those mean little eyes had never left mine, the gun barrels never wavered; he would have had no scruples about shooting through Hans to get at me.

With an elbow he poked awkwardly at a button alongside the light switch; a click and a whine; I turned my head to see a heavy steel shutter sliding down smoothly behind the car to seal us off from the outside world.

Apart from the slightly exotic shutter, we were in an ordinary-looking suburban-type garage wide enough for one car, long enough for two; at the far end stood a motor bike on its stand and an untidy work-bench cluttered with tools. To the left of the bench was the door and the goon with the gun.

As my eyes returned to him, he jerked his head and said something unintelligible in a gravelly voice. I indicated the prostrate Wayne. "Shouldn't we do something about him?"

He repeated what he had said before, this time more forcibly, with an additional and unmistakable gesture of the gun. He then made me stick my hands in the air like they do in the movies, which made me feel slightly foolish and theatrical.

As I shoved myself off the wall and moved towards him, he backed away warily towards the bench to give me airspace. He should have stayed where he was; the smell he gave off was on a direct pipeline to the zoo. I found myself longing for a whiff of Verne Wayne's Ikon, a thought which brought me up with a jolt. The Oversight Deliberate—and sneaky at that. He hadn't been wearing Ikon tonight. If he had, I'd have been on to him way back at Mölker Bastei and he knew it. He was no mean operator, I thought sourly.

On the move again I realised the Beholla, taped to the inside of my left thigh, was now hanging on by a few remaining short hairs. The pain was excruciating, each step removing another hair with the exquisite precision of a Chinese torture. "Don't worry about me," I told Gorilla Face as I limped past, "it's just the way I walk."

The door led into a dimly lit, deeply carpeted passage with angry-looking red walls offset by white paintwork. The double-barrelled gun prompted my progress every so often, so I went willingly enough until we came to a staircase which I negotiated one step at a time for fear of dislodging the Beholla altogether.

"Would you allow me to visit your lavatory?" I asked in German as I found my way upwards. I was thinking more of the necessity of retaping the gun to my leg than of any personal needs. He didn't understand German either, so I tried him with French; that too fell on stony ground. I didn't try Hungarian because the only words of Hungarian I know are Zoltán Kodály and Béla Bartók, and they wouldn't have helped. "You'll be sorry," I said in English, "when I piss all over your carpet."

There was no time for more. We had arrived.

The room on the first floor into which he shepherded me was the brainchild of a twenty-first-century cubist; polished steel, green glass and gleaming Perspex dazzled the eye; every surface, shape and object was rectangular. Until I walked into that room, I never realised how soothing a curve could be. I longed for an arch, a crescent, a bend or a parabola—anything spherical, round, hoop-shaped—a football even, and it's not often I long for a football. The nearest thing to a football was the head of the man behind the rectangular desk in the middle of the rectangular white carpet, which is probably why my distracted eyes almost immediately came to rest on it. The head was more pear-shaped than spherical and quite bald, but it was comforting to look at. I was sure that as time went by I would find it less comforting, but for the moment I was prepared to settle for it.

"Herr Savage," said the head with the slightest of inclinations, "you are welcome."

The greeting, in perfect English, was as clinically devoid of welcome as his surroundings were of spheres. "Please sit," he added, indicating the visitor's chair opposite the desk.

He got rid of Gorilla Face with an abrupt and dismissive gesture. I heard the heavy thump of feet over carpet and registered the slight hiss as the door closed stealthily behind him. Another steel door. The silence was intense. The eyes which regarded me with a certain amount of quizzical curiosity were the sort of eyes which I might have expected from the villain of the piece—hooded and dark, with lazy lids doing their best to keep themselves open.

Waiting for me to sit, he whiled away the time by measuring his green glass blotter with a Perspex ruler; he went on quietly, "You are an imprudent young man, Mr. Savage. Your performance in the garage was altogether worthy of the late Mark Sutherland." He touched a switch.

Three television sets placed at strategic points of the room flickered and glowed. I was treated to a private showing of that performance in colour and in triplicate from the moment I hurtled out of the car head first into Verne Wayne's stomach to the closing scene as I limped past Gorilla Face with the immortal words "Don't worry about me, it's just the way I walk."

The screen went blank.

"Mark Sutherland's agent," I told him drily, "would object to an appearance on 'Candid Camera' without a contract."

My eyes roved inquisitively about the room. The walls were pale green and quite restful to the eye. A door which glinted a little, I thought, was situated immediately opposite me; there appeared to be no windows, but I was willing to believe they were steel-shuttered and visible only during the day. I registered a couple of video recorders, tape decks, a cassette player, amplifiers, speakers, a compact-looking computer and other electronic equipment I didn't know about. Four shelves running the full length of the right wall groaned beneath the weight of literally hundreds of pre-recorded commercial video cassettes, many of whose titles I could read from where I sat—*The Godfather, Death Wish, The Omen, Friday the Thirteenth, The Damned* . . .

He pressed another button. Again the screens glowed. I sat stonily in my glass chair and watched myself in a scene from one of the movies I'd made for Andrew Elliot back in the seventies, *Cry Havoc!*—violent, sadistic and at one moment quite sickening, all in the cause of King and Country.

I hated watching myself on the screen. It was like opening up a can of worms. "I didn't come here to watch old movies," I said abruptly.

The screens became dark. "What *did* you come for, Herr Savage?"

I stared at him. "May I use your toilet? All that running about—you know?"

He smiled. "The door behind me. The bathroom is to your left."

At the door I asked, "Do you have a camera in there too?" I didn't wait for a reply; I noticed in passing that the door was steel.

The bathroom was grand and pink with gilt fittings—tasteless and horrid. I peered around for a prying lens, made a face in the mirror in case there was one behind it, then, dropping my pants, I released the gun, tore off the sticking plaster and seemed to remove most of my suffering leg with it. I left the skewer where it was—there were even more hairs down there—and tucked the gun into my waistband at the small of my back.

Outside the bathroom door once again I paused for a second listening. Where dead silence had been before, I could now hear the faintest wailing of music, laughter and the chatter of voices, also the unmistakable pop of a champagne cork, coming, it seemed, from beneath my feet.

I leant against the wall and did up a shoe-lace, ears straining to isolate the various sounds. The music had a rhythm to it—not the ubiquitous Viennese waltz—one instrument predominating. What the hell was it? A zither? Less strident than a zither . . . the strings struck with a hammer rather than plucked.

Someone closed a door somewhere; I stood in utter silence; I had heard enough. I knew exactly where I was. The wailing violins, voices, champagne corks; a restaurant. The instrument was the cymbalom, as unique to Hungary as bagpipes were to Scotland. *The Kekszakallu.*

Somewhat smugly I returned to the steel keep of Bluebeard's Castle to find Bluebeard himself sitting motionless, waiting for me, just as I had left him. I settled into my glass chair nodding affably at the placid face opposite.

He was a slim loose-framed man in or about his middle sixties. The face had interesting features if not particularly good, the most impressive being the deep-set watchful eyes; the nose was Wagnerian, overhanging a lipless mouth; the unusually heavy jowls gave his head the pear-shaped look. He wore a white dinner jacket and black tie.

He didn't say, "Hello again," or "Better?" or anything like that. He simply introduced himself. "My name is Stephan Hertz and I am interested to make your acquaintance, Mr. Savage. I was an admirer of your erstwhile histrionic ability; I am less enthusiastic about your current activities. However, you asked for an . . . audience; is that the right word?" When I said nothing, he added, "Whatever you have to say, now is the time to say it."

He clasped his slender hands on the desk before him. I noted the green scarab ring on his right forefinger and wondered whether I ought to offer to kiss it. "Speak," he invited softly.

I gave a resigned sigh. "I am here in Vienna, as you well know, to find someone whom Alicia Sternberg believes to be her son."

"And you believe I know of his whereabouts?"

"I know you don't, otherwise your mob wouldn't always be baying at my heels."

He gave a thin smile. "You make me sound like a gangster."

"Mr. Hertz, I don't give a damn who or what you are. My only concern is to set Madame Sternberg's mind at rest. My motive for sitting at your feet at this moment is to suggest that we save each other time and trouble by combining forces."

"And what shall we do when we find him? Divide him between us?"

I shrugged. "My own brief is simple enough. Is he or is he not Lorenz Sternberg? If and when that is established, you can have him."

"Suppose he turns out to be your cousin?"

"Two days ago I never knew I had a cousin. It won't break my heart to wake up tomorrow and find I still haven't got one. I can probably live without him. From what I gather, he's also wanted by the police, so even if he is my cousin, a happy reunion with his mother is unlikely to be permanent."

He steepled his bony fingers and studied me over them. "You sound remarkably uninvolved. Would you hand him over to the police?"

"If they don't get him, the Israelis will."

"And if neither succeed," he said in a neutral voice, "I will."

The momentary glint of malevolence in the sunken eyes turned my stomach. "You really do want him, don't you?" His head nodded twice. "Is there any point in my asking why?"

He deliberated for a second or two. "He has something of mine."

"Like?"

"One million dollars." It was as if the walls of the room were padded with thick rubber. "At a rough estimate," he added with a half smile, "eighteen and three-quarter million Austrian schillings; sounds more impressive, don't you think?"

"And is he carrying it around with him?"

"For his sake, I hope he is. In cut and polished diamonds." I probably looked disbelieving, for he added, "I think it was your own Ian Fleming who suggested that a man could carry diamonds enough on his naked body to set himself up for life."

"Has this anything to do with my aunt?"

"Why should it concern her?"

"With Verne Wayne as your sidekick you must know she—er—deals in diamonds."

He laid his hands flat on his green blotter and gave them an inscrutable stare. "She *did* deal in diamonds."

"What are you talking about?"

He took a patient breath. He chose his words with fastidious care. "The diamond business is tough and competitive; you are intelligent enough to appreciate that. Madame Sternberg is, I believe, eighty-four years old, and whilst in possession of most of her faculties, her age and uncertain health, to say nothing of the possibility of her sudden and sad demise, has necessitated the need for placing her affairs in, shall we say, more capable hands."

I gaped at him. "Verne Wayne's?"

He repeated his thin smile. "Why not? He has always managed her business affairs."

"And how long have you managed *his?*"

"That's unworthy of you, Mr. Savage. Verne Wayne and I are a partnership. Madame Sternberg has not smuggled a diamond in more than two years."

"Is she aware of that?"

"I imagine not."

I was on my feet and halfway round the desk when the door opened behind me.

"Mark," said a warning voice. I turned. Wayne stood in the doorway, Luger in hand. He was pale and *distrait,* his normally immaculate white hair ruffled; even from where I stood, I could see that his hand trembled a little. The long overcoat hung loosely like a black shroud.

I stared at him for a long still moment. "When did my aunt give you power of attorney?" Clumsily he pushed the door closed behind him. "When?" I repeated.

His eyes shifted uneasily. "We'll talk about it later."

"Now!" I said loudly. "We'll talk about it now." His eyes sought Hertz. "He's not going to help. All he's likely to do is leave you in the shit. And if you can't produce a power of attorney signed by my aunt then you're up to your eyeballs in it already, I promise you that."

"You are in no position to promise anything, Mr. Savage," interrupted Stephan Hertz as if he'd just come out of a doze. "Circumstances being what they are, we have to come to some sort of mutual agreement; otherwise I fail to see how we can possibly allow you to . . . er . . ." He trailed off with a helpless little gesture.

"You mean you'll keep me here?"

He spread reasonable hands. "That will be up to you; as I say, we must try to come to an agreement. And even then we shall require something more than promises; we shall need guarantees."

I glanced at Wayne. His eyes were bloodshot; he was sweating a little. The blow on the back of the head had done him no good at all; he looked as if he might fold up at any moment.

Hertz had just said something and I had missed it. "I'm sorry, would you repeat that?"

The steel of his displeasure flickered like forked lightning in his eyes. "I'm sorry," I said again. "My mind was wandering."

He tucked away his impatience behind hooded lids and leaned back in his chair, hands folded quietly in his lap as if he'd done with me.

I made a face at Wayne, who swayed gently on his feet. I moved in to give him a hand. The gun jerked up. "Oh, put it away, for God's sake," I told him wearily.

"Sit, Verne," snapped Hertz. "Keep him covered."

Verne slumped into the chair vacated by me. For the first time Hertz seemed to realise there might be something seriously wrong with him. "Are you all right?"

Verne nodded.

"He's just had a bang on the head, that's all," I said in a jolly voice. "A touch of the concussions, I shouldn't wonder."

"Be silent."

I was standing to the right of his desk studying his array of switches and buttons with a covert eye. A switchboard at his left hand lay just below the flat surface of the desk and sloped downward at a gentle angle so he didn't have to crane his neck; each button was numbered, each switch labelled. I wasn't near enough to make out any of them. What I did see quite plainly before he snarled at me to sit were the words "Studio I and Studio II." The place was either full of artists or film studios. The surrounding gadgets and video cassettes lining the walls suggested the latter. Did he make his own movies?

I seated myself primly on the chair he had indicated beside his desk; Wayne was on my right. "You are trespassing on private property . . ."

"Excuse me." I held up a mild hand. "I asked for an audience, if you remember. I was then kidnapped and brought here at the point of a gun with a stinking raincoat over my head. If you're afraid of your private property being pried into, you might have arranged a meeting in more public surroundings—like downstairs, for instance, over a glass of champagne. That would have been friendly."

I saw him blench a little as his eyes flicked momentarily to Wayne. "You know where you are?"

I stared at him blandly. "Of course I know where I am. And so does everyone else. That is why it's going to be awkward for you if I fail to turn up at my usual haunts tomorrow."

For the first time he was losing his cool. I enjoyed watching his unease. "*Where* are you?"

I crossed my fingers hoping to God I'd got it right. "Bluebeard's Castle?" I put a question mark on the end.

He turned abruptly to Wayne, and I could sense the cold fury in him as he gave tongue in that guttural gobbledygook I took to be Hungarian.

Wayne answered in the same language; he was no slouch; I tried hard to pick something out of the cacophony, but it was like probing about in undercooked Christmas pudding for a lost threepenny bit. I heard the words "Alicia Sternberg" and another which could have been "Meier" but the jumble of alien sounds isolated nothing with clarity.

Whatever he said was the source of considerable depression for Hertz. He went into his Gloomy Place, the forefinger of his left hand tapping an irritable tattoo on the scarab ring.

A decision arrived as he came back to us. "Do you doubt my ability to keep you incarcerated, Mr. Savage?"

I shrugged. "You know what they say: Steel doors do not a prison make."

His smile was frosty yet encouraging. "What then are the alternatives?"

"First, you could let me go. Second . . ." I hesitated.

"Dispose of you?"

"The very word I was looking for."

I thought for a moment. "To dispose of someone is to admit that that someone is treading on your heels and is a threat to your well-being. But I know nothing about you except that you live surrounded by metal doors and electronic gadgetry. I don't even know whether you can stand up or not—I haven't yet seen you on your feet; for all I know, you could be chair-bound. You don't look dangerous, but then neither did Himmler. And nobody crossed *him* and lived to tell the tale. So it must be your business which is at stake and must be protected; the business which is being part-financed by my great aunt Alice without her knowledge and which is being threatened not only by my poor bumblings but by the disappearance of someone who has a million dollars of yours rattling around loose in his pocket. How's that?"

He nodded slowly. "I'm beginning to wish you were working for me."

"I'd do a lot better than those creepy zombies of yours."

"One more question, Mr. Savage, and then I'm through." He paused, a slow smile wreathing his lipless mouth. "What *is* my business?" He leaned forward, his forearms on the desk, hands clasped.

"You run a successful Hungarian restaurant and night-club called the Kékszákallú."

The smile broadened. "Not against the law."

"I never said it was. What *is* against the law is the business for which the night-club is a front." He waited. "I would say that you, Mr. Hertz, are into the nastier aspects of video; that you are, in fact, a video pirate, distributing your wares throughout Europe and using those same networks through which my aunt and those like her are smuggling their diamonds, drugs, guns and whatever." The smile had gone. He drew a breath. I held up a hand. "I haven't finished yet. Not content with pirating and distributing other people's more sensational and lurid works, you are also into the movie business itself. On these premises you make your own movies—sex, violence, horror, torture, the bluest of blue movies—all things nasty." I smiled at him. "How am I doing?"

He was staring down at his hands; by a trick of the light I could see a pulse thudding away at his temples. If I listened intently, I thought, I would be able to hear it.

I looked at Wayne. Sweat was beading on his forehead. He was looking in my direction; when I smiled at him, there was no reaction. The muzzle of the gun was propped against his left arm, which lay limply in his lap. If it came to the crunch, serious opposition on his part could be discounted.

Hertz stirred, leaned back, hands on the arms of his chair, the left less than six inches from the switchboard; a prod of a finger could call up the cavalry. His smile was almost attractive. "Are your conclusions speculative or do you have concrete evidence of such practices?"

"Oh, speculative, of course."

He went off at a tangent. "Why should you disapprove, I wonder? In the course of your acting career you must surely have been asked to perform roles distasteful to you. The clip I showed you just now, for example, was, I would have thought, highly distasteful. I could name a dozen actors who would have refused to play it."

I nodded. "I'm sure you could. It depends how far any one particular actor is committed, whether he believes that sort of home truth should be made available to the public. Rape and murder happen every day, the nine o'clock news is full of them. If you're making a movie—a quality movie—and the intention and presentation is sincere, then in my opinion such things ought to be included—provided they're not there for sensationalism and for the satisfaction of the wanking brigade. There's nothing explicit in that sequence, is there?"

He was shaking his head slowly. "That, I think, is a dishonest appraisal."

I didn't see his hand move, but once again the television screens flickered into life and again I was treated to the vision of myself, khaki-clad and brutal; the same sequence began to roll. I stirred impatiently and suddenly froze.

What next happened on the screen had never been shot on the studio floor —not the floor I had been on. A large close-up of my own face, a swift cut to that of the girl, then back to the khaki-clad body of someone else, not me, the camera panning slowly from the chest downward without showing the face; hands, not mine, unbuttoning the battle blouse, removing the trouser belt; another cut to the girl tied spread-eagled to the bed, then back to the slowly stripping figure of the soldier, not me, Christ, not me! the trousers about the ankles, underpants, the frontal nudity, obscene and brutal, stark exposure . . .

The screens went dark. "And so it goes on," purred the voice of Hertz. "Blow by blow, every explicit detail from beginning to end—the girl too; nothing barred, all revealed, made with the courage and the honesty your own director lacked. So simple, you see. Just a question of attention to detail, matching studio lighting, backgrounds, clothing and a few willing and immodest actors whose name, alas, is Legion. A few feet of film, selected shots cut into the original and hey presto! Mark Sutherland is endowed with a masculinity he never knew he possessed—though I'm sure the eager ladies of our clandestine audience would not consider it an overstatement of your obvious potential."

I sat as if I had been pole-axed. I should have been smashing his nasty pear-shaped head into a pulp—not just sitting there staring at him, feeling sick.

"You are silent at last, Mr. Savage."

I made a Herculean effort to get myself off my knees. "Is this your idea of blackmail?"

He laughed aloud. "Blackmail? I want nothing from you other than your intelligent understanding of the situation."

"You will prevent that film from being distributed on condition I keep my mouth shut about your set-up here, is that it?"

"My dear boy, that film was distributed months ago; you have been ogled and yearned after in darkened drawing-rooms the world over: 'The previously unscreened, unabridged version of *Cry Havoc!*' They're screaming for it. The world, Mr. Savage, is my oyster. I supply a need." He regarded me for a moment, a playful glint in his eye. "I'll make you an offer."

"The answer is no."

"Work for me."

I was watching him closely. He meant it; I really believe he meant it. He needed my silence that much. Like I needed my life.

I hunched in my chair, ostensibly considering the offer. I flicked a glance at Wayne. His eyes were closed, his head drooping at an odd angle; the gun rested in the same position, but the finger on the trigger was flaccid.

"What do you say?" asked Hertz. There was an air of suppressed excitement about him.

I wagged a doubtful head at him. "I haven't acted in years. I fell off a horse and smashed myself up—I don't have to tell you that, I'm sure. I became a drunk and a junkie. But even so, I never actually enjoyed being a film star; too much effort and not enough privacy. Why should I want to go back to all that?"

"Perhaps because the alternative is even less attractive? My way you will have a new career, money as much as you need, and, not least, your continued good health."

"I need time to think."

He gave a sad shake of his head. "I need an answer."

I looked at Wayne. "He's asleep," I said.

Hertz called his name. He opened his eyes blearily and peered at us. Hertz spoke to him in Hungarian. The glaze cleared slowly from Wayne's eyes; he nodded and listened and nodded again, glancing at me doubtfully a couple of times. He spoke slurringly and with some difficulty, then climbed gingerly to his feet, the gun still in his hand.

Hertz turned to me. "He tells me you are carrying an offensive weapon which belongs to him—a meat skewer. May I have it, please?" My vindictive glare at Wayne fell on stony ground. I slowly rolled up my trouser-leg. There it was, half hidden by my sock and buried in the hairs of my leg. I eased the silver blade gently from its moorings and drew it forth. "I'll hang on to the plaster if you don't mind," I said and placed the skewer on his desk, where it turned green in the light refracted through an ashtray.

He handed it to Wayne, who promptly retreated to the doorway waving the Luger at me in a vague sort of way. No one was prepared to trust me.

Hertz said, "Your answer, Mr. Savage."

I nodded. "Okay. But before I actually put my life on the line, I'd like to see the facilities. Studios, dressing-rooms and so on." For a second I thought he was about to demur. "If I'm going to work for you, I'd like to see what I'm letting myself into."

He and Wayne exchanged glances; Wayne shrugged. Hertz said, "Fair enough, why not?" and rose to his feet. "There, you see," he said with a sunny smile. "I am not chair-bound after all."

I could also see that he packed a gun in a shoulder-holster, only the slightest bulge betraying its presence beneath the dinner jacket, tailored, I was sure, with shoulder-holster in mind. I wondered how quick he was on the draw. For his age he looked pretty trim. He probably did early morning exercises on his executive rowing machine and jogged around the Stadtpark in blue satin shorts and a T-shirt.

He and Wayne exchanged Hungarian words in the course of which Hertz patted his shoulder-holster with affection, suggesting that he was quite capable of looking after himself. Wayne, now slightly more alert, nodded and departed. We watched the steel door close behind him.

I said, "Maybe he should see a doctor."

Hertz gave a lopsided smile. "I shall deduct the bill from your first month's salary. You also damaged young Hans Schmidt, you know, quite considerably; I've had him sent to the hospital. You are a violent man, Mr. Savage."

"When provoked."

"Quite. Come."

Wisely he made me precede him, through the door into the passage where the bathroom was, a further door, up a short flight of steps and into a wide carpeted corridor where several doors stood open. "Dressing-rooms," he said, inviting me to enter one of them. Unlike what I expected, it really did look like a dressing-room; none of your kitchen tables with cracked mirrors propped against the walls. Here was a green carpeted floor and comfortable armchairs, mirrors festooned with light bulbs, adequate hanging space for clothes, and two wash basins. Like any other dressing-room recently occupied by actors, the place was a shambles: tissues, towels, beer cans, filthy ashtrays and burnt-out cigarettes . . .

"What a disgusting lot we are," I growled, wondering why even the best of us could make dressing-rooms look like the stews.

The clothes—costumes—on hangers against the wall were fascinating and evocative. Studded black leather was predominant—jackets, shirts, jeans; tough-looking black ankle-boots on a shelf below them. From the table amidst a clutter of gauntlets and studded belts I picked up a black leather hood made to zip over the entire head and buckle about the neck with a studded strap; the empty eyeholes and zipped slash for the mouth gave it a doubly sinister appearance.

I looked at Hertz. He shrugged. "It's that sort of movie."

"What's it called?"

"*Lederkameraden.*"

"You surprise me."

With a certain amount of pride he showed me a superbly equipped make-up room which was on a par with any I had come across in a major studio. The *pièce de résistance*, however, came in the form of the sound-stage, Studio I. That really was something. Small for a film studio—about thirty feet square—it was nevertheless quite large enough for the kind of intimate movies Hertz had in mind. I didn't have to look at the hardware twice to realise that it was the best money could buy: cameras, microphones, sound equipment, lighting console, booms, monitors, floods, arc lamps, all neat and compact, scaled down, no floor space wasted.

With such equipment it was easy to understand how possible it was to shoot and match up additional sequences and cut them in to commercially made products. To embark upon such an undertaking would require an immense amount of specific know-how and high-priced professionalism—directors, cameramen, designers, make-up artists, editors, actors—the list was endless and the mind boggled. Could it be worth the effort, I wondered, let alone the expense? The answer was in the clip he had shown me; crude and outrageous though it was, it had been brilliantly executed and even I couldn't see the joins. It worked, that was all that mattered. And the price of titillation on the commercial market these days was astronomical. He really had something going for him.

Despite my built-in nausea, I was impressed and was moved to say as much, which seemed to please him.

I was not so enchanted by what had evidently been going on in the studio during the working day.

The setting was a modern torture chamber with all the tried and trusted mediaeval instruments thrown in for good measure. I'm happy to say I didn't know the names of all of them, but I recognised an Iron Maiden and a rack, thumbscrews, something very sinister which looked like Caxton's printing press, branding-irons and a flogging triangle; manacles and ankle-irons in bright steel were attached to the walls. The most alarming collection of adult playthings I had seen outside Warwick Castle.

To bring it up to date there were electrical contrivances I didn't begin to understand, though I could make an educated guess as to which parts of the human body they could be attached. Along one of the walls was a full-length leather-topped operating table which came complete with steel manacles for neck, wrists and ankles.

On a small adjacent table lay an awesome collection of whips and taws, a cat-o'-nine-tails, knotted ropes and canes. A bull-whip which must have been all of eight feet long caught my eye; the end of the lash glistened oddly. I touched it with the tip of my finger.

"Jesus," I whispered, turning to Hertz as he stood modestly by, watching what he thought was my admiration. "It's blood. That's real blood."

He smiled. "Many of our actors are the genuine article. A tremendous asset. Our clientele prefer the real thing to staged representation. And the lads get paid handsomely. What more could they ask? All this and heaven too. Where else could they find satisfaction with such sophisticated equipment and so generous a reward? They love being on display, showing off their bodies, revelling in leather. And of course, to crown it all, they are able to watch themselves on the screen, all in glorious Technicolor."

I'd had enough. "You sound like a madam in a whore-house. What are you running, a studio or a male knocking-shop? Does all this crap turn *you* on?"

He had become suddenly very still; the smile had gone. "Mr. Savage," he said quietly, "I am fast losing patience. The offer I have made is to our mutual benefit. I buy your silence in return for the exploitation of your talents as an actor. Your signature to a contract can bring you nothing but advantage and profit."

I smirked at him. "And without the signature I turn up in the Danube?"

The smirk had been a mistake. He put his growing distaste of me into action.

He closed the heavy sound-proof door behind him, shot the bolt, leaned against it and drew a small revolver from his shoulder-holster. "I have no further inclination to continue this discussion." He moved towards me slowly, the gun levelled at my chest. It occurred to me as I watched his handling of the gun that he wasn't too happy with it; he needed to be too close to his target.

I let him come in a few feet further then raised my hands in surrender. "Okay, okay, you win. You've got yourself a new boy. But let's draw up a contract before I change my mind and sell you down the river."

He relaxed too quickly, too willingly, half lowering the gun, but it was the smug smile of sheer satisfaction on his lips which precipitated my attack. I lashed out at his knee with my foot, at the same moment bringing the side of my left hand down hard on his wrist; the gun fell to the floor as my right fist crunched into his jaw. He performed a curvaceous pirouette and ended up in a sprawl at my feet. Snatching up his gun, I waved it aggressively under his nose and manhandled him to his knees. He groaned in protest, but there was nothing he could do about it. I shoved him over to the fancy operating table and enquired in the nastiest possible manner if he would mind lying on it, giving him a gentle jab in the ribs to help him on his way.

He obeyed meekly enough. If there had been any fight in him before, there was none now.

The manacles were spring-operated—I had no idea how they were released, but that was his problem, not mine. In a matter of seconds I had snapped them all into place, ankles, wrists and neck. He was clearly in some pain and flinched away from my hands as they worked on him. He made no effort to speak; he had no need; the black hatred in his eyes said it all.

When it was done and he was secure, I stood panting over him, leaning against the table. "There, Mr. Hertz—hoist, as they say, with your own petard." I reached out a hand and grasped the bull-whip, drawing its sticky lash across his throat. His eyes widened with fright and apprehension; sweat beaded his face. I twisted the leather thong beneath his head and looped it gently about his neck. "I wish I thought I could bring myself to use this," I told him. I flung the heavy butt of the whip across his body and moved to the door. "I'll be back in a couple of minutes," I said, "with the law."

Releasing the bolt, I pulled open the heavy door with caution; reinforcements could have arrived.

They had.

The twin barrels of the Gorilla's shotgun were inches from my eyes. I slammed the door viciously in his face at the very moment he pulled the trigger. For a second or two I was so stunned that I didn't even know whether this was the big death scene or not. I stood with my forehead pressed against the cold metal of the door wondering at the sudden ominous quiet which seemed to have swallowed whole the ear-splitting explosion of the gun.

It was only when I began to shake myself that I realised the door I had slammed on the barrels of that gun was sound-proofed. Sound-proofed steel.

With Hertz's revolver in my hand I slowly pulled open the door, half knowing what to expect. The reality was worse than the expectation.

The gun had exploded in his face, carrying most of it away. The confined space had compacted everything. The explosion had picked him up and flung him bodily against the opposite wall, which bore grisly testimony of the demonic impact which had slammed him into it. What was left of the gun was half embedded in his chest. I shut my smarting eyes tight and breathed in the sickening stench of cordite. I was finding it difficult to hold my stomach in check.

My mind reached out for the sound of approaching feet alerted by the shot. I could hear nothing; the place was like a grave. I forced open my eyes. I stared with sudden and compassionate fury at the grubby bandage on the man's hand. It had not been his week.

I roused myself with difficulty. I had to get away, out of there, into cold clean air.

Behind me Hertz spoke calmly. "What happened?"

"One of your men." I hardly recognised my voice. "His gun backfired . . ."

"Mr. Savage." His voice drew me back reluctantly into the studio. Prostrate and helpless though he was, he exuded a terrible danger; it crept about him like sluggish morning mist; I could almost smell it. His eyes glittered hard, bright like a snake's. He spoke quietly.

"What was it you said about Himmler? 'No one crossed him and lived to tell the tale.' You were right. I knew Himmler. You would do well to kill me now, for if we should meet again—and we shall—I will have you torn apart. Bear it in mind, Mr. Savage."

CHAPTER THIRTEEN

I hesitated briefly before locking the door on him. Maybe he would suffocate. With his latest unfriendly sentiments ringing in my ears, I didn't care whether he did or not; things would be far less fraught if he did. He'd meant every word of it. The moment he was released from his present bondage the threat of annihilation would hang over me; even if his next stop was prison, he'd still be able to reach me; putting out a contract on someone is not just the flowering of a script-writer's fertile imagination. It happens.

I locked the door, pocketed the key. Every movie studio is air-conditioned. He would survive. I hoped I would.

Without difficulty I found my way back to his rectangular office, where the temptation to smash up his switchboard was almost too much for me, only overcome by the knowledge that time, as ever, was of the essence and that the sooner I got out of the place altogether, the better it would be for my state of health.

The door which led into the garage was immovable; Wayne had probably locked it after him. Not for a second did I contemplate shooting my way out. I had learned the lesson about guns and metal doors. It took only a moment to decide on the next move: the best way out would be through the restaurant itself—if I could find it; then if anyone wanted to start a fight, he'd have a public brawl on his hands.

I had locked the doors into and out of the office and hung on to the keys if only to make things difficult for those anxious to learn the whereabouts of their leader. My pocket jangled with keys.

Adding another to their number, I let myself through a door opposite that of the garage. Stone steps led downwards into spacious nether regions where discarded scenery and props were stored—left-overs from erstwhile productions of the ministudio upstairs. I shouldered my way through painted flats and drapes musty and stinking of size, instinct telling me that eventually I might well come to the wine-cellars of the Kékszákallú from which there would be easy access to both kitchens and to the club itself.

Instinct was right. The cellars came up as a matter of course, and by some fortuitous fluke the door leading into them was unlocked. Had I been in charge of a wine-cellar, all doors into and out of it would have been locked and barred and all keys attached to my own personal watch chain. However, far be it from me to knock the present system.

Hundreds of dusty and elderly bottles glinted like diminutive warriors sleeping in racked bunks of straw. I crossed my fingers; things were going too well.

A minute later, and inevitably, I suppose, the trend came to a halt and I came to grief. An iron door firmly locked stood impregnably in my path. Failing a charge of gelignite, there was no way I could hack my way through that. I examined the lock and peered through the keyhole; the darkness beyond was impenetrable. I stood back and swore at it with impotent malice. The bloody thing had been there since the death of Marcus Aurelius.

For endless precious seconds I prowled around seeking other exits—doors, windows, traps, iron gratings, anything—and drew a blank. There were two entrances into that cellar, the one I'd come through and the one I now stood glowering at. I would just have to go back the way I had come.

My heel was actually on the swivel when I heard the scraping of a key in a lock. Fear rooted me to the spot, followed by a panic which flung me headlong behind the nearest wine-rack, jangling like a janitor. I was still on the move when the giant door swung ponderously inward. I had left the light on, of course, but there was nothing I could do about it just at that moment. The man in the dinner-jacket standing in the doorway registered it too, frowning up at the nearest lamp and shaking his head in some sort of despair; an underling would receive a rocket for negligence.

Leaving the door ajar, he stepped into the cellar and, hissing tunelessly between his teeth, passed down the aisle parallel to the one in which I crouched, his footsteps echoing mournfully beneath the low vaulting of the roof. With no time to weigh up the pros and cons I took a chance, lurched to my feet and ducked through the door with a turn of speed I had forgotten I possessed. The noise I made was like an army on the rampage—there was no way he could not have heard it. I therefore didn't dawdle but leapt for the short flight of steps before me, shoved open the door at the head of them and found myself in the clatter and bustle of an enormous and steamy kitchen surrounded by exotic smells, barbaric-looking Hungarian cooks and a number of people in fancy dress.

I slowed down, clasped my hands behind me in a princely way, and strolled down the centre aisle, dispensing nods and smiles to all and sundry as I went; reciprocal nods and smiles came from most of those in the vicinity. They probably thought I was the Man from the Ministry.

The people in fancy dress turned out to be waiters and waitresses got up in traditional costumes. One of them, a pulchritudinous young woman, gave me what I chose to interpret as the come-hither, so I fell in behind her and surged in the wake of the scarlet ribbons streaming from her embroidered head-dress, admiring the dexterity with which she bore a loaded tray shoulder-high with one hand and repelled the amorous clutchings of the male kitchen staff with the other.

With a sudden and overpowering roar of voices and music, I was engulfed in the hurly-burly of the restaurant, which seethed like an anthill, its colour, vivacity, mirrored walls and sheer volume of sound both deafening and breath-taking. Everyone within earshot was shouting and laughing at the limits of their vocal chords; everyone else was laying down a smoke-screen with enormous and expensive cigars.

In the middle of the room on a low dais was the orchestra, the tell-tale cymbalom its centrepiece. Two violinists in white full-sleeved ballet shirts and scarlet waistcoats strolled among the closely packed tables, simpering over their sobbing strings, lingering over the yearning melancholy of their traditional melodies.

I stood for a second dazed and lost.

The explosion of a champagne cork at my elbow had me reaching for my gun.

Beyond the orchestra and beneath a glittering array of chandeliers, a half-dozen broad red-carpeted steps and polished brass handrails led upwards to a series of glass doors draped with red and green velvet curtains. A footman in bright national costume was ushering a small party of newcomers in the direction of the *maître d'hôtel* who stood in sober black tails at the foot of the steps to receive them.

I wondered if I could make it that far without becoming conspicuous; I was hardly dressed for a smart night club. In one of the mirrors I caught sight of someone who looked as if he had just tunnelled his way beneath the sewers of the old city; no wonder the kitchen staff had nodded and smiled—they probably thought I was dangerous. Whilst sorting out my dishevelled hair, I saw something else in the mirror which turned me into an ice-cold block of marble. A man in a white dinner-jacket stood at the head of the steps, his bald head gleaming like a beacon. With one hand on the polished handrail Stephan Hertz swept his domain with eyes like Geiger counters.

I felt as if I had turned bright green and grown a couple of feet; I was the tallest, brightest and most conspicuous object in the place; my shoes had glued themselves to the floor. Even the violinists, immersed though they were in their schmaltzy sentimentality, had become conscious of my immovability and were bearing down upon me, soulful eyes and slobbering strings reeking with sudden and terrible danger. A waiter, edging himself around me with a loaded tray in his hands, jostled me and jolted me into some semblance of life.

As I turned from the mirror, a voice hissed my name. My numbed brain slotted into second gear. A yard away stood Hedda, her back to me, her face reflected in the mirrored wall. "Follow," she whispered, and moved off without apparently caring whether I was with her or not.

I dared not look in Hertz' direction. Invisibility was the name of the game. The advancing violins were alarmingly loud.

Hedda had disappeared. More panic shot me into third gear. Somebody said, "Pssst!" the way they do, and instead of a mirror there was a large black hole in the wall. I stepped into it. The hole closed behind me. A torch flashed on.

"Hurry," squawked Hedda, her dark form leading the way down a couple of steps and along a musty-smelling passage.

"Listen," I whispered urgently as I fell in beside her. "Get me to a phone . . . If we don't get the police here in five minutes, he'll be away and no one will ever see him again . . ."

Her only reply was to quicken her pace so that we were almost on the run; then suddenly and gloriously we were in the open air, the rain bucketing down on my unprotected head. I raised my face to it as I ran; I felt like tearing off my clothes, bathing in it.

We were now racing at full tilt down a narrow cobbled alley-way, high black walls rearing up on either side, only the flickering firefly of her torch breaking the darkness.

We burst out of the alley-way into dim street lighting; a car squealed to a halt a couple of yards away, the rear door flung open. Hedda's voice was breathless. "Get in." The torch flashed into the interior. Someone inside was reaching for me, the beam momentarily touching his face—bright blue eyes, shiny black hair. I braked in sudden alarm. I was going for the little Beholla in my waistband when Hedda shoved me roughly from behind. "Get in, for God's sake, get in!"

I lost my balance, felt myself falling. The little man opened his arms to receive me. Something struck me hard on the forehead and I lurched forward into his lap, a confusion of bright lights and heavy darkness closing over me. I remember wondering why he wasn't wearing his bloody blue button-hole . . .

*   *   *

Music . . . cleverly in time with the thudding of my head. The steady rhythm lulled me into a soporific limbo.

I tried stretching my legs and couldn't. Why couldn't I stretch my legs? I ungummed my eyes. Pain lanced through them. I shut them again.

Where was the music coming from? I had the feeling I was in prison—but a whole bloody symphony orchestra in a prison? Concentrate, Savage. The music . . . Brahms? Right? Which Brahms? The First . . . Symphony No. 1. There, that wasn't difficult, was it? Good old Brahms . . . Johannes Brahms . . .

Jesus! My eyes shot open again.

A man in an armchair sat reading beneath a shaded lamp. The rest was darkness. I still couldn't stretch my legs. Whatever I was lying on was too short to accommodate me. An undersized bed, a couch . . . I half expected to be bound in some way, gagged even, so I couldn't sound the alarm. I was neither. The music came from somewhere behind me.

Through half-closed eyes I studied the man in the chair. Something vaguely familiar nudged at my bleary consciousness; something from the past; someone I had known and forgotten—and hadn't much liked . . .

I jerked into sudden awareness.

His head turned towards me, the patch over the eye black and sinister. "Hello, cousin. You've come back to us."

He sat watching me for a few seconds, then closing his book rose languidly to his feet and leaned across me. I almost cringed. With a little *clop* of sound Brahms ceased to be.

"That'll be quite enough of that," he murmured. "Hedda thought it might help. It's given me a headache."

I levered myself gingerly on to an elbow, head thudding in dutiful response to every movement.

"Like some tea?" He was standing over me. "Better for you than alcohol in your present condition."

I nodded silently and he went off somewhere out of vision.

My eyes slowly began to adapt themselves. The room, what little I could make of it through the murk, was without personality, no specific signs of taste in either decoration or furnishings; someone had gone out, bought a lot of things and put them in a room—the overall impression was "yuk." On a low coffee-table within easy reach lay Alice's Beholla.

I listened to the mumbling of voices in another room, then he was back again, resuming his seat and edging the chair around a little so that we could see each other better. He adjusted the lamp. "This worry you?" I shook my head.

I heaved myself into a sitting position. I was on a bumpy settee, unbound, ungagged and ostensibly in friendly surroundings.

"What happened?" I asked.

"You banged your head."

"How long have I been out?"

"However long it took to get you here—plus a few minutes."

The lamp immediately above him threw his features into harsh relief; there was little to choose between either of his eyes; both were in heavy shadow, neither seemed alive; only the etched lines around his mouth moved, deepening slightly as the lips smiled.

"There was no intended violence. According to reliable information, you struck your head on the door of the car. Hedda said she had to give you a push." The smile broadened. "She's very sorry."

"I'll bet she is." I sounded sour. "I've come to the point when I can't tell the wood from the trees. You're Lorenz Sternberg, is that right?"

"Bronson," he countered quietly. "Lorenz Bronson."

"And are you a goodie or a baddie?"

He settled back in his chair, and for the first time I could see the amused gleam in his good eye. "In present company I would like to think of myself as a goodie."

"And are we related, you and I?"

"Tenuously."

"You are the son of Alicia Sternberg?"

Silent, he frowned slightly, then nodded almost with reluctance. "A long time back."

Hedda interrupted us at that moment, carrying a tray of tea things which she placed on the coffee-table alongside the gun. "Hello." She gave me an uncertain smile. "How are you feeling?"

"Confused."

Switching on a couple of shaded wall lamps which added a modicum of warmth to the dramatic starkness, she joined me on the settee and prepared to dispense tea. I noticed for the first time the blood stains on my shirt-front. I put a hand to my head and my fingers encountered a large strip of sticking plaster.

She made a wry face. "If they'd caught us, they would have killed us. I'm sorry."

"Did we get away with it?"

"For the time being."

She handed me some tea and a couple of off-white pills to go with it. "For your headache." I eyed them with suspicion. She said, "Actually they're potassium cyanide—L pills, you used to call them. But remember to crunch them, otherwise they'll do you no harm."

I washed them down with a mouthful of strong tea. I said, "I swallowed them whole."

In the silence that followed, during which she poured tea for herself and Lorenz, the muffled sound of a ship's hooter reverberated through the room. I raised my head.

Lorenz said, "We are beyond the Danube, on the north bank. In what is laughingly known as a 'safe' house."

"Sounds like one of those ghastly spy movies I used to have to act in."

He smiled over the rim of his cup. "Unfortunately spies aren't unique to the movie business."

"Are *you* a spy?"

He eyed the contents of his cup for a second. "An agent." He gave a slight shrug. "Anyone who undertakes a mission on behalf of someone else is an agent—in whatever field."

"In my field an agent is someone who takes 10 percent of everything you earn."

"Some of us do it for nothing." He smiled enigmatically.

I glanced at Hedda's quiet profile; immersed in thought, she appeared uninvolved. I said, "You knew where he was all the time?" She gave a silent nod. "Whose side are *you* on?"

"Mine," said Lorenz.

"And the man who nearly killed us all in Demel's? The one in the car? Who's he?"

"Franz?"

"Is that his name?"

"He belongs to me."

I gave him a sour smirk. "Who needs a baddie?"

He said shortly, "This is not a game."

"I never imagined it was. And if I had, tonight's performance would have convinced me otherwise." He was silent. I went on. "An hour ago I was all set with Bluebeard back there to flush you out. Now you've spoilt it all. But here you are, and I didn't need him after all."

"I rather think you did," he put in drily. "Without his assistance you wouldn't be here. Without mine you might have been at the bottom of the Danube. Did you reach any sort of agreement with him?"

"The price was a little high."

"But here I am."

"And there you are." I nodded. "Will you now please go and say hello to your mother so that I can go home?"

"No."

"No." I glanced at Hedda. "Is there any more tea in that pot? We may be in for a bumpy night."

"Mark," said Lorenz quietly, "when you leave this room, most of your questions will be answered. But before I put you into *my* picture, you must first please put me into yours. I need to know what has passed between you and . . . Bluebeard, as you call him. I believe he's the man I came here to meet."

"Well, that's handy, because he's just mad to meet you. You've got something of his, he says, and wants it quite badly—like a million dollars."

He sat communing with himself for a couple of seconds then rose slowly to his feet. I sipped at the refill Hedda had given me and watched him as he moved across the room to stand with his back to us staring at a boring-looking picture on the wall. Coming to a sudden decision, he bent his head and with a quick movement removed the eye-patch. The silence in the room was intense. I glanced at Hedda. She was gazing at him with her mouth slightly open, a child watching a conjuror about to perform an impossible trick.

When my eyes went back to Lorenz, he was turning again towards us, one hand readjusting the eye-patch. The other, closed, he held towards us.

Slowly he opened his fingers. "One million dollars."

In the palm of the hand flickered four minute sources of faceted flame. I stared at them transfixed. They were alive. If you listened, Ernst Sternberg had told his wife, they would talk to you.

I had seen diamonds before many times. Alice herself carried a comprehensive selection around with her most of the time—ears, fingers and wrists were usually festooned with them—but I had never before seen them without a setting, and somehow these four, unset, lying loose in the palm of his hand, seemed more evocative and more mesmeric than any I could remember. In that moment I believe I came close to understanding the charisma of diamonds, what they were, what they stood for, their magic, sensual fascination, and perhaps most of all their utter desirability—the sheer need to possess them . . .

Our eyes met. He was smiling. "Take them."

I shook my head. "You might not get them back."

"May I?" Hedda whispered. "Please?"

He trickled them into her cupped hand, a tiny lustrous cascade of mountain water shot through with bright sunlight, refracting the colours of the spectrum yet at the same time curiously cold and glacial.

"Beautiful . . . quite beautiful . . ." murmured Hedda; the diamonds rattled in her shifting palm like cheap beads.

"Do they belong to Stephan Hertz?" I asked.

"No, they don't." He was almost rudely emphatic. "I brought them only as a precaution against the possibility of unpleasant contingencies. He looks upon them, let us say, as his due, but they are the legitimate property of my father"—his eyes flicked up to mine—"Rodrigo Bronson."

There was a silence whilst each of us contemplated the possible conduct of further conversation. It was I who decided which direction it should take.

"You smuggled those in?" He was removing them one by one from Hedda's reluctant hand, assessing each of them with the eye of the connoisseur. He nodded. "For safety's sake only, not to evade customs duty." I looked intently at the eye-patch. He smiled and nodded again. "Not just behind the patch but behind the eye itself. In the socket. Most people are queasy about damaged eyes, so even the thought of an empty socket is more than they can reasonably bear. At home I sometimes scare the mailman out of his wits when I forget to insert the false eye. It's not a pleasant sight. All orifices of the body are regularly and diligently searched for drugs and diamonds by the authorities but not, so far—in my case at least—the empty eye-socket." He resumed his seat, idly shaking a million dollars in his fist like dice. "Now please tell me about Stephan Hertz. Who is he, what is he and what is his set-up?"

I was mildly surprised to realise that he had never actually met the man and would not have recognised him had he walked into the room wearing a name-tag.

It took me no time to tell him what I knew, which was not a great deal even if I did have the uncomfortable feeling that I had lived with Stephan Hertz for the best part of my life.

When I'd finished, we sat around in uneasy silence. Rain dripping from a guttering made the room tick like a time bomb. A series of hysterical tootings from the river were engulfed and stilled by the sepulchral blast of a larger and grander vessel. We listened to the deep throb of a ship's engines. Only when the sound had gone did Lorenz speak.

"If you fall into his hands again, you're a dead man."

I nodded. "I'll try not to worry about it."

"I suggest you stay here until he and I have settled our differences."

"You're going to kill him?" He shrugged. "And if he kills you first?"

He gave a frosty smile. "Then you'll have to make other arrangements. In such a contingency my earnest advice would be that you remove yourself speedily, certainly from Vienna, preferably from Europe. Stephan Hertz has a long arm—longer than we know."

"Who is he, Mafia?"

"He's his own private Mafia with an empire built on blackmail and extortion."

"And is the Kékszákállú the centre of his operations? Does he have interests other than the video racket?"

"These days that's almost enough, except that the law is cracking down on video piracy more successfully than it is on, say, drugs. The success of any business depends on its weakest links; the clients of his particular brand of video are pleasure seekers, more liable to brag to outsiders of their latest opprobrious acquisitions than, say, the average junkie, who will keep a still tongue in his head because he has more to lose—like his sanity, for instance. Hertz is in the diamond business certainly and that, I suspect, is the least nefarious of his interests, other possibilities being drugs and armaments. Your question about the Kékszákallú is unanswerable; it's a lift-off pad and all we have at the moment. Personally I care neither one way nor the other. I have no interest in his operations, only in him. I am as amoral as I am apolitical. What other people do to earn themselves a living or build themselves an empire is a matter of indifference to me. Anyone seriously into crime puts liberty and prosperity at risk—sometimes life; he knows the odds, and hazards his own expertise against that of the law." He added quietly, "But I am not the law, nor do I practise its niceties. In *my* book the punishment should fit the crime. Vengeance is mine and mine alone, and the Lord can say or do whatever He damn well likes."

"What exactly is your gripe against him?" I asked.

He got to his feet and with hands deep in his jacket pockets proceeded to tramp up and down the room like a ship's captain on his bridge. "My gripe, as you call it," he said in a low voice, "is blackmail and extortion, practised in this particular instance upon my father."

"Ernst Sternberg?" I don't know why I said it other than to rile him. He was so bloody self-assured and absolute.

"Rodrigo Bronson." His voice tightened a little, but his steady pacing did not slacken.

"Or Otto Brunner?" I ventured with studied care.

That had him. It stopped him dead in his tracks directly in front of me; I thought for a moment he was going to hit me. I could see the angry flexing of his jaw muscles; the single eye glittered dangerously. I could hear a million dollars' worth of diamonds grinding together in his clenched fist.

I smiled up into his face, my head pounding like a pile-driver—the little off-white pills had done nothing for it. "It occurs to me," I said deliberately, and maddeningly changing the subject, "that while we're just sitting around here passing the time of day, Mr. Hertz could have packed his bags and be well on his way to Czechoslovakia by now. My final words to him were that I would be back in a couple of minutes with the law. Whatever else he is, he's not one to drag his feet; he's certainly not going to sit there in the middle of his web waiting for a police raid, now is he? I'm sorry to bring this up at such a sensitive moment, but I do think someone ought to be doing something about it."

"Someone has, never fear." He had regained his cool without a great deal of obvious effort. "I have a dozen men watching his every move. The slightest stirring on his part and I shall be informed."

I shook my head in good-natured derision. "He's already gone. He goes to the bathroom, puts on a funny wig, takes his teeth out, changes his clothes and walks out of the place. I've read the book and seen the movie."

He smiled patiently. "Perhaps like the captain of a sinking ship he had decided to go down with it."

"Never. If there's one person who's not going down with that ship it's Captain Stephan Bloody Hertz. However"—I gave a loud shrug which almost dislocated my neck—"far be it from me to criticise your organisation, whatever that may be; if *you* don't care about him slipping through your fingers, I'm afraid I do, because if anyone's liable to be scraped up off the pavement, it's going to be me, not you. So if you don't mind, I think I'll be getting along."

When I reached for the gun on the table, nobody tried to stop me; I checked it to make sure that it was still loaded, then battled my way woozily to my feet. Hedda put out a restraining hand which was remarkably ineffective whilst Lorenz just stood smiling at me quite kindly and shaking his head. "You're perfectly safe here, Mark, believe me."

"I do believe you, for Christ's sake," I almost shouted at him, swaying a little and putting a reluctant hand on his shoulder to steady myself. "But I can't sit here for the rest of my life being safe, can I? I have things to do, places to go, people to kill. Who the hell wants to be safe with that bald-headed pervert roaming the streets. I'd sooner be out on the hunt taking my chances."

My noisy show of bravura got me nowhere. Instead of marching off bravely into the night I found myself clutching hold of him to stay upright. Together they helped me back into my seat. "What was in those bloody pills?" I threw off Hedda's arm and glared at her through a haze of dizziness.

"Aspirin . . ."

"Then there was something in the tea."

"You gave your head one hell of a bang, you know . . . you knocked yourself out."

Staring vaguely in her direction, I brought her finally into focus and was almost gratified by the look of concern in her eyes. "Give yourself time," she said quietly. "Lorenz is right. Hertz isn't going anywhere."

I gritted my teeth. "That place is a rabbit warren; it's got cellars and attics and God knows what—secret rooms and sliding panels, I shouldn't wonder. There's also a make-up department second to none. In ten minutes I could make myself unrecognisable. I could walk past my own mother and she wouldn't know me."

"Mark," said Lorenz suddenly. "Listen to me, please."

I sat back with a resigned groan, all ears for the revelations to come. For some time there was nothing at all and I was about to continue with my own diatribe when he spoke again.

"I have to tell you that I have come to an arrangement with Hertz which will ensure his staying at the Kékszakállú for at least"—he consulted his watch—"another two hours."

I stared at him. "I thought you didn't know him."

"I don't. We spoke on the telephone."

"When?"

"While you were still unconscious." He raised a hand as I was about to explode. "Please." He reseated himself. "I took the liberty of using your . . . escape for my own purposes. I apologise; but I also am not one to drag my feet. Had I waited for you to recover, he would by now be well on his way to

Czechoslovakia, as you pointed out. I told him you were with me and had not contacted the police nor would not." At the look of speechless amazement on my face, he simply smiled. "By this time you have realised that I am a much sought after individual. I am the close-hunted quarry of several sets of people. The most dangerous, the Israelis, were the only ones to jump me and almost put a stop to my mission before it had begun. They needed a trophy to carry back to Tel Aviv—a Nazi head on a pole—and for some reason believed they could get at my father through me." In the wryness of his sudden smile I sensed a feeling of guilty regret. "Rodrigo Bronson. Otto Brunner, if you will . . . There's enough of the Jew in me to appreciate and understand the Jekyll and Hyde duality of the modern Israeli mind: the resignation and endurance, the shrewdness, courage, faith; all of which, at the spin of a coin, can become an awesome ferocity, guile and a fanaticism only possible in a people of deep religious conviction and introspective politics. That girl and her brother—the one I killed—are the sort of ambassadors no country should tolerate, and Israel would be the first to agree. There is little to choose between their behaviour and that of the Nazis whom they profess to abominate. So . . . be that as it may, after a great deal of persuasive . . . encouragement they realised I was not prepared to help them reach my father, the more so when, under further duress, I was . . . obliged to inform them that Otto Brunner was not, in fact, my natural father . . ." He broke off, the tremor in his voice betraying deep mental distress.

I shifted uncomfortably and glanced at Hedda. She sat quite still, head down, staring at her hands clasped tightly in her lap; the soft light burnished her dark hair, lingered over her lowered lashes, the straightness of her nose and the warm glow of her lips. She was suddenly quite breath-takingly lovely . . .

Lorenz was speaking again. "Unlike the Nazis, they were careless and stupid. When they had finished their games, I was unconscious; when I came to, my hands and feet were still tied and only the brother was there; the others had gone. He was tired, slightly the worse for alcohol and needed someone to talk to. He sickened me with his outmoded crap about being one of God's chosen people. I asked for a drink. He came close, let me smell the wine and poured it over my chest. I wrapped my tied hands around his throat and killed him. The world is happier without such people, God's chosen or not." He sat for a while still and silent. "I had always imagined myself incapable of killing. I'm told it's easier the second time." His smile was bleak and deadly. "We shall see."

Outside, a clock was chiming. Lorenz got to his feet, glancing at his watch, and once again embarked on his restless promenading. When Hedda stirred uneasily, I took her hands boldly in mine; far from resisting the gesture, she held on to me tightly, exchanging glances with me, her eyes reflecting the concern I felt for Lorenz.

He went on, "I had no difficulty in meeting up with the organisation which had promised me safety and assistance."

"A Nazi organisation, I suppose?"

He looked amused. "A *German* organisation based in West Berlin with, it is true, the swastika as its symbol, but benevolent, Mark, benevolent. The swastika once united Germany; its present aim, I understand, is the unity of Berlin—the destruction of the Wall, politically if not literally."

I shook my head. "Impossible."

He gave Hedda a wary smile. "I'm told that if the will of the people is strong enough and courageous enough the Wall will crumble—as did those of ancient Jericho."

Again I shook my head. "It's Third World War stuff."

"I think so too. I'm afraid I have no faith in Bible stories and certainly no head for politics. However, whatever the outcome, this house is the property of that organisation and I am grateful to them; I have been safe here. Also placed at my disposal were several pairs of eyes and ears to keep me in touch with what was going on outside and, in the last couple of days, with your own particular exploits."

"Why?"

"Because I believed you would lead me to Hertz."

"I didn't even know he existed."

He smiled and spread his hands. "But you led me to him nevertheless."

Hedda removed her hands gently from mine. "Once Lorenz was safe, our only care was to keep him safe. We set up a round-the-clock watch on this house to keep it free from prowlers. The next thing was that I myself was being followed everywhere—I kept seeing this same man's face reflected in shop-windows, on trams and so on. One day when I was with Alicia, there were two of them; when Alicia and I parted company, one followed her, the other stayed with me. I knew then what they were doing. If, as Lorenz told the Israelis, he *was* Alicia's son, they were counting on the probability that he would contact his mother, or at least one of the household; so by keeping us all under surveillance one of us would surely and eventually lead them to him."

"And these were Hertz' men?"

Lorenz said, "Who else? They certainly weren't the Israelis—not the ones I knew anyway. Hertz was the only other man who knew I was in Vienna."

"Why couldn't they have been the police, these men?"

"How would the police know they were looking for Alicia Sternberg's son? The Israelis wouldn't have told them—by kidnapping me they had already placed themselves outside the law."

"So you just *assumed* they were Hertz' men?"

"A highly educated assumption, though until this evening I had no positive proof. *You* supplied that when you told us whose side Verne Wayne was on. It could only have been Wayne who passed the information on to Hertz."

"That you were Alicia's son?" He nodded. I looked at them both with deep weariness. "It's all as plain as a pikestaff, isn't it? The Israelis told

Sammy Meier, Sammy told Alice, Alice told Wayne and Wayne passed it on to Hertz."

"Well done," smiled Lorenz with an avuncular sort of pride which made me feel like an idiot.

"And Hertz wants you because you owe him a million dollars?"

"I owe him nothing."

"Which is going to surprise him?"

"Very likely."

"And upset him?"

"Considerably."

"And rather than let the police have him, you're going to walk in there, tell him he's not getting his million dollars and then calmly shoot him through the head?"

"Something like that."

"You're an even bigger nut than I am. You'll never get out of that place alive."

"You did. But set your mind at rest. Any rendezvous I make with him will certainly not be on his home ground—of that I can assure you."

Silence closed around us. The pain in my head was beginning to lift. I watched Hedda's still, quiet hands. Why had she been at the Kékszákulló tonight and not at the opera? And how had she managed to make an entrance on cue at the precise moment I had needed her? Had she really saved my life or was that part of an elaborate smoke-screen laid down to obscure other more dangerous issues? The photograph of her in cahoots with Hans Schmidt haunted me.

Lorenz was offering her a cigarette. She refused. I too shook my head. "Do you mind if I do?" he asked.

"It's your coffin, not ours," I told him dourly.

A further beat of silence, then he said quite brightly, "Talking of coffins . . ." He disappeared behind an impenetrable cloud of thick grey smoke. "Would you say that Stephan Hertz is the sort of man who would have no compunction in killing you, should your paths happen to cross again?"

I waved irritably at the wall of smoke the way non-smokers do. "I would say yes, without hesitation. Even if he didn't want to soil his own hands, he has minions enough to do it for him. In all humility I rather think he'd make a point of slipping me in on his own personal dance card." I glanced at Hedda. "I just wish I knew how he got off that operating table all on his own."

She shrugged, meeting my eye calmly. "If it was a theatrical prop, simple enough. There's always a fail-safe device to things like that surely—like a retracting dagger. We'd lose a lot of tenors and baritones if it weren't for retracting daggers. He probably just pressed a button, got up and walked away."

"So why did he let me put him there in the first place?"

"You had the gun."

She had the answers too. I turned back to Lorenz. "Why do you ask?"

"Would you be willing to meet him again?"

I stared at him. "Glug," I said.

"Exactly." He nodded thoughtfully. "But if it were in a very open and public place, what then?"

I wobbled an uncertain head. "It would depend on what you had in mind."

He got up and went off on the prowl again, taking a long drag on his cigarette and unselfishly giving us the benefit of most of the smoke. "I told him on the telephone I would call him back and arrange a meeting. One, to hand over his million dollars and two, to offer some exploratory views on a possible business merger between our two companies. My father, in failing health, I said, was open to consider proposals profitable to both sides. I think he took the bait." He came to a halt by the curtained window. "The bad news is that, in exchange, he would rather like your head on a platter. When I spoke to him, I knew nothing of his offer to set you up as his own personal film star. Was that on the level, do you think?"

"To keep me quiet, yes, I think it probably was, though now . . ."

"Suppose I were to tell him that I had been able to persuade you to accept the offer and that we would like to include such a contract in our mutual discussion? How would that be?"

"He'd never trust me. And it's too elaborate. He's a shrewd operator. He'll smell a rat."

"All right, so he's shrewd, so he might not trust you, but I'd like to bet he's also a gambler—enough of a gambler to tilt the scales in our favour. What do you say?"

He reseated himself, dunking the cigarette in his cup.

Hedda's hand was suddenly in mine. I looked at her; her eyes told me nothing. I didn't know whether she meant "Yes" or "Don't touch it with a barge-pole." When I turned again to Lorenz, he was resting back in his chair, the handsome, mutilated face shadowed again into the haunting spectre of my dead father. I had never cared for my father; now it was almost as if he had deliberately resurrected to fling one of his usual arrogant challenges at my head.

I hesitated a moment longer. "You'll tell him to come alone, of course?"

"Certainly I'll tell him, but he won't, of course, but then neither will we."

"Suppose he decides not to come at all?"

"Then it's back to the drawing-board." He leaned forward into the light, his eye glittering like a solitaire. "But he'll come, I know he'll come."

I took a further look at Hedda; she was being Garbo in one of her more inscrutable roles. I gave a heavy sigh. "When and where?"

He frowned. "Tomorrow certainly—I'll think about the where."

Silence ticked on. I said slowly, "In exchange for my head on a platter . . ." I hesitated.

He waited. "What in exchange?"

"Who you are. What you are. Why have you two fathers? Why will you not acknowledge your own mother . . . ? You know the sort of thing. Once upon a time and all that . . ."

He leaned back in his chair; the shadows closed over him.

The distant clock was striking the hour.

Midnight.

Pumpkin time . . .

CHAPTER FOURTEEN

"I remember my mother as a busy, loud, laughing woman surrounded by hordes of fashionable, noisy, scented grown-ups. She was like a reigning music-hall queen, forever departing on endless tours. When she was in Vienna, the house rocked with parties and balls at none of which I was allowed to appear. If she found time to visit me in the nursery, it was usually on her way to the opera when I was half asleep. Very occasionally I was brushed and combed and shepherded downstairs for tea and cakes, to be shown off to visitors who would pat me on the head as if it were the accolade. I was a plain child and an encumbrance—which will explain all.

"My father was a grey, elderly figure, twenty years older than my mother, remote but kindly, even loving, perhaps, for I remember him hugging me a great deal. He wore black clothes which smelled of cigar smoke. Sometimes he gave me his watch-chain to play with. Never his watch. He too was rarely at home. He had business premises somewhere beyond the Votivkirche and spent most of his waking hours there. He spoke English badly, and most of the time I couldn't understand a word he said. My mother had insisted very early on that English should be my first language, which was somewhat of a handicap here in Austria. I had a full-time English tutor and picked up German as best as I could.

"Ostensibly I was brought up by a woman named Elsa Auerbach who was large and warm, coddled me and sang funny German songs to me in bed. She made me laugh. She was the only one who did."

Reaching for another cigarette, he got up and moved to the window to light it. With his back to us the leonine head was haloed in the golden flare of the match. With one finger he drew back the curtain a little and watched the rain streaming down the window.

"It was a day like this when I first saw the soldiers, helmets and guns gleaming in the rain, some of them, on motor cycles, wearing shining water-proofs; I thought they looked wonderful, hundreds of them marching along the Ring. And so did everyone else, cheering and shouting, throwing flowers. But our house was strangely quiet, more than usually so since mother was away at the time. I remember that quiet."

He came back into the room, picked up an ashtray and promenaded solemnly to and fro before us.

"Some time later when I was out walking with Elsa—a fine cold day—I saw my father on hands and knees with several others, scrubbing the sidewalk with a scrubbing brush. Soldiers stood over them, prodding them with guns and feet, jeering at them. Other people—civilians—were standing around too, watching and laughing and throwing small coins as if it were an entertainment. Two of them were our next-door neighbours, friends of my mother's. When I made to go to my father, Elsa pulled me away. I asked why they were scrubbing the pavement. She said it was because they were Jews. Oddly enough, although I was nearly nine, I couldn't remember ever having heard the word before. 'What's a Jew?' I asked. 'You're a Jew,' Elsa said. 'And when you grow up, *you'll* be scrubbing the pavement too.' She sounded cross.

"She took me home. I never saw her again. Somebody else came and took her place."

He was at the window again peering out at the rain. In the glass I could see his wraith-like reflection.

"It was raining the night the soldiers came and took us away—my father and me." He turned suddenly and violently into the room. "Why in hell am I telling you this? It happened years before either of you were born." He glared at us for a moment almost in anger, then the fire died slowly from his eye; quietly he idled around the periphery of the room breathing heavily and filling the place with smoke. Behind us I could hear him removing Brahms from the turntable and replacing it in its sleeve. Hedda took my hand in hers. Silence.

When he spoke again, his voice was entirely without emotion. "They took us to an awful place. The rain had stopped. It was daylight. Cold. People's faces were grey. There was no colour anywhere. We huddled together for warmth. There were many of us. We had travelled by truck and train throughout the night. A woman I had never seen before wrapped her shawl about me. Held my hand. The soldiers were loud and huge, with guns and bayonets; they shouted and bullied and pushed us all against a wall, one of them counting, hitting each of us with his rifle-butt as he moved down the line. I had become separated from my father. The woman told me not to worry; he'd be back, she said. Then I saw him through a crowd of soldiers, one of a small group who had been singled out from the rest. I shouted. The woman tried to hold me back, but I pulled away, ran to him. A giant of a soldier stood in my way, yelling at me; his mouth was a black hole full of terrible sound. He was reaching down for me. I remember seeing the gun and the flash of the bayonet. I tried to duck away but ran into it instead . . ."

Hedda's finger-nails were biting deep into the palms of my hand. I sensed the hurt without feeling it.

He moved into my field of vision, pausing for a second beside me. I stared at the polished black shoes, then up into the haggard face. "That's how I lost it, this wretched eye." He almost smiled. "I don't think he had any intention of harming me. I could be wrong. Like most of his kind he was glorying in a new-found taste for power."

He sat in his chair, leaned back into it with a low gentle sigh. His cigarette glowed for the last time before it was stubbed out into the ashtray in his hand. I watched him place it carefully, meticulously, on the arm of the chair. The lingering embers of the cigarette glimmered for a moment, then died, leaving a thin blue trail of smoke.

"The next face I saw was the face of Otto Brunner. Leaning over me, whispering, soothing me. I shall never forget that. I thought he had the kindest face I had ever seen—the gentlest. I heard later of the atrocities he was said to have perpetrated in that camp—and permitted. Perversely I tried not to believe them, even when he himself, years later, talked about them. I've seen him cry like a baby, I've woken him from screaming nightmares, I once wrestled a gun from his hand when he tried to kill himself. He committed those atrocities, but somehow"—he shook his head slowly—"it's the other side of the coin, you see; the two faces of Janus. No man is wholly bad, nor for that matter, thank God, wholly good. I can speak for Otto Brunner when I say that since the war he has suffered the torments of the damned. He *is* the damned, I suppose. He deserves those torments and he knows it and endures them because he can do no other. He's tied to a wheel and will never be free—not until the day he dies.

"But to me he showed the face of kindness and gave me the sort of . . . affection I had never known. Neither of my parents cared for me as he did. That's why I have two fathers, Mark, and that's why I bear no sense of . . . filial obligation to my mother. She can go bay the moon for all I care.

"I never saw my father again—Ernst Sternberg that is. They killed him in that camp. Of all men he didn't deserve that. But then, none of them did.

"I did however see my mother again, many years later when she came to Buenos Aires to sing at the opera. I sat in the front row of the stalls only yards away from her and applauded with the rest. According to the critics, she was not at her best. I wouldn't know about that; I'm tone-deaf, you see, and that evening, for me, was sheer torture. You would think, wouldn't you, that the least she could have done would be to pass her music on to me. Whenever I think of my mother, I feel . . . deprived." The bitterness in his voice was almost tangible.

"But enough of her." He dismissed her as if she had never been. I wondered if he knew of the time, money and heartache it had cost her to set up the search for him after the war, and came to the conclusion that he must have known; Hedda would surely have told him, as Emily, her mother, must have told her.

Lorenz went on. "Had Otto Brunner not been on the spot when I was struck down, I would never have survived that morning. As it was, he saw the whole thing, took me to the infirmary and later, out of the camp to the hospital. He probably risked a great deal, but he was, after all, the *Kommandant* of the camp, so perhaps few questions were asked—if any. In those days things weren't as drastic as they later became; the Gestapo weren't so active. And what was one Jew-child when they had so many?

"Otto had a house in Mauthausen and there I came to live. I still have no idea why he behaved towards me as he did. He often said it was the horror of seeing a small boy in such pain. As time went on, his concern became affection. He was a solitary man, divorced, childless and without close friends, so it wasn't surprising that eventually he came to lavish a father's care on me. There was no record of me at the camp—he saw to that—and the fact that I was half Jewish didn't seem to worry him in the least. That he was responsible for the destruction of hundreds of other Jews also didn't seem to worry him. Janus again. And anyway it was the usual cry, wasn't it? 'Those were my orders.' I really didn't know what went on in those camps until afterwards when we were on the run. He never talked about it and we rarely had visitors. I was looked after during the daytime by a gentle elderly soul whom I came to call Mutti—she was all the mother I ever had. The memory of my father faded quickly as it usually does with children. Otto was never moved from that camp throughout the war. He's a diabetic so was unfit for combat duties anyway.

"With the disintegration of the Third Reich and the Russians coming closer by the hour, the writing was on the wall. In the midst of the panic of what-to-do-for-the-best, a stranger appeared at the house, a man in uniform, a *Standartenführer*—a colonel. He came several times. I never saw him clearly —I was bundled off to bed whenever he came. If I'd met him in the street, I wouldn't have recognised him. I knew only his uniform and the sound of his voice. I heard that voice again tonight over the telephone—older but unmistakable.

"His name was Steiger then—a personal friend, he told Otto, of the great Hermann Goering, and was in fact party to the Field Marshal's somewhat clandestine operation to 'liberate' art treasures and other valuables from occupied countries—which also meant that Steiger himself was not above creaming off some of the profits for his own personal use. He must have been a rich man even then. His present proposal, however—in exchange for a consideration—was that he would be willing to remove Otto from the path of the advancing Russians, then barely a day's march from Vienna, and smuggle him out of Europe before the Allied net closed and made escape virtually impossible. Otto jumped at the opportunity; as *Kommandant* of a concentration camp he knew he would be somewhere near the top of the Allied wanted list. He himself was quite wealthy too, so he could afford whatever Steiger was asking—he'd been in diamonds before the war with his father and grandfather and together they had apparently salted away quite a bit in Switzerland.

"He refused to go without me, and Steiger pointed out that a young boy travelling with his father would be even better cover. It would, however, cost a little more. He had no idea that I was not Otto's legitimate son. So the money was paid. With forged papers and false identities we were all set. And almost too late.

"We left Mauthausen on April 13th, the day the Russians took Vienna, less than two hundred kilometres away. The journey was a nightmare, and we made it alone, always fearing that Steiger was simply feathering his nest and heading us into a trap."

He paused, shaking his head at the memories crowding in on him. "Never, Mark," he said softly, "never cross a war-torn world in the company of a diabetic in constant need of care and medicine. It was eight months before we set foot in Latin America. By which time I had grown up. I was fifteen, with a man's responsibilities. Half the time Otto had been desperately ill, twice almost died. His suffering during that time seemed to bare his soul—certainly his conscience. Then it was that the nightmares began.

"It took time to acclimatise to Brazil. The war of course had taken its toll of Otto as it had of most people, but he was a comparatively young man and Rio de Janeiro was a diamond city talking the language of diamonds which he understood. Nevertheless, it was still some time before he was able to put up his plate announcing the formation of a new company: Rodrigo Bronson and Son. We settled down to what we hoped would be a long and profitable partnership.

"He was never a happy man, rarely smiled, never laughed. I've never heard him laugh."

Lorenz shifted in his chair, sat forward, elbows on his knees, hands clasped, staring down at them. "In the early sixties Adolf Eichmann was kidnapped by the Israelis and given a show trial with blow-by-blow coverage by the world's media. The effect of this on Otto was shattering; the nightmares and the horrors redoubled themselves. He was terrified of exposure. On the day Eichmann was hanged, he tried to blow his brains out; one day, he said, it would happen to him. Nothing gave him comfort. A sick conscience is worse than a sick body—there's no magical prescription to relieve it. He tried the church, but there was nothing there for him.

"He became morose and secretive. You could almost see the cloud of depression and despair which hung over him. His only therapy was his work.

"Last year he gave up; old, frail and sick, he finally handed the reins over to me, lock, stock and barrel, and for the first time I was allowed to see the books. He had always been close about the company's finances, and when I went through them, casually at first, I realised why. I discovered there was an annual deficit of one million dollars, withdrawn—in kind—and unaccounted for. 'Steiger,' he said when eventually I got him to talk about it. 'We are still paying Steiger.'

"It was blackmail, of course. The threat had come by long distance telephone shortly after Eichmann was hanged. It was all too easy to convince Otto of the inadvisability of ignoring that threat. Steiger even managed to suggest that he'd had a hand in the hunting down of Eichmann—a fabrication, but difficult to disprove. So there it was: for twenty-odd years, on the first day of every April, Otto had sent a million dollars' worth of diamonds by courier to Steiger in exchange for silence. So, apart from the initial payment at Mauthausen—whatever that was—Otto's so-called freedom has, to date, cost something in the region of twenty-four million dollars. I suppose one could say it's only money; that's certainly his attitude; money is the least of his troubles. Perhaps I should have let him kill himself; it might have been kinder. But a debt like his—to humanity—can never really be settled, can it? Certainly not by money, nor yet perhaps by death itself. I wonder if Eichmann's death settled anything? I doubt it. A lifetime of suffering may do it . . . I'm inclined to doubt that too.

"Well, the Israelis are on to him now, God knows how. They are a shrewd and patient people and, having got a finger on him, they now want to get him out. They even tried to use me as bait. The terrible truth is that had he known I was in their hands he would have come, crippled as he is, like a lamb to the slaughter. I know Otto and the extent of his . . . affection for me. I feel humble in the light of it. That's why I had to get away from them, why I killed to do it. Nazism, you see, still claims its victims."

He lit another cigarette, got up and moved around again, taking the ashtray with him.

"The only clue I had to Steiger's whereabouts was that he was somewhere in Vienna. I determined to hunt him down and when I found him, kill him.

"I sought out two of the couriers who had made the run before. The drop was ingenious insofar as it was conventional. No cloak-and-dagger theatricals, suggesting that Steiger was pretty sure of himself. On April 5 of each year the diamonds were deposited with a reputable diamond merchant on Kärntnerstrasse to be called for by one Van der Decken of Amsterdam. Under normal circumstances that would be the end of it; the courier's job was done and paid for. In my case, however, I needed to meet this Van der Decken, Steiger or whoever he was—I felt certain that for obvious reasons he no longer called himself Steiger. So, instead of the diamonds, I left a letter purporting to have been written by Otto, signed by him but forged by me. He wrote that he was seriously ill, had decided to hand over the business to Lorenz, his son; he thought it might be wise to conclude the matter once and for all by making one last substantial payment mutually to be agreed upon. Lorenz, having business in Vienna, would himself deliver the letter together with the payment due for the current period, which sum, however, would be retained by him until, and to ensure that, personal contact was made; he would then hand it over to none but Steiger himself. The letter ended with him begging Steiger on no account to inform his son of the reason for the diamonds changing hands. 'He knows nothing of our previous association,' he wrote. 'I have simply told him that it is an ancient debt of honour which should have been paid years ago.' "

He paused for a second, then went on. "Disingenuous perhaps, its purpose only to lure Steiger into the open. I felt sure it would—more especially since I was supposed to be ignorant of the blackmail angle. I attached a note saying that I was staying at the Imperial and would be pleased to hear from him at his earliest convenience; I had goods of considerable value to hand over to him and was eager to part with them as soon as possible."

He was standing straddle-legged in front of us, staring reflectively at his cigarette. "Do you know, I was really quite excited at the prospect of meeting him. I knew he wouldn't come alone, of course—if indeed he came at all— but I had it all worked out; every contingency was covered. Except"—he smiled wryly—"the one I hadn't thought of: the Israeli brigade.

"I was on the way back to the hotel when they jumped me—in broad daylight somewhere near the Albertinaplatz with hundreds of people milling around. The Viennese, like the British, have a way of looking but not seeing, in case they get involved in something unpleasant. They bundled me into a car, two of them sat on me and I was taken to this miserable warehouse near the river somewhere. There they stripped me, tied me up and worked me over with the delicacy I might have expected from Steiger had I fallen into his hands. In fact, for the first half-hour I thought they *were* his lot. I was astounded when I realised who they really were. It never occurred to me that I had fallen foul of anyone else—a Jewish contingent least of all.

"Well, the Jewish half of me had quite a beating that afternoon. I could only feel shame for them." He was staring again at the glowing tip of his cigarette. "Three burning cigarettes on the genitals is really something one has to experience to believe. Before I passed out I told them I was the son of Alicia Sternberg, the singer. For the first and last time in my life, I turned to my mother for help . . ."

He shrugged, smiled and took himself off to his chair, where, perching on its arm, he slowly extinguished the cigarette. "I rather think I ought to give up smoking." As he looked at us, the quiet smile faded from his lips. "And that, I think, is where we came in . . ."

CHAPTER FIFTEEN

Huddled in my damp raincoat, I stared apprehensively down the yellow beams of the headlights. She drove with a fine, swashbuckling disregard for life and limb, fast, accurate and quite firmly on the crown of the road. The steady swill of rain and the beat of the wipers made up the sum of my physical discomfort.

When I'm moderately scared, I'm apt to think in quotes because nothing original seems adequate. The one I had latched on to at that moment was Andy Marvell's "But at my back I always hear Time's winged chariot hurrying near." I sank chin and ears deeper into the sturdy protection of my high storm-collar. When I'm really scared I can't think at all. That came later when a truck the size of a high-rise block of flats hove around a corner at a dizzy angle and bore down upon us with three pairs of unblinking eyes and a horn which sounded like Gabriel's trumpet. My tongue stuck to the roof of my mouth and I shut my eyes like a child as the thing thundered past us like a war-horse at a tournament.

"Pull over," I gasped when feeling returned.

"What?"

"Pull over, please."

We rocked to a halt. The deathly silence supplied by the rain beating on the roof and the heavy thud of the wipers was comforting. I leaned over and switched off the engine. That was even better. Now it was only the rain trying to get in.

She sounded petulant. "What is it?"

"I think I'm having an attack of the vapours—ignore me."

She took it like a man. "Would you like a cigarette?"

"Yuk!"

We sat for a moment in silent reserve. I swept all my broken thoughts together into an untidy heap and began picking them over without relish.

"Will you tell me something?" She gave me no encouragement. "Why weren't you at the opera tonight?"

"Because it was ballet night and I don't dance."

"Ah . . ." The rain steamed opaquely down the windscreen and we were beginning to steam up. "How was it," was my next tentative question, "that you just happened to be around when I was running for my life?"

She turned her head and studied my profile for an unending moment. "Now you're wondering whose side *I'm* on, I suppose?"

"Listen," I rejoined tartly. "There's only one person I'm absolutely sure of at this moment and that's me, jolly old Mark Savage. Everybody else I know has got a touch of the Janus-heads, as Lorenz would have it. What were you doing at the Kékszákallú tonight?"

"I often go there." She sounded quite reasonable. "It happens to be quite a good restaurant; I eat and drink there. It's also one of the stamping-grounds of the opera crowd—chorus and principals alike—a good place to relax in, unwind after a show. Most of the cafés in the centre are packed with tourists."

I reached for my wallet and gave her the photograph of herself and others living it up at the Kékszákallú. She switched on the interior light. I laid a delicate finger on Hans Schmidt. "Who's he? The principal baritone?"

She looked at Hans Schmidt for some time in silence. "I do see what you mean," she said quietly.

"Well?"

"Well . . ." She took a deep breath. "The Kékszákallú is also a get-together place for the—er—organisation you are prepared to dislike so much—the one with the swastika. He," she tapped the photo and returned it to me, "is one of us."

"He's also one of Hertz'."

"True."

"And is Stephan Hertz one of you?"

"No, he's a loner, not a joiner. Mark, you've just got to believe that we are not about to plunge the world into another holocaust, nor are we after world domination. Our sites are parochial, not universal. Like all members of a quasi-political group, some lean to the left, some to the right, but always, somewhere in the middle, there is common ground. The Kékszákallú is that common ground. Hans Schmidt works for Stephan Hertz as I work for the State Opera. Until tonight I knew nothing positive about Hertz' operations. Hans mutters on about it sometimes, but only when he's in his cups; no one listens. At his best Hans is quite a good companion."

"At his worst he's a sod."

"He's also seen you at your worst," she rebuked me with gentle primness. "By great good fortune—*your* good fortune—I stumbled across him tonight as he was about to be whisked off to the hospital in an ambulance. He was fulminating about you and your kind—as much as he was able to fulminate with a broken voice box. He said Hertz had got you and you'd be lucky to get out of there alive, and if Hertz didn't kill you, *he* would. That was when all the pieces began to fall into place. I knew then that the man Lorenz was looking for—Steiger—was the one you had turned up—Hertz. First of all, I contacted Lorenz, then some of the gang, to set up a rescue operation. There are emergency exits to the Kékszákallú known only to a few, in case of trouble. I crawled about the place for ages trying to locate you, but every other door seemed to be locked. Then I heard the shot which killed your ape-man—his name was Albert by the way; others heard it too, doors were unlocked, people began stamping about and I managed somehow to get myself locked into his inner sanctum. I was actually skulking under his desk when he came in and blasted someone important over his telephone. He said he was sure you were still in the building somewhere and was going to the restaurant himself to watch for you there and would whoever-it-was-he-was-talking-to get all concerned to search the place from cellar to attic. When he'd gone, I followed him, and then without knowing exactly how I got there, I was in the restaurant and you were there too, looking the worse for wear and wandering about like a lost soul. So that was that. Thank God Franz was on hand with the car. You owe him an apology, by the way. He nearly fell off Demel's roof with fright. Is there anything else you want to know?"

I met her smiling eyes with a sheepish grin. "It's a tangled bloody web though, isn't it? Even you have to admit that," I frowned suddenly, recalling the true deceit which the events of the evening had thrown up. "I suppose you didn't even suspect Verne Wayne?"

As she switched off the interior light, I could see the lines of disillusionment deeply etched about her mouth. "Not for a second. I would have trusted him with my life, I really would. That's the most terrible aspect of the whole thing. Poor Alicia, she mustn't know about him. Does that mean she's left with nothing?"

I shook my head. "He'd be too shrewd for that. No, I'd say that he's simply redirected most of her smuggling traffic into his own and Hertz' pockets, though how Hertz persuaded him over to his side after so many years of faithful service to Alice, God alone knows. The books are obviously cooked quite cleverly so anyone would have to delve pretty deep to find the deficit; probably only Alice would be able to put a finger on it, and knowing her, I bet she's never even asked to see the bloody books; she trusted him implicitly. That, as you say, is what makes it such a pig of a situation. When she dies, I doubt if even probate will unearth the smuggling racket; she and Verne would have worked that one out years ago. Sammy told me you were in on it too. Is that right?"

"Only as a sort of baby courier. Sammy and I were the first links in two different runs, that's all. Each of us did it for the fun of the thing; there was no money in it, and it amused Alicia. It was a sort of game she liked playing. She barely touched the things herself. She delivered the diamonds to Sammy for his particular run to Israel and gave me mine to be passed on to the next letter-box. Verne Wayne did all the difficult wheeling and dealing."

A sudden great burst of understanding flooded over me. "Demel's!" I almost shouted. "That's it, isn't it? Demel's. The diamonds are in those flaming boxes of chocolates, right? She gave a box to Sammy when we visited him, and your mother brought one to the opera and passed it over to Alice. When I was collecting her things after the show, the box was missing and she said she'd got it in her bag, which was nonsense now I come to think of it;

that evening bag of hers wasn't big enough. Why the hell didn't I think of that before? I'm right, aren't I?"

She smiled benignly. "The diamonds were in the chocolates, and the chocolates were in the boxes. Liqueur chocolates. There's a little woman at Demel's—a little woman more highly paid than even Udo knows about—who actually makes most of the liqueur chocolates, and every now and again instead of liqueur and a cherry she slips a diamond into the mould. Ten diamonds to one box. Caratwise that's quite a shipment. And it's ingenious too, I suppose, since customs are hardly likely to burrow about among your chocolates."

I gave a woeful shake of the head. "The world isn't safe to live in any more. I shall never bite knowingly into a liqueur chocolate again. Nor will I ever trust a man with a glass eye. My motto from now on will be, All eyes on the table. I imagine the chocolate idea was Alice's?"

"It sounds like her."

"And Udo didn't know about it? They were sliding diamonds into his chocolates and he didn't know about it?" She shook her head. I regarded her with the smallest squinch of family pride. "You have to admit that I come from a most devious and fascinating stock. How much of Cousin Lorenz' saga did you know before tonight?"

"He told us only what he thought necessary."

"Us? The swastika lot you mean?"

"It's a fraternity," she said, slightly piqued, "and, for your information, has branches all over the world. We exist to help those of our persuasion who need assistance, ways and means, protection—anything reasonable. Lorenz contacted us from Antwerp on his way to Vienna requesting the use of a safe house. We knew he was Otto Brunner's son and that was all. And enough. Unfortunately the Israelis were quicker off the mark than we were. They probably had a tip-off from one of their people back in Rio. So. Then all this started and here we are sitting in the middle of nowhere in a rainstorm."

I scrubbed at the windscreen and peered out into the miserable night. "Okay, let's go again, shall we? But please, if only for my peace of mind, would it bother you if we kept to our side of the road?"

She grinned suddenly and we left the curb as from a launching pad. I closed my eyes. I had a lot to think about but not a lot of brain left to do it with. I had shot my bolt.

"Did you want to stay with Lorenz tonight?" she asked a moment later.

"Not particularly. He seems to have everything in hand. I just hope he knows what he's doing. He obviously wanted us to stay, but you've got a home to go to and I'd rather like to keep an eye on Alice while she's still with us." I asked, "Do you like him—Lorenz?"

"Very much. Difficult to think of him as Alicia's son though, turning up after all these years."

"You're not going to tell her, I hope?"

"If I'd wanted to, I'd have done so long ago."

"So why didn't you?"

"Because Lorenz asked us not to."

"Exactly. She's *his* mother."

"He's nothing like her though, is he?"

"Oddly enough he reminds me of my father sometimes."

"Oddly enough," she said, "he sometimes reminds me of you."

I wiped the condensation off the window with my forearm. A string of lights marched away to the right.

"That's the Kanal," she explained. "Franz Josefs Kai."

"Near Sammy's place? Rudolfsplatz?" I peered closely at my watch, frowning to myself. I was uneasy about Sammy.

We were crossing the bridge. She pointed. "Over there . . . behind Heinrichsgasse."

I came to a sudden decision. "Drop me off, will you?"

"Here?"

"I'd like to have a word with him."

"He'll be in bed."

"Then I'll get him up."

She pulled up with a jerk. "Why disturb him at this hour?"

I shrugged. "I don't know. I just want to make sure he *is* in bed, I suppose." She was tying herself into her rainwear. "No, you go on," I told her. "I'll find my own way back. A walk in the rain will do me good after all that hot air we've been through tonight."

"How's the head?"

"Potassium cyanide works wonders." I shoved open the door. "One last thing—look in on Alice, will you, before you turn in? Make sure she's okay."

I got out of the car and sloshed around to her window. "Go straight home," I smiled, "and don't talk to strangers." Her face was turned towards me. I leant in and touched her lips with mine. "Thank you," I said, "very much."

She sat looking at me for a still second, her eyes suddenly bright. "You sure you don't want me to come with you?"

"Home," I said. "Beauty sleep. See you tomorrow."

She waved at me, touched a gear and a pedal and shot off in a shower of spray, most of which ended up over me. Dripping forlornly, I stood and watched the red glow of her rear-lamps until they disappeared, pulling up my collar and stamping life into my feet, which were ice cold. I trudged off along Franz Josefs Kai my thoughts suddenly and disturbingly full of her.

Until I turned into Heinrichsgasse; then they were suddenly and disturbingly full of Sammy Meier. Why? Something about him was worrying me; it had sat uncomfortably at the back of my benumbed brain, which had nudged at it a couple of times and then turned to other, more pressing, matters—such as the killing of Gorilla Albert, the flight from the Kékszákallú, the bang on the head, potassium cyanide, and then of course, Lorenz and his troubles . . .

My footsteps were loud and important in the dreary wet darkness; as I turned into Rudolfsplatz, I tried to quieten them as if fearful of being heard. Why again? Who was there to hear them? Sammy would be in bed and asleep.

I passed through the gaunt jungle of scaffolding and wet green swathings of the building undergoing the face-lift. I stumbled over broken paving stones and sank ankle-deep into glutinous mud which squelched and sucked as I withdrew my ruined shoes. Rain bucketed down on all sides, thundering on the stretched and bellying tarpaulins above my head; red warning lamps glimmered dimly in the darkness. I stepped out into the road to avoid a solid curtain of water sluicing down from the roof—and stopped.

My solar plexus gave a jerk as if it had been struck and then slowly tied itself into a knot.

Immediately ahead of me stood the grey Volkswagen. For a full minute at least I stood rooted, appalled by the implications aroused at the sight of the vehicle. I moved in slowly. Sidelights were burning, the car empty. I crossed the road and stared up at the windows of the fourth floor. No glimmer of light showed. The square was deserted, the desolate splashing of rain and a sudden burst of laughter from the hotel three doors away the only sounds.

As I approached the shadowy porch, I remembered the source of my unrest about Sammy. It had been the few words in Hungarian exchanged by Hertz and Wayne which had included, I had thought, the names of Sternberg and Sammy Meier . . .

I pushed gently at the door. It creaked open. Beyond it lay black darkness relieved only by the red glow of a light switch on the wall. I'd have to risk light. I pressed the button.

The gates of the ancient elevator were closed, the elevator elsewhere. I peered up the shaft counting the floors. It stood at the fourth. Recalling the racket it made, I decided against bringing it down.

Why had the mention of those two names made such a subconscious impression on me? In what context had they been spoken?

I began the long climb swiftly, knowing that the automatic time mechanism would soon extinguish the light. On the second floor it did and I didn't renew it, continuing to move upwards in the thick darkness, more cautiously now. The house was like a house of the dead. From nowhere came a sound.

A lurch of realisation brought me to a halt. The names of Sternberg and Meier had been mentioned by Verne Wayne shortly after I had told Hertz that everyone had known of my projected visit to the Kékszakallú. He had turned to Wayne and presumably asked in Hungarian if that was true and if so, who? Wayne had said the names Alicia Sternberg and Sammy Meier. The carrot dangled for my own oath of silence had been a star-spangled career in Hertz' video films; but what, I wondered with sinking heart, had he in mind for others he believed to be in possession of facts so dangerous to him.

I quickened my pace. The dust and dirt on the top landing gritted beneath my feet. In the darkness my hand felt for the elevator gates. They were open.

I became aware of a glimmer of light, very dim but enough to realise that Sammy's front door also stood open.

I reached quietly for my gun. I stuffed my apprehension down my throat and recognised in its place the frigid, almost primeval sensation of cold fury I had known only twice in my life and which I had learnt to dread. In that mood I knew I could kill . . .

From far below came a sudden flurry of sound, the thud of the front door, loud footsteps. Someone switched on the light and pressed the elevator button; at my elbow the thing seemed to jerk and strain in response to the repeated impatient electrical impulses. Taking advantage of the loud cursings from below, I covered the short distance to Sammy's door, went through it fast and stood on the far side of it listening for movement from the apartment beyond and to the grumbling frustration from below; echoing footsteps began pounding resolutely upwards. As they approached, I pushed the door closed a fraction; it creaked appallingly. The ascending feet reached the second floor with a great groan of relief; the rattle of keys, a lock turning, more muttering and finally the reverberating crash of a closing door.

Utter silence.

I resumed my breathing, took out a handkerchief and wiped my wet face; some of the dampness was rain oozing steadily from my waterlogged hair—the rest was cold sweat. I began to wish I hadn't come. The dreaded killing mood had passed; all I had in exchange was fear. The empty waiting car downstairs, the unclosed lift gates, the open front door—all breathed danger.

At the far end of the wide hall the sitting-room door stood ajar; from it came the faint glimmer of light, low on the floor, throwing the slight rucking of the carpet into relief. Why, I wondered, so low?

Without a great deal of extra creaking I pushed shut the front door and slid the lock carefully into place. I moved noiselessly on the thick pile carpet towards the light, ears straining for the slightest sound. I splayed my fingers against the door and pushed gently; it swung slowly inwards.

The light was low because the lamp was on the floor. I viewed the room with dread. Furniture, hangings, pictures, books were piled high in grotesquely shaped humps and bundles looming black and still in the bizarre lighting like so many dead and bloated bodies on a battlefield. A maniac had gone berserk, tearing and slashing and battering. Somewhere amongst the rubble a clock ticked erratically.

I edged into the room, every sense at concert pitch, every instinct searching, listening, probing into the rooms beyond for a lurking presence. My feet crunched on glass and splintered wood, I moved towards the ticking clock because the sound of it was comforting. Reaching the lamp, I righted it, stared about me without comprehension. The ticking at my feet drew my eyes downwards. I couldn't see the clock because it lay beneath him . . .

The light bucked as the lamp shifted on its precarious base. I thought I saw him move. Kneeling beside him, I put aside the gun and laid hold of the broad shoulders. "Sammy . . . ?" With brute and frantic strength I clawed and hauled at him, levering him over on to his back; the head lolled on a fallen cushion; glazed, pain-wracked eyes stared blindly into mine. The convulsed hands had died clutching at the weapon buried somewhere beneath his rib cage; blood had seeped between the fingers, welling obscenely over his white shirt. By the sleeve of his cardigan I gently raised one of the hands; it was still warm and the movement stirred the sluggish red glint of metal—a silver meat skewer.

I released the hand and sank back on to my haunches, swaying and feeling sick. I closed my eyes.

The uneven ticking of the fallen clock faltered, missed a beat and stopped altogether. Rain gusted against the window.

Beside the clock lay the big Colt pistol I had entrusted to him. I took it up and removed the magazine. Empty. The shells, I knew, would be in the pocket of that sagging old cardigan. Man of bloody peace, I thought with an overwhelming sense of bitterness, where did it get you?

Above the beating of the rain came another sound, a hollow, soughing sound like a stealthy wind creeping through reeds. Snatching up my gun, I started to my feet. My skin seemed to tighten over my cheek-bones; my scalp crawled. Breathing—someone was breathing—in the next room.

I stared at the open door through which Sammy had brought the coffee so long ago and moved towards it. Finding it impossible to wade through the muck and litter on the floor without noise, I abandoned caution altogether and arrived at the doorway in a rush, crouching beside it, the little Beholla searching the darkness warily. The sound had stopped. I could sense him holding his breath.

I slid into the room, my back to the paler rectangle of window, and switched on the light. The kitchen. Empty.

Opposite, another door stood half open, darkness beyond it; a light switch on the outside wall suggested a bathroom. As I ranged up alongside, there came from inside a long shuddering intake of breath.

Striking down at the switch, I kicked hard on the door. There came a sharp yelp of fright.

He was huddled in a corner between the bath and a wash-basin. My first glimpse of him was of a pair of blood-stained open palms raised before his face to shield his eyes from the sudden light. He was half hidden behind a stained towel trailing from the basin. I stepped in and snatched it away. Slowly the hands came down, but no further than the mouth. The once handsome face was streaked with blood and tears, the eyes wide, uncomprehending. Even the white hair glinted with blood.

"Hello, Verne," I said quietly.

The only answer was a muffled swallowing sound. I think he half recognised me; a faint gleam of understanding flickered in the wide eyes as they flooded with sudden tears, heavy and glutinous, like gouts of glycerine. They cut through the blood stains like acid biting into metal. The blood was Sammy Meier's.

I raised the gun and levelled it at his eyes—at a range of six inches. If you have to use it, Alice had said, get in close.

"Is this close enough?" I asked aloud. I had no intention of frightening him. I seemed to be playing out some private drama of my own. It was the sound of his voice which drew me back from the brink.

"Mark . . . ? It is Mark, isn't it?"

I stared at him blankly. I had been a hair's breadth from homicide. I lowered the gun. "We must get you away from here," I muttered. "Come on . . . get up . . ."

I backed away and studied him closely as he shambled untidily to his feet, putting his weight first on the bath, then on the wash-basin. I was finding it difficult to trust the foolish, lopsided look on his face. Was it an act, or had he really lost his marbles?

I knew that the answer to both questions was in the negative. If it were an act he would have dispensed with me long ago—when I was mooning defenceless over the fallen Sammy. As for losing his marbles—momentarily perhaps as a result of shock or even of the blow he'd received on the back of the head in the garage.

"I've killed him, haven't I?" He was vaguely defensive. "Sammy . . . I've killed him, right?"

I nodded slowly as he reached out a hand for my support.

"We must get you away," I said again.

"He fought me," he muttered with a flicker of spirit. "Why did he fight me?"

"Come on." I was suddenly impatient, angry with myself and him too.

There was only one reasonable thing to do: get him to the nearest police station—where the hell was that?—hand him over, tell them what had happened and let them clean up the mess.

I helped him through the shambles of the sitting-room in the still centre of which lay the gentle Sammy—the sad, vanquished man of peace—at peace. "Blessed are the peacemakers, for they shall be called the children of God." Goodbye, Sammy, child of God.

As we stumbled in the direction of the door, I glanced around for a telephone. Even if he had one, I probably wouldn't be able to find it in the midst of all that mess. But it would be nice to ring the authorities and tell them to come and collect; I didn't know what to do with a half-crazed murderer, did I?

Propping him against the doorpost, I went off on a desultory search for a telephone. I included the bedroom, the room in which Albert the Gorilla had been lurking during my first visit, but there was no phone, no wires, no junction box; he obviously hadn't got one. Muggins would have to cope whether he liked it or not.

On my way back I caught sight of a Demel chocolate box half hidden beneath an upturned chair. Routing it out, I lifted the lid: ten chocolates nestled invitingly in their wrappings. I was tempted to bite into one, thought of my teeth's welfare and shoved the box into the pocket of my raincoat, hoping I had liberated a fortune.

I left the light on.

Verne hadn't stirred. He stood in the doorway at an awkward angle, a parcel awaiting collection, his once immaculate clothes torn and dishevelled, blood staining his shirt and hands, damp hair trailing sweatily into his eyes. I put a tentative arm about his waist and humped him into action, propelling him like a far gone drinking companion through the hall to the front door.

"What happened, for Christ's sake?" I mumbled as I pulled the door shut and heaved him over to the lift, where I sat him on the bench seat inside whilst I coped with the gates. The unnerving clanking noises aroused by the jab of my finger on the button sounded like the ghost of Jacob Marley on the loose.

I stared down at the slumped figure. "Why did you have to kill him? He wouldn't have done you any harm, you know that."

"He wanted it . . ."

"What do you mean, 'he wanted it'? Who wanted it?"

He raised his head. "What?"

"Hertz? Is that who wanted him dead?"

"Hertz said . . ."

The lift came to a jolting halt. I grabbed his shoulders and shook him hard. "What did Hertz say?"

He stared up at me blankly, wagging his head stupidly. "Something . . . don't remember . . ."

I squawked at him in fury and dragged open the gates. "Well, you'd better bloody remember." I got him to his feet and bundled him out of the lift. "Come on, for Christ's sake."

He shambled along beside me making small protesting noises at my rough handling of him. I pushed him down the steps and out into the streaming light. As the cold air hit him, he wrenched away from my grasp and, raising his face to the black sky, opened his mouth to the rain, gulping it down with suppressed grunts of enjoyment.

I opened the door of the car and urged him, still protesting, towards it. "Where we going?"

"Police station, that's where we're going. Someone's got to look after you." I shoved him inside, slammed the door and tramped around and settled into the driver's seat. "Keys," I snarled.

As he plunged a hand into his pocket, I sensed rather than saw the cunning on his face; before I could react to it, he had jumped me, lashing a hand viciously into my eyes. A myriad of tiny lights flickered in the darkness, then he punched me hard in the stomach, wrenched open the door, and dived out into the night.

I scrabbled insanely at the door handle, half fell on to the road, grazing my knee. I could hear his shambling footsteps fading fast in the direction of

Heinrichsgasse. Doubled up by the blow in the stomach, I trundled off in pursuit.

In Heinrichsgasse he was silhouetted against the lights of Franz Josefs Kai. Moving with more speed than I would have thought him capable of, he was making for the Underground station.

I burst into the lights of the wide Kai as he was ploughing across a stretch of grass on the far side of it, heading towards the parapet of the fast road which lay between him and the Kanal.

A speeding car yelped at me as I charged into its path. With a shrill squeal of tyres and brakes it swerved hideously. Teutonic imprecations were screamed at me from the driver's window. I floundered over the tramlines, to the soggy grass and on to a concrete pathway. Beyond the parapet heavy traffic raced along the sunken motorway.

I pulled up, panting, and glared about me. Not a glimpse of him. I retraced my steps a few paces. He could only have ducked behind the Underground station, which bulked in the darkness. The station itself was closed. I set off again at a smart trot and almost immediately drew up again. A large black hole yawned in front of me, steps plunging downwards into darkness; a subway.

Edging uncertainly towards the steps, I paused to listen. Other than the rush and roar of traffic I could hear nothing. A faintest glimmer of light glowed from the bowels of the earth.

My nostrils quivered. The stench was overpowering; I moved with caution. The steps were wet with slime and strewn with filth and garbage. I fought shy of the handrail.

The dimly lit subway branched off at a right angle. Beyond lay the empty sprawl of dockside, beyond that the Kanal itself. Hugging the sweating wall, I emerged carefully on to the wide expanse of concreted waterfront. Lamps set at wide intervals along the quayside shed the only light; enough to see that no other living person was in sight.

Hunching into my soggy raincoat and blinking through the sheeting rain, I wondered whether I had taken a wrong steer; he could just as easily have made for the Underground.

What the hell, growled an inner voice. Leave him, for God's sake; let him work out his own salvation; let him rot.

I was on the move again, skirting the densest of the shadows but probing each for a darker shape within. A huge poster carrying a life-sized silhouette of a man straddled against a white background had me leaping for my gun; I almost shot it off the wall.

I edged towards the water. Between me and the Kanal proper was what looked like a disused landing-stage reached only by a rickety iron foot-bridge spanning twenty feet or so of evil-smelling water astir with driftwood and other flotsam. An attempt had been made to discourage the use of the bridge by an entanglement of barbed wire stranded across the iron ladder and handrails which gave access to it. The rusted wire had long since been hacked through.

Shielding my eyes against the rain, I stared across at the stone island. It looked deserted, but an occasional bollard and a couple of abandoned packing-cases large enough to conceal a man loomed in the darkness.

I hesitated only for a second, then picked my way carefully through the wire and across the bridge. The island was no more than a dozen feet across and as many yards long. To the right was the Saltztorbrücke, to the left, further away, what could only be the Augarten Bridge.

Treading quietly, gun in hand, I made a wary circuit of the packing-cases. Further away, towards the Saltztorbrücke, black against the oily glint of the water, loomed other unidentifiable objects. I moved towards them.

Glistening tarpaulins flapped wetly around a forgotten jumble of junk rotted over the years and smelling like an abandoned graveyard. I kicked it around, burrowing about among the filth and debris, listening to the scurry and scratching of tiny claws and wishing I were elsewhere. Hope died. I had lost him.

As I shoved the gun into my pocket, something creaked as if a sudden weight had been placed upon it. I was in the act of turning when an invisible hand grabbed at my ankle. Momentarily off balance, I went down with a crash; he was on me before I reached the flat, tearing at my face and throat, snapping and growling like a mad dog.

After the day and night I had just lived through, I was in no condition to put up much of a fight with a raving lunatic, but I rose to the occasion with a vigour and brutality which astounded even me. I kicked and slashed, went for his eyes and genitals and at one moment even resorted to my teeth.

It was not the sort of battle Lord Queensberry and his lot would have approved of, but to hell with Lord Queensberry and his bloody rules. Sod the rules! We slogged and clawed and pounded, wearing each other down until there would seem to be nothing left.

It was his years which eventually told against him. I could sense him weakening, staggering with fatigue, hear the struggle for breath, but far from letting up, I increased my efforts. I didn't care how bloody old he was; if he'd gone down on his knees and begged for mercy, I would have kicked his teeth in. He had killed Sammy Meier without provocation, double-crossed Alice . . .

A final hammer blow full in his face delivered with every ounce of weight and strength behind it sent him splaying like a starfish out into the wet night and down into the black waters of the Kanal, where, like a damp rag doll, he lay slurping on the surface for what seemed to be an interminable time, heaving sluggishly as if still searching for breath. I sank to my knees, trembling and twitching with exhaustion. Without emotion I watched him roll over on to his face and sink slowly beneath the surface, the oily water closing over him gently as a benediction. He was gone.

No thought of rescue occurred to me. I knelt there thinking of nothing, conscious of the relief of stillness, the deadly bruising of my body and the blood which flowed from my nostrils. I hurt.

The rain washed away the blood; the bone-piercing cold of freezing sweat persuaded me at last to my feet. I stumbled away from that awful place moving on feet which belonged to someone else, swaying across the iron bridge and clawing through the rusted wire. Emerging from the murk of that evil-smelling tunnel and slime-laden steps was like rising from the dead . . .

I sat shivering on a friendly wayside bench, breathing deeply and painfully. With a damp handkerchief I tried to clean myself up. Then hauling myself to my feet, I lurched off in search of a telephone. I jabbed out the number of a police station and gave them Sammy's address almost before they had lifted the receiver. "You'll find a dead man there. The man who killed him is somewhere in the Kanal. You'll find him too, I expect."

"And who are you, sir? Your name and address, if you please." There was no emotion in the voice. I could see his pencil poised over the paper.

I hung up and went home.

CHAPTER SIXTEEN

Bright sunlight streamed into the room, hurting my eyes. I lay on my side and stared without comprehension at an inept portrait of Winston Churchill in a messy wig. I closed down again wondering what he was doing there. In the russet darkness behind my lids I saw Verne Wayne floating face downwards in a sea of red-black water. I came to abruptly, half rolled over on to my back and yelped with unexpected pain.

"Jesus," I whispered as the spasm subsided.

I moved an arm, flexed my hand; from fingertips to shoulder was one long agony of torture. I experimented with a leg—I'd never walk again. I gave a low protesting moan.

"Good morning," said a voice behind me, gentle and full of care. I tried without success to turn my head.

"You'd better come round the other side," I muttered. "My neck won't work." Even my tongue hurt.

She came and stood between me and whoever it was in the wig. L. v. B., that's who it was. Who else? I screwed up my eyes, which felt like balls of hell-fire. "Hi," I said faintly, "I think I may be dying."

She crouched on the edge of the bed, as gently as a mother hen on an unhatched egg. I silently applauded her care; any undue vibration and I might well have disintegrated.

"You're in a terrible state," she told me in case I hadn't noticed. "What happened?"

I was silent for a time, not trusting myself to speak. My throat felt restricted. I touched her hand. "I killed Verne Wayne." I heard the quick intake of breath. "He's in the Kanal somewhere . . ." I felt tears coming; she sensed them too.

"Don't talk now." She got up. "I brought you some tea."

She nailed me up into some sort of sitting position, almost unbearable on account of a previously undiscovered bruised right buttock. I gave her a tired smile. "What are you doing in a chap's bedroom anyway?" I had become tardily aware that beneath the duvet I was naked.

"I came up to see if everything was all right. Just as well I did. The door was wide open and you were sprawled on the bed with nothing on." I blinked at her; she shook her head. "Not a stitch." She laid a cool finger on my bruised lips. "You looked lovely—almost better than in clothes. I took pity on you and hid you away."

I gave her a lopsided grin. "I was in something of a state. I seem to remember clambering into a hot bath so I wouldn't be stiff in the morning . . . there's a laugh . . . ! Sorry and all that."

"It was a pleasure." She glanced at her watch. "I was going to let you sleep it off, but Lorenz has been on the phone, wants you to meet him."

"He's coming out?"

"The Clock Museum. Midday."

"But it's not safe for him—all those crazy fanatics . . ."

"That's his worry."

"Where are my clothes?" I made some incoherent noises and several painful and unsuccessful attempts to get out of bed, but she gently pushed me back. "Tea first, then some breakfast."

I sat in a frustrated heap and watched her moving over to a table by the window where she had parked a tray of tea things. She was wearing a skirt of white pleated linen topped by a soft yellow shirt. Her legs were long and slim —I hadn't seen her legs before.

"If he can get to the Clock Museum, then he can bloody well lug himself over here to see his mother," I grumbled half to myself. "Least he can do. How is she this morning?" I had, in fact, checked up on her last night when I'd got in—just in case—and found her tucked up and sleeping peacefully.

Hedda shrugged as she brought over the tea. "All the doctor says is that she's been overdoing it, but we all know that. She's just lying there fretting about Lorenz, though whether it would be good for her to meet him is another matter. The shock of seeing him could finish her off altogether."

I sipped at the tea, swilling it around my mouth with care; there was a tooth on the loose in there somewhere. She was back again, this time with a small steaming bowl of something in her hand and a roll of cotton wool. "What's this, breakfast?"

"Face. Those cuts and bruises need attention." She was gentle and I was more than willing. She asked quietly, "Was it a fair fight?"

"No."

"Why not?"

"Because he was twice my age, that's why not. But . . ." I hesitated, shaking my head. The vision of Sammy rose up in my mind's eye, lying on his back in that shambles of a room, eyes glazed, hands clutching at that fearsome weapon . . .

"But?"

"He killed Sammy." Her hand faltered. I closed my eyes, which didn't prevent the tears from seeping through the lids. "He stabbed him—with a meat skewer."

There was a long silence. She dabbed steadily at my bruised face with something astringent.

I told her the whole story. She was bathing my split knuckles when I finished, and said nothing. She had tidied up and put away the basin before she spoke again. She stood over me holding my hand. "It was a terrible thing to happen—to both of you—but perhaps it's better this way. He would have . . ."

"I should have fished him out of there."

"To suffer more?"

"We don't know that . . ."

"Oh come on, Mark," she exclaimed with a sudden spurt of asperity. "He'd have gone through hell if the law had got him. You know that as well as I do."

"But he didn't know what he was doing. He tore that place to pieces. He was demented."

"So they would have shut him up somewhere for the rest of his life. It's no good thinking like that. It's done; there's nothing you or anyone else can do about it now."

"Dear Christ, I can't ever remember being so mad. I wanted to kill him. The only difference between him and me was that I *knew* what I was doing and he didn't."

"Mark, shut up!" Her eyes flared. "Please . . . shut up." She sat on the bed beside me. "Listen. You're not to tell anyone about this. No one. Do you understand? Not Alicia, not my mother—least of all my mother! Lorenz, if you like, but no one else. As far as the world is concerned, Verne killed Sammy and then threw himself into the Kanal. And that's that. There's nothing to connect you with his death." She paused fearfully. "Is there?"

I thought for a moment and shook my head. Her voice softened. "Be sensible, Mark dear. You're going to have to live with it anyway, but leave it at that. Please . . . ?" She stared at me earnestly until my eyes met hers. "Promise?" I nodded. She leaned in and touched my cheek with her lips.

"Dear Mark," she whispered. Her voice trembled slightly. "I wish we weren't half a world apart." I held on to her suddenly, but she pushed me gently away. "I'll get your clothes. You left them strewn all over the bathroom. None of them seem to be much good any more. Your raincoat will have to go straight to the cleaners."

"Which reminds me," I said, pulling myself together and joining in the game of mind over matter, "one of its pockets contains a fortune liberated from Sammy's flat."

She had returned my cup to the tray and now held up the Demel box. "This fortune, you mean?"

"You've been through my pockets."

"I thought it might be a gun."

For the first time I remembered Alice's Beholla. My heart sank. If I'd dropped it on the dockside, I'd have to get back there fast before anyone else laid hands on it—like the police. If they picked it up, it would lead them straight to Alice.

"The gun," said Hedda quietly as if reading my worries, "was in the other pocket." She was beside me again, Demel box in one hand, the Beholla in the other.

I gave a fervent sigh of relief. Even that hurt.

She laid both articles on the duvet. "They just about sum up Vienna for me. Guns and bloody chocolates. Lorenz' Janus head again." I opened the box and stared at the innocuous-looking contents. "Have one?"

She made a face. "What shall we do with them? If we send them off on their usual spree, they'll end up in Stephan Hertz' pocket."

"I have a feeling he's not going to need pockets much longer." I unwrapped one of the chocolates and bit into it. She watched with amused indulgence. My teeth juddered gently as they contacted quartz. I removed the chocolate coating like the top of a boiled egg. "Brilliant," I whispered. It was, too—not only the method but the merchandise nestling comfortably in its chocolate bed. With two fingers I extracted the glowing diamond and popped the rest into my mouth.

The jewel flashed exotically in the palm of my hand. "Garbo in *Ninotchka* called the diamonds she was trying to sell the tears of Russia." I looked at her earnestly. "You remind me of Garbo, you know." She coloured and touched her cheek with sudden embarrassment. I smiled away the compliment. "I think we simply eat the chocolates, keep the fillings and stash them away somewhere among Alice's assets. How about that?"

She nodded. "Why not?"

I offered her the box. She helped herself to a chocolate worth something in the region of a thousand pounds. "Cheers," I said.

*　　　*　　　*

It was the opening day of the Spring Festival. Saturday, 7 May. After the soggy meteorological excesses of the previous day, the warm sunshine brought out the ever resilient Viennese in their massed thousands to bask in the park, watch the peacocks, sing along with Strauss, imbibe coffee by the bucketful and promenade idly through the shopping precincts. Dancing and music in the streets, from pop to Strauss, hurdy-gurdy to Alp-horn. Brass bands, string quartets, glee singers and solemn male-voice choirs had converged on the city from all points of Europe's compass.

Vienna turned its brightest face to the sun, the shadows consigned to the darker places of the mind.

Even for me the tension of the past days slackened a little as I limped along the Graben early for my appointment at the Clock Museum. I was quite glad to get away from *chez* Alice, not only because I had grown inordinately fond of Hedda and needed time and space to think about it, but because my allegiance to Aunt Alice demanded that, sooner rather than later, I would be obliged to come clean on the subject of Lorenz. If she asked me outright whether or not I had found him, I would be hard pressed to keep the shifty, fish-like stare out of my eye.

So I had asked Hedda to give her my love and regards and had slunk manfully out of the house by the back door.

In the boring tradition of the P.I.'s Handbook I had snuck into doorways, retraced my steps a couple of times and twice boarded trams to descend at the next stop. It was a wearing business being a P.I., but at least I knew I was not being tailed. The last thing I needed was to lead anyone who might still be interested straight into the arms of Lorenz.

I stood for a moment watching a quartet of twelve-foot-long Alp-horns being blown with sonorous "eptitude" by a quartet of human beings in Tyrolean hats. But even there personal problems intruded, for the players stood at the base of the Plague Column on which Hedda's father had been hanged, a Nazi dagger buried in his stomach . . .

I did a circuit of the monument, shouldered my way through the crowd, skirted the church and so into Steindlgasse.

Hedda was a new one on me and I didn't begin to understand my fascination for her, except that she reminded me of Garbo, a boyhood goddess of mine. Usually I fell for the younger variety—and who wasn't younger than I felt at the moment?—like compact lady vets who straddled large motor cycles dressed in leather, and tall blonde nubile film stars. On the spur of the moment I had once married an actress who looked like a fully equipped Venus de Milo and divorced her some unhappy years later on the painful horns of a marital dilemma. But Hedda . . . She was something else, older and tougher, someone who blasted her way through opera and sieg-heiled the memory of Adolf Hitler with the worst of them. And yet . . .

Behind the Am Hof church I came at last to Schulhof and the Clock Museum. The place is built on a corner and like Demel's has narrow winding stone steps leading ever upwards. They were clearly jealous of their exhibits, fiercely locked doors having to be negotiated on each of the three floors occupied by the museum.

The man with the cash box gave my battered face an old-fashioned look as I presented him with the entrance fee, but having taken the money, there was not a lot he could do about it. As I stepped into the first room, all hell was let loose, and I stood for a frozen moment thinking I had triggered off something; the cacophony which broke over my defenceless head was mindboggling. It was a trap, I thought; take cover . . .

It was twelve o'clock striking. I will take their word for it that the place contains some nine hundred exhibits, and of those, only a small percentage are of the striking, booming, chiming, clanging, pinging variety; together they made a sound like the end of the world.

The place was packed with tourists, most of whom like me were riveted to the spot waiting for the din to die down. When it was all over the steady creak and squeak of the polished wooden floors being trampled underfoot took its place.

Lorenz hadn't specified any particular room and since there were three floors and fifteen rooms, I decided to take in a modicum of horological culture until he showed up.

I was standing in Room 4 positively aghast at the complexities of a monstrous black clock only slightly smaller than the Albert Memorial which told us not only the time and the day of the week and something about moon nodes, but also the revolving times of Saturn and Jupiter, when a voice at my elbow asked in English if I happened to have the time on me, as his watch had stopped. It was Lorenz, of course, doing his little joke, the sort of thing I might have said under similar circumstances; I put it down to a family weakness. "Hello," he added mildly. "Been fighting again, I see."

He had grown a moustache since last night and was wearing a pair of black sun-glasses overshadowed by a jaunty green Tyrolean hat; the flower in his buttonhole, which looked like edelweiss and probably wasn't, went over the top a bit, I thought, but otherwise he was sober in a dark grey suit, club tie, black shoes and a silver-topped walking stick. He looked like a distinguished elderly actor who in England would have been knighted long ago.

He tore me away from my giant black clock and led me around on the creaking boards, eyeing the exhibits, pointing at them knowledgeably and talking of other things. Between the first and second floors we paused on the dimly lit staircase and talked in low voices, our words echoing around us. He was apologetic about the cloak-and-dagger rendezvous, but such a meeting, he said, was safer than most, and he had wanted to get away from his "safe" house. He had, he added mysteriously, things to see to and transactions to put into motion before, as he put it, the shops closed.

He was rightly moved by my appearance and demanded a full explanation. In mid-flow we were forced upwards to the next floor by a closely knit wedge of American tourists, one of whom—the leader of the pack—wore the gilt-encrusted cap of an admiral of the fleet.

On the next floor we stood staring at something called an astronomical bracket clock which told us what time the sun was due to set in India. He

said, "So there is only Stephan Hertz to settle with. That's good. And tonight, as they say, is the night."

He shepherded me into a quieter room. "The opening ceremony of the
Spring Festival is at nine o'clock this evening at the City Hall. I'm told there
are speeches, song and dance and all kinds of revelry—plus several thousand
people milling around."

He smiled through his black glasses. "In numbers is safety." It sounded
like a quote, but I'm sure it wasn't. "I may need your help—join me there?"

"Try to keep me away."

"Good. They've erected a stage of sorts in front of the City Hall. I think
it's the President who's due to speak at nine, so there'll be quite a bit of
security about, which needn't bother us if we don't panic—in fact, they
might help rather than hinder."

An influx of visitors drove us again out on to the staircase. As the door
closed behind us, Lorenz said quietly, his lips twisting into an unpleasing
smile, "No expense spared, you see, for the last rites of Stephan Hertz. All
Vienna will be present to pay their respects. A public send-off in *excelsis*."

He gave a short suppressed laugh; the echoes snatched at it, hollowed it
out and sent it scampering up and down the stairwell like the rustle of rats in
a sewer. My skin came out in goose pimples.

The admiral of the fleet turned up again at that moment—louder this
time, and leading his flotilla of battle-worn veterans with the sort of grim
determination one might have looked for at Trafalgar. He remembered us
from our previous encounter on the lower floor and stared at us with hot-eyed
suspicion as he sidled by. We flattened ourselves against the wall and let them
all bunch past; a woman with blue hair told her friend in a stage whisper,
"There's those two men again," and said it without moving her lips.

When they had gone, Lorenz decided he'd had enough. "Let's go," he
muttered.

My aching limbs liked the descent no better than the climb. I clung to the
handrail and clambered down with the panting vigour of a ninety-year-old. I
found him standing at the bottom awaiting me with studied patience.

"It's all right for you," I complained tetchily. "I ache. All bloody over."

He led the way into the bright sunlight. I found myself wondering why he
had chosen that particular locale as a meeting place. "Quite simple," he said
in answer to my query. "Your friend Franz—of Demel's rooftop fame—
thought I might find the museum interesting." He glanced sideways at me.
"I collect clocks, you know." No, I thought, I didn't know. "So I decided
business should be mixed with pleasure; the museum, he tells me, houses one
of the finest collections in the world. I've been in there for over an hour.
Fascinating, really fascinating."

"Louis XVI collected clocks," I told him, airing a modicum of learning.

"No, he didn't. He made them. Poor chap."

I shut up and fell in alongside as he turned on his heel and strolled along
the narrow cobbled street towards Am Hof.

"I talked to Hertz this morning. He was surprisingly amenable. He either has something dastardly up his sleeve or he badly needs his million dollars. I suspect both. Though of course the possibility of a merger with an ailing Rodrigo Bronson and Son could be vastly attractive to him. I told him there was no way I was going to endanger myself by appearing anywhere in daylight, either at his office or in a public place. I laid it on quite thick, you understand. When I asked him if he could meet me tonight somewhere, he said, no, he couldn't, he was due at the celebrations at the Rathaus. It won't surprise you to know that, as well as everything else, he is apparently something impressive in city council circles. I said, 'Okay, why don't we meet there,' and he jumped at it. Simple as that. It fitted my plans like the last piece of a jigsaw puzzle. Fate is on our side. One sinister note: he asked specifically if you would be coming with me; I said I'd drag you along. Which suggests that there may be fireworks other than those officially scheduled. Are you game?"

"I've already said so."

"Then we'll meet up at the Rathaus steps during the speeches—Hertz can't get away until that's over. Since the crowds will be phenomenal, I suggest we join forces on the steps on the city side of the stage. Suit you?" I said it did and he nodded. "Don't be late," he added, "or you'll miss the star performance. Timing will be of the essence."

We had crossed the square in silence before he spoke again.

"I'm leaving Vienna tomorrow and there's one more thing I have to do." He stopped suddenly and stared vaguely at a plaque set into the wall of one of the houses. "My mother. I've been reconsidering. Perhaps I should see her. If only to say goodbye. I shan't come back." He looked at me, a worried frown on his face. "Can we do that, Mark?"

"When?"

He shrugged. "When better than now? If she's fit to see me—now. There won't be another opportunity."

* * *

She was sitting bolt upright in her bed still working on the morning crossword puzzle. She greeted me with a cheery wave of her gold-plated pen. "Thought you'd left me. Where have you been?" She registered the parlous condition of my face. "And look at you! Hedda mentioned that you'd been in a fight of some sort; she didn't say you'd been disfigured. Who was it this time?"

"A friend."

She snorted. "Let us hope your enemies never catch up with you." She looked a little sheepish. "My fault again, I suppose?"

"I'm afraid so. I have to defend your honour, you know. All the boys at school are talking about you. Finished your puzzle?"

"Don't be silly."

I sat on the bed and kissed her cheek. "Enough about me, how are you?"

She made a growling sound as she pulled her bed-jacket about her and screwed up her face into a theatrical facsimile of discontent. "Bored. I just want to get out and about again. That dreadful Emily Hargreaves treats me like a child. Won't let me get up."

I took her hand. "There's no need to call Emily names. If you felt like getting up, you would and there'd be no arguing about it. So enough of that."

"You're as bad as she is." She sighed with heavy duplicity. "I did so want to get to the festival tonight. I haven't missed it in years."

"Well, you're going to have to miss it tonight," I told her, squeezing her hand.

"Will you be going?"

I hedged artfully and told her they had a lovely day for it. "It's great fun," she went on as if I hadn't spoken. "They stop all the traffic on the Ringstrasse so there's plenty of room for the crowds. There are fireworks and speeches—the ballet do *The Blue Danube* in front of the Rathaus. At nine o'clock the Rathaus lights up like a Christmas tree from the very top right down to ground level. And the Turks will be there too, marching and dancing—big lovely men. Get Hedda to take you. She'd love to, I'm sure."

"She's singing tonight."

"Of course she is. *Luisa Miller*—that boring old opera. Well, anyway, try to get along on your own. It'll be worth it. Perhaps Verne will go with you. You like Verne, don't you? Such a nice man. I don't know what I'd have done without him all these years; he's so patient. It was actually he who first suggested I should get you to come over to find Lorenz . . ." She broke off suddenly and I felt her hand twitch in mine. Here it comes, I thought. "No news, I suppose?" she asked in a small hesitant voice.

The tiny hand was cold and bony. I stared down at it in silence for a second, on the back of it the ugly blemishes she hated so much. She turned the hand gently in mine until the withered palm was uppermost. It was trembling slightly. I looked up; she was staring at me wide-eyed.

"You've found him." It was a statement, not a question, tentative and so quiet as to be almost inaudible.

"We found each other."

I watched the tears well up and brim over. I reached for a tissue. She took it, pressed it tremulously against her cheek, the tears soaking into it. Not for a second did she take her eyes from mine. "Oh, Mark, you've found him . . . I knew you would, I just knew it . . . Is he . . . ?" Her voice faltered.

I nodded. "He's your Lorenz."

Her eyes closed; she reached silently towards me, both arms outstretched. I went into them and held her tightly as she wept quietly on my shoulder. "I knew he was alive . . . I knew it," she whispered. I patted her shoulder and made comforting noises. "Thank you, Mark, dear Mark . . . thank you."

"Now," I said firmly, easing her away from me. "Tidy yourself up, or he'll wish he'd never come."

Her hands gripped my shoulder, her eyes wide with sudden alarm. "He's here?"

"Outside."

Not without anxiety I watched her closely as she dabbed at her eyes and cheeks. The tears had gone. Reaching for a hand mirror, she blinked at herself with dismay. "I look a hundred and twenty. What will he think of me? In that drawer over there you'll find some rouge . . ."

"No," I told her resolutely. "No rouge. You're all right as you are. You're his mother, for God's sake, not his girl-friend. You don't want to look like bloody Tosca."

She gave her well-known hoot of laughter and I knew all was well; the worst was over. She snatched up more tissues, blew her nose, glared at herself in the mirror and tugged aggressively at the lank strands of trailing grey hair. "At least," she begged, "let me have a wig."

"No wig." I pointed a finger at her. "If you're good enough for me, you're good enough for him, right?"

"Right," she barked back.

She composed herself by numbers, closing her eyes and drawing deep massive breaths as if preparing for a performance of Brünnhilde. I got to my feet and stared fondly down at her. Our eyes met. "How do I look?"

"Like a million dollars."

She touched my hand. "Wheel him in." I went to the door. "Nephew." I turned. "I shall never forget what you've done."

"It was nothing," I lied strenuously. "And I did it for the money, not for you." I held up a finger as she was about to interrupt. "But don't be disappointed if he isn't wearing a sailor-suit."

Lorenz, hat in hand and leaning elegantly on his walking stick, was poised at the head of the grand staircase glooming down at his mother's picture gallery. I came up quietly behind him.

"I was born in this house," he said softly almost to himself. "Many's the time I've slid down this bannister." He pointed suddenly with his stick at the pictures. "Those," he said, "are monstrous, don't you think?"

"Those," I reminded him tersely, "are about all she's got." He met my eyes with an indifferent shrug. "Please be gentle with her," I added. "She's sick and elderly."

"You're coming in with me, aren't you?" he asked with an uncharacteristic show of panic.

"As far as the door."

I led him protesting to the bedroom.

What she had done to herself in the thirty seconds I had been away I had no way of knowing. I can only say that I stood rooted in the doorway with amazement plastered over my face. She had relinquished forty years. She looked quite radiant, upright among her pillows, a diva among divas; her eyes were translucent.

"Here he is . . ." I muttered awkwardly, stepping aside to let him pass. I couldn't take my eyes off her; only his coming between us brought me out of a trance.

"Hello, mother." He said it as if he'd just dropped in for tea.

I swear she saw him as a nine-year-old boy in a sailor-suit.

"Lorenz . . ." She raised her hands towards him . . .

I closed the door.

CHAPTER SEVENTEEN

When the sun had gone, the cold returned. A thin, reedy wind keened and skittered about the streets. The stars were bright and frigid, remote in their cold black velvet sky.

Overcoats and scarves, woollen hats and gloves were the sensible and popular order of the day. I joined the garrulous crowds converging on the Rathaus, shivering relentlessly in my still-damp raincoat, my gloveless hands thrust deep into its pockets. As Alice had predicted, the Ringstrasse had been closed to traffic and all tramped heartily along the tramlines, some, more playful than others, making tram noises to keep the rest of us on our toes.

I envied them, wished my thoughts too could be occupied with Strauss waltzes and Turkish marches, fireworks and the fun of being allowed to promenade in the middle of the main road without fear of being picked off by a tram. But each step I took brought me, I knew, to further violence and more bloodshed. Since my arrival in Vienna I had been steeped in it. I'd had my fill and was sick to the stomach. I even contemplated turning back. Maybe there was an empty seat going for that boring old opera Alice had been so rude about; it would be nice to catch a glimpse of the delectable Hedda knocking herself out in the chorus. I peered at my watch. The bloody thing would be half over.

The crowd ganged up on me anyway and thrust me forward towards the impressive and floodlit Burgtheater, which was as far as we were all going, for the theatre faced the Rathaus, the Ringstrasse and the wide expanse of the park flowing between them like a river, decked out tonight with all the brash finery of carnival. Glittering decorations and fairy lights flickered among the burgeoning trees; side-shows and highly coloured canvas-topped stalls offered souvenirs for sale and hot dogs and ice-creams and freshly cooked Viennese specialities.

Opposite the Burgtheater and beyond the wooden stage on which an entertainment of some sort was already in progress glowered the vast black edifice of the neo-Gothic City Hall, its clock-tower thrusting up against the stars; at its pinnacle the symbolic figure of the Rathausmann, the only portion of the building illuminated, shimmered in golden light, his unfurled pennant glinting as if caught by a sudden gust of wind.

The clock stood at eight thirty-five.

Quietly I elbowed my way through the throng. I thought about Lorenz with murder in his heart, and the knowledge scared me. But less than twenty-four hours ago the same madness had possessed me, so who was I to rebel against further slaughter?

A laughing red-faced man thrust a bottle of schnapps into my hand. *"Trinken, Freund, trinken Sie!"* he yelled above the metallic squawking of the sound system. He had the face of a circus clown. I snatched at the bottle, upended it and swallowed recklessly; the raw spirit blazed its way down my throat. *"Danke,"* I yelled breathlessly, returning the bottle; his eyes bulged like hard-boiled eggs. *"Danke schön!"*

It was the first hard stuff I had encountered since I had been "dried out" centuries before. That way, I thought, madness lay; and that way, countered my other half, untold miracles could be accomplished . . .

I quickened my steps, surged off to the left. The bodily hurts which had plagued me since morning had gradually receded during the day; only my arms and shoulders complained as I ploughed through the throng, massed and almost static now that the time was approaching for the festivities to commence. The loose tooth in my mouth burned like hell-fire after the unexpected libation of 70 per cent-proof spirit. But I was feeling better; my head had cleared, and the business in hand was taking on a less onerous aspect.

A shout of laughter and applause signalled the close of the current entertainment. I was drowned in the sudden uproar of sound. I fought my way around a tree in whose lower branches swung a motley crowd of screaming children—and came face to face with Hedda. She was as startled as I.

"What are you doing here?" I yelled. "You're supposed to be at the opera."

"Well, I'm not," she shouted back defiantly. "I have other things to do." She turned away.

I seized her wrist. "What other things?"

She struggled in my grasp. "Let me go, Mark, *please.* You'll wreck everything."

I held her for a second longer, leaning in closer to her. "Are you in this too? With Lorenz?"

"Of course I am. We all are. Now let me go . . ."

She clawed painfully at my hand, broke away and in a matter of seconds was lost in the crowd.

I glanced up at the clock: eight forty-five.

I forged ahead. The stage was now to my right, the City Hall steps almost devoid of onlookers—they commanded only a restricted view of the proceedings, and that from the rear of the stage; the podium from which the President was to speak was completely invisible. Security barricades, set up between the steps and the hall's main entrance prevented further progress. Lorenz was nowhere in sight.

A brazen fanfare bringing a throaty roar from the assembly was followed by a stirring performance of the national anthem.

Respectful but shivering, I stood remote and erect until it had finished, peering over my shoulder into the thick pall of shadow which hung like a shifting curtain behind the Gothic arches. The freshening wind whipped achingly at my scarred face.

Latecomers, finding all other vantage points occupied, were now gravitating towards the steps, huddled into scarves and coat collars and stamping their feet with cold. I eyed each new arrival with hope, some with suspicion. As they increased in number, I melted into deeper shadow, backing away, allowing them pride of place.

A sudden yell of applause greeted the appearance of the President, who launched forthrightly into his speech of inauguration, the rounded, patriotic phrases ringing plangently around the vast arena of upturned faces . . .

The hairs on the back of my neck stirred. I was under observation. I turned slowly . . . a succession of empty arches and the cloistered darkness beyond, nothing more.

A cold trickle of sweat slid insidiously beneath my collar.

Reluctantly I moved towards the deeper shadows. It was difficult to believe that within a few yards of the President I might be suddenly and recklessly mown down; each step I took was with the sombre knowledge that it could be my last.

There were two of them muffled in long black overcoats, upturned collars and scarves, hats rammed to their eyebrows. Their faces were blank patches of nothingness. Weapons glinted in their hands.

A voice behind me said, "Good evening, Mr. Savage," and, turning with consummate actorship, I said, "And good evening to you, Mr. Hertz," in a voice as carefully regulated as a luncheon party at the British Embassy. I was proud of myself. Inside I quaked.

There wasn't much to be seen of him either. In an overcoat and under a hat he looked like anyone else; only the voice was distinctive, and its affability wouldn't have deceived anyone. He said, "I was expecting Mr. Bronson," to which I replied that I was too, and if he would be patient, I was sure he'd be along at any minute.

A loaded silence sat between us for a couple of seconds whilst he listened with half an ear to the President's speech. To fill in I remarked with a somewhat jocular turn of phrase, "You managed to extract yourself from your predicament back at the ranch then?"

He laughed aloud. "Oh, Mr. Savage," he cried with a gentle snarl, "how I wish you were working for me. We could have such fun together. And make so much money! Mr. Bronson suggested you might be willing to reconsider your rejection of my offer. Is that so?"

I gave him a judicial smile, which he couldn't see because of the dark. "Rather than wrangle with you, I'll join you," I told him. "I would hate to be on the run for the rest of my life."

He liked that too. We were getting along fine and only paused in our pleasantries to allow for the immense uproar of cheering which erupted from the crowd. It was almost as if they were applauding me, but in fact it was all for the President, who had completed his peroration and given the signal for the illumination of the City Hall. Alice had said it was like a Christmas tree; the lights came on in stages—from the top downwards. The faces of the crowd suddenly blazed with light . . . For our part we seemed to recede even further—into darkness.

Public proceedings distracted me from my immediate problems, so much so that I was quite unnerved when the two shadowy gunmen who had been hulking somewhere behind me now formed up alongside, one with a gun in his back and the other two fingers of somebody else's hand; gun and hand were the property of Lorenz, who followed them in with smiling urbanity. "Relieve these gentlemen of their guns, Mark, will you please?"

They were big, heavy weapons, difficult to handle; I plunged them away from prying eyes into the pockets of my misshapen raincoat. Without their guns the two men stood docile and sulky alongside and slightly to the rear of their master.

"Mr. Hertz?" greeted Lorenz. "My name is Lorenz Bronson."

Hertz eyed him in silence with what looked like a glimmer of amusement. Lorenz added, "I said 'alone,' Mr. Hertz—I thought I'd made that quite clear. And why an armed bodyguard?"

Through the loudspeakers came the shimmering pianissimo whisper of violins heralding Vienna's second national anthem, *The Blue Danube;* to a tumultuous welcome the ballet company swept on to the stage.

When the applause had waned, Hertz murmured, "I distrust you, Mr. Bronson. I also have good reason to be wary of Mr. Savage, and I have less than a little confidence in this rendezvous, which is bizarre—to say the least."

"Send your men away," instructed Lorenz. Hertz muttered something over his shoulder; the men backed off. "Right away." More muttering and the men turned their backs and disappeared into the crowd. Lorenz, his gun covering Hertz, delved into his overcoat pocket.

The waltz swelled and the crowd began to sway.

In his hand Lorenz held a tiny suede leather sachet. "One million dollars," he smiled, "in exchange for your gun."

"I carry no gun," said Hertz, raising his voice above the swooping undulations of the orchestra. The shadows of the revolving dancers flickered across his face; it was like watching an early movie. His hand reached out for the prize . . .

A swift flurry of movement and we were surrounded by a sudden rush of men in uniform, encircling us like a swarm of flies, ugly-looking carbines at the ready within inches of us.

"Police," snapped the one in the long leather coat and impressive cap. "You will please come with us."

Transferring his attention to Lorenz, he eyed him coolly, relieved him of his gun, passed it to one of his men and again extended his hand—this time for the diamonds. The moments which ticked by before Lorenz, with a resigned sigh, placed the little sachet into the gloved palm were among the longest I have ever been made to live through. The leathered fingers closed over the bag, which then disappeared into the man's pocket.

I hesitated, glancing about me with dismay.

We were on our own; we might have been on another planet for all the interest our little drama aroused; all eyes were riveted on the swoop and swirl of the dance. In response to a peremptory tap of a gun muzzle on my arm, I moved off with the others, my eyes lingering for a second on the ballerinas in their thin blue dresses; they must have been bloody cold.

Closely guarded, we were shepherded around a corner of the building, Stephan Hertz keeping up a monotonous chatter of protest, informing the man in the leather coat who he was and what he did and what sort of repercussions might be expected when the mayor came to hear of this outrage against the person of one of his closest associates.

Lorenz marched glumly beside me.

"What the hell's going on?" I growled.

In the darkness I could almost hear his shrug. "Someone's been talking, I guess."

With a feeling of sickness I thought of Hedda prowling alone through the crowd looking guilty as hell; I wondered again why she wasn't on stage singing her head off in *Luisa Miller*. Keeping my thoughts to myself, I turned instead to worrying about me and the situation I'd got myself into. I had ample cause for worry, God knows. I had done away with Verne Wayne, and whether or not in fair fight the Viennese authorities would find it interesting listening. Lorenz too had killed. As far as I could see, the obnoxious Stephan Hertz was the only one who would get away with anything less than life.

We arrived at a side entrance to the City Hall, where the man in charge of comings and goings had words with our leather-clad leader. After some discussion we were passed through without difficulty. My pockets were clanking with guns. I drew nearer to Lorenz. "I have three bloody guns in my pocket," I informed him in a low voice. "What say we shoot our way out? Why didn't they search us? How do they know we're not all armed to the teeth?" He made no reply. I might as well not have opened my mouth.

We marched across an echoing open courtyard, through another door and into a lofty hall with an impressive set of stairs soaring upwards. No one seemed to be about, which seemed odd; they were probably all at the festival.

"Where are you taking us?" demanded Hertz tetchily as we squeezed into an elevator, leaving behind a couple of policemen who couldn't get in. We shot upwards.

"We have an emergency security office on the premises," the head one told him.

"Security, security!" screamed Hertz with not a little heat. "What has security to do with me?"

The man in the leather coat slid open the gates at an upper floor and made no comment.

Lorenz' face was expressionless as he left the elevator; a tension hung over him which had nothing to do with our present predicament. I hoped he had something up his sleeve for the future, because I hadn't. I also began to wonder what the hell a security office was doing on the fourth floor or wherever we were.

Up here the chandeliers weren't quite so grand and the place breathed industry rather than wine, women and song. Presently the head man flung open one half of a double door and we tramped into a square well-furnished room with a lofty ceiling and tall windows overlooking the Ringstrasse. The chandeliers were burning and the windows open. From far below came the lilting strains of *The Blue Danube*.

The moment the door was closed the atmosphere changed. The policemen visibly wilted, as if they had been through some sort of strain; one of them flung his carbine on to a lacquered table-top, pushed back his tight-fitting cap and with a muffled oath scratched industriously at his crotch; everyone, except their three prisoners, began to chatter; Stephan Hertz stared at them with bewilderment.

Lorenz turned suddenly and smiled. The man in the leather coat nodded. The little sachet of diamonds changed hands once again. Now I stood and stared too. Except for the music of the waltz the room had become suddenly quiet.

"Now, Mr. Hertz," smiled Lorenz, "you were saying?"

Hertz' jaw dropped even further. Lorenz continued. "Forgive the subterfuge. I could think of no other way for us to be alone and in safety—from each other! Perhaps we might move on to the terrace, where we shall be even more private. Mark, will you join us?"

He made his way to the open window, and after a second I followed, glaring at the police force, now thoroughly relaxed and lounging around like a football team after the match and in the process of lighting up cigarettes. A sharp word from their leader on his way to the door and the cigarettes went back where they came from. The man peered into the corridor, reclosed the door, locked it and took up a stand with his back towards it.

My feeling of apprehension was fast becoming one of dread. Lorenz' sudden show of affability did not ring true and neither did anything else; the policemen weren't policemen, their uniforms theatrical costumes hired for the occasion . . .

The terrace, as Lorenz had called it, was not so much a terrace as a balcony, high up on the face of the clock tower. I moved to the parapet and looked over. We were immediately above the stage, diminished by distance to the size of a boxing ring; the tiny foreshortened figures of the dancers whirled and pirouetted like clockwork toys. The sea of heads was a pincushion stuck full with multi-coloured pins. Beyond and all around glittered the lights of Vienna, closest of all the Burgtheater, a bright jewel set in blue velvet.

I turned away breathless as the wind gusted icily into my face. I met Lorenz' eyes. He was smiling.

Hertz hovered uncertainly in the lighted window watching us, still bereft of words.

"Isn't that the most perfect view," Lorenz was saying. "As a small boy I was taken by my father on the Ferris wheel. I remember looking down over the city and thinking how beautiful it was—even then, young as I was. But this . . ." He pointed, "Look, over there, beyond the Stephansdom, see it? The *Riesenrad*—the Giant Wheel . . . Do you see the lights?"

Hertz was at his elbow. "Your father?" He had found his voice again. "Rodrigo Bronson is not your father?"

Lorenz smiled at him, the black patch lending a piratical malignancy to his features which turned my blood cold. "My father, Mr. Hertz, was one Ernst Sternberg, a diamond merchant here in Vienna . . . a Jew . . ."

The word remained suspended in the cold air like a threat. Even the music below seemed to hesitate, suspended and motionless for a second, as if taking breath before hurtling towards its final dizzying crescendo and explosive conclusion.

The roar of the crowd rose like a bank of sound. I stared down over the parapet, Lorenz beside me. The dancers were taking their calls. "What *is* all this, Lorenz?" I hissed between my teeth. "What are you up to?"

He turned his head and eyed me coldly. He swung on Hertz and raised his voice. "I'm here to discharge a debt, isn't that so . . . Herr Steiger?" Above the tumult of the applause it was difficult to hear anything. Lorenz raised his voice only slightly. "I owe you one million dollars." The little sachet of diamonds was in his hand. Hertz was staring at him as if in a trance. "Steiger?" he whispered.

A stealthy movement behind me made me turn my head. Two of the pseudo-policemen stood silhouetted in the window. "My name is Stephan Hertz . . ." muttered Hertz; fear was beginning to eat into him.

Lorenz, ignoring the remark, placed the bag carefully on Hertz' outstretched palm. "That, Herr Steiger, represents the final payment of Otto Brunner's debt to you. I say that before witnesses. At a rough estimate, I would say Otto's payments have amounted to twenty-five million dollars, give or take a dollar. Fair exchange, do you think, for the passage of one frightened man and a small boy across an alien border?"

The applause was beginning to subside as the dancers withdrew from their final call. In spite of himself Hertz had upended the little bag into his hand. The diamonds sparkled liquidly in his palm. He looked up, greed mingled with terror disfiguring his face. "You were the boy—the small boy with Otto?"

Lorenz smiled. "Yes, Herr Steiger, I was the boy."

Now at last the applause had finally ceased. As if waiting for a cue, Lorenz stepped aside. The two men behind moved in swiftly, one on each side of Hertz, lifted him bodily and flung him screaming into space.

The diamonds flashed like meteors as they spun from his hand; his hat flew off, his coat-tails flapped like the feathers of a wounded bird . . .

I stood dumb with horror staring at the plunging, flailing screaming body. Every head in the crowd seemed to lift at the same moment. Heads became faces bathed in bright light. Every tongue was still.

Even from where I stood, I heard the hollow crunch of the body as it struck the centre of the empty, waiting stage, to lie, black and ugly, sprawled and twisted like a dead spider. The sound of the stunned crowd moved in like a tidal wave.

Backing incredulously from the parapet, I turned my head. The two men had gone. Lorenz still smiled. His lips moved. He was saying something I couldn't hear. He moved to the window, tugging at my arm, urging me back into the room beyond, empty now of all but ourselves. He hurried me along, half pushing, half pulling at me.

Sound came back to my ears with a rush. "Hurry, for God's sake," he was saying.

We pounded along the wide corridor; the lift gates were open, the men in uniform already ensconced. We crowded in, someone slammed the gates. We plunged earthwards with a whine.

I was engulfed in nightmare; I stared bemused at the set faces around me, wondering which of them had belonged to the two men who had flung Hertz to his death.

The gates clashed open. The guards we had left below stood waiting. In a body we moved fast, the uniformed men with carbines at the ready. We crossed the empty courtyard, through the hollow hall. The man on duty, startled by our reappearance, stood aside as one of our number yelled that someone had thrown himself from an upper window.

We burst into the street; to our left came the troubled growlings of the crowd, from somewhere else the insistent wailing of an approaching siren. Lorenz restrained me as I was about to take off at speed. "Don't draw attention to yourself," he muttered, guiding me away from the noise of the crowd into the quieter reaches of the street. "There's no hurry. I have a car waiting."

"You've thought of bloody everything, haven't you?" I snarled.

The blare of the siren was coming closer by the second.

We were half-way across the road when the ambulance swept around the corner and bore down upon us, headlights ablaze, the baying of its siren crippling the eardrums. Lorenz shouted a warning. I stood rooted to the spot, fully expecting to be snatched up and savaged by the screaming vehicle. At the last minute I leapt out of its path, dived for the safety of the pavement opposite . . . red lamps warning of footpath obstructions, the latticed rearing of shrouded scaffolding. I saw too late the great wooden sleepers directly in my path. I crashed headlong on to my face. My ankle cracked like a whip; the screech of pain I heard came from my own lips. Lorenz was behind me, his hands on my shoulders.

"I've broken my fucking ankle," I groaned.

The pain was excruciating. He helped me carefully to my knees. "Try it," he whispered with hoarse urgency, "try to stand. You may have just sprained it . . ."

"It's broken, I tell you," I shouted at him. "I heard it go."

"Come on, come on," he soothed. "Try . . ."

He placed my arm about his shoulders and slowly straightened me up; I hung on to him like a rag doll. "Put your foot down . . . carefully . . . try the weight . . ."

It was learning to walk all over again, but more painful; it took some of my weight. "If you'd broken it, you wouldn't be able to do that at all," he muttered with some relief. "You've probably torn some ligaments. Stay here. I'll get the car. It's just around the corner."

"No. Just get me there. I'll be all right."

He did and I wasn't.

I sprawled into the waiting car with him almost on top of me in his effort to support my weight. "Jesus," I muttered. "It's bloody agony."

The other person in the car was Hedda. I was past being surprised or curious about her. Through a haze of misery I was conscious only of her questioning him as they straightened me out and spread me over the back seat. "We'll have to get him to a hospital if it's broken."

"It isn't broken," I told her wearily. "Something snapped, but it wasn't bone. Just get me home. I'll be okay. Get me home; tie me up with something."

In the end they took me to a doctor she knew, a big burly man who looked like a prize-fighter and behaved like Goliath; he picked me up off his doorstep and carried me into his surgery as if I were a laundry basket.

I hadn't broken anything; damaged ligaments, he said. He strapped it up and told me everything would swell up and go black, but I was not to worry. "Keep your weight off it and rest."

"I can't rest. I'm going home tomorrow."

"Where's home?"

"England."

"No," he said firmly. "Never. Not England"—as if England was the last place anyone with a damaged ligament should go. He had probably heard about our Health Service.

Hedda decided to take me back to the house, where she would hand the car over to Lorenz, who would then take himself off to wherever he wanted to go.

I lay on the back seat with my leg up, brooding over the horrendous events of the evening.

Lorenz sensed what I was on about. "You are shocked by my methods, Mark?" he asked over his shoulder.

" 'Appalled' is the word," I told him tartly.

After a short silence he said, "Well, it's done now and it may interest you to know that I have not a twinge of conscience. I came to pay a debt; I've done so and it has cost me something more than a million dollars, but I am well satisfied. It was worth every last cent."

His smugness irked me. "You are from sterner stock than I."

"From the *same* stock, cousin, remember? Anyway, tomorrow I get myself out of your hair. I return home on the first available flight and shall probably never see you again." He turned his head to smile at me. "I have enjoyed meeting you, even under such . . . exceptional circumstances." He hesitated. "Will you please give my regards to your aunt?"

The car drew to a halt. Hedda sat silent at the wheel.

I closed my eyes and gritted my teeth. "How did it go?" I asked with reluctance.

"The meeting with your aunt?"

"With your mother," I snapped.

"She seemed happy enough," he said slowly. "Difficult to tell. She holds herself so well in control. We have little in common, she and I—except perhaps an iron will." He swung himself about in his seat and looked at me directly. "You must please not judge me by my attitude towards her. We don't choose our parents, any more than they can choose their children. My mother was incapable of combining parenthood with a professional career. And who can blame her? Who has the *right* to blame her? I, Mark, have the right, and I do. Fortunately for her she was relieved of those responsibilities by a stranger with a murky past who took them on himself and gave me the sort of care and . . . affection I needed. By doing so he may have redeemed himself, who knows? And if we believe in anything at all, redemption is what the world should be about. Fortunately I hold no such beliefs, and that allows me to deal with the present as I see fit, with no regard for latter-day reprisals or rewards.

"Stephan Hertz was an offence to society and to me; both society and I are now rid of him and I do not propose to defend my action." He raised a hand as I was about to interrupt. "And before you point out that the action which killed him was not mine, let me tell you that those two hoodlums can now retire and live happily ever after on the proceeds of a single night's work."

I stared at him woodenly and in silence for a long and distasteful moment. I turned to Hedda. "Get me out of here, will you, please?"

CHAPTER EIGHTEEN

Alice died that night. Gently and, as far as anyone knew, without pain—in her sleep, with a smile on her face. The world-famous diva, Alicia Sternberg, was dead.

I knew nothing of it until several hours after the event.

I was fast acquiring the habit of regaining consciousness in that dismal Beethoven mausoleum feeling as if I had been fed through a combine harvester.

On this occasion my eyes opened to shrouded darkness, a pale glimmer of light filtering through heavy curtains. As usual, everything was on the throb. The melancholy beat of rain belabouring the windows seemed to intensify the silence of the house; even the traffic outside sounded subdued. Then I remembered it was Sunday and became even more depressed. I have never been able to cope with Sundays. Sometimes I wonder if God himself is able to cope with it, sitting up there on his own with the shops closed and the railway timetables up the spout, nothing to do but listen to all that dismal hymn droning. I couldn't help feeling he might prefer *The Blue Danube* to *Rock of Ages*—at least it would give him a bit of a laugh. And he had to have a sense of humour or he'd never have thought of us in the first place.

I peered at the green digits of my wrist-watch. Eleven-thirty. Where was everybody? I switched on the bedside lamp, frowned at L. v. B. on the wall and gingerly removed the duvet from my foot. My heart sank. Goliath was right. My toes were bright blue in process of turning black. Above the strapping the knee was also blue. I wondered if Hedda had put me to bed again; that too was becoming a habit. This time she had allowed me to hang on to my multi-coloured Jockey shorts.

Tea would be nice. Why didn't someone come and say hello, or goodbye or something? Anything.

I manipulated my leg on to the floor, put two ounces of weight on it and almost passed out. I fell back on the bed in a sweat and thought about amputation, stared at my blue toes and delivered myself of my usual and unimaginative expletive. The door swung open silently as if I had said "Open sesame."

Emily Hargreaves. I whipped the duvet over me. "Hi," I crowed cheerfully. "I was wondering where everybody had got to."

"We thought we'd let you sleep," she said in a subdued voice, and, making for the windows, drew back the curtains. I switched off the lamp and was about to wish her the top of the morning when the words died in my throat.

She was twenty years older, her face haggard, eyes ugly, red-rimmed and tear-stained. She stood dark against the window, her hands, imprisoning a handkerchief, clasped tightly over her stomach.

We stared at each other wordlessly.

"Alice?" I said at last.

She nodded a couple of times. "She's gone." The tears squeezed through her tightly closed lids. Dabbing at them convulsively, she stumbled over to the bed, where she collapsed in a dejected heap of sobbing heart-break. When I laid a comforting hand on her shoulder, she clutched at it like a life-raft, hanging on to it in a Herculean effort to control her grief. "During the night . . . none of us with her . . . she just . . ." She shook her head and blew her nose. "I'm sorry, Mark . . . it's been such a shock—to happen like that and none of us there . . ." She blinked at me through the tears. "Hedda tells me you've been hurt again."

"I bashed up my ankle, that's all. Is there anything I can do?"

She shook her head. "The doctor's gone. It's all straightforward, he says. Quite peaceful it was, he says . . . as if"—she renewed her struggle against tears—"as if she had made up her mind . . . no pain, no trouble—just closed her eyes and went. She was even smiling as if . . ."

I pressed her hand. "Well, we've been expecting it long enough, haven't we? Maybe it's for the best. At least she . . . found her son."

I broke off as the face of Lorenz rose before me, that set malignant smile possessing it like an evil entity.

She nodded, blinking into her soggy handkerchief. "Thanks to you . . . last night she was all . . . lit up inside . . . as if a miracle had happened. And I suppose it had, in a way."

After a moment I said, "Did you meet him?"

She hesitated, eyes lowered. "For a few minutes, yes—I met him. She called me to come up."

"And?" This time the silence was profound. "He wasn't what you expected. Not the little boy in the sailor-suit?"

She frowned slightly. "He was . . . out of another world."

I nodded, allowed another moment of silence, then said, "Well, let's hope he's on his way back there."

Momentarily startled, she raised her head. "But the funeral—he'll stay for the funeral surely?"

I shook my head gently. "No. He won't stay for the funeral."

She caught the coldness in my voice. "Didn't you like him?"

Oh God, I thought miserably, how the hell do I know whether I liked him or not; he was a battlefield over which both sides had fought and left their dead.

I said aloud, "I don't think I really understood him—and what we don't understand we're inclined to knock, aren't we?"

We sat for a quiet spell listening to the rain. "It's a beastly morning," she murmured half to herself.

"Emily . . ." She turned her head. "Is she alone?" She nodded. "I'd like to see her."

She stared at me through waterlogged eyes, then, gathering herself together, brought me a bathrobe and I levered myself on to the edge of the bed. She eyed my foot anxiously. "You really ought not to, you know, not on that foot . . ."

"If I don't see her now, I never will. Everyone will be around . . ."

With the stalwart support of her shoulder I made slow and painful progress, negotiated the stairs by a series of teeth-juddering hops, coming finally to rest at the door of Alice's bedroom. She hesitated. I said, "Just get me to the bedside."

The room was as it had been that first night, curtains tightly closed, flickering candlelight, the canopied four-poster riding the golden glow like a black-sailed vessel straining at anchor.

Emily helped me to the bedside. About to withdraw, she slid the handle of Alice's stick into my hand. "It'll help you," she whispered. "Take it."

The candles flickered and stilled as the door closed noiselessly behind her.

No one had covered her face. She lay quiet and still, smiling at me through closed lids. I found myself smiling back with no urgent sense of loss, just affection. As before, the slight tremor of candle flame drew from her lips that sly wreathing curl of humour. The bluish bruising of death was visible but only fleetingly. She looked half her age, content and at rest—even the folded hands seemed in that light to be without blemish. Someone, Emily of course, had arrayed her in the wig she had worn at the opera—the one I preferred.

I lowered myself gently on to the bed beside her and laid a hand on hers. It felt warm, probably because I was so cold. "Emily said," I whispered, "that I could borrow your stick. I'll bring it back . . ." I kissed her cheek and with the support of the stick regained my feet with ease.

I turned at the door for a last glimpse of her. "*Shalom,*" I murmured, the word coming to me from nowhere. "*Shalom,* Alice . . ."

*   *   *

Hedda said, "He's gone. I waved him off at the airport."

"I hope he's satisfied."

"Apparently his father died last night."

"Otto Brunner?" I shook my head with disbelief. "It's a general exodus— Alice, Brunner, Hertz—it's the end of an era. Sammy, Verne. Perhaps Brunner and Alice will get together and exchange notes—maybe he'll tell her where she went wrong." I smiled up at her. "Take your coat off and come and say hello. Or aren't you stopping?"

She rustled out of her rain-wet Klepper, spread it over a chair, then came to perch on the bed beside me. "How do you feel?"

I gave her a wan grin. "Like I've had an internal operation. And you?"

She sat for a while in silence, eyes turned away, then, reaching for my hand, spread her cool palm softly against mine. "Sick," she whispered. "It's been a bad time. Not for anything would I go through it again."

"Did you know what was going to happen last night?"

"God, no. I was there to smooth the way should it have been necessary. The ballet company had access to the hall, I had access to the ballet company, and I told the opera I had a throat infection. Lorenz needed someone on the inside. In the event, I did nothing except stand around and keep an eye on various guards who might have got in the way." After a second she added almost defensively, "Stephan Hertz was an evil man. We shouldn't feel bad about it." Her tone suggested that she wasn't feeling all that good about it either.

"What do the press say?"

"Suicide."

I made a derisive sound. "A suicide hides away in a quiet corner. Why couldn't he have just shoved him in the river . . . like I did Verne . . ."

Her hand gripped mine tightly. "He wanted a public execution."

"And by Christ he got it."

"By this time tomorrow he'll be back in Brazil again—safe and sound."

"I wouldn't be too sure of that. Have you wondered whatever became of his Jewish pals? Are they going to give up, do you think, now he's gone back? Or will they have another go at getting him out?"

"They won't want him now that Brunner's gone."

"He killed that blasted girl's brother, didn't he? And she's all the bloody Eumenides rolled into one. If I were Lorenz, I'd be inclined to keep my hat well down for the next few years." She was staring at me intently, not listening to a word I was saying. "What is it?" I asked. "What's up?"

"You aren't married, are you?" The question was like a bullet from a gun.

"Not at the moment, no. I was once, but by special dispensation of the divorce court I am no longer." I eyed her soberly, shaken slightly by the question. "What brought that on?"

She shrugged. "I was just . . . thinking how difficult it would be to be . . . close to someone like you, always coming home to find you laid up in bed with broken legs and cuts and bruises and the like . . ."

I grinned. "I do have my trouble-free moments, you know. But not to worry; when I get back, I'll put Mitch on to the dangerous assignments and I'll stick to jealous wives and lost dogs."

"Mitch, your assistant?" I nodded. "I don't envy him."

"Her. She's a lady." Our eyes met. I winked at her. "And it's not like that."

She said after a second's hesitation, "I wish . . ." She stared at me with that look in her eye.

I nodded slowly. "So do I . . . God, so do I." I squeezed her hand. "We'd never make a go of it though, would we? It would never work out." Our eyes shifted away. "In bed perhaps . . . wow! But it's not all bed, more's the pity and all that."

"Perhaps . . ." Again the hesitation, a small smile lifting the corners of her mouth. "Perhaps . . . we could try it some time—before you go. Once. Perhaps? Twice even . . . ?"

The suggestion seeped into my bloodstream like a slow dose of adrenalin. "You're on," I whispered a little hoarsely. "Just as soon as I get my leg off."

With the promise of things to come I drew her close and kissed her long and lingeringly. Her response made me wonder whether bed for the rest of my life might not be the answer to my troubles. After all, politics change. Bed doesn't.

* * *

The demise of Alicia Sternberg made front-page news the world over. The fact that she had, as it were, cried wolf on four previous occasions diminished neither the public loss nor the magisterial sonority of her obituaries. Even the London *Times* gave her a picture and a column. As her only living relative I was mentioned twice.

Other headlines dealt with the brutal stabbing of one Samuel Meier of Rudolfsplatz and the suicide of his presumed killer, an American business associate of the late Alicia Sternberg, Laverne Bruce Wayne. The police, said one paper, were anxious to interview the anonymous caller who, on the night of the murder, had reported not only the death of Herr Meier but also the whereabouts of Wayne's body, later recovered from the Donau Kanal. Death had been caused by drowning. Foul play was not suspected.

The Beethoven room was littered with newspapers faithfully delivered by the grief-stricken Emily, who, in the face of her sorrow over Alice, bore up remarkably well with the additional tragedies of Sammy and Verne. On the second day she informed me that *da Caruso*, the record shop on the Operngasse, had devoted an entire window display to photographs and recordings of "the deeply mourned Alicia Sternberg," and wasn't that wonderful?

I mooned around the quiet house like the ghost of Christmas-yet-to-come, humping about on Alice's stick and wishing to God I could go home. But with Lorenz gone the least I could do was to hang on for the funeral and hope that the leg would be well enough to hop aboard a jet immediately afterwards.

Hedda got Goliath to come along and have a look at it. He was hugely pleased and laughed a lot at my black toes and knee. When I told him that the entire leg was about to explode, the laugh faded and he visibly saddened. Could he not perhaps, I suggested, loose the bandage a little? No, he said, not for one week, and departed.

Hedda sympathised but could do little more than cheer me on with conversation, reading matter and *The Times* crossword puzzle. There came a moment on Thursday evening just before she was due to leave for the opera when each of us felt that an excursion into fornication was about to take place; neither, however, seemed capable of taking the initiative, and we withdrew to our separate corners to languish in collapsed and frustrated heaps until the urge wore off.

On Friday afternoon I rang Mitch and told her I had solved the mystery.

"The papers said she died," said Mitch.

"I'm going to the funeral tomorrow."

"Did she pay you before she went?" I stared in silence at the phone. "Mark?"

"You're a miserable money-grubber, Mitch."

"Are you mentioned in her will?"

"Mitch . . ."

"You're her only living relative, aren't you?"

"I'm going to hang up, Mitch."

"What's the matter? Are you all right?"

"I've broken my leg."

"I don't believe you."

"All right then, I haven't broken my leg."

"That's better. So you're coming home when?"

"Sunday. I'll have the leg sent on by parcel post."

"Goodbye, Mark."

"Goodbye, Mitch."

Having a telephone conversation with Mitch is like being plugged into a failed life-support machine. I sat and thought about her for several unproductive minutes, then wandered off to Hedda's room only to find her missing. She had given me *carte blanche* as far as her room was concerned, so I thumped around on my stick for a bit, stared out of the window, looked at her books, none of which I had read, and finally, seating myself at her table, drew towards me a writing pad she used for shopping lists.

I would write a book, that's what I'd do. Bored out of my tiny mind and waiting for my leg to fall off or whatever it was going to do, I would write a book—tell the unknowing world of my experiences. I picked up a ball-point pen.

"I should never have gone back to Vienna," I wrote and sat back to admire it, well pleased. Short, snazzy and to the point. Dear reader, please read on . . .

"What are you doing?" asked Hedda, coming in at that moment and looking like a cool green lampshade in her Klepper cape.

"Writing a book."

She peered over my shoulder. "Is that it?" I nodded. "Not very long, is it?"

Writing a book, I explained, would be excellent therapy, keep me off the streets and prevent me from going out of my skull. When, however, she enfolded me in her lascivious cape and asked whether, apart from writing a book, I was doing anything special for the rest of the afternoon, I abandoned the idea.

The rest of the afternoon turned out to be very special indeed. Dating from those restive and exhilarating moments, my hurt mind and bruised limbs began their upward surge towards recovery.

* * *

The day of the funeral was the most perfect Vienna could produce. Pale sunlight, cool blue skies, the air gentle and still, not a branch or a leaf stirring —almost as if nature had given up breathing to listen.

The great sprawl of the Zentral Friedhof exuded peace. Unlike any other cemetery I know, it has no sense of the gloomy dead lying in ambush ready to burst their cerements and lurch from their graves on the Day of Judgement. There is, rather, the feeling that they're content to be there, resting and undisturbed, until somebody comes along with his trumpet and frightens the death out of them.

Because I was, as it were, a nearest and dearest, I was directed to stand alongside the grave and listen to all those emotive phrases I had never cared for . . . *"Man that is born of woman hath but a short time to live and is full of misery"* . . . *"In the midst of life we are in death . . ."*

I sometimes wonder why we're here at all.

"Thou knowest, Lord, the secrets of our hearts." I caught Hedda's eye across the open grave.

I was handed a little trowel and sprinkled earth on the lowered coffin. Sorry Alice, I apologised silently as the earth thudded hollowly on the casket. *"Earth to earth, ashes to ashes . . ."*

It was over at last. Alice, dear Alice, lay in the earth. The great and brilliant Alicia Sternberg . . . *"dust to dust"* . . . as if she'd never been. I glanced around. She had *been*, all right, there was no doubt about that, and had made her not inconsiderable mark on the pages of the world's musical diary. I had never seen so many people at a funeral—half Vienna seemed to be there. I smiled secretly to myself. She had caught her 71 tram without a lot of bother, and her most private wishes had come true too. Within a few yards of her lay the great Lotte Lehmann and Hilde Konetzni. And less than a stone's throw away, snug in their exclusive Valhalla, slumbered Beethoven, Schubert, Brahms, Gluck, the Strausses and the rest . . .

People I had never seen before nor would see again came and shook my hand as if she had belonged to me—kind saddened strangers in black hats and dark ties. Then was the time I felt like mourning—to get away some-where on my own.

Hedda was waiting to drive me back. The devastated Emily, surrounded by friends, had already departed. I said, "Hang on a second, will you? Someone I need to have words with."

Fresh spring flowers in green metal vases . . . the small square plot of ground surrounded by low iron rails backed by bright burgeoning trees . . .

the slender white obelisk with its golden lyre and its circled gilded butterfly in flight . . . at its base the single word: BEETHOVEN.

The silence was intense. The liquid ravishments of a blackbird added to the stillness. A red squirrel froze for a moment, still as stone, studying me with beady blatant eyes.

I stood for a long time doing nothing, just staring at the grave, then, leaning heavily on Alice's stick, I turned away. My ankle hurt like hell.

Hedda was watching me. "Friend of yours?"

"A household god," I told her. "I hope he and old Franz next door are still on the music jag—Alice was looking forward to eavesdropping . . ."

*   *   *

She wore a red beret to the airport, a matching red skirt and an olive-green jumper. I was glad she wasn't in mourning. Alice would have hated it.

Back at the house Emily had engulfed me tearfully in her arms and kissed me wetly on the cheek. She was in black, of course, which made her look even paler than she was. When I mentioned Alice's stick, she had told me to keep it—"She would have liked you to have it."

I limped across the tarmac to the 737, turned at the foot of the gangway. The red beret glowed brightly behind the huge windows of the observation area. I raised my stick briefly, a flutter of a white hand. I mounted the gangway. My seat number was on the aisle, so I didn't see her again.

When the plane took off, I tried not to think of her. The head of the man sitting beside me filled the window, so I couldn't take a last look at Vienna even had I wanted to. I had the nightmares to be getting on with; they'd keep me occupied for some time to come.

I refused the plastic lunch. The emptiness in me wasn't hunger. There was a chance she might come to England for a visit, she had said . . . sometime.

I read the free newspaper from cover to cover. Page 2 was interesting. "Video Pirates," ran the headline. The police, said the report, had uncovered a video-pirating concern run in conjunction, it seemed, with the Hungarian restaurant and night-club the Kékszákallú in District 9, the club being used as a front. More than a hundred video recording machines and several thousand pirated video cassettes had been seized by the authorities pending further investigations. "It has also been ascertained that pornographic video films intended for world-wide distribution were being shot on the premises. Several arrests have been made and charges preferred. No names, at present, are available to the public, but further interest in the case will doubtless be aroused by the fact that the late Herr Stephan Hertz, who last week plunged to his death at the Spring Festival before the City Hall, was the owner/ proprietor of the Kékszákallú and the adjoining premises. The police are anxious to interview the woman whose telephone call on Wednesday evening led them to place the night club under surveillance. The Kékszákallú has been temporarily closed to allow for further investigation.

I speculated for a moment or two on the identity of the woman the police were anxious to interview. One way and another, the police were having a pretty anxious time of it. Well done, Hedda!

I sat back and closed my eyes, listened to the man in the next seat tearing at his bread roll with his teeth . . .

When the trolley trundled down the aisle with duty-free goods, I bought a bottle of Ma Griffe for Mitch. It wouldn't do to go back empty-handed. Then we were on the final approach to Heathrow and a pretty young hostess-lady with red hair and violet eyes was shaking my shoulder and wondering whether I would be kind enough to fasten my seat-belt.

I was limping out through the Nothing-to-Declare exit when a customs man looking for something to do called, "Excuse me, sir . . ."

I sighed heavily, turned on the ferrule of Alice's stick, humped over to him and dropped my inoffensive overnight bag on his table. He was young, fair, clean-shaven and had pale blue eyes. His hat was too big.

"What?" I asked curtly.

"It's Mr. Sutherland, isn't it?"

"No, it isn't, it's Mr. Savage. Mr. Sutherland died."

He looked confused but rallied on. "Thought I recognised you, sir. My wife is a great fan of yours."

Having got me there, he didn't know what to do with me. He stuttered a bit. "You have nothing to declare, sir?"

"Otherwise I wouldn't be going out this way." I nodded at the notice in case he couldn't read.

"Sorry, Mr. Sutherland . . . Savage . . . but we are expected to make spot checks occasionally. May I?"

I made no answer as his fingers hovered over my bag. He was welcome. It contained the filthiest selection of old clothes he would probably ever en-counter in his line of business; he thought so too; they made him feel like a rag-picker. He closed the zip hurriedly.

"I wonder if I might bother you for an autograph . . . er . . ." He pro-duced an official notebook and a ball-point. "Would you put 'To Marjorie' please, Mr. . . . er . . . she would be so . . ."

"My name's Savage now," I said, writing.

"Ah," he muttered. I wrote "Mark Sutherland." Did it mean anything to anyone any more? I wondered. I looked up into his shy smile. I grinned at him.

"Thank you," I said. "Tell Marjorie she has excellent taste."

"You've had an accident," he remarked as I gathered up stick and bag.

"An ambulance ran over me."

"That was lucky," he laughed. I paused and looked back. The laugh faded. "In a way . . . being an ambulance, I mean . . ."

Silly sod, I thought, as I waved him goodbye.

*   *   *

Mitch was her usual collected self when I pushed panting into the office late
next morning after a devastating encounter with the seventy-eight steps outside. Her collection faltered, however, when she saw I was on a stick. "You
did break your leg!" I eyed her coolly. She gave a lame shrug. "I never know
when you're telling the truth."

I went up on my points to kiss her forehead. "It's not actually *broken*
broken," I relented. "Some of the ligaments went for a burton."

Then, of course, she started treating me like a cripple, putting an arm
around my waist and holding my hand, shepherding me soothingly towards
my office. I shook her off. "I've just come all the way from Vienna on my
own. I can just about make it to my desk, thank you all the same."

"How was it?"

"Vienna?" She nodded. "How about some of your delectable coffee?"

I stood Alice's stick against the desk. When Mitch returned with coffee, I
pushed the bottle of perfume across the desk. "An offering," I said, shame-
faced. "Peace?"

She undid the wrapping, squinted at the box and came fumbling around
the desk to give me a thank-you kiss. She's a clumsy soul, but then there's so
much of her. She crashed into Alice's stick and almost landed in my lap. I
fielded her adroitly and groped around for the stick. She handed it to me
silently.

"You've busted it," I told her. She took it back and examined it myopi-
cally. "That stick belonged to Auntie Alice."

"The silver band's a bit loose, that's all." She twisted and tugged at it.

"Well, don't make it worse." I removed it from her grasp. She was right.
When I tried to screw it back, the top of the handle shot up a couple of
inches on a spring. "Christ," I said, "it's a trick stick."

We stared at it. "A sword stick perhaps," suggested Mitch.

Carefully I levered off the handle; it just came away. No sword. I peered
inquisitively into the hollow cane. Nothing. I upended it carefully over the
desk.

A glittering stream of brightness cascaded on to the blotter. My mouth
went quite dry. Neither of us spoke for a long time, then Mitch whispered
hoarsely, "Diamonds?"

I was counting slowly. "One for each year of a happy marriage," I said
quietly. "Eleven of them."

Mitch knelt on the floor and rested her chin on the desk. Together we
stared in awed silence at the fortune before us.

"Oh, Alice, Alice," I muttered at last. "What the hell am I going to do
with them?"

It was only then that I recalled the callow customs man in the hat which
was too big for him, and the exit sign which said Nothing to Declare.

I broke out into a cold sweat . . .